THE CONSPIRATORS

Or, The Chevalier D'harmental.

by

Alexandre Dumas

British Library Cataloguing-in-Publication Data
A catalogue record for this book is available from the
British Library

Contents

Alexandre Dumas

Alexandre Dumas was born in Villers-Cotterêts, France in 1802. His parents were poor, but their heritage and good reputation – Alexandre's father had been a general in Napoleon's army – provided Alexandre with opportunities for good employment. In 1822, Dumas moved to Paris to work for future king Louis Philippe I in the Palais Royal. It was here that he began to write for magazines and the theatre.

In 1829 and 1830 respectively, Dumas produced the plays Henry III and His Court and Christine, both of which met with critical acclaim and financial success. As a result, he was able to commit himself full-time to writing. Despite the turbulent economic times which followed the Revolution of 1830, Dumas turned out to have something of an entrepreneurial streak, and did well for himself in this decade. He founded a production studio that turned out hundreds of stories under his creative direction, and began to produce serialised novels for newspapers which were widely read by the French public. It was over the next two decades, as a now famous and much loved author of romantic and adventuring sagas, that Dumas produced his best-known works – the D'Artagnan romances, including The Three Musketeers, in 1844, and The Count of Monte Cristo, in 1846.

Dumas made a lot of money from his writing, but he was almost constantly penniless as a result of his extravagant lifestyle and love of women. In 1851 he fled his creditors to Belgium, and then Russia, and then Italy, not returning to Paris until 1864. Dumas died in Puys, France, in 1870, at the age of 68. He is now enshrined in the Panthéon of Paris alongside fellow authors Victor Hugo and Emile Zola. Since his death, his fiction has been translated into almost a hundred languages, and has formed the basis for more than 200 motion pictures.

CHAPTER I.
CAPTAIN ROQUEFINETTE.

On the 22d of March, in the year of our Lord 1718, a young cavalier of high bearing, about twenty-six or twenty-eight years of age, mounted on a pure-bred Spanish charger, was waiting, toward eight o'clock in the morning, at that end of the Pont Neuf which abuts on the Quai de l'Ecole.

He was so upright and firm in his saddle, that one might have imagined him to be placed there as a sentinel by the Lieutenant-General of Police, Messire Voyer d'Argenson. After waiting about half an hour, during which time he impatiently examined the clock of the Samaritaine, his glance, wandering till then, appeared to rest with satisfaction on an individual who, coming from the Place Dauphine, turned to the right, and advanced toward him.

The man who thus attracted the attention of the young chevalier was a powerfully-built fellow of five feet ten, wearing, instead of a peruke, a forest of his own black hair, slightly grizzled, dressed in a manner half-bourgeois, half-military, ornamented with a shoulder-knot which had once been crimson, but from exposure to sun and rain had become a dirty orange. He was armed with a long sword slung in a belt, and which bumped ceaselessly against the calves of his legs. Finally, he wore a hat once furnished with a plume and lace, and which—in remembrance, no doubt, of its past splendor—its owner had stuck so much over his left ear, that it seemed as if only a miracle of equilibrium could keep it in its place. There was altogether in the countenance and in the carriage and bearing of the man (who seemed from forty to forty-five years of age, and who advanced swaggering and keeping the middle of the road, curling his mustache with one hand, and with the other signing to the carriages to give place), such a character of insolent carelessness, that the cavalier who watched him smiled involuntarily, as he murmured to himself, "I believe this is my man."

In consequence of this probability, he walked straight up to the new-comer, with the evident intention of speaking to him. The latter, though he evidently did not know the cavalier, seeing that he was going to address him, placed himself in the third position, and waited, one hand on his sword and the other on his mustache, to hear what the person who was coming up had to say to him. Indeed, as the man with the orange ribbon had foreseen, the young cavalier stopped his horse by him, and touching his hat—"Sir," said he, "I think I may conclude, from your appearance and manner, that you are a gentleman; am I mistaken?"

"No, palsam-bleu!" replied he to whom this strange question was addressed, touching his hat in his turn. "I am delighted that my appearance speaks so well for me, for, however little you would think that you were giving me my proper title, you may call me captain."

"I am enchanted that you are a sol[Pg 240]dier; it is an additional security to me that you are incapable of leaving a brave man in distress."

"Welcome, provided always the brave man has no need

8

of my purse, for I confess, freely, that I have just left my last crown in a cabaret on the Port de la Tonnelle."

"Nobody wants your purse, captain; on the contrary, I beg you to believe that mine is at your disposal."

"To whom have I the honor to speak?" asked the captain, visibly touched by this reply, "and in what can I oblige you?"

"I am the Baron Rene de Valef," replied the cavalier.

"I think," interrupted the captain, "that I knew, in the Flemish wars, a family of that name."

"It was mine, since we are from Liege." The two speakers exchanged bows.

"You must know then," continued the Baron de Valef, "that the Chevalier Raoul d'Harmental, one of my most intimate friends, last night, in my company, picked up a quarrel, which will finish this morning by a meeting. Our adversaries were three, and we but two. I went this morning to the houses of the Marquis de Gacé and Comte de Sourgis, but unfortunately neither the one nor the other had passed the night in his bed; so, as the affair could not wait, as I must set out in two hours for Spain, and that we absolutely require a second, or rather a third, I installed myself on the Pont Neuf with the intention of addressing the first gentleman who passed. You passed, and I addressed myself to you."

"And you have done right, pardieu! rest satisfied, baron, I am your man. What hour is fixed for the meeting?"

"Half-past nine this morning."

"Where will it take place?"

"At the Port Maillot."

"Diable! there is no time to lose; but you are on horseback and I am on foot; how shall we manage that?"

"There is a way, captain."

"What is it?"

"It is that you should do me the honor of mounting behind me."

"Willingly, baron."

"I warn you, however," added the young cavalier, with a slight smile, "that my horse is rather spirited."

"Oh, I know him!" said the captain, drawing back a step, and looking at the beautiful animal with the eye of a connoisseur; "if I am not mistaken, he was bred between the mountains of Grenada and the Sierra Morena. I rode such a one at Almanza, and I have often made him lie down like a sheep when he wanted to carry me off at a gallop, only by pressing him with my knees."

"You reassure me. To horse then, captain."——"Here I am, baron."

And without using the stirrup, which the young cavalier left free for him, with a single bound the captain sprang on to the croup.

The baron had spoken truly; his horse was not accustomed to so heavy a load, therefore he attempted to get rid of it. Neither had the captain exaggerated, and the animal soon felt that he had found his master; so that, after a few attempts, which had no other effect than to show to the passers-by the address of the two cavaliers, he became obedient, and went at a swinging trot down the Quai de l'Ecole, which at that time was nothing but a wharf, crossed at the same pace the Quai du Louvre and the Quai des Tuileries, through the gate of the Conference, and leaving on the left the road to Versailles, threaded the great avenue of the Champs-Elysées, which now leads to the triumphal Arc de l'Etoile. Arrived at the Pont d'Antin, the Baron de Valef slackened his horse's pace a little, for he found that he had ample time to arrive at the Port Maillot at the hour fixed.

The captain profited by this respite.

"May I, without indiscretion, ask why we are going to fight? I wish, you understand, to know that, in order to regulate my conduct toward my adversary, and to know whether it is worth killing him."

"That is only fair," answered the baron; "I will tell you everything as it passed. We were supping last night at La Fillon's. Of course you know La Fillon, captain?"

He attacked the captain with such fury that their swordsengaged at the hilt.

He attacked the captain with such fury that their swords engaged at the hilt.—*Page* 244.

Link to larger image

[Pg 241]"Pardieu! it was I who started her in the world, in 1705, before my Italian campaign."

"Well," replied the baron, laughing, "you may boast of a pupil who does you honor. Briefly, I supped there tete-à-tete with D'Harmental."

"Without any one of the fair sex?"

"Oh, mon Dieu, yes! I must tell you that D'Harmental

is a kind of Trappist, only going to La Fillon's for fear of the reputation of not going there; only loving one woman at a time, and in love for the moment with the little D'Averne, the wife of the lieutenant of the guards."

"Very good!"

"We were there, chatting, when we heard a merry party enter the room next to ours. As our conversation did not concern anybody else, we kept silence, and, without intending it, heard the conversation of our neighbors. See what chance is. Our neighbors talked of the only thing which we ought not to have heard."

"Of the chevalier's mistress, perhaps?"

"Exactly. At the first words of their discourse which reached me, I rose, and tried to get Raoul away, but instead of following me, he put his hand on my shoulder, and made me sit down again. 'Then Philippe is making love to the little D'Averne?' said one. 'Since the fete of the Marechal d'Estrée, where she gave him a sword-belt with some verses, in which she compared him to Mars,' replied another voice. 'That is eight days ago,' said a third. 'Yes,' replied the first. 'Oh! she made a kind of resistance, either that she really held by poor D'Harmental, or that she knew that the regent only likes those who resist him. At last this morning, in exchange for a basketful of flowers and jewels, she has consented to receive his highness.'"

"Ah!" said the captain, "I begin to understand; the chevalier got angry."

"Exactly. Instead of laughing, as you or I would have

done, and profiting by this circumstance to get back his brevet of colonel, which was taken from him under pretext of economy, D'Harmental became so pale that I thought he was going to faint; then, approaching the partition, and striking with his fist, to insure silence, 'Gentlemen,' said he, 'I am sorry to contradict you, but the one who said that Madame d'Averne had granted a rendezvous to the regent, or to any other, has told a lie.'

"'It was I who said it, and who repeat it, and if it displeases you, my name is Lafare, captain of the guards.' 'And mine, Fargy,' said a second voice. 'And mine, Ravanne,' said the third. 'Very well, gentlemen,' replied D'Harmental, 'to-morrow, from nine to half-past, at the Port Maillot.' And he sat down again opposite me. They talked of something else, and we finished our supper. That is the whole affair, captain, and you now know as much as I."

The captain gave vent to a kind of exclamation which seemed to say, "This is not very serious;" but in spite of this semi-disapprobation, he resolved none the less to support, to the best of his power, the cause of which he had so unexpectedly been made the champion, however defective that cause might appear to him in principle; besides, even had he wished it, he had gone too far to draw back. They had now arrived at the Port Maillot, and a young cavalier, who appeared to be waiting, and who had from a distance perceived the baron and the captain, put his horse to the gallop, and approached rapidly; this was the Chevalier d'Harmental.

"My dear chevalier," said the Baron de Valef, grasping his hand, "permit me, in default of an old friend, to present to you a new one. Neither Sourgis nor Gacé were at home. I met this gentleman on the Pont Neuf, and told him our embarrassment, and he offered himself to free us from it, with the greatest good will."

"I am doubly grateful to you then, my dear Valef," replied the chevalier, casting on the captain a look which betrayed a slight astonishment. "And to you, monsieur," continued he. "I must excuse myself for making your acquaintance by mixing you up thus with an unpleasant affair. But you will afford me one day or another an opportunity to[Pg 242] return your kindness, and I hope and beg that, an opportunity arising, you would dispose of me as I have of you."

"Well said, chevalier," replied the captain, leaping to the ground; "and in speaking thus you might lead me to the end of the world. The proverb is right: 'It is only mountains that don't meet.'"

"Who is this original?" asked D'Harmental of Valef, while the captain stamped the calls with his right foot, to stretch his legs.

"Ma foi! I do not know," said Valef, "but I do know that we should be in a great difficulty without him. Some poor officer of fortune, without doubt, whom the peace has thrown abroad like so many others; but we will judge him by-and-by, by his works."

"Well!" said the captain, becoming animated with the exercise he was taking, "where are our adversaries?"

"When I came up to you," replied D'Harmental, "they had not arrived, but I perceived at the end of the avenue a kind of hired carriage, which will serve as an excuse if they are late; and indeed," added the chevalier, pulling out a beautiful watch set with diamonds, "they are not behind time, for it is hardly half-past nine."

"Let us go," said Valef, dismounting and throwing the reins to D'Harmental's valet, "for if they arrive at the rendezvous while we stand gossiping here, it will appear as though we had kept them waiting."

"You are right," said D'Harmental; and, dismounting, he advanced toward the entrance of the wood, followed by his two companions.——"Will you not take anything, gentlemen," said the landlord of the restaurant, who was standing at his door, waiting for custom.

"Yes, Maitre Durand," replied D'Harmental, who wished, in order that they might not be disturbed, to make it appear as if they had come from an ordinary walk, "breakfast for three. We are going to take a turn in the avenue, and then we shall come back." And he let three louis fall into the hands of the inn-keeper.

The captain saw the shine of the three gold pieces one after another, and quickly reckoned up what might be had at the "Bois de Boulogne" for seventy-two francs; but as he knew whom he had to deal with, he judged that a little advice from him would not be useless; consequently, in his turn approaching the maitre d'hotel—

"Listen, my friend," said he; "you know that I understand

15

the price of things, and that no one can deceive me about the amount of a tavern bill. Let the wines be good and varied, and let the breakfast be copious, or I will break your head! Do you understand?"

"Be easy, captain," answered Durand, "it is not a customer like you whom I would deceive."

"All right; I have eaten nothing for twelve hours. Arrange accordingly."

The hotel-keeper bowed, as knowing what that meant, and went back to his kitchen, beginning to think that he had made a worse bargain than he had hoped.

As to the captain, after having made a last sign of recognition, half amicable, half threatening, he quickened his pace, and rejoined the chevalier and the baron, who had stopped to wait for him.

The chevalier was not wrong as to the situation of the hired carriage. At the turn of the first alley he saw his three adversaries getting out of it. They were, as we have already said, the Marquis de Lafare, the Comte de Fargy, and the Chevalier de Ravanne.

Our readers will now permit us to give them some short details of these three personages, who will often reappear in the course of this history. Lafare, the best known of the three, thanks to the poetry which he has left behind him, was a man of about thirty-six or thirty-eight years, of a frank and open countenance, and of an inexhaustible gayety and good humor. Always ready to engage with all comers, at table, at play, or at arms, and that without malice or bitterness; much run after by the fair sex, and much beloved by the regent, who had named him his captain of the guards, and who, during the ten years in which he had admitted him[Pg 243] into his intimacy, had found him his rival sometimes, but his faithful servant always. Thus the prince, who had the habit of giving nicknames to all his boon companions, as well as to his mistresses, never called him any other than "bon enfant." Nevertheless, for some time the popularity of Lafare, established as it was by agreeable antecedents, was fast lowering among the ladies of the court and the girls of the opera. There was a report current that he was going to be so ridiculous as to become a well-behaved man. It is true that some people, in order to preserve his reputation for him, whispered that this apparent conversion had no other cause than the jealousy of Mademoiselle de Conti, daughter of the duchess, and granddaughter of the great Conde, who it was said honored the regent's captain of the guards with a particular affection. His alliance with the Duc de Richelieu, who on his side was supposed to be the lover of Mademoiselle de Charolais, gave consistency to this report.

The Comte de Fargy, generally called "Le Beau Fargy," thus substituting the title which he had received from nature for that which his fathers had left him was cited, as his name indicates, as the handsomest man of his time, which in that age of gallantry imposed obligations from which he had never recoiled, and from which he had always come with honor. Indeed, it was impossible to be a more perfect figure than he was. At once strong and graceful, supple and active, he seemed to unite all the different perfections of a hero of romance of that time. Add to this a charming head, uniting the most opposite styles of beauty; that is to say, black hair and blue eyes, strongly-marked features, and a complexion like a woman. Unite with all these, wit, loyalty, the greatest courage, and you will have an idea of the high consideration which Le Fargy must have enjoyed from the society of that mad period.

As to the Chevalier de Ravanne, who has left us such strange memoirs of his early life, that, in spite of their authenticity, one is tempted to believe them apocryphal, he was still but a youth, rich and of noble birth, who entered into life by a golden door, and ran into all its pleasures with the fiery imprudence and eagerness of his age. He carried to excess, as so many do at eighteen, all the vices and all the virtues of his day. It will be easily understood how proud he was to serve as second to men like Lafare and Fargy in a meeting which was likely to "make a noise."

CHAPTER II.
THE MEETING.

As soon as Lafare, Fargy, and Ravanne saw their adversaries appear at the corner of the path, they walked to meet them. Arrived at ten paces from each other, they all took off their hats and bowed with that elegant politeness which was a characteristic of the aristocracy of the eighteenth century, and advanced some steps thus bareheaded with a smile on their lips, so that to the eyes of the passer-by, ignorant of the cause of their réunion, they would have appeared like friends enchanted to meet.

"Gentlemen," said the Chevalier d'Harmental, to whom the first word by right belonged, "I hope that neither you nor we have been followed; but it is getting late, and we might be disturbed here. I think it would be wise in us to find a more retired spot, where we shall be more at ease to transact the little business which we have in hand."

"Gentlemen," said Ravanne, "I know one which will suit you, a hundred yards from here—a true cover."

"Come, let us follow the child," said the captain; "innocence leads to safety."

Ravanne turned round, and examined, from head to foot, our friend with the yellow ribbons.

"If you are not previously engaged, my strapping friend," said he, in a bantering tone, "I claim the preference."

"Wait a moment, Ravanne," interrupted Lafare; "I have some explanations to give to Monsieur d'Harmental."

"Monsieur Lafare," replied the chevalier, "your courage is so well known, that the explanations you offer me are a[Pg 244] proof of delicacy for which I thank you; but these explanations would only delay us uselessly, and we have no time to lose."

"Bravo!" cried Ravanne, "that is what I call speaking, chevalier. As soon as we have cut each other's throats, I hope you will grant me your friendship. I have heard you much spoken of in good quarters, and have long wished to make your acquaintance."

"Come, come, Ravanne," said Fargy, "since you have undertaken to be our guide, show us the way."

Ravanne sprang into the wood like a young fawn: his five companions followed. At the end of about ten minutes' walking, during which the six adversaries had maintained the most profound silence, either from fear of being heard, or from that natural feeling which makes a man in the moment of danger reflective for a time, they found themselves in the midst of a glade, surrounded on all sides by a screen of trees.

"Well," said Ravanne, looking round him in a satisfied manner, "what do you say to the locality?"

"I say that if you boast of having discovered it," said the captain, "you are a strange kind of Christopher Columbus. If you had told me it was here you were coming, I could have guided you with my eyes shut."——"Well," replied Ravanne, "we will endeavor that you shall leave it in the same manner."

"It is with you that my business lies, Monsieur de Lafare," said D'Harmental, throwing his hat on the ground.

"Yes, monsieur," replied the captain of the guards, following the example of the chevalier; "and at the same time I know that nothing could give me more honor and more pain than a rencontre with you, particularly for such a cause."

D'Harmental smiled as a man on whom this flower of politeness was not lost, but his only answer was to draw his sword.

"It appears, my dear baron," said Fargy, addressing himself to Valef, "that you are on the point of setting out for Spain."

"I ought to have left last night; and nothing less than the pleasure I promised myself in seeing you this morning would have detained me till now, so important is my errand."

"Diable! you distress me," said Fargy, drawing, "for if I should have the misfortune to retard you, you are the man to bear me deadly malice."

"Not at all. I should know that it was from pure friendship, my dear count," replied Valef; "so do your best, I beg, for I am at your orders."

"Come, then, monsieur," said Ravanne to the captain, who was folding his coat neatly, and placing it by his hat, "you see that I am waiting for you."

"Do not be impatient, my fine fellow," said the old soldier, continuing his preparations with the phlegm natural to him; "one of the most essential qualities in arms is sang-froid. I was like you at your age; but after the third or fourth sword-blow I received, I understood that I was on the wrong road, and I returned to the right path. There," added he, at last drawing his sword, which I have said was of extreme length.

"Peste!" said Ravanne, throwing a glance on his adversary's weapon, "what a charming implement you have there! It reminds me of the great spit in my mother's kitchen; and I am grieved that I did not order the maitre-d'hotel to bring it me, as a match to yours."

"Your mother is a worthy woman, and her 'cuisine' is a good one; I have heard both spoken of with great praise, Monsieur le Chevalier," replied the captain with an almost paternal manner; "I should be grieved to take you from one or the other for a trifle like that which procures me the honor of crossing swords with you. Suppose, then, that you are only taking a lesson from your fencing-master, and keep the distance."

The recommendation was useless. Ravanne was exasperated by his adversary's calmness, to which, in spite of his courage, his young and ardent blood did not allow him to attain. He attacked the captain with such fury that their swords engaged at the hilt. The captain made a step back.

[Pg 245]"Ah! you give ground, my tall friend."

"To give ground is not to fly, my little chevalier," replied the captain; "it is an axiom of the art which I advise you to consider; besides, I am not sorry to study your play. Ah! you are a pupil of Berthelot, apparently; he is a good master, but he has one great fault: it is not teaching to parry. Stay, look at this," continued he, replying by a thrust in "seconde" to a straight thrust; "if I had lunged, I should have spitted you like a lark."

Ravanne was furious, for he had felt on his breast the

point of his adversary's sword, but so lightly that he might have taken it for the button of a foil. His anger redoubled at the conviction that he owed his life to the captain, and his attacks became more numerous and more furious than ever.

"Stop, stop," said the captain; "now you are going crazy, and trying to blind me; fie! fie! young man; at the chest, morbleu! Ah! at the face again; you will force me to disarm you. Again! Go and pick up your sword, young man; and come back hopping on one leg to calm yourself."

And with a sudden twist he whipped Ravanne's sword out of his hand and sent it flying some twenty paces from him. This time Ravanne profited by the advice. He went slowly to pick up his sword, and came back quietly to the captain; but the young man was as pale as his satin vest, on which was apparent a small drop of blood.

"You are right, captain," said he, "and I am still but a child; but this meeting will, I hope, help to make a man of me. Some passes more, if you please, that it may not be said you have had all the honors."

And he put himself on guard. The captain was right; the chevalier only required to be calm to make him a formidable adversary: thus, at the first thrust of this third engagement, he saw that he must attend solely to his own defense; but his superiority in the art of fencing was too decided for his young adversary to obtain any advantage over him. The matter ended as it was easy to foresee. The captain disarmed Ravanne a second time; but this time he went and picked up the sword himself, and with a politeness of which at first one might have supposed him incapable.

"Monsieur le Chevalier," said he, extending his hand to Ravanne, "you are a brave young man; but believe in an old frequenter of schools and taverns, who was at the Flemish wars before you were born, at the Italian when you were in your cradle, and at the Spanish while you were a page; change your master. Leave Berthelot, who has already taught you all he knows, and take Bois-Robert; and may the devil fly away with me, if in six months you are not as good a fencer as myself."

"Thanks for your lesson," said Ravanne, taking the hand of the captain, while two tears, which he could not restrain, flowed down his cheeks; "I hope it will profit me."

And, receiving his sword, he did what the captain had already done—sheathed it. They then both cast their eyes on their companions to see how things were going. The combat was over. Lafare was seated on the ground, with his back leaning against a tree: he had been run through the body, but happily the point of the sword had struck against a rib, and had glanced along the bone, so that the wound seemed at first worse than it really was; still he had fainted—the shock had been so violent. D'Harmental was on his knees before him, endeavoring to staunch the blood with his handkerchief. Fargy and Valef had wounded each other at the same moment. One was struck in the thigh, the other run through the arm; both had apologized, promising to be friends for the future.

"Look, young man," said the captain, showing Ravanne

these different episodes of the field of battle. "Look on that, and meditate. There is the blood of three brave gentlemen flowing—probably for a folly."

"Faith, captain," answered Ravanne, quite calmed down, "I believe you are right, and that you are the only one of us all that has got common sense."

[Pg 246]At that moment Lafare opened his eyes and recognized D'Harmental in the man who was tending him.

"Chevalier," said he, "take a friend's advice; send me a kind of surgeon whom you will find in the carriage, and whom I brought with me in case of accident. Then gain Paris as fast as possible. Show yourself to-night at the opera ball, and if they ask you about me, say that it is a week since you have seen me. As to me, you may be quite easy. Your name shall not pass my lips; and if you get into any unpleasant discussion with the police, let me know at once, and we will manage so that the affair shall have no consequences."

"Thanks, Monsieur le Marquis," answered D'Harmental, "I quit you because I leave you in better hands than mine; otherwise, believe me, nothing should have separated me from you until I had seen you in your bed."

"Pleasant journey, my dear Valef," said Fargy, "for I do not think that scratch will hinder your going. On your return, do not forget that you have a friend at No. 14, Place Louis-le-Grand."

"And you, my dear Fargy, if you have any commission for Madrid, you have but to say so, and you may rely upon its being executed with the exactitude and zeal of a true comrade."

And the two friends shook hands as if nothing had passed.

"Adieu, young man, adieu," said the captain to Ravanne; "do not forget the advice which I have given you. Give up Berthelot, and take to Bois-Robert. Be calm—give ground when it is necessary—parry in time, and you will be one of the best fencers in the kingdom of France. My implement sends its compliments to your mother's great spit."

Ravanne, in spite of his presence of mind, could not find anything to reply to the captain; so he contented himself with bowing and going up to Lafare, who appeared to be the most seriously wounded.

As to D'Harmental, Valef, and the captain, they rapidly gained the path, where they found the coach, and inside, the surgeon, who was enjoying a nap. D'Harmental woke him; and showing him the way he must go, told him that the Marquis de Lafare and the Comte de Fargy had need of his services. He also ordered his valet to dismount and follow the surgeon in order to aid him; then, turning toward the captain—

"Captain," said he, "I do not think that it would be prudent to go and eat the breakfast which we have ordered; therefore receive my thanks for the assistance you have rendered me, and in remembrance of me, as it seems you are on foot, will you accept one of my two horses? you can take one by chance; they are both good, and neither will fail you if you have need to go eight or ten leagues in the hour."

"Faith, chevalier," answered the captain, casting a look on the horse which had been so generously offered to him, "there was no need for that. Their blood and their purses are things which gentlemen lend each other every day; but you make the offer with so good a grace that I know not how to refuse you. If you ever have need of me, for anything whatever, remember that I am at your service."

"If that case should occur, where should I find you, monsieur?" said D'Harmental, smiling.

"I have no fixed residence, chevalier, but you may always hear of me by going to La Fillon's and asking for La Normande, and inquiring of her for Captain Roquefinette."

And as the two young men mounted their horses, the captain did the same, not without remarking to himself that D'Harmental had left him the best of the three. Then, as they were near a four-cross road, each one took his own way at a gallop.

The Baron de Valef re-entered by the Barriere de Passy, and returned straight to the arsenal to receive the commissions of the Duchesse de Maine, to whose establishment he belonged, and left the same day for Spain.

Captain Roquefinette made two or three tours round the Bois de Boulogne, walking, trotting, and galloping, in order to appreciate the different qualities of his[Pg 247] horse; and having satisfied himself that it was, as the chevalier had told him, a fine and pure-blooded animal, he returned to Durand's hotel, where he ate, all alone, the breakfast which had been ordered for three. The same day, he took his horse

27

to a dealer and sold it for sixty louis. It was about half what it was worth; but one must be prepared to make sacrifices, if one wishes to realize promptly.

As to the Chevalier d'Harmental, he took the road to La Muette, entered Paris by the great avenue of the Champs-Elysées, and on returning to his home in the Rue de Richelieu, found two letters waiting for him. One of these letters was in a handwriting so well known to him that he trembled from head to foot as he looked at it, and after having taken it up with as much hesitation as if it had been a burning coal, he opened it with a hand whose shaking betrayed the importance he attached to it. It read as follows:

"My dear Chevalier—No one is master of his own heart—you know that; and it is one of the misfortunes of our nature not to be able to love the same person, or the same thing, long at a time. As to myself, I wish at least to have, beyond other women, the merit of never deceiving the man who has been my lover. Do not come, then, at your accustomed hour, for you will be told that I am not at home; and I am so scrupulous that I would not willingly endanger the soul even of a valet or a waiting-maid by making them tell so great a lie.

"Adieu, my dear chevalier. Do not retain too unkind a remembrance of me, and behave so that ten years hence I may still think what I think now—that is to say, that you are one of the noblest gentlemen in France.

"Sophie d'Averne."

"Mon Dieu!" cried D'Harmental, striking his fist on a

beautiful buhl table, which he smashed to bits, "if I have killed that poor Lafare I shall never forgive myself."

After this outburst, which comforted him a little, the poor fellow began to walk backward and forward between the door and the window in a manner that showed that he still wanted more deceptions of the same sort in order to arrive at the perfection of moral philosophy which the faithless beauty preached to him. Then, after two or three turns, he saw the other letter, which he had entirely forgotten, lying on the floor. He passed it once or twice, looking at it with a supreme indifference. At last, seeming to think that it would make some diversion on the first, he picked it up disdainfully, opened it slowly, looked at the writing, which was unknown to him, searched for the signature, but there was none; and then, led on by the mysterious air of it, he read as follows:

"Chevalier—If you have in your mind a quarter of the romance, or in your heart half the courage, that your friends give you credit for, some one is ready to offer you an enterprise worthy of you, and the result of which will be at the same time to avenge you on the man you hate most in the world, and to conduct you to a goal more brilliant than you can have hoped for in your wildest dreams. The good genius who will lead you thither by an enchanted road, and in whom you must trust entirely, will expect you this evening at ten o'clock at the opera ball. If you come there unmasked, he will come to you; if you come masked, you will know him by the violet ribbon which he will wear on his left shoulder. The watchword is 'open sesame;' speak boldly, and a cavern will open to you as wonderful as that of Ali Baba."

"Bravo!" said D'Harmental; "if the genius in the violet ribbons keeps only half his promise, by my honor he has found his man!"

CHAPTER III.
THE CHEVALIER.

The Chevalier Raoul d'Harmental, with whom, before going further, it is necessary that our readers make a better acquaintance, was the last of one of the best families of Nivernais. Although that family had never played an impor[Pg 248]tant part in history, yet it did not want a certain notoriety, which it had acquired partly alone and partly by its alliances. Thus the father of the chevalier, the Sire Gaston d'Harmental, had come to Paris in 1682, and had proved his genealogical tree from the year 1399, an heraldic operation which would have given some trouble to more than one duke and peer. In another direction, his maternal uncle, Monsieur de Torigny, before being named chevalier of the order in the promotion of 1694, had confessed, in order to get his sixteen quarterings recognized, that the best part of his scutcheon was that of the D'Harmentals, with whom his ancestors had been allied for three hundred years. Here, then, was enough to satisfy the aristocratic demands of the age of which we write.

The chevalier was neither poor nor rich—that is to say, his father, when he died, had left him an estate in the environs of Nevers, which brought him in from 20,000 to 25,000 livres a year. This was enough to live well in the country, but the chevalier had received an excellent education, and was very ambitious; therefore he had at his majority, in 1711, quitted his home for Paris. His first visit was to the Comte de Torigny, on whom he counted to introduce him at court. Unfortunately, at that time the Comte de Torigny was absent from home; but as he remembered with pleasure the family of D'Harmental, he recommended his nephew to the Chevalier de Villarceaux, who could refuse nothing to his friend the Comte de Torigny, and took the young man to Madame de Maintenon.

Madame de Maintenon had one good quality—she always continued to be the friend of her old lovers. She received the Chevalier d'Harmental graciously, thanks to the old recollections which recommended him to her, and some days afterward, the Marechal de Villars coming to pay his court to her, she spoke a few such pressing words in favor of her young protégé, that the marechal, delighted to find an opportunity of obliging this queen "in partibus," replied that from that hour he attached the chevalier to his military establishment and would take care to offer him every occasion to justify his august protectress's good opinion of him.

It was a great joy to the chevalier to see such a door opened to him. The coming campaign was definitive. Louis XIV. had arrived at the last period of his reign—the period of reverses. Tallard and Marsin had been beaten at Hochstett, Villeroy at Ramilies, and Villars himself, the hero of Friedlingen, had lost the famous battle of Malplaquet against Marlborough and Eugene. Europe, kept down for a time by Colbert and Louvois, rose against France, and the situation of affairs was desperate.

The king, like a despairing invalid who changes his

doctor every hour, changed ministers every day. Each new attempt but revealed a new weakness. France could not sustain war and could not obtain peace. Vainly she offered to abandon Spain, and limit her frontier. This was not sufficient humiliation. They exacted that the king should allow the hostile armies to cross France, in order to chase his grandson from the throne of Spain; and also that he should give up, as pledges, Cambray, Mettray, La Rochelle, and Bayonne, unless he preferred dethroning him himself, by open force, during the following year.

These were the conditions on which a truce was granted to the conqueror of the plains of Senef, Fleurus, of Steerekirk, and of La Marsalle; to him who had hitherto held in the folds of his royal mantle peace and war; to him who called himself the distributer of crowns, the chastiser of nations, the great, the immortal; to him in whose honor, during the last half century, marbles had been sculptured, bronzes cast, sonnets written, and incense poured.

Louis XIV. had wept in the full council. These tears had produced an army, which was intrusted to Villars.

Villars marched straight to the enemy, whose camp was at Denain, and who slept in security while watching the agony of France. Never had greater responsibility rested on one head. On one blow of Villars hung the salvation of France. [Pg 249] The allies had established a line of fortifications between Denain and Marchiennes, which, in their pride of anticipation, Albemarle and Eugene called the grand route to Paris.

Villars resolved to take Denain by surprise, and, Albemarle conquered, to conquer Eugene. In order to succeed in this audacious enterprise, it was necessary to deceive, not only the enemy's army, but also his own, the success of this coup de main being in its impossibility.

Villars proclaimed aloud his intention of forcing the lines of Landrecies. One night, at an appointed hour, the whole army moves off in the direction of that town. All at once the order is given to bear to the left. His genius throws three bridges over the Scheldt. Villars passes over the river without obstacle, throws himself into the marshes considered impracticable, and where the soldier advances with the water up to his waist; marches straight to the first redoubts; takes them almost without striking a blow; seizes successively a league of fortifications; reaches Denain; crosses the fosse which surrounds it, penetrates into the town, and on arriving at the place, finds his young protégé, the Chevalier d'Harmental, who presents to him the sword of Albemarle, whom he has just taken prisoner.

At this moment the arrival of Eugene is announced. Villars returns, reaches, before him, the bridge over which he must pass, takes possession of it, and awaits him. There the true combat takes place, for the taking of Denain had been but a short skirmish. Eugene makes attack after attack, returns seven times to the head of the bridge, his best troops being destroyed by the artillery which protects it, and the bayonets which defend it. At length, his clothes riddled with balls, and bleeding from two wounds, he mounts his third horse, the conqueror of Hochstett and Malplaquet retreats crying with rage and biting his gloves with fury. In six hours the aspect of things has changed. France is saved, and Louis XIV. is still Le Grand Roi.

D'Harmental had conducted himself like a man who wished to gain his spurs at once. Villars, seeing him covered with blood and dust, recalled to his mind by whom he had been recommended to him; made him draw near, while, in the midst of the field of battle, he wrote on a drum the result of the day.

"Are you wounded?" asked he.

"Yes, Monsieur le Marechal, but so slightly that it is not worth speaking of."

"Have you the strength to ride sixty leagues, without resting an hour, a minute, a second?"

"I have the strength for anything that will serve the king or you."

"Then set out instantly; go to Madame de Maintenon; tell her from me what you have seen, and announce to her the courier who will bring the official account."

D'Harmental understood the importance of the mission with which he was charged, and bleeding and dusty as he was, he mounted a fresh horse and gained the first stage. Twelve hours afterward he was at Versailles.

Villars had foreseen what would happen. At the first words which fell from the mouth of the chevalier, Madame de Maintenon took him by the hand, and conducted him to the king. The king was at work with Voisin, but, contrary to his habit, in his room, for he was a little indisposed.

Madame de Maintenon opened the door, pushed D'Harmental to the feet of the king, and raising her hands to heaven:

"Sire," said she, "give thanks to God, for your majesty knows we are nothing by ourselves, and it is from Him comes every blessing."

"What has happened, monsieur? Speak," said the king quickly, astonished to see this young man, whom he did not know, at his feet.

"Sire," replied the chevalier, "the camp at Denain is taken. Albemarle is a prisoner. Prince Eugene has taken flight; and the Marechal de Villars places his victory at your majesty's feet."

Louis XIV. turned pale, in spite of his command over himself. He felt his limbs fail him, and leaned against the table for support.

[Pg 250]"What ails you, sire?" said Madame de Maintenon, hastening to him.

"It is, madame, that I owe you everything," said Louis XIV.; "you save the king, and your friends save the kingdom."

Madame de Maintenon bowed and kissed the king's hand respectfully.

Then Louis XIV., still pale and much moved, passed behind the great curtain which hid the alcove containing his bed, and they heard a prayer of thanksgiving. He then reappeared, grave and calm, as if nothing had happened.

"And now, monsieur," said he, "tell me the details."

D'Harmental gave an account of that marvelous battle, which came as by a miracle to save the monarchy; then, when he had finished:

"And have you nothing to tell of yourself?" asked Louis XIV. "If I may judge by the blood and dust with which you are yet covered, you did not remain idle."

"Sire, I did my best," said D'Harmental, bowing; "but if there is really anything to tell, I will, with your permission, leave it to the Marechal de Villars."

"It is well, young man; and if he forgets you by chance, we shall remember. You must be fatigued. Go and rest. I am pleased with you."

D'Harmental retired joyously, Madame de Maintenon conducting him to the door; he kissed her hand again, and hastened to profit by the royal permission. For twenty hours he had neither eaten, drunk, nor slept. On his awaking, they gave him a packet which had been brought from the minister of war. It was his brevet as colonel. Two months afterward peace was made. Spain gave up half its monarchy, but France remained intact. Louis XIV. died. Two distinct and irreconcilable parties were in existence. That of the bastards, centering in the Duc de Maine, and that of the legitimate princes, represented by the Duc d'Orleans. If the Duc de Maine had had the will, the perseverance, the courage of his wife, Louise Benedicte de Conde, perhaps, supported as he was by the royal will, he might have triumphed; but he had to defend himself in broad day, as he was attacked; and the Duc de Maine, weak in mind and heart, dangerous only because he was a coward, was only good at underhand deeds.

He was threatened openly, and his numerous artifices and wiles were of no use to him. In one day, and almost without a struggle, he was precipitated from that height to which he had been raised by the blind love of the old king. His fall was heavy, and above all disgraceful; he retired mutilated, abandoning the regency to his rival, and only preserving, out of all the favors accumulated upon him, the superintendence of the royal education, the command of the artillery, and the precedence over the dukes and peers.

The decree, which had just passed the parliament, struck the old court and all attached to it. Letellier did not wait to be exiled. Madame de Maintenon took refuge at Saint Cyr, and Monsieur le Duc de Maine shut himself up in the beautiful town of Sceaux, to finish his translation of Lucrece.

The Chevalier d'Harmental saw, as a passive spectator, these different intrigues, waiting till they should assume a character which would permit him to take part in them. If there had been an open and armed contest, he would have taken that side to which gratitude called him. Too young and too chaste, if we may say so, in politics, to turn with the wind of fortune, he remained faithful to the memory of the old king, and to the ruins of the old court.

His absence from the Palais Royal, round which hovered all those who wished to take a place in the political sky, was interpreted as opposition; and one morning, as he had received the brevet which gave him a regiment, he received the decree which took it from him.

D'Harmental had the ambition of his age. The only career open to a gentleman was that of arms. His debut had been brilliant, and the blow which at five-and-twenty took from him his hopes for the future was profoundly painful.

He ran to Monsieur de Villars, in whom[Pg 251] he had found so warm a protector. The marshal received him with the coldness of a man who not only wishes to forget the past, but also to see it forgotten.

D'Harmental understood that the old courtier was about to change his skin, and retired discreetly. Though the age was essentially that of egotism, the chevalier's first experience of it was bitter to him; but he was at that happy time of life when a disappointed ambition is rarely a deep or lasting grief.

Ambition is the passion of those who have no other, and the chevalier had all those proper to five-and-twenty years of age; besides, the spirit of the times did not tend to melancholy, that is a modern sentiment, springing from the overthrow of fortunes and the weakness of man. In the eighteenth century it was rare to dream of abstract things, or aspire to the unknown: men went straight to pleasure, glory, or fortune, and all who were handsome, brave or intriguing could attain them. That was the time when people were not ashamed to be happy. Now mind governs matter so much that men dare not avow that they are happy.

After the long and somber winter of Louis XIV.'s old age appeared all at once the joyous and brilliant spring of a young royalty. Every one basked in this new sun, radiant and benevolent, and went about buzzing and careless, like the bees and butterflies on the first fine day. The Chevalier d'Harmental had retained his sadness for a week; then he mixed again in the crowd, and was drawn in by the whirlpool which threw him at the feet of a pretty woman.

For three months he had been the happiest man in the world. He had forgotten Saint Cyr, the Tuileries, and the Palais Royal. He did not know whether there was a Madame de Maintenon, a king, or a regent. He only knew that it is sweet to live when one is loved, and he did not see why he should not live and love forever. He was still in this dream, when, as we have said, supping with his friend, the Baron de Valef, at La Fillon's, in the Rue Saint Honore, he had been all at once brutally awakened by Lafare. Lovers are often unpleasantly awakened, and we have seen that D'Harmental was not more patient under it than others. It was more pardonable in the chevalier, because he thought he loved truly, and that in his juvenile good faith he thought nothing could replace that love in his heart.

Thus Madame d'Averne's strange but candid letter, instead of inspiring him with the admiration which it merited at that time, had at first overwhelmed him. It is the property of every sorrow which overtakes us to reawaken past griefs which we believed dead, but which were only sleeping. The soul has its scars as well as the body, and they are seldom so well healed but a new wound can reopen them.

D'Harmental again began to feel ambitious. The loss of his mistress had recalled to him the loss of his regiment. It required nothing less than the second letter, so unexpected and mysterious, to divert him from his grief. A lover of our days would have thrown it from him with disdain, and would have despised himself if he had not nursed his grief so as to make himself poetically melancholy for a week; but a lover in the regency was much more accommodating. Suicide was scarcely discovered, and if by chance people fell into the water, they did not drown as long as there was the least little straw to cling to. D'Harmental did not affect the coxcombry of sadness. He decided, sighing, it is true, that he would go to the opera ball; and for a lover betrayed in so unforeseen and cruel a manner this was something; but it must be confessed, to the shame of our poor species, that he was chiefly led to this philosophic determination by the fact that the letter was written in a female hand.

CHAPTER IV.
A BAL-MASQUE OF THE PERIOD.—THE BAT.

The opera balls were then at their height. It was an invention of the Chevalier de Bullon, who only obtained pardon for assuming the title of Prince d'Auvergne, nobody exactly knew why, by rendering this service to the dissipated society of the time. It was he who had invented[Pg 252] the double flooring which put the pit on a level with the stage: and the regent, who highly appreciated all good inventions, had granted him in recompense a pension of two thousand livres, which was four times what the Grand Roi had given to Corneille. That beautiful room, with its rich and grave architecture, which the Cardinal de Richelieu had inaugurated by his "Mirame," where Sully and Quinault's pastorals had been represented, and where Moliere had himself played his principal works, was this evening the rendezvous of all that was noble, rich, and elegant.

D'Harmental, from a feeling of spite, very natural in his situation, had taken particular pains with his toilet. When he arrived, the room was already full, and he had an instant's fear that the mask with the violet ribbons would not find him, inasmuch as the unknown had neglected to assign a place of meeting, and he congratulated himself on having come unmasked. This resolution showed great confidence in the discretion of his late adversaries, a word from whom would have sent him before the Parliament, or at least to the Bastille. But so much confidence had the gentlemen of that day in each other's good faith, that, after having in the morning passed his sword through the body of one of the regent's favorites, the chevalier came, without hesitation, to seek an adventure at the Palais Royal. The first person he saw there was the young Duc de Richelieu, whose name, adventures, elegance, and perhaps indiscretions, had already brought him so much into fashion. It was said that two princesses of the blood disputed his affections, which did not prevent Madame de Nesle and Madame de Polignac from fighting with pistols for him, or Madame de Sabran, Madame de Villars, Madame de Mouchy, and Madame de Tencin, from sharing his heart.

He had just joined the Marquis de Canillac, one of the regent's favorites, whom, on account of the grave appearance he affected, his highness called his mentor. Richelieu began to tell Canillac a story, out loud and with much gesticulation. The chevalier knew the duke, but not enough to interrupt a conversation; he was going to pass, when the duke seized him by the coat.

"Pardieu!" he said, "my dear chevalier, you are not de trop. I am telling Canillac an adventure which may be useful to him as nocturnal lieutenant to the regent, and to you, as running the same danger as I did. The history dates from to-day—a further merit, as I have only had time to tell it to about twenty people, so that it is scarcely known. Spread it, you will oblige me, and the regent also."

D'Harmental frowned. The duke had chosen his time badly. At this moment the Chevalier de Ravanne passed, pursuing a mask. "Ravanne!" cried Richelieu, "Ravanne!"

"I am not at leisure," replied he.

"Do you know where Lafare is?"

"He has the migraine."

"And Fargy?"

"He has sprained himself." And Ravanne disappeared in the crowd, after bowing in the most friendly manner to his adversary of the morning.

"Well, and the story?" asked Canillac.

"We are coming to it. Imagine that some time ago, when I left the Bastille, where my duel with Gacé had sent me, three or four days after my reappearance Rafé gave me a charming little note from Madame de Parabere, inviting me to pass that evening with her. You understand, chevalier, that it is not at the moment of leaving the Bastille that one would despise a rendezvous, given by the mistress of him who holds the keys. No need to inquire if I was punctual; guess who I found seated on the sofa by her side. I give you a hundred guesses."

"Her husband," said Canillac.

"On the contrary, it was his royal highness himself. I was so much the more astonished, as I had been admitted with some mystery; nevertheless, as you will understand, I would not allow myself to appear astonished. I assumed a composed and modest air, like yours, Canillac, and saluted the marquise with such profound respect, that the regent laughed.[Pg 253] I did not expect this explosion, and was a little disconcerted. I took a chair, but the regent signed to me to take my place on the sofa. I obeyed.

"'My dear duke,' he said, 'we have written to you on a serious affair. Here is this poor marchioness, who, after being separated from her husband for two years, is threatened with an action by this clown, under pretext that she has a lover.' The marchioness tried to blush, but finding she could not, covered her face with her fan. 'At the first word she told me of her position,' continued the regent, 'I sent for D'Argenson, and asked him who this lover could be.'

"'Oh, monsieur, spare me!' said the marchioness.— 'Nonsense, my little duck; a little patience.'—'Do you know what the lieutenant of police answered me, my dear duke?'— 'No,' said I, much embarrassed.—'He said it was either you or me.'—'It is an atrocious calumny,' I cried.—'Don't be excited, the marchioness has confessed all.'

"'Then,' I replied, 'if the marchioness has confessed all, I do not see what remains for me to tell.'—'Oh!' continued the regent, 'I do not ask you for details. It only remains for us, as accomplices, to get one another out of the scrape.'—'And what have you to fear, monseigneur?' I asked. 'I know that, protected by your highness's name, I might brave all. What have we to fear?'—'The outcry of Parabere, who wants me to make him a duke.'

"'Well, suppose we reconcile them,' replied I.—'Exactly,' said his highness, laughing; 'and you have had the same idea as the marchioness.'—'Pardieu, madame, that is an honor for me. There must be a kind of apparent reconciliation between this tender couple, which would prevent the marquis from incommoding us with the scandal of an action.'—'But the difficulty,' objected Madame de Parabere, 'is, that it is two years since he has been here; and, as he piques himself on his jealousy and severity, what can we say? He has made a vow, that if any one sets foot here during his absence, the law should avenge him.'

"'You see, Richelieu, this becomes rather uncomfortable,' added the regent.—'Peste! It does indeed.'—'I have some means of coercion in my hands, but they do not go so far as to force a husband to be reconciled to his wife, and to receive her at his house.'—'Well,' replied I, 'suppose we bring him here.'—'There is the difficulty.'—'Wait a moment. May I ask if Monsieur de Parabere still has a weakness for champagne and burgundy?'—'I fear so,' said the marchioness.—'Then, monseigneur, we are saved. I invite the marquis to supper, with a dozen of mauvais sujets and charming women. You send Dubois.'—'What! Dubois?' asked the regent.

"'Certainly; one of us must remain sober. As Dubois cannot drink, he must undertake to make the marquis drink; and when everybody is under the table, he can take him away from us and do what he likes with him. The rest depends on the coachman.'—'Did I not tell you, marchioness,' said the regent, 'that Richelieu would give us good advice? Stop, duke,' continued he; 'you must leave off wandering round certain palaces; leave the old lady to die quietly at St. Cyr, the lame man to rhyme at Sceaux, and join yourself with us. I will give you, in my cabinet, the place of that old fool D'Axelles; and affairs will not perhaps be injured by it.'—'I dare say,' answered I. 'The thing is impossible; I have other plans.'—'Obstinate fellow!' murmured the regent."

"And Monsieur de Parabere?" asked the Chevalier d'Harmental, curious to know the end of the story.—"Oh! everything passed as we arranged it. He went to sleep at my house, and awoke at his wife's. He made a great noise, but there was no longer any possibility of crying scandal. His carriage had stopped at his wife's hotel, and all the servants saw him enter. He was reconciled in spite of himself. If he dares again to complain of his beautiful wife, we will prove to him, as clearly as possible, that he adores her without knowing it; and that she is the most innocent of women— also without his knowing it."

"Chevalier!" at this moment a sweet[Pg 254] and flute-like voice whispered in D'Harmental's ear, while a little hand rested on his arm.

"You see that I am wanted."

"I will let you go on one condition."

"What is it?"

"That you will tell my story to this charming bat, charging her to tell it to all the night-birds of her acquaintance."

"I fear," said D'Harmental, "I shall not have time."

"Oh! so much the better for you," replied the duke, freeing the chevalier, whom till then he had held by the coat; "for then you must have something better to say."

And he turned on his heel, to take the arm of a domino, who, in passing, complimented him on his adventure. D'Harmental threw a rapid glance on the mask who accosted him, in order to make sure that it was the one with whom he had a rendezvous, and was satisfied on seeing a violet ribbon on the left shoulder. He hastened to a distance from Canillac and Richelieu, in order not to be interrupted in a conversation which he expected to be highly interesting.

The unknown, whose voice betrayed her sex, was of middle height, and young, as far as one could judge from the elasticity of her movements. As M. de Richelieu had already remarked, she had adopted the costume best calculated to hide either graces or defects. She was dressed as a bat—a costume much in vogue, and very convenient, from its perfect simplicity, being composed only of two black skirts. The manner of employing them was at the command of everybody. One was fastened, as usual, round the waist; the masked head was passed through the placket-hole of the other. The front was pulled down to make wings; the back raised to make horns. You were almost certain thus to puzzle an interlocutor, who could only recognize you by the closest scrutiny.

The chevalier made all these observations in less time than it has taken to describe them; but having no knowledge of the person with whom he had to deal, and believing it to be some love intrigue, he hesitated to speak; when, turning toward him:

"Chevalier," said the mask, without disguising her voice, assuming that her voice was unknown to him, "do you know that I am doubly grateful to you for having come, particularly in the state of mind in which you are? It is unfortunate that

I cannot attribute this exactitude to anything but curiosity."

"Beautiful mask!" answered D'Harmental, "did you not tell me in your letter that you were a good genius? Now, if really you partake of a superior nature, the past, the present and the future must be known to you. You knew, then, that I should come; and, since you knew it, my coming ought not to astonish you."

"Alas!" replied the unknown, "it is easy to see that you are a weak mortal, and that you are happy enough never to have raised yourself above your sphere, otherwise you would know that if we, as you say, know the past, the present and the future, this science is silent as to what regards ourselves, and that the things we most desire remain to us plunged in the most dense obscurity."

"Diable! Monsieur le Genie," answered D'Harmental, "do you know that you will make me very vain if you continue in that tone; for, take care, you have told me, or nearly so, that you had a great desire that I should come to your rendezvous."

"I did not think I was telling you anything new, chevalier. It appeared to me that my letter would leave you no doubt as to the desire I felt of seeing you."

"This desire, which I only admit because you confess it, and I am too gallant to contradict you—had it not made you promise in your letter more than is in your power to keep?"

"Make a trial of my science; that will give you a test of my power."

"Oh, mon Dieu! I will confine myself to the simplest thing. You say you are acquainted with the past, the present and the future. Tell me my fortune."

"Nothing easier; give me your hand."

D'Harmental did what was asked of him.

[Pg 255]"Sir," said the stranger, after a moment's examination, "I see very legibly written by the direction of the 'adducta,' and by the arrangement of the longitudinal lines of the palm, five words, in which are included the history of your life. These words are, courage, ambition, disappointment, love, and treason."

"Peste!" interrupted the chevalier, "I did not know that the genii studied anatomy so deeply, and were obliged to take their degrees like a Bachelor of Salamanca!"

"Genii know all that men know, and many other things besides, chevalier."

"Well, then, what mean these words, at once so sonorous and so opposite? and what do they teach you of me in the past, my very learned genius?"

"They teach me that it is by your courage alone that you gained the rank of colonel, which you occupied in the army in Flanders; that this rank awakened your ambition; that this ambition has been followed by a disappointment; that you hoped to console yourself for this disappointment by love; but that love, like fortune, is subject to treachery, and that you have been betrayed."

"Not bad," said the chevalier; "and the Sybil of Cuma could not have got out of it better. A little vague, as in all horoscopes, but a great fund of truth, nevertheless. Let us come to the present, beautiful mask."

"The present, chevalier? Let us speak softly of it, for it smells terribly of the Bastille."

The chevalier started in spite of himself, for he believed that no one except the actors who had played a part in it could know his adventure of the morning.

"There are at this hour," continued the stranger, "two brave gentlemen lying sadly in their beds, while we chat gayly at the ball; and that because a certain Chevalier d'Harmental, a great listener at doors, did not remember a hemistich of Virgil."

"And what is this hemistich?" asked the chevalier, more and more astonished.

"'Facilis descensus Averni,'" said the mask, laughing.

"My dear genius," cried the chevalier, trying to peep through the openings in the stranger's mask, "that, allow me to inform you, is a quotation rather masculine."

"Do you not know that genii are of both sexes?"

"Yes; but I had never heard that they quoted the Æneid so fluently."

"Is not the quotation appropriate? You speak to me of the Sybil of Cuma; I answer you in her language. You ask for existing things; I give them you. But you mortals are never satisfied."

"No; for I confess that this knowledge of the past and the present inspires me with a terrible desire to know the future."

"There are always two futures," said the mask; "there is the future of weak minds, and the future of strong minds. God has given man free will that he might choose. Your future depends on yourself."

"But we must know these two futures to choose the best."

"Well, there is one which awaits you, somewhere in the environs of Nevers, in the depth of the country, among the rabbits of your warren, and the fowls of your poultry-yard. This one will conduct you straight to the magistrate's bench of your parish. It is an easy ambition, and you have only to let yourself go to attain it. You are on the road."

"And the other?" replied the chevalier, visibly piqued at the supposition that in any case such a future could be his.

"The other," said the stranger, leaning her arm on that of the young man, and fixing her eyes on him through her mask; "the other will throw you back into noise and light— will make you one of the actors in the game which is playing in the world, and, whether you gain or lose, will leave you at least the renown of a great player."

"If I lose, what shall I lose?" asked the chevalier.

"Life, probably."

The chevalier tossed his head contemptuously.

"And if I win?" added he.

"What do you say to the rank of colo[Pg 256]nel of horse, the title of Grandee of Spain, and the order of the Saint Esprit, without counting the field-marshal's baton in prospective?"

"I say that the prize is worth the stake, and that if you can prove to me that you can keep your promise, I am your man."

"This proof," replied the mask, "must be given you by another, and if you wish to have it you must follow me."

"Oh!" said D'Harmental, "am I deceived, and are you but a genius of the second order—a subaltern spirit, an intermediate power? Diable! this would take away a little of my consideration for you."

"What does it matter if I am subject to some great enchantress, and she has sent me to you?"

"I warn you that I do not treat with ambassadors."

"My mission is to conduct you to her."

"Then I shall see her?"

"Face to face."——"Let us go, then."

"Chevalier, you go quickly to the work; you forget that before all initiations there are certain indispensable ceremonies to secure the discretion of the initiated."

"What must I do?"

"You must allow your eyes to be bandaged, and let me lead you where I like. When arrived at the door of the temple, you must take a solemn oath to reveal nothing concerning the things you may hear, or the people you may see."

"I am ready to swear by the Styx," said D'Harmental, laughing.

"No, chevalier," said the mask, in a grave voice; "swear only by your honor; you are known, and that will suffice."

"And when I have taken this oath," asked the chevalier, after an instant's reflection, "will it be permitted to me to retire, if the proposals made are not such as a gentleman may entertain?"

"Your conscience will be your sole arbiter, and your word the only pledge demanded of you."

"I am ready," said the chevalier.

"Let us go, then," said the mask.

The chevalier prepared to cross the room in a straight line toward the door; but perceiving three of his friends, who might have stopped him on the way, he made a turn, and described a curve which would bring him to the same end.

"What are you doing?" asked the mask.

"I am avoiding some one who might detain us."

"Ah!" said the mask, "I began to fear."

"Fear what?" asked D'Harmental.

"To fear that your ardor was diminished in the proportion of the diagonal to the two sides of a square."

"Pardieu!" said D'Harmental, "this is the first time, I believe, that ever a rendezvous was given to a gentleman at an opera ball to talk anatomy, ancient literature, and mathematics. I am sorry to say so, but you are the most pedantic genius I ever met in my life."

The bat burst out laughing, but made no reply to this sally, in which was betrayed the spite of the chevalier at not being able to recognize a person who appeared to be so well acquainted with his adventures; but as this only added to his curiosity, both descended in equal haste, and found themselves in the vestibule.

"What road shall we take?" asked the chevalier. "Shall we travel underground, or in a car drawn by griffins?"

"With your permission, chevalier, we will simply go in a carriage; and though you appear to doubt it, I am a woman, and rather afraid of the dark."

"Permit me, then, to call my carriage," said the chevalier.

"Not at all; I have my own."

"Call it then."

"With your permission, chevalier, we will not be more proud than Mahomet with the mountain; and as my carriage cannot come to us, we will go to it."

At these words the bat drew the chevalier into the Rue St. Honore. A carriage without armorial bearings, with two dark-colored horses, waited at the corner of the street. The coachman was on his seat, enveloped in a great cape which hid the lower part of his face, while a three-cornered hat covered his forehead and eyes. A footman held the door open with one hand, and with the other held his handkerchief so as to conceal his face.

[Pg 257]"Get in," said the mask.

D'Harmental hesitated a moment. The anxiety of the servants to preserve their incognito, the carriage without blazon, the obscure place where it was drawn up, and the advanced hour of the night, all inspired the chevalier with a sentiment of mistrust; but reflecting that he gave his arm to a woman, and had a sword by his side, he got in boldly. The mask sat down by him, and the footman closed the door.

"Well, are we not going to start?" said the chevalier, seeing that the carriage remained motionless.

"There remains a little precaution to be taken," said the mask, drawing a silk handkerchief from her pocket.

"Ah! yes, true," said D'Harmental; "I had forgotten. I give myself up to you with confidence."

And he advanced his head. The unknown bandaged his eyes; then said—

"Chevalier, you give me your word of honor not to remove this bandage till I give you permission?"

"I do."

"It is well."

Then, raising the glass in front, she said to the coachman—

"You know where, Monsieur le Comte."

And the carriage started at a gallop.

CHAPTER V.
THE ARSENAL.

They both maintained a profound silence during the route. This adventure, which at first had presented itself under the appearance of an amorous intrigue, had soon assumed a graver aspect, and appeared to turn toward political machinations. If this new aspect did not frighten the chevalier, at least it gave him matter for reflection. There is a moment in the affairs of every man which decides upon his future. This moment, however important it may be, is rarely prepared by calculation or directed by will. It is almost always chance which takes a man as the wind does a leaf, and throws him into some new and unknown path, where, once entered, he is obliged to obey a superior force, and where, while believing himself free, he is but the slave of circumstances and the plaything of events.

It was thus with the chevalier. Interest and gratitude attached him to the party of the old court. D'Harmental, in consequence, had not calculated the good or the harm that Madame de Maintenon had done France. He did not weigh in the balance of genealogy Monsieur de Maine and Monsieur d'Orleans. He felt that he must devote his life to those who had raised him from obscurity, and knowing the old king's will, regarded as a usurpation Monsieur d'Orleans' accession to the regency.

Fully expecting an armed reaction against this power, he looked around for the standard which he should follow.

Nothing that he expected happened; Spain had not even protested. Monsieur de Maine, fatigued by his short contest, had retired into the shade. Monsieur de Toulouse, good, easy, and almost ashamed of the favors which had fallen to the share of himself and his elder brother, would not permit even the supposition that he could put himself at the head of a party. The Marshal de Villeroy had made a feeble and systemless opposition. Villars went to no one, but waited for some one to come to him. D'Axelles had changed sides, and had accepted the post of secretary for foreign affairs. The dukes and peers took patience, and paid court to the regent, in the hope that he would at last take away from the Dukes of Maine and Toulouse the precedence which Louis XIV. had given them.

Finally, there was discontent with, and even opposition to, the government of the Duc d'Orleans, but all impalpable and disjointed. This is what D'Harmental had seen, and what had resheathed his half-drawn sword: he thought he was the only one who saw another issue to affairs, and he gradually came to the conclusion that that issue had no existence, except in his own imagination, since those who should have been most interested in that result seemed to regard it as so impossible, that they did not even attempt to attain to it.

Although the carriage had been on the[Pg 258] road nearly half an hour, the chevalier had not found it long: so deep were his reflections, that, even if his eyes had not been bandaged, he would have been equally ignorant of what streets they passed through.

At length he heard the wheels rumbling as if they were passing under an arch. He heard the grating of hinges as the gate opened to admit him, and closed behind him, and directly after, the carriage, having described a semi-circle, stopped.

"Chevalier," said his guide, "if you have any fear, there is still time to draw back; if, on the contrary, you have not changed your resolution, come with me."

D'Harmental's only answer was to extend his hand.

The footman opened the door; the unknown got out first, and then assisted the chevalier. His feet soon encountered some steps; he mounted six—still conducted by the masked lady—crossed a vestibule, passed through a corridor, and entered a room.

"We are now arrived," said the unknown, "you remember our conditions; you are free to accept or refuse a part in the piece about to be played, but, in case of a refusal, you promise not to divulge anything you may see or hear."

"I swear it on my honor," replied the chevalier.

"Now, sit down; wait in this room, and do not remove the bandage till you hear two o'clock strike. You have not long to wait."

At these words his conductress left him. Two o'clock soon struck, and the chevalier tore off the bandage. He was alone in the most marvelous boudoir possible to imagine. It was small and octagonal, hung with lilac and silver, with furniture and portieres of tapestry. Buhl tables, covered with splendid china; a Persian carpet, and the ceiling painted by

Watteau, who was then coming into fashion. At this sight, the chevalier found it difficult to believe that he had been summoned on grave matters, and almost returned to his first ideas.

At this moment a door opened in the tapestry, and there appeared a woman who, in the fantastic preoccupation of his spirit, D'Harmental might have taken for a fairy, so slight, small, and delicate was her figure. She was dressed in pearl gray satin, covered with bouquets, so beautifully embroidered that, at a short distance, they appeared like natural flowers; the flounces, ruffles, and head-dress was of English point; it was fastened with pearls and diamonds. Her face was covered with a half-mask of black velvet, from which hung a deep black lace. D'Harmental bowed, for there was something royal in the walk and manner of this woman which showed him that the other had been only an envoy.

"Madame," said he, "have I really, as I begin to believe, quitted the earth for the land of spirits, and are you the powerful fairy to whom this beautiful palace belongs?"

"Alas! chevalier," replied the masked lady, in a sweet but decided voice, "I am not a powerful fairy, but, on the contrary, a poor princess, persecuted by a wicked enchanter, who has taken from me my crown, and oppresses my kingdom. Thus, you see, I am seeking a brave knight to deliver me, and your renown has led me to address myself to you."

"If my life could restore you your past power, madame," replied D'Harmental, "speak; I am ready to risk it with joy. Who is this enchanter that I must combat; this giant that

I must destroy? Since you have chosen me above all, I will prove myself worthy of the honor. From this moment I engage my word, even if it cost me my life."

"If you lose your life, chevalier, it will be in good company," said the lady, untying her mask, and discovering her face, "for you would lose it with the son of Louis XIV., and the granddaughter of the great Conde."

"Madame la Duchesse de Maine!" cried D'Harmental, falling on one knee; "will your highness pardon me, if, not knowing you, I have said anything which may fall short of the profound respect I feel for you."

"You have said nothing for which I am not proud and grateful, chevalier, but,[Pg 259] perhaps, you now repent. If so, you are at liberty to withdraw."

"Heaven forbid, madame, that having had the honor to engage my life in the service of so great and noble a princess, I should deprive myself of the greatest honor I ever dared to hope for. No, madame; take seriously, I beg, what I offered half in jest; my arm, my sword, and my life."

"I see," said the Duchesse de Maine, with that smile which gave her such power over all who approached her, "that the Baron de Valef did not deceive me, and you are such as he described. Come, I will present you to our friends."

The duchess went first, D'Harmental followed, astonished at what had passed, but fully resolved, partly from pride, partly from conviction, not to withdraw a step.

The duchess conducted him to a room where four new personages awaited him. These were the Cardinal de Polignac, the Marquis de Pompadour, Monsieur de Malezieux, and the Abbe Brigaud.

The Cardinal de Polignac was supposed to be the lover of Madame de Maine. He was a handsome prelate, from forty to forty-five years of age; always dressed with the greatest care, with an unctuous voice, a cold face, and a timid heart; devoured by ambition, which was eternally combated by the weakness of his character, which always drew him back where he should advance; of high birth, as his name indicated, very learned for a cardinal, and very well informed for a nobleman.

Monsieur de Pompadour was a man of from forty-five to fifty, who had been a minion of the dauphin's, the son of Louis XIV., and who had so great a love for his whole family, that, seeing with grief that the regent was going to declare war against Philip V., he had thrown himself, body and soul, into the Duc de Maine's party. Proud and disinterested, he had given a rare example of loyalty, in sending back to the regent the brevet of his pensions and those of his wife, and in refusing for himself and the Marquis de Courcillon, his son-in-law, every place offered to them.

Monsieur de Malezieux was a man of from sixty to sixty-five, Chancellor of Dombes and Lord of Chatenay: he owed this double title to the gratitude of M. de Maine, whose education he had conducted. A poet, a musician, an author of small comedies, which he played himself with infinite spirit; born for an idle and intellectual life; always occupied in procuring pleasure for others, and above all for Madame de Maine, whom he adored, he was a type of the Sybarite of the eighteenth century, but, like the Sybarites who, drawn by the aspect of beauty, followed Cleopatra to Actium, and were killed around her, he would have followed his dear Bénédicte through fire and water, and, at a word from her, would, without hesitation, and almost without regret, have thrown himself from the towers of Notre-Dame.

The Abbe Brigaud was the son of a Lyons merchant. His father, who was commercially related with the court of Spain, was charged to make overtures, as if on his own account, for the marriage of the young Louis XIV. with the young Maria Theresa of Austria. If these overtures had been badly received, the ministers of France would have disavowed them; but they were well received, and they supported them.

The marriage took place; and, as the little Brigaud was born about the same time as the dauphin, he asked, in recompense, that the king's son should stand godfather to his child, which was granted to him. He then made acquaintance with the Marquis de Pompadour, who, as we have said, was one of the pages of honor. When he was of an age to decide on his profession, he joined the Fathers of the Oratory. He was a clever and an ambitious man, but, as often happens to the greatest geniuses, he had never had an opportunity of making himself known.

Some time before the period of which we are writing, he met the Marquis de Pompadour, who was seeking a man of spirit and enterprise as the secretary of Madame de Maine. He told him to what the situation would expose him at the present time. Brigaud weighed for an[Pg 260] instant the good and evil chances, and, as the former appeared to predominate, he accepted it.

Of these four men, D'Harmental only knew the Marquis de Pompadour, whom he had often met at the house of Monsieur de Courcillon, his son-in-law, a distant relation of the D'Harmentals.

When D'Harmental entered the room, Monsieur de Polignac, Monsieur de Malezieux, and Monsieur de Pompadour were standing talking at the fireplace, and the Abbe Brigaud was seated at a table classifying some papers.

"Gentlemen," said the Duchesse de Maine, "here is the brave champion of whom the Baron de Valef has spoken to us, and who has been brought here by your dear De Launay, Monsieur de Malezieux. If his name and antecedents are not sufficient to stand sponsor for him, I will answer for him personally."

"Presented thus by your highness," said Malezieux, "we shall see in him not only a companion, but a chief, whom we are ready to follow wherever he may lead."

"My dear D'Harmental," said the Marquis de Pompadour, extending his hand to him, "we were already relations, we are now almost brothers."

"Welcome, monsieur!" said the Cardinal de Polignac, in the unctuous tone habitual to him, and which contrasted so strangely with the coldness of his countenance.

The Abbe Brigaud raised his head with a movement resembling that of a serpent, and fixed on D'Harmental two little eyes, brilliant as those of the lynx.

"Gentlemen," said D'Harmental, after having answered each of them by a bow, "I am new and strange among you, and, above all, ignorant of what is passing, or in what manner I can serve you; but though my word has only been engaged to you for a few minutes, my devotion to your cause is of many years' standing. I beg you, therefore, to grant me the confidence so graciously claimed for me by her highness. All that I shall ask after that will be a speedy occasion to prove myself worthy of it."

"Well said!" cried the Duchesse de Maine; "commend me to a soldier for going straight to the point! No, Monsieur d'Harmental, we will have no secrets from you, and the opportunity you require, and which will place each of us in our proper position—"

"Excuse me, Madame la Duchesse," interrupted the cardinal, who was playing uneasily with his necktie, "but, from your manner, the chevalier will think that the affair is a conspiracy."

"And what is it then, cardinal?" asked the duchess, impatiently.

"It is," said the cardinal, "a council, secret, it is true, but in no degree reprehensible, in which we only seek a means of remedying the misfortunes of the state, and enlightening France on her true interests, by recalling the last will of the king, Louis XIV."

"Stay, cardinal!" said the duchess, stamping her foot; "you will kill me with impatience by your circumlocutions. Chevalier," continued she, addressing D'Harmental, "do not listen to his eminence, who at this moment, doubtless, is thinking of his Lucrece. If it had been a simple council, the talents of his eminence would soon have extricated us from our troubles, without the necessity of applying to you; but it is a bona fide conspiracy against the regent—a conspiracy which numbers the king of Spain, Cardinal Alberoni, the Duc de Maine, myself, the Marquis de Pompadour, Monsieur de Malezieux, l'Abbe Brigaud, Valef, yourself, the cardinal himself the president; and which will include half the parliament and three parts of France. This is the matter in hand, chevalier. Are you content, cardinal? Have I spoken clearly, gentlemen?"

"Madame—" murmured Malezieux, joining his hands before her with more devotion than he would have done before the Virgin.

"No, no; stop, Malezieux," said the duchess, "but the cardinal enrages me with his half-measures. Mon Dieu! are these eternal waverings worthy of a man? For myself, I do not ask a sword, I do not ask a dagger; give me but a nail, and I,[Pg 261] a woman, and almost a dwarf, will go, like a new Jael, and drive it into the temple of this other Sisera. Then all will be finished; and, if I fail, no one but myself will be compromised."

Monsieur de Polignac sighed deeply; Pompadour burst out laughing; Malezieux tried to calm the duchess; and Brigaud bent his head, and went on writing as if he had heard nothing. As to D'Harmental, he would have kissed the hem of her dress, so superior was this woman, in his eyes, to the four men who surrounded her.

At this moment they heard the sound of a carriage, which drove into the courtyard and stopped at the door. The person expected was doubtless some one of importance, for there was an instant silence, and the Duchesse de Maine, in her impatience, went herself to open the door.

"Well?" asked she.

"He is here," said a voice, which D'Harmental recognized as that of the Bat.

"Enter, enter, prince," said the duchess; "we wait for you."

CHAPTER VI.
THE PRINCE DE CELLAMARE.

At this invitation there entered a tall, thin, grave man, with a sunburned complexion, who at a single glance took in everything in the room, animate and inanimate. The chevalier recognized the ambassador of their Catholic majesties, the Prince de Cellamare.

"Well, prince," asked the duchess, "what have you to tell us?"

"I have to tell you, madame," replied the prince, kissing her hand respectfully, and throwing his cloak on a chair, "that your highness had better change coachmen. I predict misfortune if you retain in your service the fellow who drove me here. He seems to me to be some one employed by the regent to break the necks of your highness and all your companions."

Every one began to laugh, and particularly the coachman himself, who, without ceremony, had entered behind the prince; and who, throwing his hat and cloak on a seat, showed himself a man of high bearing, from thirty-five to forty years old, with the lower part of his face hidden by a black handkerchief.

"Do you hear, my dear Laval, what the prince says of you?"

"Yes, yes," said Laval; "it is worth while to give him Montmorencies to be treated like that. Ah, M. le Prince, the first gentlemen in France are not good enough for your coachmen! Peste! you are difficult to please. Have you many coachmen at Naples who date from Robert the Strong?"

"What! is it you, my dear count?" said the prince, holding out his hand to him.

"Myself, prince! Madame la Duchesse sent away her coachman to keep Lent in his own family, and engaged me for this night. She thought it safer."

"And Madame la Duchesse did right," said the cardinal. "One cannot take too many precautions."

"Ah, your eminence," said Laval, "I should like to know if you would be of the same opinion after passing half the night on the box of a carriage, first to fetch M. d'Harmental from the opera ball, and then to take the prince from the Hotel Colbert."

"What!" said D'Harmental, "was it you, Monsieur le Comte, who had the goodness—"

"Yes, young man," replied Laval; "and I would have gone to the end of the world to bring you here, for I know you. You are a gallant gentleman; you were one of the first to enter Denain, and you took Albemarle. You were fortunate enough not to leave half your jaw there, as I did in Italy. You were right, for it would have been a further motive for taking away your regiment, which they have done, however."

"We will restore you that a hundredfold," said the duchess; "but now let us speak of Spain. Prince, you have news from Alberoni, Pompadour tells me."

"Yes, your highness."

"What are they?"

"Both good and bad. His majesty Philip V. is in one of his melancholy moods and will not determine upon anything. [Pg 262] He will not believe in the treaty of the quadruple alliance."

"Will not believe in it!" cried the duchess; "and the treaty ought to be signed now. In a week Dubois will have brought it here."

"I know it, your highness," replied Cellamare, coldly; "but his Catholic majesty does not."

"Then he abandons us?"

"Almost."

"What becomes, then, of the queen's fine promises, and the empire she pretends to have over her husband?"

"She promises to prove it to you, madame," replied the prince, "when something is done."

"Yes," said the Cardinal de Polignac; "and then she will fail in that promise."

"No, your eminence! I will answer for her."

"What I see most clearly in all this is," said Laval, "that we must compromise the king. Once compromised, he must go on."

"Now, then," said Cellamare, "we are coming to business."

"But how to compromise him," asked the Duchesse de Maine, "without a letter from him, without even a verbal message, and at five hundred leagues' distance?"

"Has he not his representative at Paris, and is not that representative in your house at this very moment, madame?"

"Prince," said the duchess, "you have more extended

powers than you are willing to admit."

"No; my powers are limited to telling you that the citadel of Toledo and the fortress of Saragossa are at your service. Find the means of making the regent enter there, and their Catholic majesties will close the door on him so securely that he will not leave it again, I promise you."

"It is impossible," said Monsieur de Polignac.

"Impossible! and why?" cried D'Harmental. "On the contrary, what is more simple? Nothing is necessary but eight or ten determined men, a well-closed carriage, and relays to Bayonne."

"I have already offered to undertake it," said Laval.

"And I," said Pompadour.

"You cannot," said the duchess; "the regent knows you; and if the thing failed, you would be lost."

"It is a pity," said Cellamare, coldly; "for, once arrived at Toledo or Saragossa, there is greatness in store for him who shall have succeeded."

"And the blue ribbon," added Madame de Maine, "on his return to Paris."

"Oh, silence, I beg, madame," said D'Harmental; "for if your highness says such things, you give to devotion the air of ambition, and rob it of all its merit. I was going to offer myself for the enterprise—I, who am unknown to the regent—but now I hesitate; and yet I venture to believe myself worthy of the confidence of your highness, and able to justify it."——"What, chevalier!" cried the duchess, "you would risk—"

"My life; it is all I have to risk. I thought I had already offered it, and that your highness had accepted it. Was I mistaken?"

"No, no, chevalier," said the duchess quickly; "and you are a brave and loyal gentleman. I have always believed in presentiments, and from the moment Valef pronounced your name, telling me that you were what I find you to be, I felt of what assistance you would be to us. Gentlemen, you hear what the chevalier says; in what can you aid him?"

"In whatever he may want," said Laval and Pompadour.

"The coffers of their Catholic majesties are at his disposal," said the Prince de Cellamare, "and he may make free use of them."

"I thank you," said D'Harmental, turning toward the Comte de Laval and the Marquis de Pompadour; "but, known as you are, you would only make the enterprise more difficult. Occupy yourselves only in obtaining for me a passport for Spain, as if I had the charge of some prisoner of importance: that ought to be easy."

"I undertake it," said the Abbe Brigaud: "I will get from D'Argenson a paper all prepared, which will only have to be filled in."

[Pg 263]"Excellent Brigaud," said Pompadour; "he does not speak often, but he speaks to the purpose."

"It is he who should be made cardinal," said the duchess, "rather than certain great lords of my acquaintance; but as soon as we can dispose of the blue and the red, be easy, gentlemen, we shall not be miserly. Now, chevalier, you have heard what the prince said. If you want money—"

"Unfortunately," replied D'Harmental, "I am not rich enough to refuse his excellency's offer, and so soon as I have arrived at the end of about a million pistoles which I have at home, I must have recourse to you."

"To him, to me, to us all, chevalier, for each one in such circumstances should tax himself according to his means. I have little ready money, but I have many diamonds and pearls; therefore want for nothing, I beg. All the world has not your disinterestedness, and there is devotion which must be bought."

"Above all, be prudent," said the cardinal.

"Do not be uneasy," replied D'Harmental, contemptuously. "I have sufficient grounds of complaint against the regent for it to be believed, if I were taken, that it was an affair between him and me, and that my vengeance was entirely personal."

"But," said the Comte de Laval, "you must have a kind of lieutenant in this enterprise, some one on whom you can count. Have you any one?"

"I think so," replied D'Harmental; "but I must be informed each morning what the regent will do in the evening. Monsieur le Prince de Cellamare, as ambassador, must have his secret police."

"Yes," said the prince, embarrassed, "I have some people who give me an account."——"That is exactly it," said D'Harmental.

"Where do you lodge?" asked the cardinal.

"At my own house, monseigneur, Rue de Richelieu, No.

74."

"And how long have you lived there?"

"Three years."

"Then you are too well known there, monsieur; you must change quarters. The people whom you receive are known, and the sight of strange faces would give rise to questions."

"This time your eminence is right," said D'Harmental. "I will seek another lodging in some retired neighborhood."

"I undertake it," said Brigaud; "my costume does not excite suspicions. I will engage you a lodging as if it was destined for a young man from the country who has been recommended to me, and who has come to occupy some place in an office."

"Truly, my dear Brigaud," said the Marquis de Pompadour, "you are like the princess in the 'Arabian Nights,' who never opened her mouth but to drop pearls."

"Well, it is a settled thing, Monsieur l'Abbe," said D'Harmental; "I reckon on you, and I shall announce at home that I am going to leave Paris for a three months' trip."

"Everything is settled, then," said the Duchesse de Maine joyfully. "This is the first time that I have been able to see clearly into our affairs, chevalier, and we owe it to you. I shall not forget it."

"Gentlemen," said Malezieux, pulling out his watch, "I would observe that it is four o'clock in the morning, and that we shall kill our dear duchesse with fatigue."

"You are mistaken," said the duchess; "such nights rest me, and it is long since I have passed one so good."

"Prince," said Laval, "you must be contented with the coachman whom you wished discharged, unless you would prefer driving yourself, or going on foot."

"No, indeed," said the prince, "I will risk it. I am a Neapolitan, and believe in omens. If you overturn me it will be a sign that we must stay where we are—if you conduct me safely it will be a sign that we may go on."

"Pompadour, you must take back Monsieur d'Harmental," said the duchess.

"Willingly," said the marquis. "It is a long time since we met, and we have a hundred things to say to each other."

"Cannot I take leave of my sprightly[Pg 264] bat?" asked D'Harmental; "for I do not forget that it is to her I owe the happiness of having offered my services to your highness."

"De Launay," cried the duchess, conducting the Prince of Cellamare to the door, "De Launay, here is Monsieur le Chevalier d'Harmental, who says you are the greatest sorceress he has ever known."

"Well!" said she who has left us such charming memoirs, under the name of Madame de Staël, "do you believe in my prophecies now, Monsieur le Chevalier?"

"I believe, because I hope," replied the chevalier. "But now that I know the fairy that sent you, it is not your predictions that astonish me the most. How were you so well informed about the past, and, above all, of the present?"

"Well, De Launay, be kind, and do not torment the chevalier any longer, or he will believe us to be two witches, and be afraid of us."

"Was there not one of your friends, chevalier," asked De Launay, "who left you this morning in the Bois de Boulogne to come and say adieu to us."

"Valef! It is Valef!" cried D'Harmental. "I understand now."

"In the place of Œdipus you would have been devoured ten times over by the Sphinx."

"But the mathematics; but the anatomy; but Virgil?" replied D'Harmental.

"Do you not know, chevalier," said Malezieux, mixing in the conversation, "that we never call her anything here but our 'savante?' with the exception of Chaulieu, however, who calls her his flirt, and his coquette; but all as a poetical license. We let her loose the other day on Du Vernay, our doctor, and she beat him at anatomy."

"And," said the Marquis de Pompadour, taking D'Harmental's arm to lead him away, "the good man in his disappointment declared that there was no other girl in France who understood the human frame so well."

"Ah!" said the Abbe Brigaud, folding his papers, "here is the first savant on record who has been known to make a bon-mot. It is true that he did not intend it."

And D'Harmental and Pompadour, having taken leave of the duchess, retired laughing, followed by the Abbe Brigaud, who reckoned on them to drive him home.

"Well," said Madame de Maine, addressing the Cardinal de Polignac, "does your eminence still find it such a terrible thing to conspire?"

"Madame," replied the cardinal, who could not understand that any one could laugh when their head was in danger, "I will ask you the same question when we are all in the Bastille."

And he went away with the good chancellor, deploring the ill-luck which had thrown him into such a rash enterprise.

The duchess looked after him with a contempt which she could not disguise: then, when she was alone with De Launay:

"My dear Sophy," said she, "let us put out our lantern, for I think we have found a man."

CHAPTER VII.
ALBERONI.

When D'Harmental awoke, he wondered if all had been a dream. Events had, during the last thirty-six hours, succeeded each other with such rapidity, that he had been carried away, as by a whirlpool, without knowing where he was going. Now for the first time he had leisure to reflect on the past and the future.

These were times in which every one conspired more or less. We know the natural bent of the mind in such a case. The first feeling we experience, after having made an engagement in a moment of exaltation, is one almost of regret for having been so forward. Little by little we become familiarized with the idea of the dangers we are running. Imagination removes them from our sight, and presents instead the ambitions we may realize. Pride soon becomes mingled with it, as we think that we have become a secret power in the State. We walk along proudly, with head erect, passing contemptuously those who lead an ordinary life; we cradle ourselves in our hopes, and[Pg 265] wake one morning conquering or conquered; carried on the shoulders of the people, or broken by the wheels of that machine called the government.

Thus it was with D'Harmental. After a few moments' reflection, he saw things under the same aspect as he had done the day before, and congratulated himself upon having taken the highest place among such people as the Montmorencies and the Polignacs. His family had transmitted to him much of that adventurous chivalry so much in vogue under Louis XIII., and which Richelieu with his scaffolds, and Louis XIV. with his antechambers, had not quite been able to destroy. There was something romantic in enlisting himself, a young man, under the banners of a woman, and that woman a granddaughter of the great Conde.

D'Harmental lost no time in preparing to keep the promises he had made, for he felt that the eyes of all the conspirators were upon him, and that on his courage and prudence depended the destinies of two kingdoms, and the politics of the world. At this moment the regent was the keystone of the arch of the European edifice; and France was beginning to take, if not by arms, at least by diplomacy, that influence which she had unfortunately not always preserved. Placed at the center of the triangle formed by the three great Powers, with eyes fixed on Germany, one arm extended toward England, and the other toward Spain, ready to turn on either of these three States that should not treat her according to her dignity, she had assumed, under the Duc d'Orleans, an attitude of calm strength which she had never had under Louis XIV.

This arose from the division of interests consequent on the usurpation of William of Orange, and the accession of Philip V. to the throne of Spain. Faithful to his old hatred against the stadtholder, who had refused him his daughter, Louis XIV. had constantly advanced the pretensions of James II., and, after his death, of the Chevalier de St. George. Faithful to his compact with Philip V., he had constantly aided his grandson against the emperor, with men and money; and, weakened by this double war, he had been reduced to the shameful treaty of Utrecht; but at the death of the old king all was changed, and the regent had adopted a very different line of conduct. The treaty of Utrecht was only a truce, which had been broken from the moment when England and Holland did not pursue common interests with those of France.

In consequence, the regent had first of all held out his hand to George I., and the treaty of the triple alliance had been signed at La Haye, by Dubois, in the name of France; by General Cadogan, for England; and by the pensioner, Heinsiens, for Holland. This was a great step toward the pacification of Europe, but the interests of Austria and Spain were still in suspense. Charles VI. would not recognize Philip V. as king of Spain; and Philip V., on his part, would not renounce his rights over those provinces of the Spanish empire which the treaty of Utrecht had given to the emperor.

It was in the hopes of bringing these things about that the regent had sent Dubois to London, where he was pursuing the treaty of the quadruple alliance with as much ardor as he had that of La Haye. This treaty would have neutralized the pretensions of the State not approved by the four Powers. This was what was feared by Philip V. (or rather the Cardinal d'Alberoni).

It was not thus with Alberoni; his was one of those extraordinary fortunes which one sees, always with new astonishment, spring up around the throne; one of those caprices of destiny which chance raises and destroys;

like a gigantic waterspout, which advances on the ocean, threatening to annihilate everything, but which is dispersed by a stone thrown from the hand of a sailor; or an avalanche, which threatens to swallow towns, and fill up valleys, because a bird in its flight has detached a flake of snow on the summit of the mountain.

Alberoni was born in a gardener's cottage, and as a child he was the bell-ringer. When still a young man he exchanged his smock-frock for a surplice, but was of a merry and jesting disposition. The Duke[Pg 266] of Parma heard him laugh one day so gayly, that the poor duke, who did not laugh every day, asked who it was that was so merry, and had him called. Alberoni related to him some grotesque adventure. His highness laughed heartily; and finding that it was pleasant to laugh sometimes, attached him to his person. The duke soon found that he had mind, and fancied that that mind was not incapable of business.

It was at this time that the poor bishop of Parma came back, deeply mortified at his reception by the generalissimo of the French army. The susceptibility of this envoy might compromise the grave interests which his highness had to discuss with France. His highness judged that Alberoni was the man to be humiliated by nothing, and he sent the abbe to finish the negotiation which the bishop had left unfinished. M. de Vendome, who had not put himself out for a bishop, did not do so for an abbe, and received the second ambassador as he had the first; but, instead of following the example of his predecessor, he found in M. de Vendome's own situation so much subject for merry jests and strange praises, that the affair was finished at once, and he came back to the duke with everything arranged to his desire.

This was a reason for the duke to employ him a second time. This time Vendome was just going to sit down to table, and Alberoni, instead of beginning about business, asked if he would taste two dishes of his cooking, went into the kitchen, and came back, a "soupe au fromage" in one hand, and macaroni in the other. De Vendome found the soup so good that he asked Alberoni to take some with him at his own table. At dessert Alberoni introduced his business, and profiting by the good humor of Vendome, he twisted him round his finger.

His highness was astonished. The greatest genius he had met with had never done so much. The next time it was M. de Vendome who asked the duke of Parma if he had nothing else to negotiate with him. Alberoni found means of persuading his sovereign that he would be more useful to him near Vendome than elsewhere, and he persuaded Vendome that he could not exist without "soupe au fromage" and macaroni.

M. de Vendome attached him to his service, allowed him to interfere in his most secret affairs, and made him his chief secretary. At this time Vendome left for Spain. Alberoni put himself in communication with Madame des Ursins; and when Vendome died, she gave him, near her, the same post he had occupied near the deceased.

This was another step. The Princesse des Ursins began to

get old, an unpardonable crime in the eyes of Philip V. She resolved to place a young woman near the king, through whom she might continue to reign over him. Alberoni proposed the daughter of his old master, whom he represented as a child, without character, and without will, who would claim nothing of royalty but the name. The princess was taken by this promise. The marriage was decided on, and the young princess left Italy for Spain.

Her first act of authority was to arrest the Princesse des Ursins, who had come to meet her in a court dress, and to send her back, as she was, with her neck uncovered, in a bitter frost, in a carriage of which the guard had broken the window with his elbow, first to Burgos, and then to France, where she arrived, after having been obliged to borrow fifty pistoles from her servants. After his first interview with Elizabeth Farnese, the king announced to Alberoni that he was prime minister. From that day, thanks to the young queen, who owed him everything, the ex-ringer of bells exercised an unlimited empire over Philip V.

Now this is what Alberoni pictured to himself, having always prevented Philip V. from recognizing the peace of Utrecht. If the conspiracy succeeded—if D'Harmental carried off the Duc d'Orleans, and took him to the citadel of Toledo, or the fortress of Saragossa—Alberoni would get Monsieur de Maine recognized as regent, would withdraw France from the quadruple alliance, throw the Chevalier de St. George with the fleet on the English coast,[Pg 267] and set Prussia, Sweden, and Russia, with whom he had a treaty of alliance, at variance with Holland. The empire would then profit by their dispute to retake Naples and Sicily; would assure Tuscany to the second son of the king of Spain; would reunite the Catholic Netherlands to France, give Sardinia to the Dukes of Savoy, Commachio to the pope, and Mantua to the Venetians. He would make himself the soul of the great league, of the south against the north; and if Louis XV. died, would crown Philip V. king of half the world.

All these things were now in the hands of a young man of twenty-six years of age; and it was not astonishing that he should be, at first, frightened at the responsibility which weighed upon him.

As he was still in deep thought, the Abbe Brigaud entered. He had already found a lodging for the chevalier, at No. 5, Rue du Temps-Perdu; a small furnished room, suitable to a young man who came to seek his fortune in Paris. He brought him also two thousand pistoles from the Prince of Cellamare.

D'Harmental wished to refuse them, for it seemed as if he would be no longer acting according to conscience and devotion; but Brigaud explained to him that in such an enterprise there are susceptibilities to conquer, and accomplices to pay; and that besides, if the affair succeeded, he would have to set out instantly for Spain, and perhaps make his way by force of gold. Brigaud carried away a complete suit of the chevalier's, as a pattern for a fresh one suitable for a clerk in an office. The Abbe Brigaud was a useful man.

D'Harmental passed the rest of the day in preparing for

his pretended journey, and removed, in case of accident, every letter which might compromise a friend; then went toward the Rue St. Honore, where—thanks to La Normande—he hoped to have news of Captain Roquefinette. In fact, from the moment that a lieutenant for his enterprise had been spoken of, he had thought of this man, who had given him, as his second, a proof of his careless courage. He had instantly recognized in him one of those adventurers always ready to sell their blood for a good price, and who, in time of peace, when their swords are useless to the State, place them at the service of individuals.

On becoming a conspirator one always becomes superstitious, and D'Harmental fancied that it was an intervention of Providence which had introduced him to Roquefinette. The chevalier, without being a regular customer, went occasionally to the tavern of La Fillon. It was quite fashionable at that time to go and drink at her house. D'Harmental was to her neither her son, a name which she gave to all her "habitués," nor her gossip, a word which she reserved for the Abbe Dubois, but simply Monsieur le Chevalier; a mark of respect which would have been considered rather a humiliation by most of the young men of fashion. La Fillon was much astonished when D'Harmental asked to see one of her servants, called La Normande.

"Oh, mon Dieu! Monsieur le Chevalier!" said she, "I am really distressed; but La Normande is waiting at a dinner which will last till to-morrow evening."

"Plague! what a dinner!"

"What is to be done?" replied La Fillon. "It is a caprice of an old friend of the house. He will not be waited on by any one but her, and I cannot refuse him that satisfaction."

"When he has money, I suppose?"

"You are mistaken. I give him credit up to a certain sum. It is a weakness, but one cannot help being grateful. He started me in the world, such as you see me, monsieur—I, who have had in my house the best people in Paris, including the regent. I was only the daughter of a poor chair-bearer. Oh! I am not like the greater part of your beautiful duchesses, who deny their origin; nor like two-thirds of your dukes and peers, who fabricate genealogies for themselves. No! what I am, I owe to my own merit, and I am proud of it."

"Then," said the chevalier, who was not particularly interested by La Fillon's history, "you say that La Normande will[Pg 268] not have finished with this dinner till to-morrow evening?"

"The jolly old captain never stays less time than that at table, when once he is there."

"But, my dear presidente" (this was a name sometimes given to La Fillon, as a certain quid pro quo for the presidente who had the same name as herself), "do you think, by chance, your captain may be my captain?"

"What is yours called?"

"Captain Roquefinette."

"It is the same."

"He is here?"

"In person."

"Well, he is just the man I want; and I only asked for La Normande to get his address."

"Then all is right," said the presidente.

"Have the kindness to send for him."

"Oh! he would not come down for the regent himself. If you want to see him you must go up."

"Where?"

"At No. 2, where you supped the other evening with the Baron de Valef. Oh! when he has money, nothing is too good for him. Although he is but a captain, he has the heart of a king."

"Better and better," said D'Harmental, mounting the staircase, without being deterred by the recollection of the misadventure which had happened to him in that room; "that is exactly what I want."

If D'Harmental had not known the room in question, the voice of the captain would soon have served him for a guide.

"Now, my little loves," said he, "the third and last verse, and together in the chorus." Then he began singing in a magnificent bass voice, and four or five female voices took up the chorus.

"That is better," said the captain; "now let us have the 'Battle of Malplaquet."

"No, no," said a voice; "I have had enough of your battle."

"What! enough of it—a battle I was at myself?"

"That is nothing to me. I like a romance better than all your wicked battle-songs, full of oaths." And she began to sing "Linval loved Arsene—"

"Silence!" said the captain. "Am I not master here? As long as I have any money I will be served as I like. When I have no more, that will be another thing; then you may sing what you like; I shall have nothing to say to it."

It appeared that the servants of the cabaret thought it beneath the dignity of their sex to subscribe to such a pretension, for there was such a noise that D'Harmental thought it best to announce himself.

"Pull the bobbin, and the latch will go up," said the captain.

D'Harmental followed the instruction which was given him in the words of Little Red Riding-hood; and, having entered, saw the captain lying on a couch before the remains of an ample dinner, leaning on a cushion, a woman's shawl over his shoulders, a great pipe in his mouth, and a cloth rolled round his head like a turban. Three or four servants were standing round him with napkins in their hands. On a chair near him was placed his coat, on which was to be seen a new shoulder-knot, his hat with a new lace, and the famous sword which had furnished Ravanne with the facetious comparison to his mother's spit.

"What! is it you?" cried the captain. "You find me like Monsieur de Bonneval—in my seraglio, and surrounded by my slaves. You do not know Monsieur de Bonneval, ladies: he is a pasha of three tails, who, like me, could not bear romances, but who understood how to live. Heaven preserve me from such a fate as his!"

"Yes, it is I, captain," said D'Harmental, unable to prevent laughing at the grotesque group which presented itself. "I see you did not give me a false address, and I congratulate you on your veracity."

"Welcome, chevalier," said the captain. "Ladies, I beg you to serve monsieur with the grace which distinguishes you, and to sing him whatever songs he likes. Sit down, chevalier, and eat and drink as if you were at home, particularly as it is[Pg 269] your horse we are eating and drinking. He is already more than half gone, poor animal, but the remains are good."

"Thank you, captain, I have just dined; and I have only one word to say to you, if you will permit it."

"No, pardieu! I do not permit it," said the captain, "unless it is about another engagement—that would come before everything. La Normande, give me my sword."

"No, captain; it is on business," interrupted D'Harmental.

"Oh! if it is on business, I am your humble servant; but I am a greater tyrant than the tyrants of Thebes or Corinth—Archias, Pelopidas, Leonidas, or any other that ends in 'as,' who put off business till to-morrow. I have enough money to last till to-morrow evening; then, after to-morrow, business."

"But at least after to-morrow, captain, I may count upon you?"

"For life or death, chevalier."

"I believe that the adjournment is prudent."

"Prudentissimo!" said the captain. "Athenais, light my pipe. La Normande, pour me out something to drink."

"The day after to-morrow, then, captain?"

"Yes; where shall I find you?"

"Listen," replied D'Harmental, speaking so as to be heard by no one but him. "Walk, from ten to eleven o'clock in the morning, in the Rue du Temps Perdu. Look up; you will be called from somewhere, and you must mount till you meet some one you know. A good breakfast will await you."

"All right, chevalier," replied the captain; "from ten to eleven in the morning. Excuse me if I do not conduct you to the door, but you know it is not the custom with Turks."

The chevalier made a sign with his hand that he dispensed with this formality, and descended the staircase. He was only on the fourth step when he heard the captain begin the famous song of the Dragoons of Malplaquet, which had perhaps caused as much blood to be shed in duels as there had been on the field of battle.

CHAPTER VIII.
THE GARRET.

The next day the Abbe Brigaud came to the chevalier's house at the same hour as before. He was a perfectly punctual man. He brought with him three things particularly useful to the chevalier; clothes, a passport, and the report of the Prince of Cellamare's police respecting what the regent was going to do on the present day, March 24, 1718. The clothes were simple, as became the cadet of a bourgeois family come to seek his fortune in Paris. The chevalier tried them on, and, thanks to his own good looks, found that they became him admirably.

The abbe shook his head. He would have preferred that the chevalier should not have looked quite so well; but this was an irreparable misfortune. The passport was in the name of Signior Diego, steward of the noble house of Oropesa, who had a commission to bring back to Spain a sort of maniac, a bastard of the said house, whose mania was to believe himself regent of France. This was a precaution taken to meet anything that the Duc d'Orleans might call out from the bottom of the carriage; and, as the passport was according to rule, signed by the Prince de Cellamare, and "viséd" by Monsieur Voyer d'Argenson, there was no reason why the regent, once in the carriage, should not arrive safely at Pampeluna, when all would be done.

The signature of Monsieur Voyer d'Argenson was imitated with a truth which did honor to the caligraphers of the Prince de Cellamare. As to the report, it was a chef-d'œuvre of clearness; and we insert it word for word, to give an idea of the regent's life, and of the manner in which the Spanish ambassador's police was conducted. It was dated two o'clock in the morning.

"To-day the regent will rise late. There has been a supper in his private rooms; Madame d'Averne was there for the first time instead of Madame de Parabere. The other women were the Duchesse de Falaris, and Saseri, maid of honor to madame. The men were the Marquis de Broglie, the Count de Nocé, the Mar[Pg 270]quis de Canillac, the Duc de Brancas, and the Chevalier de Simiane. As to the Marquis de Lafare and Monsieur de Fargy, they were detained in bed by an illness, of which the cause is unknown. At noon there will be a council. The regent will communicate to the Ducs de Maine and de Guiche the project of the treaty of the quadruple alliance, which the Abbe Dubois has sent him, announcing his return in three or four days.

"The rest of the day is given entirely to paternity. The day before yesterday the regent married his daughter by La Desmarets, who was brought up by the nuns of St. Denis. She dines with her husband at the Palais Royal, and, after dinner, the regent takes her to the opera, to the box of Madame Charlotte de Baviere. La Desmarets, who has not seen her daughter for six years, is told that, if she wishes to see her, she can come to the theater. The regent, in spite of his caprice for Madame d'Averne, still pays court to Madame de Sabran, who piques herself on her fidelity—not to her husband, but to the Duc de Richelieu. To advance his affairs, the regent has appointed Monsieur de Sabran his maitre-d'hotel."

"I hope that is business well done," said the Abbe Brigaud.

"Yes, my dear abbe," replied D'Harmental; "but if the regent does not give us greater opportunities than that for executing our enterprise, it will not be easy for us to take him to Spain."

"Patience, patience," said Brigaud; "if there had been an opportunity to-day you would not have been able to profit by it."

"No; you are right."

"Then you see that what God does is well done. He has left us this day; let us profit by it to move."

This was neither a long nor difficult business. D'Harmental took his treasure, some books, and the packet which contained his wardrobe, and drove to the abbe's house. Then he sent away his carriage, saying he should go into the country in the evening, and would be away ten or twelve days. Then, having changed his elegant clothes for those that the abbe had brought him, he went to take possession of his new lodging. It was a room, or rather an attic, with a closet, on the fourth story, at No. 5, Rue du Temps Perdu. The proprietor of the house was an acquaintance of the Abbe Brigaud's; therefore, thanks to his recommendation, they had gone to some expense for the young provincial. He found beautifully white curtains, very fine linen, and a well-furnished library; so he saw at once that, if not so well off as in his own apartments, he should be tolerably comfortable.

Madame Denis (this was the name of the abbe's friend) was waiting to do the honors of the room to her future lodger. She boasted to him of its convenience, and promised him that there would be no noise to disturb him from his work. To all which he replied in such a modest manner, that on going down to the first floor, where she lived, Madame Denis particularly recommended him to the care of the porter and his wife. This young man, though in appearance he could certainly compete with the proudest seigneurs of the court, seemed to her far from having the bold and free manners which the young men of the time affected. 'Tis true that the Abbe Brigaud, in the name of his pupil's family, had paid her a quarter in advance.

A minute after, the abbe went down to Madame Denis's room and completed her good opinion of his young protege by telling her that he received absolutely nobody but himself and an old friend of his father's. The latter, in spite of brusk manners, which he had acquired in the field, was a highly respectable gentleman.

D'Harmental used this precaution for fear the apparition of the captain might frighten Madame Denis if she happened to meet him. When he was alone, the chevalier, who had already taken the inventory of his own room, resolved to take that of the neighborhood. He was soon able to convince himself of the truth of what Madame Denis had said about the quietness of the street, for it was not more than ten or twelve feet wide; but[Pg 271] this was to him a recommendation, for he calculated that if pursued he might, by means of a plank passed from one window to that opposite, escape to the other side of the street. It was, therefore, important to establish amicable relations with his opposite neighbors.

Unfortunately, they did not seem much disposed to sociability; for not only were the windows hermetically sealed, as the time of year demanded, but the curtains behind them were so closely drawn, that there was not the smallest opening through which he could look. More favored than that of Madame Denis, the house opposite had a fifth story, or rather a terrace. An attic room just above the window so carefully closed, opened on this terrace. It was probably the residence of a gardener, for he had succeeded, by means of patience and labor, in transforming this terrace into a garden, containing, in some twelve feet square, a fountain, a grotto, and an arbor.

It is true that the fountain only played by means of a superior reservoir, which was fed in winter by the rain, and in summer by what he himself poured into it. It is true that the grotto, ornamented with shell work, and surrounded by a wooden fortress, appeared fit only to shelter an individual of the canine race. It is true that the arbor, entirely stripped of its leaves, appeared for the time fit only for an immense poultry cage. As there was nothing to be seen but a monotonous series of roofs and chimneys, D'Harmental closed his window, sat down in an armchair, put his feet on the hobs, took up a volume by the Abbe Chaulieu, and began to read the verses addressed to Mademoiselle de Launay, which had a double interest for him, since he knew the heroine.

The result of this reading was that the chevalier, while smiling at the octogenarian love of the good abbe, discovered that he, less fortunate, had his heart perfectly unoccupied. For a short time he had thought he had loved Madame d'Averne, and had been loved by her; but on her part this deep affection did not withstand the offer of some jewels from the regent, and the vanity of pleasing him.

Before this infidelity had occurred, the chevalier thought that it would have driven him to despair. It had occurred, and he had fought, because at that time men fought about everything which arose, probably from dueling being so strictly forbidden. Then he began to perceive how small a place this love had held in his heart. A real despair would not have allowed him to seek amusement at the bal-masque, in which case the exciting events of the last few days would not have happened.

The result of this was, that the chevalier remained convinced that he was incapable of a deep love, and that he was only destined for those charming wickednesses so much in vogue. He got up, and began to walk up and down his room; while thus employed he perceived that the window opposite was now wide open. He stopped mechanically, drew back his curtain, and began to investigate the room thus exposed.

It was to all appearance occupied by a woman. Near the window, on which a charming little Italian greyhound rested her delicate paws, was an embroidery frame. Opposite the window was an open harpsichord between two music stands, some crayon drawings, framed in black wood with a gold bead, were hung on the walls, which were covered with a Persian paper. Curtains of Indian chintz, of the same pattern as the paper, hung behind the muslin curtains. Through a second window, half open, he could see the curtains of a recess which probably contained a bed. The rest of the furniture was perfectly simple, but almost elegant, which was due evidently, not to the fortune, but to the taste of the modest inhabitant.

An old woman was sweeping, dusting, and arranging the room, profiting by the absence of its mistress to do this household work, for there was no one else to be seen in the room, and yet it was clear it was not she who inhabited it. All at once the head of the greyhound—whose great eyes had been wandering till then, with the aristocratic indifference characteristic[Pg 272] of that animal—became animated. She leaned her head over into the street; then, with a miraculous lightness and address, jumped on to the window-sill, pricking up her long-ears, and raising one of her paws. The chevalier understood by these signs that the tenant of the little room was approaching. He opened his window directly; unfortunately it was already too late, the street was solitary.

At the same moment the greyhound leaped from the window into the room and ran to the door. D'Harmental concluded that the young lady was mounting the stairs. In order to see her at his ease, he threw himself back and hid behind the curtain, but the old woman came to the window and closed it. The chevalier did not expect this denouement. There was nothing for him but to close his window also, and to come back and put his feet on the hobs. This was not amusing, and the chevalier began to feel how solitary he should be in this retreat. He remembered that formerly he also used to play and draw, and he thought that if he had the smallest spinet and some chalks, he could bear it with patience.

He rang for the porter, and asked where he could procure these things. The porter replied that every increase of furniture must be at his own expense. That if he wished for a harpsichord he must hire it, and that as to pencils, he could get them at the shop at the corner of the Rue de Clery.

D'Harmental gave a double louis to the porter, telling him that in half an hour he wished to have a spinet and some pencils. The double louis was an argument of which he had before found the advantage; reproaching himself, however, with having used it this time with a carelessness which gave the lie to his apparent position, he recalled the porter, and told him that he expected for his double louis to have, not only paper and pencils, but a month's hire of his instrument.

The porter replied that as he would speak as if it were for himself, the thing was possible; but that he must certainly pay the carriage. D'Harmental consented, and half an hour afterward was in possession of the desired objects. Such a wonderful place is Paris for every enchanter with a golden wand. The porter, when he went down, told his wife that if the new lodger was not more careful of his money, he would ruin his family, and showed her two crowns of six francs, which he had saved out of the double louis. The woman took the two crowns from the hands of her husband, calling him a drunkard, and put them into a little bag, hidden under a heap of old clothes, deploring the misfortune of fathers and mothers who bleed themselves to death for such good-for-nothings. This was the funeral oration of the chevalier's double louis.

CHAPTER IX.
A CITIZEN OF THE RUE DU TEMPS PERDU.

During this time D'Harmental was seated before the spinet, playing his best. The shopkeeper had had a sort of conscience, and had sent him an instrument nearly in tune, so that the chevalier began to perceive that he was doing wonders, and almost believed he was born with a genius for music, which had only required such a circumstance to develop itself. Doubtless there was some truth in this, for in the middle of a brilliant shake he saw, from the other side of the street, five little fingers delicately raising the curtain to see from whence this unaccustomed harmony proceeded. Unfortunately, at the sight of these fingers the chevalier forgot his music, and turned round quickly on the stool, in hopes of seeing a face behind the hand.

This ill-judged maneuver ruined him. The mistress of the little room, surprised in the act of curiosity, let the curtain fall. D'Harmental, wounded by this prudery, closed his window. The evening passed in reading, drawing, and playing. The chevalier could not have believed that there were so many minutes in an hour, or so many hours in a day. At ten o'clock in the evening he rang for the porter, to give orders for the next day; but no one answered; he had been in bed a long[Pg 273] time, and D'Harmental learned that there were people who went to bed about the time he ordered his carriage to pay visits.

D'HARMENTAL

This set him thinking of the strange manners of that unfortunate class of society who do not know the opera, who do not go to supper-parties, and who sleep all night and are awake all day. He thought you must come to the Rue du Temps Perdu to see such things, and promised himself to amuse his friends with an account of this singularity. He was glad to see also that his neighbor watched like himself. This showed in her a mind superior to that of the vulgar inhabitants of the Rue du Temps Perdu. D'Harmental believed that people only watched because they did not wish to sleep, or because they wanted to be amused. He forgot all those who do so because they are obliged. At midnight the light in the opposite windows was extinguished; D'Harmental also went to his bed. The next day the Abbe Brigaud appeared at eight o'clock. He brought D'Harmental the second report of secret police. It was in these terms:

"Three o'clock, a.m.

"In consequence of the regular life which he led yesterday, the regent has given orders to be called at nine.

"He will receive some appointed persons at that time.

"From ten to twelve there will be a public audience.

"From twelve till one the regent will be engaged with La Vrilliere and Leblanc.

"From one to two he will open letters with Torcy.

"At half-past two there will be a council, and he will pay the king a visit.

"At three o'clock he will go to the tennis court in the Rue du Seine, to sustain, with Brancas and Canillac, a challenge against the Duc de Richelieu, the Marquis de Broglie, and the Comte de Gacé.

"At six he will go to supper at the Luxembourg with the Duchesse de Berry, and will pass the evening there.

"From there he will come back, without guards, to the Palais Royal, unless the Duchesse de Berry gives him an escort from hers."

"Without guards, my dear abbe! what do you think of that?" said D'Harmental, beginning to dress; "does it not make your mouth water?"

"Without guards, yes," replied the abbe; "but with footmen, outriders, a coachman—all people who do not fight much, it is true, but who cry very loud. Oh! patience, patience, my young friend. You are in a great hurry to be a grandee of Spain."

"No, my dear abbe, but I am in a hurry to give up living in an attic where I lack everything, and where I am obliged to dress myself alone, as you see. Do you think it is nothing to go to bed at ten o'clock, and dress in the morning without a valet?"

"Yes, but you have music," replied the abbe.

"Ah! indeed!" replied D'Harmental. "Abbe, open my window, I beg, that they may see I receive good company. That will do me honor with my neighbors."

"Ho! ho!" said the abbe, doing what D'Harmental asked; "that is not bad at all."

"How, not bad?" replied D'Harmental; "it is very good, on the contrary. It is from Armida: the devil take me if I expected to find that in the fourth story of a house in the Rue du Temps Perdu."

"Chevalier, I predict," said the abbe, "that if the singer be young and pretty, in a week there will be as much trouble to get you away as there is now to keep you here."

"My dear abbe," said D'Harmental, "if your police were as good as those of the Prince de Cellamare, you would know that I am cured of love for a long time, and here is the proof. Do not think I pass my days in sighing. I beg when you go down you will send me something like a pâté, and a dozen bottles of good wine. I trust to you. I know you are a connoisseur; besides, sent by you, it will seem like a guardian's attention. Bought[Pg 274] by me, it would seem like a pupil's debauch; and I have my provincial reputation to keep up with Madame Denis."

"That is true. I do not ask you what it is for, but I will send it to you."

"And you are right, my dear abbe. It is all for the good of the cause."

"In an hour the pâté and the wine will be here."

"When shall I see you again?"

"To-morrow, probably."

"Adieu, then, till to-morrow."

"You send me away."

"I am expecting somebody."

"All for the good of the cause?"

"I answer you, go, and may God preserve you."

"Stay, and may the devil not get hold of you. Remember

that it was a woman who got us turned out of our terrestrial paradise. Defy women."

"Amen," said the chevalier, making a parting sign with his hand to the Abbe Brigaud.

Indeed, as the abbe had observed, D'Harmental was in a hurry to see him go. The great love for music, which the chevalier had discovered only the day before, had progressed so rapidly that he did not wish his attention called away from what he had just heard. The little which that horrible window allowed him to hear, and which was more of the instrument than of the voice, showed that his neighbor was an excellent musician. The playing was skillful, the voice sweet and sustained, and had, in its high notes and deep vibrations, something which awoke an answer in the heart of the listener. At last, after a very difficult and perfectly executed passage, D'Harmental could not help clapping his hands and crying bravo! As bad luck would have it, this triumph, to which she had not been accustomed, instead of encouraging the musician, frightened her so much, that voice and harpsichord stopped at the same instant, and silence immediately succeeded to the melody for which the chevalier had so imprudently manifested his enthusiasm.

In exchange, he saw the door of the room above (which we have said led on to the terrace) open, and a hand was stretched out, evidently to ascertain what kind of weather it was. The answer of the weather seemed reassuring, for the hand was almost directly followed by a head covered by a little chintz cap, tied on the forehead by a violet ribbon; and the head was only a few instants in advance of a neck and shoulders clothed in a kind of dressing-gown of the same stuff as the cap. This was not quite enough to enable the chevalier to decide to which sex the individual, who seemed so cautious about exposing himself to the morning air, belonged. At last, a sort of sunbeam having slipped out between two clouds, the timid inhabitant of the terrace appeared to be encouraged to come out altogether. D'Harmental then saw, by his black velvet knee-breeches, and by his silk stockings, that the personage who had just entered on the scene was of the masculine gender.

It was the gardener of whom we spoke. The bad weather of the preceding days had, without doubt, deprived him of his morning walk, and had prevented him from giving his garden his ordinary attention, for he began to walk round it with a visible fear of finding some accident produced by the wind or rain; but, after a careful inspection of the fountain, the grotto, and the arbor, which were its three principal ornaments, the excellent face of the gardener was lighted by a ray of joy, as the weather was by the ray of sun. He perceived, not only that everything was in its place, but that the reservoir was full to overflowing. He thought he might indulge in playing his fountain, a treat which, ordinarily, following the example of Louis XIV., he only allowed himself on Sundays. He turned the cock, and the jet raised itself majestically to the height of four or five feet. The good man was so delighted that he began to sing the burden of an old pastoral song which D'Harmental had heard when he was a baby, and, while repeating—

"Let me go And let me play Beneath the hazel-tree,"

he ran to the window, and called aloud, "Bathilde! Bathilde!"

[Pg 275]The chevalier understood that there was a communication between the rooms on the third and fourth stories, and some relation between the gardener and the musician, and thought that perhaps if he remained at the window she would not come on to the terrace; therefore he closed his window with a careless air, taking care to keep a little opening behind the curtain, through which he could see without being seen. What he had foreseen happened. Very soon the head of a charming young girl appeared on the terrace; but as, without doubt, the ground, on which he had ventured with so much courage, was too damp, she would not go any further. The little dog, not less timid than its mistress, remained near her, resting its white paws on the window, and shaking its head in silent denial to every invitation. A dialogue was established between the good man and the young girl, while D'Harmental had leisure to examine her at ease.

She appeared to have arrived at that delicious time of life when woman, passing from childhood to youth, is in the full bloom of sentiment, grace, and beauty. He saw that she was not less than sixteen nor more than eighteen years of age, and that there existed in her a singular mixture of two races. She had the fair hair, thick complexion, and graceful neck of an English woman, with the black eyes, coral lips, and pearly teeth of a Spaniard.

As she did not use either rouge or white, and as that time powder was scarcely in fashion, and was reserved for aristocratic heads, her complexion remained in its natural freshness, and nothing altered the color of her hair.

The chevalier remained as in an ecstasy—indeed, he had never seen but two classes of women. The fat and coarse peasants of the Nivernais, with their great feet and hands, their short petticoats, and their hunting-horn shaped hats; and the women of the Parisian aristocracy, beautiful without doubt, but of that beauty fagged by watching and pleasure, and by that reversing of life which makes them what flowers would be if they only saw the sun on some rare occasions, and the vivifying air of the morning and the evening only reached them through the windows of a hot-house. He did not know this intermediate type, if one may call it so, between high society and the country people, which had all the elegance of the one, and all the fresh health of the other. Thus, as we have said, he remained fixed in his place, and long after the young girl had re-entered, he kept his eyes fixed on the window where this delicious vision had appeared.

The sound of his door opening called him out of his ecstasy: it was the pâté and the wine from Abbe Brigaud making their solemn entry into the chevalier's garret. The sight of these provisions recalled to his mind that he had now something better to do than to abandon himself to contemplation, and that he had given Captain Roquefinette a rendezvous on the most important business. Consequently he looked at his watch, and saw that it was ten o'clock. This was, as the reader will remember, the appointed hour. He sent away the man who had brought the provisions, and said he would lay the cloth himself; then, opening his window once more, he sat down to watch for the appearance of Captain Roquefinette.

He was hardly at his observatory before he perceived the worthy captain coming round the corner from the Rue Gros-Chenet, his head in the air, his hand on his hip, and with the martial and decided air of a man who, like the Greek philosopher, carries everything with him. His hat, that thermometer by which his friends could tell the secret state of its master's finances, and which, on his fortunate days was placed as straight on his head as a pyramid on its base, had recovered that miraculous inclination which had so struck the Baron de Valef, and thanks to which, one of the points almost touched his right shoulder, while the parallel one might forty years later had given Franklin, if Franklin had known the captain, the first idea of his electric kite.

Having come about a third down the street, he raised his head as had been arranged, and saw the chevalier just[Pg 276] above him. He who waited, and he who was waited for, exchanged nods, and the captain having calculated the distance at a glance, and recognized the door which ought to belong to the window above, jumped over the threshold of Madame Denis's poor little house with as much familiarity as if it had been a tavern. The chevalier shut the window, and drew the curtains with the greatest care—either in order that his pretty neighbor might not see him with the captain, or that the captain might not see her.

An instant afterward D'Harmental heard the sound of his steps, and the beating of his sword against the banisters. Having arrived at the third story, as the light which came from below was not aided by any light from above, he found himself in a difficulty, not knowing whether to stop where he was, or mount higher. Then, after coughing in the most significant manner, and finding that this call remained unnoticed—

"Morbleu!" said he. "Chevalier, as you did not probably bring me here to break my neck, open your door or call out, so that I may be guided either by the light of heaven, or by the sound of your voice; otherwise I shall be lost, neither more nor less than Theseus in the labyrinth."

And the captain began to sing in a loud voice—

"Fair Ariadne, I beg of you, Help me, by lending me your clew. Toutou, toutou, toutaine, toutou!"

The chevalier ran to his door and opened it.

"My friend," said the captain, "the ladder up to your pigeon-house is infernally dark; still here I am, faithful to the agreement, exact to the time. Ten o'clock was striking as I came over the Pont-Neuf."

CHAPTER X.
THE AGREEMENT.

The chevalier extended his hand to Roquefinette, saying:

"Yes, you are a man of your word, but enter quickly; it is important that my neighbors should not notice you."

"In that case I am as dumb as a log," answered the captain; "besides," added he, pointing to the pâté and the bottles which covered the table, "you have found the true way of shutting my mouth."

The chevalier shut the door behind the captain and pushed the bolt.

"Ah! ah! mystery—so much the better, I am fond of mystery. There is almost always something to be gained when people begin by saying 'hush.' In any case you cannot do better than address yourself to your servant," continued the captain, resuming his mythological language. "You see in me the grandson of Hippocrates, the god of silence. So do not be uneasy."

"That is well, captain," answered D'Harmental, "for I confess that what I have to say to you is of sufficient importance for me to claim your discretion beforehand."

"It is granted, chevalier. While I was giving a lesson to little Ravanne, I saw, out of a corner of my eye, that you were a skillful swordsman, and I love brave men. Then, in return for a little service, only worth a fillip, you made me a present of a horse which was worth a hundred louis, and I love generous men. Thus you are twice my man, why should

I not be yours once?"

"Well," said the chevalier, "I see that we understand each other."

"Speak, and I will listen," answered the captain, assuming his gravest air.

"You will listen better seated, my dear guest. Let us go to breakfast."

"You preach like St. John with the golden mouth, chevalier," said the captain, taking off his sword and placing that and his hat on the harpsichord; "so that," continued he, sitting down opposite D'Harmental, "one cannot differ from you in opinion. I am here; command the maneuver, and I will execute it."

"Taste that wine while I cut the pate."

"That is right," said the captain, "let us divide our forces, and fight the enemy separately, then let us re-unite to exterminate what remains."

And joining practice to theory, the captain seized the first bottle by the neck,[Pg 277] drew the cork, and having filled a bumper, drank it off with such ease that one would have said that nature had gifted him with an especial method of deglutition; but, to do him justice, scarcely had he drunk it than he perceived that the liquor, which he had disposed of so cavalierly, merited a more particular attention than he had given it.

"Oh!" said he, putting down his glass with a respectful slowness, "what have I done, unworthy that I am? I drink nectar as if it were trash, and that at the beginning of the feast! Ah!" continued he, shaking his head, "Roquefinette, my friend, you are getting old. Ten years ago you would have known what it was at the first drop that touched your palate, while now you want many trials to know the worth of things. To your health, chevalier."

And this time the captain, more circumspect, drank the second glass slowly, and set it down three times before he finished it, winking his eyes in sign of satisfaction. Then, when he had finished—

"This is hermitage of 1702, the year of the battle of Friedlingen. If your wine-merchant has much like that, and if he will give credit, let me have his address. I promise him a good customer."

"Captain," answered the chevalier, slipping an enormous slice of pate on to the plate of his guest, "my wine-merchant not only gives credit, but to my friends he gives altogether."

"Oh, the honest man!" cried the captain. Then, after a minute's silence, during which a superficial observer would have thought him absorbed in the appreciation of the pate, as he had been an instant before in that of the wine, he leaned his two elbows on the table, and looking at D'Harmental with a penetrating glance between his knife and fork—

"So, my dear chevalier," said he, "we conspire, it seems, and in order to succeed we have need of poor Captain Roquefinette."

"And who told you that, captain?" broke in the chevalier, trembling in spite of himself.

"Who told me that, pardieu! It is an easy riddle to answer.

A man who gives away horses worth a hundred louis, who drinks wine at a pistole the bottle, and who lodges in a garret in the Rue du Temps Perdu, what should he be doing if not conspiring?"

"Well, captain," said D'Harmental, laughing, "I shall never be discreet; you have divined the truth. Does a conspiracy frighten you?" continued he, filling his guest's glass.

"Frighten *me*! Who says that anything on earth can frighten Captain Roquefinette?"

"Not I, captain; for at the first glance, at the first word, I fixed on you as my second."

"Ah! that is to say, that if you are hung on a scaffold twenty feet high, I shall be hung on one ten feet high, that's all!"

"Peste! captain," said D'Harmental, "if one always began by seeing thing in their worst light, one would never attempt anything."

"Because I have spoken of the gallows?" answered the captain. "That proves nothing. What is the gallows in the eyes of a philosopher? One of the thousand ways of parting from life, and certainly one of the least disagreeable. One can see that you have never looked the thing in the face, since you have such an aversion to it. Besides, on proving our noble descent, we shall have our heads cut off, like Monsieur de Rohan. Did you see Monsieur de Rohan's head cut off?" continued the captain, looking at D'Harmental. "He was a handsome young man, like you, and about your age. He conspired, but the thing failed. What would you have?

Everybody may be deceived. They built him a beautiful black scaffold; they allowed him to turn toward the window where his mistress was; they cut the neck of his shirt with scissors, but the executioner was a bungler, accustomed to hang, and not to decapitate, so that he was obliged to strike three or four times to cut the head off, and at last he only managed by the aid of a knife which he drew from his girdle, and with which he chopped so well that[Pg 278] he got the neck in half. Bravo! you are brave!" continued the captain, seeing that the chevalier had listened without frowning to all the details of this horrible execution. "That will do—I am your man. Against whom are we conspiring? Let us see. Is it against Monsieur le Duc de Maine? Is it against Monsieur le Duc d'Orleans? Must we break the lame one's other leg? Must we cut out the blind one's other eye? I am ready."

"Nothing of all that, captain; and if it pleases God there will be no blood spilled."

"What is going on then?"

"Have you ever heard of the abduction of the Duke of Mantua's secretary?"

"Of Matthioli?"——"Yes."

"Pardieu! I know the affair better than any one, for I saw them pass as they were conducting him to Pignerol. It was the Chevalier de Saint-Martin and Monsieur de Villebois who did it; and by this token they each had three thousand livres for themselves and their men."

"That was only middling pay," said D'Harmental, with a disdainful air.

"You think so, chevalier? Nevertheless three thousand livres is a nice little sum."

"Then for three thousand livres you would have undertaken it?"

"I would have undertaken it," answered the captain.

"But if instead of carrying off a secretary it had been proposed to you to carry off a duke?"

"That would have been dearer."

"But you would have undertaken it all the same?"

"Why not? I should have asked double—that is all."

"And if, in giving you double, a man like myself had said to you, 'Captain, it is not an obscure danger that I plunge you into; it is a struggle in which I am myself engaged, like you, and in which I venture my name, my future, and my head:' what would you have answered?"

"I would have given him my hand, as I now give it you. Now what is the business?"

The chevalier filled his own glass and that of the captain.

"To the health of the regent," said he, "and may he arrive without accident at the Spanish frontier, as Matthioli arrived at Pignerol."

"Ah! ah!" said the captain, raising his glass. Then, after a pause, "And why not?" continued he, "the regent is but a man after all. Only we shall neither be hanged nor decapitated; we shall be broken on the wheel. To any one else I should say that a regent would be dearer, but to you, chevalier, I have only one price. Give me six thousand livres, and I will find a dozen determined men."

"But those twelve men, do you think that you may trust them?"

"What need for their knowing what they are doing? They shall think they are only carrying out a wager."

"And I," answered D'Harmental, "will show you that I do not haggle with my friends. Here are two thousand crowns in gold, take them on account if we succeed; if we fail we will cry quits."

"Chevalier," answered the captain, taking the bag of money and poising it on his hand with an indescribable air of satisfaction, "I will not do you the injustice of counting after you. When is the affair to be?"

"I do not know yet, captain; but if you find the pate to your taste, and the wine good, and if you will do me the pleasure of breakfasting with me every day as you have done to-day, I will keep you informed of everything."

"That would not do, chevalier," said the captain. "I should not have come to you three mornings before the police of that cursed Argenson would have found us out. Luckily he has found some one as clever as himself, and it will be some time before we are at the bar together. No, no, chevalier, from now till the moment for action, the less we see of one another the better; or rather, we must not see each other at all. Your street is not a long one, and as it opens at one end on the Rue du Gros-Chenet, and at the other on the Rue Montmartre, I shall have no reason for coming through it. Here," continued he, detaching his shoulder-knot,[Pg 279] "take this ribbon. The day that you want me, tie it to a nail

116

outside your window. I shall understand it, and I will come to you."

"How, captain!" said D'Harmental, seeing that his companion was fastening on his sword. "Are you going without finishing the bottle? What has the wine, which you appeared to appreciate so much a little while ago, done to you, that you despise it so now?"

"It is just because I appreciate it still that I separate myself from it; and the proof that I do not despise it," said the captain, filling his glass, "is that I am going to take an adieu of it. To your health, chevalier; you may boast of having good wine. Hum! And now, n—o, no, that is all. I shall take to water till I see the ribbon flutter from your window. Try to let it be as soon as possible, for water is a liquid that does not suit my constitution."

"But why do you go so soon?"

"Because I know Captain Roquefinette. He is a good fellow; but when he sits down before a bottle he must drink, and when he has drunk he must talk; and, however well one talks, remember that those who talk much always finish by making some blunder. Adieu, chevalier. Do not forget the crimson ribbon; I go to look after our business."

"Adieu, captain," said D'Harmental, "I am pleased to see that I have no need to preach discretion to you."

The captain made the sign of the cross on his mouth with his right thumb, placed his hat straight on his head, raised his sword for fear of its making a noise or beating against the wall, and went downstairs as silently as if he had feared that every step would echo in the Hotel d'Argenson.

CHAPTER XI.
PROS AND CONS.

The chevalier remained alone; but this time there was, in what had just passed between himself and the captain, sufficient matter for reflection to render it unnecessary for him to have recourse either to the poetry of the Abbe Chaulieu, his harpsichord, or his chalks. Indeed, until now, he had been only half engaged in the hazardous enterprise of which the Duchesse de Maine and the Prince de Cellamare had shown him the happy ending, and of which the captain, in order to try his courage, had so brutally exhibited to him the bloody catastrophe. As yet he had only been the end of a chain, and, on breaking away from one side, he would have been loose. Now he was become an intermediate ring, fastened at both ends, and attached at the same time to people above and below him in society. In a word, from this hour he no longer belonged to himself, and he was like the Alpine traveler, who, having lost his way, stops in the middle of an unknown road, and measures with his eye, for the first time, the mountain which rises above him and the gulf which yawns beneath his feet.

Luckily the chevalier had the calm, cold, and resolute courage of a man in whom fire and determination—those two opposite forces—instead of neutralizing, stimulated each other. He engaged in danger with all the rapidity of a sanguine man; he weighed it with all the consideration of a phlegmatic one. Madame de Maine was right when she said to Madame de Launay that she might put out her lantern, and that she believed she had at last found a man.

But this man was young, twenty-six years of age, with a heart open to all the illusions and all the poetry of that first part of existence. As a child he had laid down his playthings at the feet of his mother. As a young man he had come to exhibit his handsome uniform as colonel to the eyes of his mistress; indeed, in every enterprise of his life some loved image had gone before him, and he threw himself into danger with the certainty that, if he succumbed, there would be some one surviving who would mourn his fate.

But his mother was dead, the last woman by whom he had believed himself loved had betrayed him, and he felt alone in the world—bound solely by interest to men to whom he would become an obstacle as soon as he ceased to be an in[Pg 280]strument, and who, if he broke down, far from mourning his loss, would only see in it a cause of satisfaction. But this isolated position, which ought to be the envy of all men in a great danger, is almost always (such is the egotism of our nature) a cause of the most profound discouragement. Such is the horror of nothingness in man, that he believes he still survives in the sentiments which he has inspired, and he in some measure consoles himself for leaving the world by thinking of the regrets which will accompany his memory, and of the pity which will visit his tomb. Thus, at this instant, the chevalier would have given everything to be loved, if it was only by a dog.

He was plunged in the saddest of these reflections when,

passing and repassing before his window, he noticed that his neighbor's was open. He stopped suddenly, and shook his head, as if to cast off the most somber of these thoughts; leaning his elbow on the table, and his head on his hand, he tried to give a different direction to his thoughts by looking at exterior objects.

The young girl whom he had seen in the morning was seated near her window, in order to benefit by the last rays of daylight; she was working at some kind of embroidery. Behind her the harpsichord was open, and, on a stool at her feet, her greyhound slept the light sleep of an animal destined by nature to be the guard of man, waking at every noise which arose from the street, raising its ears, and stretching out its elegant head over the window-sill; then it lay down again, placing one of its little paws upon its mistress's knees. All this was deliciously lighted up by the rays of the sinking sun, which penetrated into the room, sparkling on the steel ornaments of the harpsichord and the gold beading of the picture-frames. The rest was in twilight.

Then it seemed to the chevalier (doubtless on account of the disposition of mind he was in when this picture had struck his eye) that this young girl, with the calm and sweet face, entered into his life, like one of those personages who always remain behind a veil, and make their entrance on a piece in the second or third act to take part in the action, and, sometimes, to change the denouement.

Since the age when one sees angels in one's dreams, he had seen no one like her. She was a mixture of beauty, candor, and simplicity, such as Greuze has copied, not from nature, but from the reflections in the mirror of his imagination. Then, forgetting everything, the humble condition in which without doubt she had been born, the street where he had found her, the modest room which she had inhabited, seeing nothing in the woman except the woman herself, he attributed to her a heart corresponding with her face, and thought what would be the happiness of the man who should first cause that heart to beat; who should be looked upon with love by those beautiful eyes, and who, in the words, "I love you!" should gather from those lips, so fresh and so pure, that flower of the soul—a first kiss.

Such are the different aspects which the same objects borrow from the situation of him who looks at them. A week before, in the midst of his gayety, in his life which no danger menaced, between a breakfast at the tavern and a stag-hunt, between a wager at tennis and a supper at La Fillon's, if D'Harmental had met this young girl, he would doubtless have seen in her nothing but a charming grisette, whom he would have had followed by his valet-de-chambre, and to whom, the next day, he would have outrageously offered a present of some twenty-five louis.

But the D'Harmental of a week ago existed no more. In the place of the handsome seigneur—elegant, wild, dissipated, and certain of life—was an insulated young man, walking in the shade, alone, and self-reliant, without a star to guide him, who might suddenly feel the earth open under his feet, and the heavens burst above his head. He had need of a support, so feeble was he; he had need of love, he had need of poetry. It was not then wonderful that, searching for a Madonna to whom to address his prayers, he raised in his imagination this young and beautiful girl from the material and prosaic sphere in which he found her, and[Pg 281] that, drawing her into his own, he placed her, not such as she was, doubtless, but such as he wished her to be, on the empty pedestal of his past adorations.

All at once the young girl raised her head, and happened to look in his direction, and saw the pensive figure of the chevalier through the glass. It appeared evident to her that the young man remained there for her, and that it was at her he was looking. Then a bright blush spread over her face. Still she pretended she had seen nothing, and bent her head once more over her embroidery. But a minute afterward she rose, took a few turns round her room; then, without affectation, without false prudery, but nevertheless with a certain embarrassment, she returned and shut the window. D'Harmental remained where he was, and as he was; continuing, in spite of the shutting of the window, to advance into the imaginary country where his thoughts were straying.

Once or twice he thought that he saw the curtain of his neighbor's window raised, as if she wished to know whether he whose indiscretion had driven her from her place was still at his. At last a few masterly chords were heard; a sweet harmony followed; and it was then D'Harmental who opened his window in his turn.

123

He had not been mistaken, his neighbor was an admirable musician; she executed two or three little pieces, but without blending her voice with the sound of the instrument; and D'Harmental found almost as much pleasure in listening to her as he had found in looking at her. Suddenly she stopped in the midst of a passage. D'Harmental supposed either that she had seen him at his window, and wished to punish him for his curiosity, or that some one had come in and interrupted her. He retired into his room, but so as not to lose sight of the window, and soon discovered that his last supposition was the true one.

A man came to the window, raised the curtain, and pressed his fat, good-natured face against the glass, while with one hand he beat a march against the panes. The chevalier recognized, in spite of a sensible difference which there was in his toilet, the man of the water-jet whom he had seen on the terrace in the morning, and who, with a perfect air of familiarity, had twice pronounced the name of "Bathilde."

This apparition, more than prosaic, produced the effect which might naturally have been expected; that is to say, it brought D'Harmental back from imaginary to real life. He had forgotten this man, who made such a strange and perfect contrast with the young girl, and who must doubtless be either her father, her lover, or her husband. But in either of these cases, what could there be in common between the daughter, the wife, or the mistress of such a man, and the noble and aristocratic chevalier? The wife! It is a misfortune of her dependent situation that she rises and falls according to the grandeur or vulgarity of him on whose arm she leans; and it must be confessed that the gardener was not formed to maintain poor Bathilde at the height to which the chevalier had raised her in his dreams.

Then he began to laugh at his own folly; and the night having arrived, and as he had not been outside the door since the day before, he determined to take a walk through the town, in order to assure himself of the truth of the Prince de Cellamare's reports. He wrapped himself in his cloak, descended the four stories, and bent his steps toward the Luxembourg, where the note which the Abbe Brigaud had brought him in the morning said that the regent was going to supper without guards.

Arrived opposite the palace of the Luxembourg, the chevalier saw none of those signs which should announce that the Duc d'Orleans was at his daughter's house: there was only one sentinel at the door, while from the moment that the regent entered a second was generally placed there. Besides, he saw no carriage waiting in the court, no footmen or outriders; it was evident, then, that he had not come. The chevalier waited to see him pass, for, as the regent never breakfasted, and took nothing but a cup of[Pg 282] chocolate at two o'clock in the afternoon, he rarely supped later than six o'clock; but a quarter to six had struck at the St. Surplice at the moment when the chevalier turned the corner of the Rue de Conde, and the Rue de Vaugirard.

The chevalier waited an hour and a half in the Rue de Tournon, going from the Rue du Petit-Lion to the palace,

125

without seeing what he had come to look for. At a quarter to eight he saw some movement in the Luxembourg. A carriage, with outriders armed with torches, came to the foot of the steps. A minute after three women got in; he heard the coachman call to the outriders, "To the Palais Royal;" and the outriders set off at a gallop, the carriage followed, the sentinel presented arms; and, quickly as the elegant equipage with the royal arms of France passed, the chevalier recognized the Duchesse de Berry, Madame de Mouchy, her lady of honor, and Madame de Pons, her tire-woman.

There had been an important error in the report sent to the chevalier; it was the daughter who went to the father, not the father who came to the daughter.

Nevertheless, the chevalier still waited, for some accident might have happened to the regent, which detained him at home. An hour after he saw the carriage repass. The Duchesse de Berry was laughing at a story which Broglie was telling her. There had not then been any serious accident; it was the police of the Prince de Cellamare, then, that were at fault.

The chevalier returned home about ten o'clock without having been met or recognized. He had some trouble to get the door opened, for, according to the patriarchal habits of Madame Denis's house, the porter had gone to bed, and came out grumbling to unfasten the bolts. D'Harmental slipped a crown into his hand, saying to him, once for all, that he should sometimes return late, but that each time that he did so he would give him the same; upon which the porter thanked him, and assured him that he was perfectly welcome to come home at any time he liked, or even not to return at all.

On returning to his room, D'Harmental saw that his neighbor's was lighted up; he placed his candle behind a piece of furniture, and approached the window, so that, as much as the muslin curtains allowed, he could see into her room, while she could not see into his.

She was seated near a table, drawing, probably, on a card which she held on her knees, for he saw her profile standing out black against the light behind her. Shortly another shadow, which the chevalier recognized as that of the good man of the terrace, passed twice between the light and the window. At last the shade approached the young girl, she offered her forehead, the shadow imprinted a kiss on it, and went away, with his candle in his hand. Directly afterward the windows of the fifth story were lighted up. All these little circumstances spoke a language which it was impossible not to understand. The man of the terrace was not the husband of Bathilde, he must be her father.

D'Harmental, without knowing why, felt overjoyed at this discovery; he opened his window as softly as he could, and leaned on the bar, which served him as a support, with his eyes fixed on the shadow. He fell into the same reverie out of which he had been startled that morning by the grotesque apparition of his neighbor. In about an hour the girl rose, put down her card and crayons on the table, advanced toward the alcove, knelt on a chair before the second window, and offered up her prayers. D'Harmental understood that her laborious watch was finished, but remembering the curiosity of his beautiful neighbor, when he had begun to play the first time, he wished to see if he could prolong that watch, and he sat down to his spinet. What he had foreseen happened; at the first notes which reached her, the young girl, not knowing that from the position of the light he could see her shadow through the curtains, approached the window on tiptoe, and thinking herself hidden, she listened to the melodious instrument, which, like the nightingale, awoke to sing in the middle of the night.

The concert would have probably con[Pg 283]tinued thus for some hours, for D'Harmental, encouraged by the result produced, felt an energy and an ease of execution such as he had never known before. Unluckily, the occupier of the third floor was undoubtedly some clown, no lover of music, for D'Harmental heard suddenly, just below his feet, the noise of a stick knocking on the ceiling with such violence that he could not doubt that it was a warning to him to put off his melodious occupation till a more suitable period. Under other circumstances, D'Harmental would have sent the impertinent adviser to the devil, but reflecting that any ill-feeling on the lodger's part would injure his own reputation with Madame Denis, and that he was playing too heavy a game to risk being recognized, and not to submit philosophically to all the inconveniences of the new position which he had adopted, instead of setting himself in opposition to the rules established without doubt between Madame Denis and her lodgers, he obeyed the intimation, forgetting in what manner that intimation had been given him.

On her part, as soon as she heard nothing more, the young girl left the window, and as she let the inner curtains fall behind her, she disappeared from D'Harmental's eyes. For some time longer he could still see a light in her room; then the light was extinguished. As to the window on the fifth floor, for some time that had been in the most perfect darkness. D'Harmental also went to bed, joyous to think that there existed a point of sympathy between himself and his neighbor.

The next day the Abbe Brigaud entered the room with his accustomed punctuality. The chevalier had already been up more than an hour; he had gone twenty times to his window, but without seeing his neighbor, although it was evident that she was up, even before himself; indeed, on waking he had seen the large curtains put up in their bands. Thus he was disposed to let out his ill-humor on any one.

"Ah! pardieu! my dear abbe," said he, as soon as the door was shut; "congratulate the prince for me on his police; it is perfectly arranged, on my honor!"

"What have you got against them?" asked the abbe, with the half-smile which was habitual to him.

"What have I! I have, that, wishing to judge for myself, last evening, of its truth, I went and hid myself in the Rue Tournon. I remained there four hours, and it was not the regent who came to his daughter, but Madame de Berry who went to her father."

"Well, we know that."

"Ah! you know that!" said D'Harmental.

"Yes, and by this token, that she left the Luxembourg at five minutes to eight, with Madame de Mouchy and Madame de Pons, and that she returned at half-past nine, bringing Broglie with her, who came to take the regent's place at table."

"And where was the regent?"

"The regent?"

"Yes."

"That is another story; you shall learn. Listen, and do not lose a word; then we shall see if you will say that the prince's police is badly arranged."

"I attend."

"Our report announced that at three o'clock the duke-regent would go to play tennis in the Rue de Seine."

"Yes."

"He went. In about half an hour he left holding his handkerchief over his eyes. He had hit himself on the brow with the racket, and with such violence that he had torn the skin of his forehead."

"Ah, this then was the accident!"

"Listen. Then the regent, instead of returning to the Palais Royal, was driven to the house of Madame de Sabran. You know where Madame de Sabran lives?"

"She lived in the Rue de Tournon, but since her husband has become maitre d'hotel to the regent, she lives in the Rue des Bons Enfants, near the Palais Royal."

"Exactly; but it seems that Madame de Sabran, who until

now was faithful to Richelieu, was touched by the pitiable state in which she saw the prince, and wished to justify the proverb, 'Unlucky[Pg 284] at play, lucky at love.' The prince, by a little note, dated half-past seven, from the drawing-room of Madame de Sabran, with whom he supped, announced to Broglie that he should not go to the Luxembourg, and charged him to go in his stead, and make his excuses to the Duchesse de Berry."

"Ah, this then was the story which Broglie was telling, and at which the ladies were laughing."

"It is probable; now do you understand?"

"Yes; I understand that the regent is not possessed of ubiquity, and could not be at the house of Madame de Sabran and at his daughter's at the same time."

"And you only understand that?"

"My dear abbe, you speak like an oracle; explain yourself."

"This evening, at eight o'clock, I will come for you; we will go to the Rue des Bons Enfants together. To me the locality is eloquent."

"Ah! ah!" said D'Harmental, "I see; so near the Palais Royal, he will go on foot. The hotel which Madame de Sabran inhabits has an entrance from the Rue des Bons Enfants; after a certain hour they shut the passage from the Palais Royal, which opens on the Rue des Bons Enfants: and he will be obliged, on his return, to follow either the Cour des Fontaines, or the Rue Neuve des Bons Enfants, and then we shall have him. Mordieu! you are a great man, and if Monsieur de Maine does not make you cardinal, or at least archbishop, there will be no justice done."

"I think, therefore, that now you must hold yourself in readiness."

"I am ready."

"Have you the means of execution prepared?"——"I have."

"Then you can correspond with your men?"

"By a sign."

"And that sign cannot betray you?"

"Impossible."

"Then all goes well, and we may have breakfast; for I was in such haste to tell you the good news that I came out fasting."

"Breakfast, my dear abbe! you speak coolly; I have nothing to offer you, except the remains of the paté and two or three bottles of wine, which, I believe, survived the battle."

"Hum! hum," murmured the abbe; "we will do better than that, my dear chevalier."

"I am at your orders."

"Let us go down and breakfast with our good hostess, Madame Denis."

"And why do you want me to breakfast with her? Do I know her?"

"That concerns me. I shall present you as my pupil."

"But we shall get a detestable breakfast."

"Comfort yourself. I know her table."

"But this breakfast will be tiresome."

"But you will make a friend of a woman much known

in the neighborhood for her good conduct, for her devotion to the government—a woman incapable of harboring a conspirator. Do you understand that?"

"If it be for the good of the cause, abbe, I sacrifice myself."

"Moreover, it is a very agreeable house, where there are two young people who play—one on the spinet, and the other on the guitar—and a young man who is an attorney's clerk; a house where you may go down on Sunday evenings to play lots."

"Go to the devil with your Madame Denis. Ah! pardon, abbe, perhaps you are her friend. In that case, imagine that I have said nothing."

"I am her confessor," replied the Abbe Brigaud, with a modest air.

"Then a thousand excuses, my dear abbe; but you are right indeed. Madame Denis is still a beautiful woman, perfectly well preserved, with superb hands and very pretty feet. Peste! I remember that. Go down first; I will follow."

"Why not together?"

"But my toilet, abbe. Would you have me appear before the Demoiselles Denis with my hair in its present state? One must try to look one's best—que diable! Besides, it is better that you should announce me: I have not a confessor's privilege."

[Pg 285]"You are right. I will go down and announce you, and in ten minutes you will arrive—will you not?"

"In ten minutes."

"Adieu!"——"Au revoir!"

133

The chevalier had only told half the truth. He might have remained partly to dress, but also in the hope of seeing his beautiful neighbor, of whom he had dreamed all the night, but in vain. He remained hidden behind the curtains of his window: those of the young girl with the fair hair and the beautiful black eyes remained closed. It is true that, in exchange, he could perceive his neighbor, who, opening his door, passed out, with the same precaution as the day before, first his hand, then his head; but this time his boldness went no further, for there was a slight fog, and fog is essentially contrary to the organization of the Parisian bourgeois. Our friend coughed twice, and then, drawing in his head and his arm, re-entered his room like a tortoise into his shell. D'Harmental saw with pleasure that he might dispense with buying a barometer, and that this neighbor would render him the same service as the butterflies which come out in the sunshine, and remain obstinately shut up in their hermitages on the days when it rains.

The apparition had its ordinary effect, and reacted on poor Bathilde. Every time that D'Harmental perceived the young girl, there was in her such a sweet attraction that he saw nothing but the woman—young, beautiful, and graceful, a musician and painter—that is to say, the most delicious and complete creature he had ever met. But when, in his turn, the man of the terrace presented himself to the chevalier's gaze, with his common face, his insignificant figure—that indelible type of vulgarity which attaches to certain individuals—directly a sort of miraculous transition took place in the chevalier's mind. All the poetry disappeared, as a machinist's whistle causes the disappearance of a fairy palace. Everything was seen by a different light. D'Harmental's native aristocracy regained the ascendency. Bathilde was then nothing but the daughter of this man—that is to say, a grisette: her beauty, her grace, her elegance, even her talents, were but an accident—an error of nature—something like a rose flowering on a cabbage-stalk. The chevalier shrugged his shoulders as he stood before the glass, began to laugh, and to wonder at the impression which he had received. He attributed it to the preoccupation of his mind, to the strange and solitary situation, to everything, in fact, except its true cause—the sovereign and irresistible power of distinction and beauty. D'Harmental went down to his hostess disposed to find the Demoiselles Denis charming.

CHAPTER XII.
THE DENIS FAMILY.

Madame Denis did not think it proper that two young persons as innocent as her daughters should breakfast with a young man who, although he had been only three days in Paris, already came in at eleven o'clock at night, and played on the harpsichord till two in the morning. In vain the Abbe Brigaud affirmed that this double infraction of the rules of her house should in no degree lower her opinion of his pupil, for whom he could answer as for himself. All he could obtain was that the young ladies should appear at the dessert; but the chevalier soon perceived that if their mother had ordered them not to be seen, she had not forbidden them to be heard, for scarcely were they at table, round a veritable devotée's breakfast, composed of a multitude of little dishes, tempting to the eye and delicious to the palate, when the sounds of a spinet were heard, accompanying a voice which was not wanting in compass, but whose frequent errors of intonation showed lamentable inexperience. At the first notes Madame Denis placed her hand on the abbe's arm, then, after an instant's silence, during which she listened with a pleased smile to that music which made the chevalier's flesh creep, "Do you hear?" she said. "It is our Athenais who is playing, and it is Emilie who sings."

[Pg 286]The Abbe Brigaud, making signs that he heard perfectly, trod on D'Harmental's foot under the table, to hint that this was an opportunity for paying a compliment.

"Madame," said the chevalier, who understood this appeal to his politeness perfectly, "we are doubly indebted to you; for you offer us not only an excellent breakfast, but a delightful concert."

"Yes," replied Madame Denis, negligently, "it is those children: they do not know you are here, and they are practicing; but I will go and tell them to stop."

Madame Denis was going to rise.

"What, madame!" said D'Harmental, "because I come from Ravenne do you believe me unworthy to make acquaintance with the talents of the capital?"

"Heaven preserve me, monsieur, from having such an opinion of you," said Madame Denis, maliciously, "for I know you are a musician; the lodger on the third story told me so."

"In that case, madame, perhaps he did not give you a very high idea of my merit," replied the chevalier, laughing, "for he did not appear to appreciate the little I may possess."

"He only said that it appeared to him a strange time for music. But listen, Monsieur Raoul," added Madame Denis, "the parts are changed now, my dear abbe, it is our Athenais who sings, and it is Emilie who accompanies her on the guitar."

It appeared that Madame Denis had a weakness for Athenais, for instead of talking as she did when Emilie was singing, she listened from one end to the other to the romance of her favorite, her eyes tenderly fixed on the Abbe Brigaud, who, still eating and drinking, contented himself with nodding his head in sign of approbation. Athenais sang a little more correctly than her sister, but for this she made up by a defect at least equivalent in the eyes of the chevalier. Her voice was equally vulgar.

As to Madame Denis, she beat wrong time with her head, with an air of beatitude which did infinitely more honor to her maternal affection than to her musical intelligence.

A duet succeeded to the solos. The young ladies appeared determined to give their whole repertoire. D'Harmental, in his turn, sought under the table for the abbe's feet, to crush at least one, but he only found those of Madame Denis, who, taking this for a personal attention, turned graciously toward him.

"Then, Monsieur Raoul," she said, "you come, young and inexperienced, to brave all the dangers of the capital?"

"Yes," said the Abbe Brigaud, taking upon himself to answer, for fear that D'Harmental might not be able to resist answering by some joke. "You see in this young man, Madame Denis, the son of a friend who was very dear to me" (the abbe put his table-napkin up to his eyes), "and whom, I hope, will do credit to the care I have bestowed on his education."

"And monsieur is right," replied Madame Denis; "for, with his talents and appearance, there is no saying to what he may attain."

"Ah! but, Madame Denis," said the Abbe Brigaud, "if you spoil him thus I shall not bring him to you again. My dear Raoul," continued the abbe, addressing him in a paternal manner, "I hope you will not believe a word of all this." Then, whispering to Madame Denis, "Such as you see him, he might have remained at Sauvigny, and taken the first place after the squire. He has three thousand livres a year in the funds."

"That is exactly what I intend giving to each of my daughters," replied Madame Denis, raising her voice, so as to be heard by the chevalier, and giving a side-glance to discover what effect the announcement of such magnificence would have upon him.

Unfortunately for the future establishment of the Demoiselles Denis, the chevalier was not thinking of uniting the three thousand livres which this generous mother gave to her daughters to the thousand crowns a year which the Abbe Brigaud had bestowed on him. The shrill treble of Mademoiselle Emilie, the contralto of Mademoiselle Athenais, the accompaniment of both, had recalled to his recollec[Pg 287]tion the pure and flexible voice and the distinguished execution of his neighbor. Thanks to that singular power which a great preoccupation gives us over exterior objects, the chevalier had escaped from the charivari which was executed in the adjoining room, and was following a sweet melody which floated in his mind, and which protected him, like an enchanted armor, from the sharp sounds which were flying around him.

"How he listens!" said Madame Denis to Brigaud. "'Tis worth while taking trouble for a young man like that. I shall have a bone to pick with Monsieur Fremond."

"Who is Monsieur Fremond?" said the abbe, pouring himself out something to drink.

"It is the lodger on the third floor. A contemptible little fellow, with twelve hundred francs a year, and whose temper has caused me to have quarrels with every one in the house; and who came to complain that Monsieur Raoul prevented him and his dog from sleeping."

"My dear Madame Denis," replied the abbe, "you must not quarrel with Monsieur Fremond for that. Two o'clock in the morning is an unreasonable time; and if my pupil must sit up till then, he must play in the daytime and draw in the evening."

"What! Monsieur Raoul draws also!" cried Madame Denis, quite astonished at so much talent.

"Draws like Mignard."

"Oh! my dear abbe," said Madame Denis, "if you could but obtain one thing."

"What?" asked the abbe.

"That he would take the portrait of our Athenais."

The chevalier awoke from his reverie, as a traveler, asleep on the grass, feels a serpent glide up to him, and instinctively understands that a great danger threatens him.

"Abbe!" cried he, in a bewildered manner, "no folly!"

"Oh! what is the matter with your pupil?" asked Madame Denis, quite frightened.

Happily, at the moment when the abbe was seeking a subterfuge, the door opened, and the two young ladies entered blushing, and, stepping from right to left, each made a low courtesy.

"Well!" said Madame Denis, affecting an air of severity,

"what is this? Who gave you permission to leave your room?"

"Mamma," replied a voice which the chevalier recognized, by its shrill tones, for that of Mademoiselle Emilie, "we beg pardon if we have done wrong, and are willing to return."

"But, mamma," said another voice, which the chevalier concluded must belong to Mademoiselle Athenais, "we thought that it was agreed that we were to come in at dessert."

"Well, come in, since you are here; it would be ridiculous now to go back. Besides," added Madame Denis, seating Athenais between herself and Brigaud, and Emilie between herself and the chevalier, "young persons are always best— are they not, abbe?—under their mother's wing."

And Madame Denis presented to her daughters a plate of bon-bons, from which they helped themselves with a modest air which did honor to their education.

The chevalier, during the discourse and action of Madame Denis, had time to examine her daughters.

Mademoiselle Emilie was a tall and stiff personage, from twenty-two to twenty-three, who was said to be very much like her late father; an advantage which did not, however, suffice to gain for her in the maternal heart an affection equal to what Madame Denis entertained for her other two children. Thus poor Emilie, always afraid of being scolded, retained a natural awkwardness, which the repeated lessons of her dancing-master had not been able to conquer.

Mademoiselle Athenais, on the contrary, was little, plump, and rosy; and, thanks to her sixteen or seventeen years, had what is vulgarly called the devil's beauty. She did not resemble either Monsieur or Madame Denis, a singularity which had often exercised the tongues of the Rue St. Martin before she went to inhabit the house which her husband had bought in[Pg 288] the Rue du Temps Perdu. In spite of this absence of all likeness to her parents, Mademoiselle Athenais was the declared favorite of her mother, which gave her the assurance that poor Emilie wanted. Athenais, however, it must be said, always profited by this favor to excuse the pretended faults of her sister.

Although it was scarcely eleven o'clock in the morning, the two sisters were dressed as if for a ball, and carried all the trinkets they possessed on their necks, arms, and ears.

This apparition, so conformable to the idea which D'Harmental had formed beforehand of the daughters of his landlady, gave him a new subject for reflection. Since the Demoiselles Denis were so exactly what they ought to be, that is to say, in such perfect harmony with their position and education, why was Bathilde, who seemed their equal in rank, as visibly distinguished as they were vulgar? Whence came this immense difference between girls of the same class and age? There must be some secret, which the chevalier would no doubt know some day or other. A second pressure of the Abbe Brigaud's foot against his made him understand that, however true his reflections were, he had chosen a bad moment for abandoning himself to them. Indeed, Madame Denis took so sovereign an air of dignity, that D'Harmental saw that he had not an instant to lose if he wished to efface from her mind the bad impression which his distraction had caused.

"Madame," said he directly, with the most gracious air he could assume, "that which I already see of your family fills me with the most lively desire to know the rest. Is not your son at home, and shall not I have the pleasure of seeing him?"

"Monsieur," answered Madame Denis, to whom so amiable an address had restored all her good humor, "my son is with M. Joulu, his master; and, unless his business brings him this way, it is improbable that he will make your acquaintance."

"Parbleu! my dear pupil," said the Abbe Brigaud, extending his hand toward the door; "you are like Aladdin. It is enough for you to express a wish, and it is fulfilled."

Indeed, at this moment they heard on the staircase the song about Marlborough, which at this time had all the charm of novelty; the door was thrown open, and gave entrance to a boy with a laughing face, who much resembled Mademoiselle Athenais.

"Good, good, good," said the newcomer, crossing his arms, and remarking the ordinary number of his family increased by the abbe and the chevalier. "Not bad, Madame Denis; she sends Boniface to his office with a bit of bread and cheese, saying, 'Beware of indigestion,' and, in his absence, she gives feasts and suppers. Luckily, poor Boniface has a good nose. He comes through the Rue Montmartre; he snuffs the wind, and says, 'What is going on there at No. 5, Rue du Temps Perdu?' So he came, and here he is. Make a place for one."

And, joining the action to the word, Boniface drew a

chair to the table, and sat down between the abbe and the chevalier.

"Monsieur Boniface," said Madame Denis, trying to assume a severe air, "do you not see that there are strangers here?"

"Strangers!" said Boniface, taking a dish from the table, and setting it before himself; "and who are the strangers? Are you one, Papa Brigaud? Are you one, Monsieur Raoul? You are not a stranger, you are a lodger." And, taking a knife and fork, he set to work in a manner to make up for lost time.

"Pardieu! madame," said the chevalier, "I see with pleasure that I am further advanced than I thought I was. I did not know that I had the honor of being known to Monsieur Boniface."

"It would be odd if I did not know you," said the lawyer's clerk, with his mouth full; "you have got my bedroom."

"How, Madame Denis!" said D'Harmental, "and you left me in ignorance that I had the honor to succeed in my room to the heir apparent of your family?[Pg 289] I am no longer astonished to find my room so gayly fitted up; I recognize the cares of a mother."

"Yes, much good may it do you; but I have one bit of advice to give you. Don't look out of window too much."

"Why?" asked D'Harmental.

"Why? because you have a certain neighbor opposite you."

"Mademoiselle Bathilde," said the chevalier, carried away by his first impulse.

"Ah! you know that already?" answered Boniface; "good, good, good; that will do."——"Will you be quiet, monsieur!" cried Madame Denis.

"Listen!" answered Boniface; "one must inform one's lodgers when one has prohibited things about one's house. You are not in a lawyer's office; you do not know that."

"The child is full of wit," said the Abbe Brigaud in that bantering tone, thanks to which it was impossible to know whether he was serious or not.

"But," answered Madame Denis, "what would you have in common between Monsieur Raoul and Bathilde?"

"What in common? Why, in a week, he will be madly in love with her, and it is not worth loving a coquette."

"A coquette?" said D'Harmental.

"Yes, a coquette, a coquette," said Boniface; "I have said it, and I do not draw back. A coquette, who flirts with the young men and lives with an old one, without counting that little brute of a Mirza, who eats up all my bon-bons, and now bites me every time she meets me."

"Leave the room, mesdemoiselles," cried Madame Denis, rising and making her daughters rise also. "Leave the room. Ears so pure as yours ought not to hear such things."

And she pushed Mademoiselle Athenais and Mademoiselle Emilie toward the door of their room, where she entered with them.

As to D'Harmental, he felt a violent desire to break Boniface's head with a wine-bottle. Nevertheless, seeing the absurdity of the situation, he made an effort and restrained himself.

"But," said he, "I thought that the bourgeois whom I saw on the terrace—for no doubt it is of him that you speak, Monsieur Boniface—"

"Of himself, the old rascal; what did you think of him?"

"That he was her father."

"Her father! not quite. Mademoiselle Bathilde has no father."

"Then, at least, her uncle?"

"Her uncle after the Bretagne fashion, but in no other manner."

"Monsieur," said Madame Denis, majestically coming out of the room, to the most distant part of which she had doubtless consigned her daughters, "I have asked you, once for all, not to talk improprieties before your sisters."

"Ah, yes," said Boniface, "my sisters; do you believe that, at their age, they cannot understand what I said, particularly Emilie, who is three-and-twenty years old?"

"Emilie is as innocent as a new-born child," said Madame Denis, seating herself between Brigaud and D'Harmental.

"I should advise you not to reckon on that. I found a pretty romance for Lent in our innocent's room. I will show it to you, Pere Brigaud; you are her confessor, and we shall see if you gave her permission to read her prayers from it."

"Hold your tongue, mischief-maker," said the abbe, "do you not see how you are grieving your mother?"

Indeed Madame Denis, ashamed of this scene passing before a young man on whom, with a mother's foresight, she had already begun to cast an eye, was nearly fainting. There is nothing in which men believe less than in women's faintings, and nothing to which they give way more easily. Whether he believed in it or not, D'Harmental was too polite not to show his hostess some attention in such circumstances. He advanced toward her with his arms extended. Madame Denis no sooner saw this support offered to her than she let herself fall, and, throwing her head back, fainted in the chevalier's arms.

"Abbe," said D'Harmental, while Boniface profited by the circumstance to fill[Pg 290] his pockets with all the bonbons left on the table, "bring a chair."

The abbe pushed forward a chair with the nonchalance of a man familiar with such accidents, and who is beforehand quite secure as to the result.

They seated Madame Denis, and D'Harmental gave her some salts, while the Abbe Brigaud tapped her softly in the hollow of the hand; but, in spite of these cares, Madame Denis did not appear disposed to return to herself; when all at once, when they least expected it, she started to her feet as if by a spring, and gave a loud cry.

D'Harmental thought that a fit of hysterics was following the fainting. He was truly frightened, there was such an accent of reality in the scream that the poor woman gave.

"It is nothing," said Boniface, "I have only just emptied the water-bottle down her back. That is what brought her to; you saw that she did not know how to manage it. Well, what?" continued the pitiless fellow, seeing Madame Denis look angrily at him; "it is I; do you not recognize me, Mother Denis? It is your little Boniface, who loves you so."

"Madame," said D'Harmental, much embarrassed at the situation, "I am truly distressed at what has passed."

"Oh! monsieur," cried Madame Denis in tears, "I am indeed unfortunate."

"Come, come; do not cry, Mother Denis, you are already wet enough," said Boniface; "you had better go and change your linen; there is nothing so unhealthy as wet clothes."

"The child is full of sense," said Brigaud, "and I think you had better follow his advice."

"If I might join my prayers to those of the abbe," said D'Harmental, "I should beg you, madame, not to inconvenience yourself for us. Besides, we were just going to take leave of you."

"And you, also, abbe?" said Madame Denis, with a distressed look at Brigaud.

"As for me," said Brigaud, who did not seem to fancy the part of comforter, "I am expected at the Hotel Colbert, and I must leave you."

"Adieu, then," said Madame Denis, making a curtsey, but the water trickling down her clothes took away a great part of its dignity.

"Adieu, mother," said Boniface, throwing his arms round her neck with the assurance of a spoiled child. "Have you nothing to say to Maître Joulu?"

"Adieu, mauvais sujet," replied the poor woman, embracing her son, and yielding to that attraction which a mother cannot resist; "adieu, and be steady."

"As an image, mother, on condition that you will give us a nice little dish of sweets for dinner."

He joined the Abbe Brigaud and D'Harmental, who were already on the landing.

"Well, well," said the abbe, lifting his hand quickly to his waistcoat pocket, "what are you doing there?"

"Oh, I was only looking if there was not a crown in your pocket for your friend Boniface."

"Here." said the abbe, "here is one, and now leave us alone."

"Papa Brigaud," said Boniface, in the effusion of his gratitude, "you have the heart of a cardinal, and if the king only makes you an archbishop, on my honor you will be robbed of half. Adieu, Monsieur Raoul," continued he, addressing the chevalier as familiarly as if he had known him for years. "I repeat, take care of Mademoiselle Bathilde if you wish to keep your heart, and give some sweetmeats to Mirza if you care for your legs;" and holding by the banister, he cleared the first flight of twelve steps at one bound, and reached the street door without having touched a stair.

Brigaud descended more quietly behind him, after having given the chevalier a rendezvous for eight o'clock in the evening.

As to D'Harmental, he went back thoughtfully to his attic.

CHAPTER XIII.
THE CRIMSON RIBBON.

What occupied the mind of the chevalier was neither the denouement of the drama where he had chosen so important[Pg 291] a part, nor the admirable prudence of the Abbe Brigaud in placing him in a house which he habitually visited almost daily, so that his visits, however frequent, could not be remarkable. It was not the dignified speeches of Madame Denis, nor the soprano of Mademoiselle Emilie. It was neither the contralto of Mademoiselle Athenais, nor the tricks of M. Boniface. It was simply poor Bathilde, whom he had heard so lightly spoken of; but our reader would be mistaken if he supposed that M. Boniface's brutal accusation had in the least degree altered the sentiments of the chevalier for the young girl, for an instant's reflection showed him that such an alliance was impossible.

Chance might give a charming daughter to an undistinguished father. Necessity may unite a young and elegant woman to an old and vulgar husband, but a liaison, such as that attributed to the young girl and the bourgeois of the terrace, can only result from love or interest. Now between these two there could be no love; and as to interest, the thing was still less probable; for, if they were not in absolute poverty, their situation was certainly not above mediocrity— not even that gilded mediocrity of which Horace speaks, with a country house at Tibur and Montmorency, and which results from a pension of thirty thousand sestercia from the

Augustan treasury, or a government annuity of six thousand francs—but that poor and miserable mediocrity which only provides from day to day, and which is only prevented from becoming real poverty by incessant labor.

D'Harmental gathered from all this the certainty that Bathilde was neither the daughter, wife, nor mistress of this terrible neighbor, the sight of whom had sufficed to produce such a strange reaction on the growing love of the chevalier. If she was neither the one nor the other, there was a mystery about her birth; and if so, Bathilde was not what she appeared to be. All was explained, her aristocratic beauty, her finished education. Bathilde was above the position which she was temporarily forced to occupy: there had been in the destiny of this young girl one of those overthrows of fortune, which are for individuals what earthquakes are for towns, and she had been forced to descend to the inferior sphere where he found her.

The result of all this was, that the chevalier might, without losing rank in his own estimation, allow himself to love Bathilde. When a man's heart is at war with his pride, he seldom wants excuses to defeat his haughty enemy. Bathilde had now neither name nor family, and nothing prevented the imagination of the man who loved her from raising her to a height even above his own; consequently, instead of following the friendly advice of M. Boniface, the first thing D'Harmental did was to go to his window and inspect that of his neighbor. It was wide open. If, a week ago, any one had told the chevalier that such a simple thing as an open window would have made his heart beat, he would have laughed at the idea. However, so it was; and after drawing a long breath, he settled himself in a corner, to watch at his ease the young girl in the opposite room, without being seen by her, for he was afraid of frightening her by that attention which she could only attribute to curiosity, but he soon perceived that the room was deserted.

D'Harmental then opened his window, and at the noise he made in doing so, he saw the elegant head of the greyhound, which, with his ears always on the watch, and well worthy of the trust that her mistress had reposed in her, in making her guardian of the house, was awake, and looking to see who it was that thus disturbed her sleep.

Thanks to the indiscreet counter-tenor of the good man of the terrace and the malice of M. Boniface, the chevalier already knew two things very important to know— namely, that his neighbor was called Bathilde, a sweet and euphonious appellation, suitable to a young, beautiful, and graceful girl; and that the greyhound was called Mirza, a name which seemed to indicate a no less distinguished rank in the canine aristocracy. Now as nothing is to be disdained when we wish[Pg 292] to conquer a fortress, and the smallest intelligence from within is often more efficacious than the most terrible machines of war, D'Harmental resolved to commence opening communications with the greyhound; and with the most caressing tone he could give to his voice, he called Mirza. Mirza, who was indolently lying on the cushion, raised her head quickly, with an expression of unmistakable astonishment; and, indeed, it must have appeared strange to the intelligent little animal, that a man so perfectly unknown to her as the chevalier should address her by her Christian name. She contented herself with fixing on him her uneasy eyes, which, in the half-light where she was placed, sparkled like two carbuncles, and uttering a little dull sound which might pass for a growl.

D'Harmental remembered that the Marquis d'Uxelle had tamed the spaniel of Mademoiselle Choin, which was a much more peevish beast than any greyhound in the world, with roast rabbits' heads; and that he had received for this delicate attention the baton of Maréchal de France; and he did not despair of being able to soften by the same kind of attention the surly reception which Mademoiselle Mirza had given to his advances: so he went toward the sugar-basin; then returned to the window, armed with two pieces of sugar, large enough to be divided ad infinitum.

The chevalier was not mistaken; at the first piece of sugar which fell near her, Mirza negligently advanced her head; then, being by the aid of smell made aware of the nature of the temptation offered to her, she extended her paw toward it, drew it toward her, took it in her teeth, and began to eat it with that languid air peculiar to the race to which she belonged. This operation finished, she passed over her mouth a little red tongue, which showed, that in spite of her apparent indifference, which was owing, no doubt, to her excellent education, she was not insensible to the surprise her neighbor had prepared for her; instead of lying down again on the cushion as she had done the first time, she remained seated, yawning languidly, but wagging her tail, to show that she would wake entirely, after two or three such little attentions as she had just had paid to her.

D'Harmental, who was well acquainted with the habits of all the King Charles' dogs of the pretty women of the day, understood the amiable intentions of Mirza, and not wishing to give her time to change her mind, threw a second piece of sugar, taking care that it should fall at such a distance as to oblige her to leave her cushion to get it. This test would decide whether she was most inclined to laziness or greediness. Mirza remained an instant uncertain, but then greediness carried the day, and she went across the room to fetch the piece of sugar, which had rolled under the harpsichord. At this moment a third piece fell near the window, and Mirza came toward it; but there the liberality of the chevalier stopped; he thought that he had now given enough to require some return, and he contented himself with calling Mirza in a more imperative tone, and showing her the other pieces of sugar which he held in his hand.

Mirza this time, instead of looking at the chevalier with uneasiness or disdain, rested her paws on the window, and began to behave as she would to an old acquaintance. It was finished; Mirza was tamed.

The chevalier remarked that it was now his turn to play the contemptuous with Mirza, and to speak to her, in order to accustom her to his voice; however, fearing a return of pride on the part of his interlocutor, who sustained her part in the dialogue by little whines and grumblings, he threw her a fourth piece of sugar, which she seized with greater avidity from having been kept waiting. This time, without being called, she came to take her place at the window. The chevalier's triumph was complete. So complete, that Mirza, who the day before had given signs of so superior an intelligence in discovering Bathilde's return, and in running to the door as she descended the staircase, this time discovered neither the one nor the other, so that her mistress, entering all at once, surprised her in the midst of[Pg 293] these coquetries with her neighbor. It is but just to say, however, that at the noise the door made in opening Mirza turned, and recognizing Bathilde, bounded toward her, lavishing on her the most tender caresses; but we must add, to the shame of the species, that this duty once accomplished, she hastened back to the window. This unusual action on the part of the dog naturally guided Bathilde's eyes toward the cause which occasioned it. Her eyes met those of the chevalier.

Bathilde blushed: the chevalier bowed; and Bathilde, without knowing what she was doing, returned the salute.

Her first impulse was to go and close the window, but an instinctive feeling restrained her. She understood that this was giving importance to a thing which had none, and that to put herself on the defensive was to avow herself attacked. In consequence, she crossed to that part of the room where her neighbor's glance could not reach. Then, at the end of a few minutes, when she returned, she found that he had closed his window. Bathilde understood that there was discretion in this action, and she thanked him. Indeed, the chevalier had just made a masterstroke. On the terms which he was on with his neighbor, it was impossible that both windows should remain open at once; if the chevalier's window was open, his neighbor's must be shut; and he knew that when that was closed, there was not a chance of seeing even the tip of Mirza's nose behind the curtain; while if, on the contrary, his window was closed, hers might possibly remain open, and he could watch her passing to and fro, or working, which was a great amusement for a poor devil condemned to absolute seclusion; besides, he had made an immense step:—he had saluted Bathilde, and she had returned it. They were no longer strangers to each other, but, in order that their acquaintance might advance, he must be careful not to be too brusk.

To risk speaking to her after the salute would have been risking too much; it was better to allow Bathilde to believe that it was all the effect of chance. Bathilde did not believe it, but she appeared to do so. The result was that she left her window open, and, seeing her neighbor's closed, sat down by her own with a book in her hand. As to Mirza, she jumped on to the stool at her mistress's feet, but instead of resting her head as usual on the knees of the young girl, she placed it on the sill, of the window, so much was she occupied with the generous unknown. The chevalier seated himself in the middle of his room, took his pencils, and thanks to a corner of his curtain skillfully raised, he sketched the delicious picture before him. Unfortunately the days were short, and toward three o'clock the little light which the clouds and rain had permitted to descend to the earth began to decline, and Bathilde closed her window. Nevertheless, even in this short time the chevalier had finished the young girl's head, and the likeness was perfect. There was her waving hair, her fine transparent skin, the graceful curve of her swan-like neck; in fact, all to which art can attain with one of those inimitable models which are the despair of artists.

When night closed in, the Abbe Brigaud arrived. The chevalier and he wrapped themselves in their mantles, and went toward the Palais Royal; they had, it will be remembered, to examine the ground. The house in which Madame de Sabran lived, since her husband had been named maitre d'hotel to the regent, was No. 22, between the Hotel de la Roche-Guyon and the passage formerly called Passage du Palais Royal, because it was the only one leading from the Rue des Bons Enfants to the Rue de Valois. This passage, now called Passage du Lycée, was closed at the same time as the other gates of the garden; that is to say, at eleven o'clock in the evening; therefore, having once entered a house in the Rue des Bons Enfants, unless it had a second door opening on the Rue de Valois, no one could return to the Palais Royal after eleven o'clock without making the round, either by the Rue Neuve des Petits-Champs, or by the Cour des Fontaines.

Thus it was with Madame de Sabran's house; it was an exquisite little hotel,[Pg 294] built toward the end of the last century, some five-and-twenty years before, by a merchant who wished to ape the great lords and have a petite maison of his own. It was a one-storied house, with a stone gallery, on which the servants' attics opened, and surmounted by a low tilted roof. Under the first-floor windows was a large balcony which jutted out three or four feet, and extended right across the house; but some iron ornaments, similar to the balcony, and which reached to the terrace, separated the two windows on each side from the three in the center, as is often done when it is desired to interrupt exterior communications. The two facades were exactly similar, only, as the Rue de Valois was eight or ten feet lower than that of the Bons Enfants, the ground-floor windows and door opened on a terrace, where was a little garden, filled in spring with charming flowers, but which did not communicate with the street, the only entrance being, as we have said, in the Rue des Bons Enfants.

This was all our conspirators could wish; the regent, once entered into Madame de Sabran's house, would—provided he stayed after eleven o'clock, which was probable—be taken as in a trap, and nothing would be easier than to carry out their plan in the Rue des Bons Enfants, one of the most deserted and gloomy places in the neighborhood; moreover, as this street was surrounded by very suspicious houses, and frequented by very bad company, it was a hundred to one that they would not pay any attention to cries which were too frequent in that street to cause any uneasiness, and that if the watch arrived, it would be, according to the custom of that estimable force, long after their intervention could be of any avail. The inspection of the ground finished, the plans laid, and the number of the house taken, they separated; the abbe to go to the Arsenal to give Madame de Maine an account of the proceedings, and D'Harmental to return to his attic.

As on the preceding night, Bathilde's room was lighted, but this time the young girl was not drawing but working; her light was not put out till one o'clock in the morning. As to the good man, he had retired long before D'Harmental returned. The chevalier slept badly; between a love at its commencement and a conspiracy at its height, he naturally experienced some sensations little favorable to sleep; but toward morning fatigue prevailed, and he only awoke on feeling himself violently shaken by the arm. Without doubt the chevalier was at that moment in some bad dream, of which this appeared to him the end, for, still half asleep, he stretched out his hand toward the pistols which were at his side.

"Ah, ah!" cried the abbe, "an instant, young man. What a hurry you are in! Open your eyes wide—so. Do you not recognize me?"

"Ah!" said D'Harmental, laughing, "it is you, abbe. You did well to stop me. I dreamed that I was arrested."

"A good sign," said the Abbe Brigaud: "you know that dreams always go by contraries. All will go well."

"Is there anything new?" asked D'Harmental.

"And if there were, how would you receive it?"

"I should be enchanted. A thing of this kind once undertaken, the sooner it is finished the better."

"Well, then," said Brigaud, drawing a paper from his pocket and presenting it to the chevalier, "read, and glorify the name of the Lord, for you have your wish."

D'Harmental took the paper, unfolded it as calmly as if it were a matter of no moment, and read as follows:

"*Report of the 27th of March.*

"Two in the Morning.

"To-night at ten o'clock the regent received a courier from London, who announces for to-morrow the arrival of the Abbe Dubois. As by chance the regent was supping with madame, the dispatch was given to him in spite of the late hour. Some minutes before, Mademoiselle de Chartres had asked permission of her father to perform her devotions at the Abbey of Chelles, and he had promised to[Pg 295] conduct her there; but on the receipt of this letter his determination was changed and he has ordered the council to meet at noon.

"At three o'clock the regent will pay his majesty a visit at the Tuileries. He has asked for a tete-à-tete, for he is beginning to be impatient at the obstinacy of the Marechal de Villeroy, who will always be present at the interviews between the regent and his majesty. Report says that if this obstinacy continue, it will be the worse for the marshal.

"At six o'clock, the regent, the Chevalier de Simiane, and the Chevalier de Ravanne, will sup with Madame de Sabran."

"Ah, ah!" said D'Harmental; and he read the last sentence, weighing every word.

"Well, what do you think of this paragraph?" asked the abbe.

The chevalier jumped from his bed, put on his dressing-gown, took from his drawer a crimson ribbon, a hammer and a nail, and having opened his window (not without throwing a stolen glance at that of his neighbor), he nailed the ribbon on to the outer wall.

"There is my answer," said he.

"What the devil does that mean?"

"That means," said D'Harmental, "that you may go and tell Madame de Maine that I hope this evening to fulfill my promise to her. And now go away, my dear abbe, and do not come back for two hours, for I expect some one whom it would be better you should not meet."

The abbe, who was prudence itself, did not wait to be told twice, but pressed the chevalier's hand and left him. Twenty minutes afterward Captain Roquefinette entered.

CHAPTER XIV.
THE RUE DES BONS ENFANTS.

The evening of the same day, which was Sunday, toward eight o'clock, at the moment when a considerable group of men and women, assembled round a street singer who was playing at the same time the cymbals with his knees and the tambourine with his hands, obstructed the entrance to the Rue de Valois, a musketeer and two of the light horse descended a back staircase of the Palais Royal, and advanced toward the Passage du Lycée, which, as every one knows, opened on to that street; but seeing the crowd which barred the way, the three soldiers stopped and appeared to take council. The result of their deliberation was doubtless that they must take another route, for the musketeer, setting the example of a new maneuver, threaded the Cour des Fontaines, turned the corner of the Rue des Bons Enfants, and walking rapidly—though he was extremely corpulent—arrived at No. 22, which opened as by enchantment at his approach, and closed again on him and his two companions.

At the moment when they commenced this little detour, a young man, dressed in a dark coat, wrapped in a mantle of the same color, and wearing a broad-brimmed hat pulled down over his eyes, quitted the group which surrounded the singer, singing himself, to the tune of Les Pendus, "Vingt-quatre, vingt-quatre, vingt-quatre," and advancing rapidly toward the Passage du Lycée, arrived at the further end in time to see the three illustrious vagabonds enter the house as we have said. He threw a glance round him, and by the light of one of the three lanterns, which lighted, or rather ought to have lighted, the whole length of the street, he perceived one of those immense coalheavers, with a face the color of soot, so well stereotyped by Greuze, who was resting against one of the posts of the Hotel de la Roche-Guyon, on which he had hung his bag. For an instant he appeared to hesitate to approach this man; but the coalheaver having sung the same air and the same burden, he appeared to lose all hesitation, and went straight to him.

"Well, captain," said the man in the cloak, "did you see them?"

"As plainly as I see you, colonel—a musketeer and two light horse; but I could not recognize them. However, as[Pg 296] the musketeer hid his face in his handkerchief, I presume it was the regent."

"Himself; and the two light horse are Simiane and Ravanne."

"Ah, ah! my scholar," said the captain, "I shall have great pleasure in seeing him again: he is a good boy."

"At any rate, captain, take care he does not recognize you."

"Recognize me! It must be the devil himself to recognize me, accoutered as I am. It is you, rather, chevalier, who should take the caution. You have an unfortunately aristocratic air, which does not suit at all with your dress. However, there they are in the trap, and we must take care they do not leave it. Have our people been told?"

"Your people, captain. I know no more of them than they do of me. I quitted the group singing the burden which was our signal. Did they hear me? Did they understand me? I know nothing of it."

"Be easy, colonel. These fellows hear half a voice, and understand half a word."

Indeed, as soon as the man in the cloak had left the group, a strange fluctuation which he had not foreseen began to take place in the crowd, which appeared to be composed only of passers-by, so that the song was not finished, nor the collection received. The crowd dispersed. A great many men left the circle, singly, or two and two, turning toward each other with an imperceptible gesture of the hand, some by the Rue de Valois, some by the Cour des Fontaines, some by the Palais Royal itself, thus surrounding the Rue des Bons Enfants, which seemed to be the center of the rendezvous. In consequence of this maneuver, the intention of which it is easy to understand, there only remained before the singer ten or twelve women, some children, and a good bourgeois of about forty years old, who, seeing that the collection was about to begin again, quitted his place with an air of profound contempt for all these new songs, and humming an old pastoral which he placed infinitely above them. It seemed to him that several men as he passed them made him signs; but as he did not belong to any secret society or any masonic lodge, he went on, singing his favorite—

"Then let me go And let me play Beneath the hazel-tree," and after having followed the Rue St. Honoré to the Barriere des Deux Sergents, turned the corner and disappeared. Almost at the same moment, the man in the cloak, who had been the first to leave the group, reappeared, and, accosting the singer—

"My friend," said he, "my wife is ill, and your music will prevent her sleeping. If you have no particular reason for remaining here, go to the Place du Palais Royal, and here is a crown to indemnify you."

"Thank you, my lord," replied the singer, measuring the social position of the giver by his generosity. "I will go directly. Have you any commissions for the Rue Mouffetard?"

"No."

"Because I would have executed them into the bargain."

The man went away, and as he was at once the center and the cause of the meeting, all that remained disappeared with him. At this moment the clock of the Palais Royal struck nine. The young man drew from his pocket a watch, whose diamond setting contrasted strangely with his simple costume. He set it exactly, then turned and went into the Rue des Bons Enfants. On arriving opposite No. 24, he found the coalheaver.

"And the singer?" asked the latter.

"He is gone."

"Good."

"And the postchaise?" asked the man in the cloak.

"It is waiting at the corner of the Rue Baillif."

"Have they taken the precaution of wrapping the wheels and horses' hoofs in rags?"

"Yes."

"Very good. Now let us wait," said the man in the cloak.

"Let us wait," replied the coalheaver. And all was silent.

An hour passed, during which a few[Pg 297] rare passers-by crossed the street at intervals, but at length it became almost deserted. The few lighted windows were darkened one after the other, and night, having now nothing to contend with but the two lanterns, one of which was opposite the chapel of St. Clare, and the other at the corner of the Rue Baillif, at length reigned over the domain which it had long claimed. Another hour passed. They heard the watch in the Rue de Valois; behind him, the keeper of the passage came to close the door.

"Good," murmured the man in the cloak; "now we are sure not to be interrupted."

"Provided," replied the coalheaver, "he leaves before day."

"If he were alone, we might fear his remaining, but Madame de Sabran will scarcely keep all three."

"Peste! you are right, captain; and I had not thought of it; however, are all your precautions taken?"——"All."

"And your men believe that it is a question of a bet?"

"They appear to believe it, at least, and we cannot ask more."

"Then it is well understood, captain. You and your people are drunk. You push me. I fall between the regent and him who has his arm. I separate them. You seize on him and gag him, and at a whistle the carriage arrives, while Simiane and Ravanne are held with pistols at their throats."

"But," answered the coalheaver, in a low voice, "if he declares his name."

The man in the cloak replied, in a still lower tone, "In conspiracies there are no half measures. If he declares himself, you must kill him."

"Peste!" said the coalheaver; "let us try to prevent his doing so."

There was no reply, and all was again silent. A quarter of an hour passed, and then the center windows were lighted up.

"Ah! ah! there is something new," they both exclaimed together.

At this moment they heard the step of a man, who came from the Rue St. Honore, and who was preparing to go the whole length of the street.

The coalheaver muttered a terrible oath; however, the man came on, but whether the darkness sufficed to frighten him, or whether he saw something suspicious moving there, it was evident that he experienced some fear. As he reached the Hotel St. Clare, employing that old ruse of cowards who wish to appear brave, he began to sing; but as he advanced, his voice trembled, and though the innocence of the song proved the serenity of his heart, on arriving opposite the passage he began to cough, which, as we know, in the gamut of terror, indicates a greater degree of fear than singing. Seeing, however, that nothing moved round him, he took courage, and, in a voice more in harmony with his present situation than with the sense of the words, he began—

"Then let me go,"

but there he stopped short, not only in his song, but in his walk; for, having perceived two men standing in a doorway, he felt his voice and his legs fail him at once, and he drew up, motionless and silent. Unfortunately, at this moment a shadow approached the window. The coalheaver saw that a cry might lose all, and moved, as if to spring on the passenger; his companion held him back.

"Captain," said he, "do not hurt this man;" and then, approaching him—"Pass on, my friend," said he, "but pass quickly, and do not look back."

The singer did not wait to be told twice, but made off as fast as his little legs and his trembling condition allowed, so that in a few minutes, he had disappeared at the corner of the Hotel de Toulouse.

"'Twas time," murmured the coalheaver; "they are opening the window."

The two men drew back as far as possible into the shade. The window was opened, and one of the light horse appeared on the balcony.

"Well?" said a voice, which the coalheaver and his companion recognized as that of the regent, from the interior of the room. "Well, Simiane, what kind of weather is it?"

"Oh!" replied Simiane, "I think it snows."

[Pg 298]"You think it snows?"

"Or rains, I do not know which," continued Simiane.

"What!" said Ravanne, "can you not tell what is falling?" and he also came on to the balcony.

"After all," said Simiane, "I am not sure that anything is falling."

"He is dead drunk," said the regent.

"I!" said Simiane, wounded in his amour propre as a toper, "I dead drunk! Come here, monseigneur, come."

Though the invitation was given in a strange manner, the regent joined his companions, laughing. By his gait it was easy to see that he himself was more than warmed.

"Ah! dead drunk," replied Simiane, holding out his hand to the prince; "well, I bet you a hundred louis that, regent of France as you are, you will not do what I do."

"You hear, monseigneur," said a female voice from the room; "it is a challenge."

"And as such I accept it."

"Done, for a hundred louis."

"I go halves with whoever likes," said Ravanne.

"Bet with the marchioness," said Simiane; "I admit no one into my games."

"Nor I," said the regent.

"Marchioness," cried Ravanne, "fifty louis to a kiss."

"Ask Philippe if he permits it."

"Yes," said the regent, "it is a golden bargain; you are sure to win. Well, are you ready, Simiane?"

"I am; will you follow me?"

"Everywhere. What are you going to do?"

"Look."

"Where the devil are you going?"

"I am going into the Palais Royal."

"How?"

"By the roofs."

And Simiane, seizing that kind of iron fan which we have said separated the windows of the drawing-room from those of the bedrooms, began to climb like an ape.

"Monseigneur," cried Madame de Sabran, bounding on to the balcony, and catching the prince by the arm, "I hope you will not follow."

"Not follow!" said the regent, freeing himself from the marchioness's arm; "do you know that I hold as a principle that whatever another man tries I can do? If he goes up to the moon, devil take me if I am not there to knock at the door as soon as he. Did you bet on me, Ravanne?"

"Yes, my prince," replied the young man, laughing.

"Then take your kiss, you have won;" and the regent seized the iron bars, climbing behind Simiane, who, active, tall, and slender, was in an instant on the terrace.

"But I hope you, at least, will remain, Ravanne?" said the marchioness.

"Long enough to claim your stakes," said the young man, kissing the beautiful fresh cheeks of Madame de Sabran. "Now, adieu," continued he, "I am monseigneur's page; you understand that I must follow him."

And Ravanne darted on to the perilous road already taken by his companions. The coalheaver and the man in the cloak uttered an exclamation of astonishment, which was repeated along the street as if every door had an echo.

"Ah! what is that?" said Simiane, who had arrived first on

the terrace.

"Do you see double, drunkard?" said the regent, seizing the railing of the terrace, "it is the watch, and you will get us taken to the guard-house; but I promise you I will leave you there."

At these words those who were in the street were silent, hoping that the duke and his companions would push the joke no further, but would come down and go out by the ordinary road.

"Oh! here I am," said the regent, landing on the terrace; "have you had enough, Simiane?"

"No, monseigneur," replied Simiane; and bending down to Ravanne, "that is not the watch," continued he, "not a musket—not a jerkin."

"What is the matter?" asked the regent.

"Nothing," replied Simiane, making a sign to Ravanne, "except that I continue my ascent, and invite you to follow me."

[Pg 299]And at these words, holding out his hand to the regent, he began to scale the roof, drawing him after him. Ravanne brought up the rear.

At this sight, as there was no longer any doubt of their intention, the coalheaver uttered a malediction, and the man in the cloak a cry of rage.

"Ah! ah!" said the regent, striding on the roof, and looking down the street, where, by the light from the open window, they saw eight or ten men moving, "what the devil is that? a plot! Ah! one would suppose they wanted to scale the house—they are furious. I have a mind to ask them what we can do to help them."

"No joking, monseigneur," said Simiane; "let us go on."

"Turn by the Rue St. Honore," said the man in the cloak. "Forward, forward."

"They are pursuing us," said Simiane; "quick to the other side; back."

"I do not know what prevents me," said the man in the cloak, drawing a pistol from his belt and aiming at the regent, "from bringing him down like a partridge."

"Thousand furies!" cried the coalheaver, stopping him, "you will get us all hanged and quartered."

"But what are we to do?"

"Wait till they come down alone and break their necks, for if Providence is just, that little surprise awaits us."

"What an idea, Roquefinette!"

"Eh! colonel; no names, if you please."

"You are right. Pardieu!"

"There is no need; let us have the idea."

"Follow me," cried the man in the cloak, springing into the passage. "Let us break open the door and we will take them on the other side when they jump down."

And all that remained of his companions followed him. The others, to the number of five or six, were already making for the Rue St. Honore.

"Let us go, monseigneur," said Simiane; "we have not a minute to lose; slide on your back. It is not glorious, but it is safe."

"I think I hear them in the passage," said the regent; "what do you think, Ravanne?"

"I do not think at all," said Ravanne, "I let myself slip."

And all three descended rapidly, and arrived on the terrace.

"Here, here!" said a woman's voice, at the moment when Simiane strode over the parapet to descend his iron ladder.

"Ah! is it you, marchioness?" said the regent; "you are indeed a friend in need."

"Jump in here, and quickly."

The three fugitives sprang into the room.

"Do you like to stop here?" asked Madame de Sabran.

"Yes," said Ravanne; "I will go and look for Canillac and his night-watch."

"No, no," said the regent; "they will be scaling your house and treating it as a town taken by assault. Let us gain the Palais Royal."

And they descended the staircase rapidly and opened the garden door. There they heard the despairing blows of their pursuers against the iron gates.

"Strike, strike, my friends," said the regent, running with the carelessness and activity of a young man, "the gate is solid, and will give you plenty of work."

"Quick, quick, monseigneur," cried Simiane, who, thanks to his great height, had jumped to the ground hanging by his arms, "there they are at the end of the Rue de Valois. Put your foot on my shoulder—now the other—and let yourself slip into my arms. You are saved, thank God."

"Draw your sword, Ravanne, and let us charge these fellows," said the regent.

"In the name of Heaven, monseigneur," cried Simiane, "follow us. I am not a coward, I believe, but what you would do is mere folly. Here, Ravanne."

And the young men, each taking one of the duke's arms, led him down a passage of the Palais Royal at the moment when those who were running by the Rue de Valois were at twenty paces from them,[Pg 300] and when the door of the passage fell under the efforts of the second troop. The whole reunited band rushed against the gate at the moment that the three gentlemen closed it behind them.

"Gentlemen," said the regent, saluting with his hand, for as to his hat, Heaven knows where that was; "I hope, for the sake of your heads, that all this was only a joke, for you are attacking those who are stronger than yourselves. Beware, to-morrow, of the lieutenant of police. Meanwhile, good-night."

And a triple shout of laughter petrified the two conspirators leaning against the gate at the head of their breathless companions.

"This man must have a compact with Satan," cried D'Harmental.

"We have lost the bet, my friends," said Roquefinette, addressing his men, who stood waiting for orders, "but we do not dismiss you yet; it is only postponed. As to the promised sum, you have already had half: to-morrow—you know where, for the rest. Good-evening. I shall be at the rendezvous to-morrow."

All the people dispersed, and the two chiefs remained alone.

"Well, colonel," said Roquefinette, looking D'Harmental full in the face.

"Well, captain," replied the chevalier; "I have a great mind to ask one thing of you."

"What?" asked Roquefinette.

"To follow me into some cross-road and blow my brains out with your pistol, that this miserable head may be punished and not recognized."

"Why so?"

"Why? Because in such matters, when one fails one is but a fool: What am I to say to Madame de Maine now?"

"What!" cried Roquefinette, "is it about that little hop-o'-my-thumb that you are bothering yourself? Pardieu! you are frantically susceptible, colonel. Why the devil does not her lame husband attend to his own affairs. I should like to have seen your prude with her two cardinals and her three or four marquises, who are bursting with fear at this moment in a corner of the arsenal, while we remain masters of the field of battle. I should like to have seen if they would have climbed walls like lizards. Stay, colonel, listen to an old fox. To be a good conspirator, you must have, first, what you have, courage; but you must also have what you have not, patience. Morbleu! if I had such an affair in my hands, I would answer for it that I would bring it to a good end, and if you like to make it over to me we will talk of that."

"But in my place," asked the colonel, "what would you say

to Madame de Maine?"

"Oh! I should say, 'My princess, the regent must have been warned by his police, for he did not leave as we expected, and we saw none but his roué companions.' Then the Prince de Cellamare will say to you, 'My dear D'Harmental, we have no resources but in you.' Madame de Maine will say that all is not lost since the brave D'Harmental remains to us. The Count de Laval will grasp your hand trying to pay you a compliment, which he will not finish, because since his jaw is broken his tongue is not active, particularly for compliments. The Cardinal de Polignac will make the sign of the cross. Alberoni will swear enough to shake the heavens—in this manner you will have conciliated everybody, saved your amour propre, and may return to hide in your attic, which I advise you not to leave for three or four days if you do not wish to be hanged. From time to time I will pay you a visit. You will continue to bestow on me some of the liberalities of Spain, because it is of importance to me to live agreeably, and keep up my spirits; then, at the first opportunity we recall our brave fellows, and take our revenge."

"Yes, certainly," said D'Harmental; "that is what any other would do, but you see I have some foolish ideas—I cannot lie."

"Whoever cannot lie cannot act," replied the captain; "but what do I see there? The bayonets of the watch; amicable institution, I recognize you there; always a quarter of an hour too late.[Pg 301] But now adieu, colonel," continued he; "there is your road, we must separate," said the captain, showing the Passage du Palais Royal, "and here is mine," added he, pointing to the Rue Neuve des Petits-Champs; "go quietly, that they may not know that you ought to run as fast as you can, your hand on your hip so, and singing 'La Mere Gaudichon.'" And the captain followed the Rue de Valois at the same pace as the watch, who were a hundred paces behind him, singing carelessly as he went.

As to the chevalier, he re-entered the Rue des Bons Enfants, now as quiet as it had been noisy ten minutes before; and at the corner of the Rue Baillif he found the carriage, which, according to its orders, had not moved, and was waiting with the door open, the servant at the step, and the coachman on his box.

"To the arsenal," said the chevalier.

"It is useless," said a voice which made D'Harmental start; "I know all that has passed, and I will inform those who ought to know. A visit at this hour would be dangerous for all."

"Is it you, abbe?" said D'Harmental, trying to recognize Brigaud in the livery in which he was disguised; "you would render me a real service in taking the news instead of me, for on my honor I do not know what to say."

"Well, I shall say," said Brigaud, "that you are a brave and loyal gentleman, and that if there were ten like you in France, all would soon be finished; but we are not here to pay compliments: get in quickly—where shall I take you?"

"It is useless," said D'Harmental; "I will go on foot."

"Get in. It is safer."

D'Harmental complied, and Brigaud, dressed as he was, came and sat beside him.

"To the corner of the Rue du Gros Chenet and the Rue de Cléry," said the abbe.

The coachman, impatient at having waited so long, obeyed quickly. At the place indicated the carriage stopped; the chevalier got out, and soon disappeared round the corner of the Rue du Temps-Perdu. As to the carriage, it rolled on noiselessly toward the Boulevards, like a fairy car which does not touch the earth.

CHAPTER XV.
JEAN BUVAT.

Our readers must now make a better acquaintance with one of the principal personages in the history which we have undertaken to relate, of whom we have scarcely spoken. We would refer to the good bourgeois, whom we have seen quitting the group in the Rue de Valois, and making for the Barrière des Sergents at the moment when the street-singer began his collection, and who, it will be remembered, we have since seen at so inopportune a moment in the Rue des Bons-Enfants.

Heaven preserve us from questioning the intelligence of our readers, so as to doubt for a moment that they had recognized in the poor devil to whom the Chevalier d'Harmental had rendered such timely assistance the good man of the terrace in the Rue du Temps-Perdu. But they cannot know, unless we tell them in detail, what he was physically, morally, and socially. If the reader has not forgotten the little we have already told him, it will be remembered that he was from forty to forty-five years of age. Now as every one knows, after forty years of age the bourgeois of Paris entirely forgets the care of his person, with which he is not generally much occupied, a negligence from which his corporeal graces suffer considerably, particularly when, as in the present instance, his appearance is not to be admired.

Our bourgeois was a little man of five feet four, short and fat, disposed to become obese as he advanced in age; and with one of those placid faces where all—hair, eyebrows, eyes, and skin—seem of the same color; in fact, one of those faces of which, at ten paces, one does not distinguish a feature. The most enthusiastic physiognomist, if he had sought to read on this countenance some high and curious destiny, would have been stopped in his examination as he mounted from his great blue eyes to his depressed forehead, or de[Pg 302]scended from his half-open mouth to the fold of his double chin. There he would have understood that he had under his eyes one of those heads to which all fermentation is unknown, whose freshness is respected by the passions, good or bad, and who turn nothing in the empty corners of their brain but the burden of some old nursery song. Let us add that Providence, who does nothing by halves, had signed the original, of which we have just offered a copy to our readers, by the characteristic name of Jean Buvat.

It is true that the persons who ought to have appreciated the profound nullity of spirit, and excellent qualities of heart of this good man, suppressed his patronymic, and ordinarily called him Le Bonhomme Buvat.

From his earliest youth the little Buvat, who had a marked repugnance for all other kinds of study, manifested a particular inclination for caligraphy: thus he arrived every morning at the College des Oratoriens, where his mother sent him gratis, with his exercises and translations full of faults, but written with a neatness, a regularity, and a beauty which it was charming to see. The little Buvat was whipped every day for the idleness of his mind, and received the writing prize every year for the skill of his hand. At fifteen years of age he passed from the Epitome Sacræ, which he had recommenced five times, to the Epitome Græcæ; but the professor soon perceived that this was too much for him, and put him back for the sixth time in the Epitome Sacræ. Passive as he appeared, young Buvat was not wanting in a certain pride. He came home in the evening crying to his mother, and complaining of the injustice which had been done him, declaring, in his grief, a thing which till then he had been careful not to confess, namely, that there were in the school children of ten years old more advanced than he was.

Widow Buvat, who saw her son start every morning with his exercises perfectly neat (which led her to believe that there could be no fault to be found with them), went the next day to abuse the good fathers. They replied that her son was a good boy, incapable of an evil thought toward God, or a bad action toward his neighbor; but that, at the same time, he was so awfully stupid that they advised her to develop, by making him a writing-master, the only talent with which nature had blessed him. This counsel was a ray of light for Madame Buvat; she understood that, in this manner, the benefit she should derive from her son would be immediate. She came back to her house, and communicated to her son the new plans she had formed for him. Young Buvat saw in this only a means of escaping the castigation which he received every morning, for which the prize, bound in calf, that he received every year was not a compensation.

He received the propositions of his mother with great joy; promised her that, before six months were over, he would be the first writing-master in the capital; and the same day, after having, from his little savings, bought a knife with four blades, a packet of quills, and two copy-books, set himself to the work. The good Oratoriens were not deceived as to the true vocation of young Buvat. Caligraphy was with him an art which almost became drawing. At the end of six months, like the ape in the Arabian Nights, he wrote six kinds of writing; and imitated men's faces, trees, and animals. At the end of a year he had made such progress that he thought he might now give out his prospectus. He worked at it for three months, day and night; and almost lost his sight over it. At the end of that time he had accomplished a chef-d'œuvre.

It was not a simple writing, but a real picture representing the creation of the world, and divided almost like the Transfiguration of Raphael. In the upper part, consecrated to Eden, was the Eternal Father drawing Eve from the side of the sleeping Adam, and surrounded by those animals which the nobility of their nature brings near to man, such as the lion, the horse, and the dog. At the bottom was the sea, in the depths of which were to be seen swimming the most fantastic fishes, and on the surface a superb three-decked[Pg 303] vessel. On the two sides, trees full of birds put the heavens, which they touched with their topmost branches, in communication with the earth, which they grasped with their roots; and in the space left in the middle of all this, in the most perfectly horizontal line, and reproduced in

182

six different writings, was the adverb "pitilessly." This time the artist was not deceived; the picture produced the effect which he expected. A week afterward young Buvat had five male and two female scholars. His reputation increased; and Madame Buvat, after some time passed in greater ease than she had known even in her husband's lifetime, had the satisfaction of dying perfectly secure about her son's future.

As to him, after having sufficiently mourned his mother, he pursued the course of his life, one day exactly like the other. He arrived thus at the age of twenty-six or twenty-seven, having passed the stormy part of existence in the eternal calm of his innocent and virtuous good nature. It was about this time that the good man found an opportunity of doing a sublime action, which he did instinctively and simply, as he did everything; but perhaps a man of mind might have passed it over without seeing it, or turned away from it if he had seen it. There was in the house No. 6, in the Rue des Orties, of which Buvat occupied the attic, a young couple who were the admiration of the whole quarter for the harmony in which they lived. They appeared made for each other. The husband was a man of from thirty-four to thirty-five years of age, of a southern origin, with black eyes, beard and hair, sunburned complexion, and teeth like pearls. He was called Albert du Rocher, and was the son of an ancient Cevenol chief, who had been forced to turn Catholic, with all his family, at the persecutions of Monsieur Baville; and half from opposition, half because youth seeks youth, he had entered the household of M. le Duc de Chartres, which was being reformed just at that time, having suffered much in the campaign preceding the battle of Steinkirk, where the prince had made his debut in arms. Du Rocher had obtained the place of La Neuville, who had been killed in that charge which, conducted by the Duc de Chartres, had decided the victory.

The winter had interrupted the campaign, but in the spring M. de Luxembourg had recalled all those officers who shared their life between war and pleasure. The Duc de Chartres, always eager to draw a sword which the jealousy of Louis XIV. had so often replaced in the scabbard, was one of the first to answer this appeal. Du Rocher followed him with all his military household. The great day of Nerwinden arrived. The Duc de Chartres had, as usual, the command of the guards; as usual he charged at their head, but so furiously that five times he found himself almost alone in the midst of the enemy. At the fifth time he had near him only a young man whom he scarcely knew; but in the rapid glance which he cast on him he recognized one of those spirits on whom one may rely, and instead of yielding, as a brigadier of the enemy's army, who had recognized him, proposed to him, he blew the proposer's brains out with his pistol. At the same instant two shots were fired, one of which took off the prince's hat, and the other turned from the handle of his sword. Scarcely had these two shots been fired when those who had discharged them fell simultaneously, thrown down by the prince's companion—one by a saber-stroke, the other by a bullet. A general attack took place on these two men, who were miraculously saved from any ball. The prince's horse, however, fell under him. The young man who was with him jumped from his, and offered it to him.

The prince hesitated to accept this service, which might cost him who rendered it so dear; but the young man, who was tall and powerful, thinking that this was not a moment to exchange politenesses, took the prince in his arms and forced him into the saddle. At this moment, M. d'Arcy, who had lost his pupil in the melée, and who was seeking for him with a detachment of light horse, came up, just as, in spite of their courage, the prince and his companion were about to be killed[Pg 304] or taken. Both were without wound, although the prince had received four bullets in his clothes. The Duc de Chartres held out his hand to his companion, and asked him his name; for, although his face was known to him, he had been so short a time in his service that he did not remember his name. The young man replied that he was called Albert du Rocher, and that he had taken the place of La Neuville, who was killed at Steinkirk.

Then, turning toward those who had just arrived—

"Gentlemen," said the prince, "you have prevented me from being taken, but this gentleman," pointing to Du Rocher, "has saved me from being killed."

At the end of the campaign, the Duc de Chartres named Du Rocher his first equerry, and three years afterward, having retained the grateful affection which he had vowed to him, he married him to a young person whom he loved, and gave her a dowry.

As M. le Duc de Chartres was still but a young man, this dowry was not large, but he promised to take charge of the advancement of his protégée. This young person was of English origin; her mother had accompanied Madame Henriette when she came to France to marry Monsieur; and after that princess had been poisoned by the Chevalier d'Effiat, she had passed, as lady-in-waiting, into the service of the Grand Dauphine; but, in 1690, the Grand Dauphine died, and the Englishwoman, in her insular pride, refused to stay with Mademoiselle Choin, and retired to a little country house which she hired near St. Cloud, where she gave herself up entirely to the education of her little Clarice. It was in the journeys of the Duc de Chartres to St. Cloud that Du Rocher made acquaintance with this young girl, whom, as we have said, he married in 1697. It was, then, these young people who occupied the first floor of the house of which Buvat had the attic. The young couple had first a son, whose caligraphic education was confided to Buvat from the age of four years. The young pupil was making the most satisfactory progress when he was carried off by the measles. The despair of the parents was great; Buvat shared it, the more sincerely that his pupil had shown such aptitude. This sympathy for their grief, on the part of a stranger, attached them to him; and one day, when the young man was complaining of the precarious future of artists, Albert du Rocher proposed to him to use his influence to procure him a place at the government library. Buvat jumped with joy at the idea of becoming a public functionary; and, a month afterward,

Buvat received his brevet as employé at the library, in the manuscript department, with a salary of nine hundred livres a year. From this day, Buvat, in the pride natural to his new position, neglected his scholars, and gave himself up entirely to the preparation of forms. Nine hundred livres, secured to the end of his life, was quite a fortune, and the worthy writer, thanks to the royal munificence, began to lead a life of ease and comfort, promising his good neighbors that if they had a second child no one but himself should teach him to write. On their parts, the poor parents wished much to give this increase of occupation to the worthy writer. God heard their desire. Toward the termination of 1702, Clarice was delivered of a daughter.

Great was the joy through the whole house. Buvat did not feel at all at his ease; he ran up and down stairs, beating his thighs with his hands, and singing below his breath the burden of his favorite song, "Then let me go, and let me play," etc. That day, for the first time since he had been appointed, that is to say, during two years, he arrived at his office at a quarter past ten, instead of ten o'clock exactly. A supernumerary, who thought that he must be dead, had asked for his place.

The little Bathilde was not a week old before Buvat wished to begin teaching her her strokes and pot-hooks, saying, that to learn a thing well, it is necessary to commence young. It was with the greatest difficulty that he was made to understand that he must wait till she was two or three years old. He resigned him[Pg 305]self; but, in expectation of

187

that time, he set about preparing copies. At the end of three years Clarice kept her word, and Buvat had the satisfaction of solemnly putting her first pen into the hands of Bathilde.

He then returned to his work with all the eagerness of anartist.

He then returned to his work with all the eagerness of an artist.—*Page* 325.

Link to larger image

It was the beginning of the year 1707, and the Duc de Chartres had become Duc d'Orleans, by the death of Monsieur, and had at last obtained a command in Spain, where he was to conduct the troops to the Marechal de Berwick. Orders were directly given to all his military household to hold themselves in readiness for the 5th of March. As first equerry, it was necessary that Albert should accompany the prince. This news, which would have formerly given him the highest joy, made him now almost sad, for the health of Clarice began to fill him with the greatest uneasiness; and the doctor had allowed the word consumption to escape him. Whether Clarice felt herself seriously attacked, or whether, more natural still, she feared only for her husband, her burst of grief was so wild that Albert himself could not help crying with her, and little Bathilde and Buvat cried because they saw the others cry.

The 5th of March arrived; it was the day fixed for the departure. In spite of her grief, Clarice had busied herself with her husband's outfit, and had wished that it was worthy of the prince whom he accompanied. Moreover, in the midst of her tears a ray of proud joy lit up her face when she saw Albert in his elegant uniform, and on his noble war-horse. As to Albert, he was full of hope and pride; the poor wife smiled sadly at his dreams for the future; but in order not to dispirit him at this moment, she shut her grief up in her own heart, and silencing her fears which she had for him, and, perhaps, also those which she experienced for herself, she was the first to say to him, "Think not of me, but of your honor."

The Duc d'Orleans and his corps d'armée entered Catalonia in the first days of April, and advanced directly, by forced marches, across Arragon. On arriving at Segorbe, the duke learned that the Marechal de Berwick held himself in readiness for a decisive battle; and in his eagerness to arrive in time to take part in the action he sent Albert on at full speed, charging him to tell the marshal that the Duc d'Orleans was coming to his aid with ten thousand men, and to pray that if it did not interfere with his arrangements, he would wait for him before joining battle.

Albert left, but bewildered in the mountains, and misled by ignorant guides, he was only a day before the army, and he arrived at the marshal's camp at the very moment when the engagement was going to commence. Albert asked where the marshal was; they showed his position, on the left of the army, on a little hill, from which he overlooked the whole plain. The Duc de Berwick was there surrounded by his staff; Albert put his horse to the gallop and made straight toward him.

The messenger introduced himself to the marshal and told him the cause of his coming. The marshal's only answer was to point to the field of battle, and tell him to return to the prince, and inform him what he had seen. But Albert had smelled powder, and was not willing to leave thus. He asked permission to wait till he could at least give him the news of a victory. At that moment a charge of dragoons seemed necessary to the marshal; he told one of his aides-de-camp to carry the order to charge to the colonel. The young man started at a gallop, but he had scarcely gone a third of the distance which separated the hill from the position of the regiment, when his head was carried off by a cannon-ball. Scarcely had he fallen from his stirrups when Albert, seizing this occasion to take part in the battle, set spurs to his horse, transmitted the order to the colonel, and instead of returning to the marshal, drew his sword, and charged at the head of the regiment.

This charge was one of the most brilliant of the day, and penetrated so completely to the heart of the imperial guard that they began to give way. The marshal had involuntarily watched the young officer throughout the melée, recognizing him by his uniform. He saw him arrive at the enemy's standard, engage in a per[Pg 306]sonal contest with him who carried it; then, when the regiment had taken flight, he saw him returning with his conquest in his arms. On reaching the marshal he threw the colors at his feet; opening his mouth to speak, instead of words, it was blood that came to his lips. The marshal saw him totter in his saddle, and advanced to support him, but before he had time to do so Albert had fallen; a ball had pierced his breast. The marshal sprung from his horse, but the brave young man lay dead on the standard he had just taken. The Duc d'Orleans arrived the day after the battle. He regretted Albert as one regrets a gallant gentleman; but, after all, he had died the death of the brave, in the midst of victory, and on the colors he himself had taken. What more could be desired by a Frenchman, a soldier, and a gentleman?

The duke wrote with his own hand to the poor widow. If anything could console a wife for the death of her husband, it would doubtless be such a letter; but poor Clarice thought but of one thing, that she had no longer a husband, and that her child had no longer a father. At four o'clock Buvat came in from the library; they told him that Clarice wanted him, and he went down directly. The poor woman did not cry, she did not complain; she stood tearless and speechless, her eyes fixed and hollow as those of a maniac. When Buvat entered, she did not even turn her head toward him, but merely holding out her hand, she presented him the letter. Buvat looked right and left to endeavor to find out what was the matter, but seeing nothing to direct his conjectures, he looked at the paper and read aloud:

"Madame—Your husband has died for France and for me. Neither France nor I can give you back your husband, but remember that if ever you are in want of anything, we are both your debtors.

"Your affectionate,

"Philippe d'Orleans."

"What!" cried Buvat, fixing his great eyes on Clarice, "M. du Rocher—it is not possible!"

"Papa is dead," said little Bathilde, leaving the corner where she was playing with her doll, and running to her mother; "is it true that papa is dead?"

"Alas! yes, my dear child!" said Clarice, finding at once words and tears. "Oh yes, it is true; it is but too true, unhappy that we are!"

"Madame," said Buvat, who had been seeking for some consolation to offer, "you must not grieve thus; perhaps it is a false report."

"Do you not see that the letter is from the Duc d'Orleans himself?" cried the poor widow. "Yes, my child, your father is dead. Weep, my child; perhaps in seeing your tears God will have pity on me;" and saying these things, the poor widow coughed so painfully that Buvat felt his own breast torn by it, but his fright was still greater when he saw that the handkerchief which she drew from her mouth was covered with blood. Then he understood that a greater misfortune threatened Bathilde than that which had just befallen her.

The apartments which Clarice occupied were now too large for her. No one was astonished when she left them for smaller ones on the second floor. Besides her grief, which annihilated all her other faculties, Clarice felt, in common with all other noble hearts, a certain unwillingness to ask, even from her county, a reward for the blood which had been spilled for it, particularly when that blood is still warm, as was that of Albert. The poor widow hesitated to present herself to the minister-at-war to ask for her due. At the end of three months, when she took courage to make the first steps, the taking of Requena and that of Saragossa had already thrown into the shade the battle of Almanza. Clarice showed the prince's letter. The secretary replied that with such a letter she could not fail in obtaining what she wanted, but that she must wait for his highness's return. Clarice looked in a glass at her emaciated face, and smiled sadly.

"Wait!" said she; "yes, it would be better, but God knows if I shall have the time."

[Pg 307]The result of this repulse was, that Clarice left her lodging on the second floor for two little rooms on the third. The poor widow had no other fortune than her husband's savings. The little dowry which the duke had given her had disappeared in the purchase of furniture and her husband's outfit. As the new lodging which she took was much smaller than the other, no one was astonished that Clarice sold part of her furniture.

The return of the Duc d'Orleans was expected in the autumn, and Clarice counted on this to ameliorate her situation; but, contrary to the usual custom, the army, instead of taking winter quarters, continued the campaign, and news arrived that, instead of returning, the duke was about to lay siege to Lerida. Now, in 1647, the great Conde himself had failed before Lerida, and the new siege, even supposing that it ever came to a successful issue, threatened to be of a terrible length.

Clarice risked some new advances. This time they had forgotten even her husband's name. She had again recourse to the prince's letter, which had its ordinary effect; but they told her that after the siege of Lerida the duke could not fail to return, and the poor widow was again obliged to wait.

She left her two rooms for a little attic opposite that of Buvat, and she sold the rest of her furniture, only keeping a table, some chairs, Bathilde's little cot, and a bed for herself.

Buvat had seen, without taking much notice, these frequent removals, but it was not very difficult to understand his neighbor's situation. Buvat, who was a careful man, had some savings which he had a great wish to put at his neighbor's service; but Clarice's pride increased with her poverty, and poor Buvat had never yet dared to make the offer. Twenty times he had gone to her with a little rouleau, which contained his whole fortune of fifty or sixty louis, but every time he left without having dared to take it out of his pocket; but one day it happened that Buvat, descending to go to business, having met the landlord who was making his quarterly round, and guessing that his neighbor might be embarrassed, even for so small a sum, took the proprietor into his own room, saying that the day before Madame du Rocher had given him the money, that he might get both receipts at once. The landlord, who had feared a delay on the part of his tenant, did not care from whence the money came, and willingly gave the two receipts.

Buvat, in the naïveté of his soul, was tormented by this good action as by a crime. He was three or four days without daring to present himself to his neighbor, so that when he returned, he found her quite affected by what she thought an act of indifference on his part. Buvat found Clarice so much changed during these few days, that he left her wiping his eyes, and for the first time he went to bed without having sung, during the fifteen turns he generally took in his bedroom—

"Then let me go," etc.

which was a proof of melancholy preoccupation.

The last days of winter passed, and brought, in passing, the news that Lerida had surrendered, and that the young and indefatigable general was about to besiege Tortosa. This was the last blow for poor Clarice. She understood that spring was coming, and with it a new campaign, which would retain the duke with the army. Strength failed her, and she was obliged to take to her bed.

The position of Clarice was frightful. She did not deceive herself as to her illness. She felt that it was mortal, and she had no one in the world to whom she could recommend her child. The poor woman feared death, not on her own account, but on her daughter's, who would not have even the stone of her mother's tomb to rest her head on, for the unfortunate have no tomb. Her husband had only distant relations, from whom she could not solicit aid; as to her own family, born in France, where her mother died, she had not even known them; besides, she understood that if there were any hope from that quarter, there was[Pg 308] no longer the time to seek it. Death was approaching.

One night Buvat, who the evening before had left Clarice devoured by fever, heard her groaning so deeply, that he jumped from his bed and dressed himself to go and offer her help; but on arriving at the door, he did not dare to enter or to knock—Clarice was sobbing and praying aloud. At this moment Bathilde woke and called her mother. Clarice drove back her tears, took her child from the cradle, and placing her on her knees on her own bed, made her repeat what prayers she knew, and between each of them Buvat heard her cry in a sad voice—

"Oh, my God! listen to my poor child!"

There was in this nocturnal scene—the child scarcely out of the cradle, and a mother half way to the grave, both addressing the Lord as their only support in the silence of night—something so deeply sad that good Buvat fell on his knees, and inwardly swore, what he had not dared to offer aloud, that though Bathilde might be an orphan, yet she should not be abandoned. God had heard the double prayers which had ascended to Him, and He had granted them.

The next day Buvat did what he had never dared to do before. He took Bathilde in his arms, leaned his good-natured round face against the charming little face of the child, and said softly—

"Be easy, poor little innocent, there are yet good people on the earth."

The little girl threw her arms round his neck and kissed him. Buvat felt that the tears stood in his eyes, and as he had often heard that you must not cry before sick people, for fear of agitating them, he drew out his watch, and assuming a gruff voice to conceal his emotion—

"Hum, it is a quarter to ten, I must go. Good-day, Madame du Rocher."

On the staircase he met the doctor, and asked him what he thought of the patient. As he was a doctor who came through charity, and did not consider himself at all bound to be considerate when he was not paid, he replied that in three days she would be dead.

Coming back at four o'clock, Buvat found the whole house in commotion. The doctor had said that they must send for the viaticum. They had sent for the curé, and he had arrived, and, preceded by the sacristan and his little bell, he had without any preparation entered the sick room. Clarice received it with her hands joined, and her eyes turned toward heaven; but the impression produced on her was not the less terrible. Buvat heard singing, and thought what must have happened. He went up directly, and found the landing and the door of the sick room surrounded by all the gossips of the neighborhood, who had, as was the custom at that time, followed the holy sacrament. Round the bed where the dying woman was extended, already so pale and motionless that if it had not been for the two great tears that ran down her cheeks, she might have been taken for a marble statue lying on a tomb, the priests were singing the prayers for the dying, and in a corner of the room the little Bathilde, whom they had separated from her mother, that she might not distract her attention during her last act of religion, was seated on the ground, not daring to cry, frightened at seeing so many people she did not know, and hearing so much she did not understand.

As soon as she saw Buvat, the child ran to him as the only person she knew in this grave assembly. Buvat took her in his arms, and knelt with her near the bed of the dying woman. At this moment Clarice lowered her eyes from the heavens toward the earth. Without doubt she had been addressing a prayer to Heaven to send a protector to her daughter. She saw Bathilde in the arms of the only friend she had in the world. With the penetrating glance of the dying she read this pure and devoted heart, and saw what he had not dared to tell her; and as she sat up in bed she held out her hand to him, uttering a cry of gratitude and joy, such as the angels only can understand; and, as if she had exhausted her remaining strength in this maternal outburst, she sank back fainting on the bed.

The religious ceremony was finished.[Pg 309] The priests retired first, then the pious followed; the indifferent and curious remained till the last. Among this number were several women. Buvat asked if there was none among them who knew a good sick-nurse. One of them presented herself directly, declared, in the midst of a chorus of her companions, that she had all the necessary virtues for this honorable situation, but that, just on account of these good qualities, she was accustomed to be paid a week in advance, as she was much sought after in the neighborhood. Buvat asked the price of this week. She replied that to any other it would be sixteen livres, but as the poor lady did not seem rich, she would be contented with twelve. Buvat, who had just received his month's pay, took two crowns from his pocket and gave them to her without bargaining. He would have given double if she had asked it.

Clarice was still fainting. The nurse entered on her duty by giving her some vinegar instead of salts. Buvat retired. As to Bathilde, she had been told that her mother was asleep. The poor child did not know the difference between sleep and death, and returned to her corner to play with her doll.

At the end of an hour Buvat returned to ask news of Clarice. She had recovered from her fainting, but though her eyes were open she did not speak. However, she recognized him, for as soon as he entered she joined her hands as if to pray, and then she appeared to seek for something under her bolster. The nurse shook her head, and approaching the patient:

"Your pillow is very well," said she, "you must not disarrange it." Then turning to Buvat, "Ah! these sick people!" added she, shrugging her shoulders, "they are always fancying that there is something making them uncomfortable: it is death, only they do not know it."

Clarice sighed deeply, but remained motionless. The nurse approached her, and passed over her lips the feather of a quill dipped in a cordial of her own invention, which she had just been to fetch at the chemist's. Buvat could not support this spectacle; he recommended the mother and child to the care of the nurse, and left.

The next day Clarice was still worse, for though her eyes were open, she did not seem to recognize any one but her daughter, who was lying near her on the bed, and whose little hand she held. On her part the child, as if she felt that this was the last maternal embrace, remained quiet and silent. On seeing her kind friend she only said, "Mamma sleeps."

It appeared to Buvat that Clarice moved as if she heard and recognized her child's voice, but it might have been only a nervous trembling. He asked the nurse if the sick woman had wanted anything. She shook her head, saying, "What would be the use? It would be money thrown away. These apothecaries make quite enough already." Buvat would have liked to stay with Clarice, for he saw that she had not long to live, but he never would have thought of absenting himself for a day from business unless he were dying himself. He arrived there, then, as usual, but so sad and melancholy that the king did not gain much by his presence. They remarked with astonishment that that day Buvat did not wait till four o'clock had struck to take off the false blue sleeves which he wore to protect his coat; but that at the first stroke of the clock he got up, took his hat, and went out. The supernumerary, who had already asked for his place, watched him as he went, then, when he had closed the door, "Well!" said he, loud enough to be heard by the chief, "there is one who takes it easy."

Buvat's presentiments were confirmed. On arriving at the house he asked the porter's wife how Clarice was.

"Ah, God be thanked!" replied she; "the poor woman is

happy; she suffers no more."

"She is dead!" cried Buvat, with that shudder always produced by this terrible word.

"About three-quarters of an hour ago," replied she; and she went on darning her stocking, and singing a merry song[Pg 310] which she had interrupted to reply to Buvat.

Buvat ascended the steps of the staircase one by one, stopping frequently to wipe his forehead; then, on arriving on the landing, where was his room and that of Clarice, he was obliged to lean his head against the wall, for he felt his legs fail him. He stood silent and hesitating, when he thought he heard Bathilde's voice crying. He remembered the poor child, and this gave him courage. At the door, however, he stopped again; then he heard the groans of the little girl more distinctly.

"Mamma!" cried the child, in a little voice broken by sobs, "will you not wake? Mamma, why are you so cold?" Then, running to the door and striking with her hand, "Come, my kind friend, come," said she; "I am alone, and I am afraid."

Buvat was astonished that they had not removed the child from her mother's room; and the profound pity which the poor little creature inspired made him forget the painful feeling which had stopped him for a moment. He then raised his hand to open the door. The door was locked. At this moment he heard the porter's wife calling him. He ran to the stairs and asked her where the key was.

"Ah!" replied she, "how stupid I am; I forgot to give it you as you passed."

Buvat ran down as quickly as he could.

"And why is the key here?" he asked.

"The landlord placed it here after he had taken away the furniture," answered she.

"What! taken away the furniture?" cried Buvat.

"Of course, he has taken away the furniture. Your neighbor was not rich, M. Buvat, and no doubt she owes money on all sides. Ah! the landlord will not stand tricks; the rent first. That is but fair. Besides, she does not want furniture any more, poor dear!"

"But the nurse, where is she?"

"When she saw that her patient was dead, she went away. Her business was finished, but she will come back to shroud her for a crown, if you like. It is generally the portress who does this: but I cannot; I am too sensitive."

Buvat understood, shuddering at all that had passed. He went up quickly. His hand shook so that he could scarcely find the lock; but at length the key turned, and the door opened. Clarice was extended on the ground on the mattress out of her bed, in the middle of the dismantled room. An old sheet was thrown over her, and ought to have hidden her entirely, but little Bathilde had moved it to seek for her mother's face, which she was kissing when he entered.

"Ah, my friend," cried she, "wake my mamma, who sleeps still. Wake her, I beg!" And the child ran to Buvat, who was watching from the door this pitiable spectacle. Buvat took Bathilde back to the corpse.

"Kiss your mother for the last time, my poor child," said

he.

The child obeyed.

"And now," said he, "let her sleep. One day God will wake her;" and he took the child in his arms and carried her away. The child made no resistance. She seemed to understand her weakness and her isolation.

He put her in his own bed, for they had carried away even the child's cot; and when she was asleep, he went out to give information of the death to the commissary of the quarter, and to make arrangements for the funeral.

When he returned, the portress gave him a paper, which the nurse had found in Clarice's hand. Buvat opened and recognized the letter from the Duc d'Orleans. This was the sole inheritance which the poor mother had left to her daughter.

CHAPTER XVI.
BATHILDE.

In going to make his declaration to the commissary of the quarter and his arrangements for the funeral, Buvat had not forgotten to look for a woman who could take care of little Bathilde, an office which he could not undertake himself; firstly, because he was entirely ignorant of its duties; and, secondly, because it[Pg 311] would be impossible to leave the child alone during the six hours he spent daily at the office. Fortunately, he knew the very person he wanted; a woman of from thirty-five to thirty-eight years of age, who had been in Madame Buvat's service, and whose good qualities he had duly appreciated. It was arranged with Nanette—for this was the good woman's name—that she should live in the house, do the cooking, take care of little Bathilde, and have fifty livres a year wages, and her board. This new arrangement must greatly change all Buvat's habits, by obliging him to have a housekeeper, whereas he had always lived as a bachelor, and taken his meals at an eating-house. He could no longer keep his attic, which was now too small for him, and next morning he went in search of a new lodging. He found one, Rue Pagevin, as he wished to be near the royal library, that he might not have too far to walk in wet weather. This lodging contained two rooms, a closet, and a kitchen. He took it on the spot, and went to buy the necessary furniture for Bathilde and Nanette's rooms; and the same evening, after his return from business, they moved to their new lodgings.

The next day, which was Sunday, Clarice was buried; so that Buvat had no need to ask for a day's leave even for this.

For the first week or two, Bathilde asked constantly for her mamma; but her friend Buvat had brought her a great many pretty playthings to console her, so that she soon began to ask for her less frequently; and as she had been told she had gone to join her father, she at length only asked occasionally when they would both come back.

Buvat had put Bathilde in the best room; he kept the other for himself, and put Nanette in the little closet.

This Nanette was a good woman, who cooked passably, and knitted and netted splendidly. In spite of these divers talents, Buvat understood that he and Nanette would not suffice for the education of a young girl; and that though she might write magnificently, know her five rules, and be able to sew and net, she would still know only half of what she should. Buvat had looked the obligation he had undertaken full in the face. His was one of those happy organizations which think with the heart, and he had understood that, though she had become his ward, Bathilde remained the child of Albert and Clarice. He resolved, then, to give her an education conformable, not to her present situation, but to the name she bore.

In arriving at this resolution, Buvat had reasoned, very simply, that he owed his place to Albert, and consequently, the income of that place belonged to Bathilde. This is how he divided his nine hundred livres a year: four hundred and fifty for music, drawing and dancing masters; four hundred and fifty for Bathilde's dowry.

Now, supposing that Bathilde, who was four years old, should marry at eighteen, the interest and the capital together would amount to something like nine or ten thousand francs. This was not much, he knew, and was much troubled by that knowledge; but it was in vain to think, he could not make it more.

To defray the expense of their living, lodgings, and clothing, for himself and Bathilde, he would again begin to give writing lessons and make copies. For this purpose he got up at five o'clock in the morning, and went to bed at ten at night. This would be all profit; for, thanks to this new arrangement, he would lengthen his life by two or three hours daily. For some time these good resolutions prospered; neither lessons nor copies were wanting; and, as two years passed before Bathilde had finished the early education he himself undertook to give her, he was able to add nine hundred francs to her little treasure. At six years old Bathilde had what the daughters of the richest and noblest houses seldom have—masters for music, drawing and dancing. Making sacrifices for this charming child was entirely pleasure; for she appeared to have received from God one of those happy organizations whose aptitude makes us believe in a former world, for they appear not so much to be learning a new thing as to be[Pg 312] remembering one formerly known. As to her beauty, which had given such early promise, it had amply fulfilled it.

Buvat was happy the whole week, while after each lesson

he received the compliments of the master, and very proud on Sundays, when, having put on his salmon-colored coat, his black velvet breeches, and chiné stockings, he took Bathilde by the hand and went for his weekly walk.

It was generally toward the Chemin des Porcherons that he directed his steps.

This was a rendezvous for bowls, and Buvat had formerly been a great lover of this game. In ceasing to be an actor, he had become a judge. Whenever a dispute arose, it was referred to him; and his eye was so correct, that he could tell at the first glance, and without fail, which ball was nearest the mark. From his judgments there was no appeal, and they were received with neither more nor less respect than those of St. Louis at Vincennes. But it must be said to his credit that his predilection for this walk was not entirely egotistical: it also led to the Marsh of the Grange Bateliere, whose black and gloomy waters attracted a great many of those dragon-flies with the gauzy wings and golden bodies which children delight to pursue. One of Bathilde's greatest amusements was to run, with her green net in her hand, her beautiful fair curls floating in the wind, after the butterflies and dragon-flies. The result of this was that Bathilde had many accidents to her white frock, but, provided she was amused, Buvat took very philosophically a spot or a tear. This was Nanette's affair. The good woman scolded well on their return, but Buvat closed her mouth by shrugging his shoulders and saying, "Bah! one can't put old heads on young shoulders."

And, as Nanette had a great respect for proverbs, which

she occasionally used herself, she generally gave way to the moral of this one. It happened also sometimes, but this was only on fete days, that Buvat complied with Bathilde's request to take her to Montmartre to see the windmills. Then they set out earlier. Nanette took dinner with them, which was destined to be eaten on the esplanade of the abbey. They did not get home till eight o'clock in the evening, but from the Cross des Porcherons Bathilde slept in Buvat's arms.

Things went on thus till the year 1712, at which time the great king found himself so embarrassed in his affairs that the only thing left for him to do was to leave off paying his employés. Buvat was warned of this administrative measure by the cashier, who announced to him one fine morning, when he presented himself to receive his month's pay, that there was no money. Buvat looked at the man with an astonished air: it had never entered into his head that the king could be in want of money. He took no further notice of this answer, convinced that some accident only had interrupted the payment, and went back to his office singing his favorite

"Then let me go," etc.

"Pardon," said the supernumerary, who after waiting for seven years had at last been named employé the first of the preceding month, "you must be very light-hearted to sing when we are no longer paid."

"What!" cried Buvat; "what do you mean?"

"I mean that I suppose you have not gone to be paid."

"Yes, I have just come from there."

"Did they pay you?"

"No; they said there was no money."

"And what do you think of that?"

"Oh! I think," said Buvat, "that they will pay the two months together."

"Oh, yes! two months together! Do you hear, Ducoudray? He thinks they will pay the two months together. He is a simple fellow, this Buvat."

"We shall see next month," replied the second clerk.

"Yes," replied Buvat, to whom this remark appeared very just, "we shall see next month."

"And if they do not pay you next month, nor the following months, what shall you do, Buvat?"

"What shall I do!" said Buvat, astonished that there could be a doubt as[Pg 313] to his resolution, "I should come just the same."

"What! if you were not paid you would come still?"

"Monsieur," said Buvat, "for ten years the king has paid me down on the nail; surely after that he has a right to ask for a little credit if he is embarrassed."

"Vile flatterer," said the clerk.

The month passed, and pay-day came again. Buvat presented himself with the most perfect confidence that they would pay his arrears; but to his astonishment they told him that there was still no money. Buvat asked when there would be any. The cashier replied that he should like to know. Buvat was quite confused, and went away; but this time without singing. The same day the clerk resigned. Now as it was difficult to replace a clerk who resigned because he was not paid, and whose work must be done all the same, the chief told Buvat, besides his own work, to do that of the missing clerk. Buvat undertook it without murmur; and as his ordinary work had left him some time free, at the end of the month the business was done.

They did not pay the third month any more than the two others—it was a real bankruptcy. But as has been seen, Buvat never bargained with his duties. What he had promised on the first impulse he did on reflection; but he was forced to attack his treasure, which consisted of two years' pay. Meanwhile Bathilde grew. She was now a young girl of thirteen or fourteen years old, whose beauty became every day more remarkable, and who began to understand all the difficulties of her position. For some time the walks in the Porcheron and the expedition to Montmartre had been given up under pretext that she preferred remaining at home to draw or play on the harpsichord.

Buvat did not understand these sedentary tastes which Bathilde had acquired so suddenly. And as, after having tried two or three times to go out without her, he found that it was not the walk itself he cared for, he resolved, as he must have air upon a Sunday, to look for a lodging with a garden. But lodgings with gardens were too dear for his finances, and having seen the lodging in the Rue du Temps-Perdu, he had the bright idea of replacing the garden by a terrace. He came back to tell Bathilde what he had seen, telling her that the only inconvenience in this lodging would be that their rooms must be separated, and that she would be obliged to sleep on the fourth floor with Nanette, and he on the fifth. This was rather a recommendation to Bathilde. For some time she had begun to feel it inconvenient that her room should be only separated by a door from that of a man still young and who was neither her father nor her husband. She therefore assured Buvat that the lodging must suit him admirably, and advised him to secure it at once. Buvat was delighted, and at once gave notice to quit his old lodgings, and at the half-term he moved. Bathilde was right; for since her black mantle sketched her beautiful shoulders—since her mittens showed the prettiest fingers in the world—since of the Bathilde of former times there was nothing left but her childish feet, every one began to remark that Buvat was young—that the tutor and the pupil were living under the same roof. In fact, the gossips who, when Bathilde was six years old, worshiped Buvat's footsteps, now began to cry out about his criminality because she was fifteen. Poor Buvat! If ever echo was innocent and pure, it was that of the room which adjoined Bathilde's, and which for ten years had sheltered his good round head, into which a bad thought had never entered, even in dreams.

But on arriving at the Rue du Temps-Perdu it was still worse. In the Rue Pagevin, where his admirable conduct to the child was known, this remembrance had protected him against calumny; but in their new quarter this was quite unknown, and their inscribing themselves under two different names prevented any idea of very near relationship. Some supposed that they saw in Bathilde the result of an old passion which the Church had forgotten to consecrate, but this idea fell at the first examination. Bathilde was[Pg 314] tall and slender, Buvat short and fat; Bathilde had brilliant black eyes, Buvat's were blue and expressionless; Bathilde's face was white and smooth, Buvat's face was bright red. In fact, Bathilde's whole person breathed elegance and distinction, while poor Buvat was the type of vulgar good-nature. The result of this was, that the women began to look at Bathilde with contempt, and that men called Buvat a lucky fellow. The previsions of the clerk who resigned were realized. For eighteen months Buvat had not touched a sou of his pay, and yet had not relaxed for a moment in his punctuality. Moreover, he was haunted with a fear that the ministry would turn away a third of the clerks for the sake of economy. Buvat would have looked on the loss of his place as a great misfortune, although it took him six hours a day which he might have employed in a lucrative manner. They took care not to dismiss a man who worked the better the less they paid him.

Bathilde began to think that there was something passing of which she was ignorant. She thought it would be no use to ask Buvat, and addressing herself to Nanette, who, after a short time, avowed all to her, Bathilde learned for the first time all she owed to Buvat; and that to pay her masters, and to amass her dowry, Buvat worked from morning till night; and that in spite of this, as his salary was not paid, he would be obliged sooner or later to tell Bathilde that they must retrench all expenses that were not absolutely necessary.

Bathilde's first impulse on learning this devotion was to

fall at Buvat's feet and express her gratitude; but she soon understood that, to arrive at her desired end, she must feign ignorance.

The next day Bathilde told Buvat, laughing, that it was throwing away money to keep her masters any longer, for she knew as much as they did; and as, in Buvat's eyes, Bathilde's drawings were the most beautiful things in the world, and as, when she sang, he was in the seventh heaven, he found no difficulty in believing her, particularly as her masters, with unusual candor, avowed that their pupil knew enough to study alone; but Bathilde had a purifying influence on all who approached her. Bathilde was not satisfied with saving expense, but also wished to increase his gains. Although she had made equal progress in music and drawing, she understood that drawing was her only resource, and that music could be nothing but a relaxation. She reserved all her attention for drawing; and as she was really very talented, she soon made charming sketches. At last one day she wished to know what they were worth; and she asked Buvat, in going to his office, to show them to the person from whom she bought her paper and crayons, and who lived at the corner of the Rue de Cléry. She gave him two children's heads which she had drawn from fancy, to ask their value. Buvat undertook the commission without suspecting any trick, and executed it with his ordinary naïveté. The dealer, accustomed to such propositions, turned them round and round with a disdainful air, and, criticising them severely, said that he could only offer fifteen francs each for them. Buvat was hurt not by the price offered, but by the disrespectful manner in which the shopkeeper had spoken of Bathilde's talent. He drew them quickly out of the dealer's hands, saying that he thanked him.

The man, thinking that Buvat thought the price too small, said that, for friendship's sake, he would go as high as forty francs for the two; but Buvat, offended at the slight offered to the genius of his ward, answered dryly that the drawings which he had shewn him were not for sale, and that he had only asked their value through curiosity. Every one knows that from the moment drawings are not for sale they increase singularly in value, and the dealer at length offered fifty francs; but Buvat, little tempted by this proposition, by which he did not even dream of profiting, took the drawings and left the shop with all the dignity of wounded pride. When he returned, the dealer was standing, as if by chance, at his door. Buvat, seeing him, kept at a distance; but the shopkeeper came to[Pg 315] him, and, putting his two hands on his shoulders, asked him if he would not let him have the two drawings for the price he had named. Buvat replied a second time, sharply, that they were not for sale. "That is a pity," replied the dealer, "for I would have given eighty francs." And he returned to his door with an indifferent air, but watching Buvat as he did so. Buvat, however, went on with a pride that was almost grotesque, and, without turning once, went straight home. Bathilde heard him, as he came up the staircase, striking his cane against the balusters, as he was in the habit of doing. She ran out to meet him, for she was very anxious to hear the result of the negotiation, and, with the remains of her childish habits, throwing her arms round his neck—

"Well, my friend," asked she, "what did M. Papillon say?"

"M. Papillon," replied Buvat, wiping his forehead, "is an impertinent rascal."

Poor Bathilde turned pale.

"How so?" asked she.

"Yes; an impertinent rascal, who, instead of admiring your drawings, has dared to criticise them."

"Oh! if that is all," said Bathilde, laughing, "he is right. Remember that I am but a scholar. But did he offer any price?"

"Yes," said Buvat; "he had impertinence enough for that."

"What price?" asked Bathilde, trembling.

"He offered eighty francs."

"Eighty francs!" cried Bathilde. "Oh! you must be mistaken."

"I tell you he offered eighty francs for the two," replied Buvat, laying a stress on each syllable.

"But it is four times as much as they are worth," said the young girl, clapping her hands for joy.

"It is possible, though I do not think so; but it is none the less true that M. Papillon is an impertinent rascal!"

This was not Bathilde's opinion; but she changed the conversation, saying that dinner was ready—an announcement which generally gave a new course to Buvat's ideas. Buvat gave back the drawings to Bathilde without further observation, and entered the little sitting-room, singing the inevitable, "Then let me go," etc.

He dined with as good an appetite as if there had been no M. Papillon in the world. The same evening, while Buvat was making copies, Bathilde gave the drawings to Nanette, telling her to take them to M. Papillon and ask for the eighty francs he had offered to Buvat. Nanette obeyed, and Bathilde awaited her return with great anxiety, for she still believed there must be some mistake as to the price. Ten minutes afterward she was quite assured, for the good woman entered with the money. Bathilde looked at it for an instant with tears in her eyes, then kneeling before the crucifix at the foot of her bed, she offered up a thanksgiving that she was enabled to return to Buvat a part of what he had done for her.

The next day Buvat, in returning from the office, passed before Papillon's door, but his astonishment was great when, through the windows of the shop, he saw the drawings. The door opened and Papillon appeared.

"So," said he, "you thought better of it, and made up your mind to part with the two drawings which were not for sale? Ah! I did not know you were so cunning, neighbor. But, however, tell Mademoiselle Bathilde, that, as she is a good girl, out of consideration for her, if she will do two such drawings every month, and promise not to draw for any one else for a year, I will take them at the same price."

Buvat was astonished; he grumbled out an answer which the man could not hear, and went home. He went upstairs and opened the door without Bathilde having heard him.

She was drawing; she had already begun another head, and perceiving her good friend standing at the door with a troubled air, she put down her paper and pencils and ran to him, asking what was the matter. Buvat wiped away two great tears,

"So," said he, "the child of my benefactors, of Clarice Gray and Albert du Rocher, is working for her bread!"

"Father," replied Bathilde, half cry[Pg 316]ing, half laughing; "I am not working, I am amusing myself."

The word "father" was substituted on great occasions for "kind friend," and ordinarily had the effect of calming his greatest troubles, but this time it failed.

"I am neither your father, nor your good friend," murmured he, "but simply poor Buvat, whom the king pays no longer, and who does not gain enough by his writing to continue to give you the education you ought to have."

"Oh! you want to make me die with grief," cried Bathilde, bursting into tears, so plainly was Buvat's distress painted on his countenance.

"I kill you with grief, my child?" said Buvat, with an accent of profound tenderness. "What have I done? What have I said? You must not cry. It wanted nothing but that to make me miserable."

"But," said Bathilde, "I shall always cry if you do not let me do what I like."

This threat of Bathilde's, puerile as it was, made Buvat tremble; for, since the day when the child wept for her mother, not a tear had fallen from her eyes.

217

"Well," said Buvat, "do as you like, but promise me that when the king pays my arrears—"

"Well, well," cried Bathilde, interrupting him, "we shall see all that later; meanwhile, the dinner is getting cold." And, taking him by the arm, she led him into the little room, where, by her jokes and gayety, she soon succeeded in removing the last traces of sadness from Buvat's face.

What would he have said if he had known all?

Bathilde thought she could do the two drawings for M. Papillon in eight or ten days; there therefore remained the half, at least, of every month, which she was determined not to lose. She, therefore, charged Nanette to search among the neighbors for some difficult, and, consequently, well-paid needlework, which she could do in Buvat's absence. Nanette easily found what she sought. It was the time for laces. The great ladies paid fifty louis a yard for guipure, and then ran carelessly through the woods with these transparent dresses. The result of this was, that many a rent had to be concealed from mothers and husbands, so that at this time there was more to be made by mending than by selling laces. From her first attempt, Bathilde did wonders; her needle seemed to be that of a fairy. Nanette received many compliments on the work of the unknown Penelope, who did by day what was undone by night. Thanks to Bathilde's industry, they began to have much greater ease in their house.

Buvat, more tranquil, and seeing that he must renounce his Sunday walks, determined to be satisfied with the famous terrace which had determined him in the choice of his house.

For a week he spent an hour morning and evening taking measures, without any one knowing what he intended to do. At length he decided on having a fountain, a grotto, and an arbor. Collecting the materials for these, and afterward building them, had occupied all Buvat's spare time for twelve months. During this time Bathilde had passed from her fifteenth to her sixteenth year, and the charming child into a beautiful woman. It was during this time that her neighbor, Boniface Denis, had remarked her, and his mother, who could refuse him nothing, after having been for information to the Rue Pagevin, had presented herself, under pretext of neighborhood, to Buvat and his ward, and, after a little while, invited them both to pass Sunday evenings with her.

The invitation was given with so good a grace that there was no means of refusing it, and, indeed, Buvat was delighted that some opportunity of amusement should be presented to Bathilde; besides, as he knew that Madame Denis had two daughters, perhaps he was not sorry to enjoy that triumph which his paternal pride assured him Bathilde could not fail to obtain over Mademoiselle Emilie and Mademoiselle Athenais. However, things did not pass exactly as he had arranged them. Bathilde soon saw the mediocrity of her rivals, so that when they spoke of drawing, and called on her to admire[Pg 317] some heads by these young ladies, she pretended to have nothing in the house that she could show, while Buvat knew that there were in her portfolio two heads, one of the infant Jesus, and one of St. John, both charming; but this was not all—the Misses Denis sang; and when they asked Bathilde to sing, she chose a simple little romance in two verses, which lasted five minutes, instead of the grand scene which Buvat had expected.

However, this conduct appeared singularly to increase the regard of Madame Denis for the young girl, for Madame Denis was not without some uneasiness with respect to the event of an artistic struggle between the young people. Bathilde was overwhelmed with caresses by the good woman, who, when she was gone, declared she was full of talents and modesty, and that she well deserved all the praises lavished upon her. A retired silk-mercer raised her voice to recall the strange position of the tutor and the pupil, but Madame Denis imposed silence on this malicious tongue by declaring that she knew the whole history from beginning to end, and that it did the greatest honor to both her neighbors. It was a small lie, however, of good Madame Denis, but it was doubtless pardoned in consideration of the intention.

As to Boniface, in company he was dumb and a nonentity; he had been this evening so remarkably stupid that Bathilde had hardly noticed him at all.

But it was not thus with Boniface, who, having admired Bathilde from a distance, became quite crazy about her when he saw her near. He began to sit constantly at his window, which obliged Bathilde to keep hers closed; for it will be remembered that Boniface then inhabited the room now occupied by the Chevalier d'Harmental. This conduct of Bathilde, in which it was impossible to see anything but supreme modesty, only augmented the passion of her neighbor. At his request, his mother went again to the Rue Pagevin, and to the Rue des Orties, where she had learned, from an old woman, something of the death-scene we have related, and in which Buvat played so noble a part. She had forgotten the names, and she only remembered that the father was a handsome young officer, who had been killed in Spain, and that the mother was a charming young woman, who had died of grief and poverty.

Boniface also had been in search of news, and had learned from his employer, who was a friend of Buvat's notary, that every year, for six years past, five hundred francs had been deposited with him in Bathilde's name, which, with the interest, formed a little capital of seven or eight thousand francs. This was not much for Boniface, who, as his mother said, would have three thousand francs a year, but at least it showed that Bathilde was not destitute. At the end of a month, during which time Madame Denis's friendship for Bathilde did not diminish, seeing that her son's love greatly increased, she determined to ask her hand for him. One afternoon, as Buvat returned from business, Madame Denis waited for him at her door, and made a sign to him that she had something to say to him. Buvat followed her politely into her room, of which she closed the door, that she might not be interrupted; and when Buvat was seated, she asked for the hand of Bathilde for her son.

Buvat was quite bewildered. It had never entered his mind that Bathilde might marry. Life without Bathilde appeared so impossible a thing that he changed color at the bare idea. Madame Denis did not fail to remark the strange effect that her request had produced on Buvat. She would not even allow him to think it had passed unnoticed. She offered him the bottle of salts which she always kept on the chimney-piece, that she might repeat three or four times a week that her nerves were very sensitive.

Buvat, instead of simply smelling the salts from a reasonable distance, put it close up under his nose. The effect was rapid. He bounded to his feet, as if the angel of Habakkuk had taken him by the hair. He sneezed for about ten minutes; then, having regained his senses, he said that he understood the honorable proposal made for Bathilde, but that he was only[Pg 318] her guardian: that he would tell her of the proposal, but must leave her free to accept or refuse.

Madame Denis thought this perfectly right, and conducted him to the door, saying that, waiting a reply, she was their very humble servant.

Buvat went home, and found Bathilde very uneasy; he was half an hour late, which had not happened before for ten years. The uneasiness of the young girl was doubled when she saw Buvat's sad and preoccupied air, and she wanted to know directly what it was that caused the abstracted mien of her dear friend. Buvat, who had not had time to prepare a speech, tried to put off the explanation till after dinner; but Bathilde declared that she should not go to dinner till she knew what had happened. Buvat was thus obliged to deliver on the spot, and without preparation, Madame Denis's proposal to Bathilde.

Bathilde blushed directly, as a young girl always does when they talk to her of marriage; then, taking the hands of Buvat, who was sitting down, trembling with fear, and looking at him with that sweet smile which was the sun of the poor writer—

"Then, my dear father," said she, "you have had enough of your daughter, and you wish to get rid of her?"

"I," said Buvat, "I who wish to get rid of you! No, my child; it is I who shall die of grief if you leave me."

"Then, my father, why do you talk to me of marriage?"

"Because—because—some day or other you must marry, and if you find a good partner, although, God knows, my little Bathilde deserves some one better than M. Boniface."

"No, my father," answered Bathilde, "I do not deserve any one better than M. Boniface, but—"——"Well—but?"

"But—I will never marry."

"What!" cried Buvat, "you will never marry?"

"Why should I? Are we not happy as we are?"

"Are we not happy?" echoed Buvat. "Sabre de bois! I believe we are."

Sabre de bois was an exclamation which Buvat allowed himself on great occasions, and which illustrated admirably the pacific inclinations of the worthy fellow.

"Well, then," continued Bathilde, with her angel's smile, "if we are happy, let us rest as we are. You know one should not tempt Providence."

"Come and kiss me, my child," said Buvat; "you have just lifted Montmartre off my stomach!"

"You did not wish for this marriage, then?"

"I wish to see you married to that wretched little imp of a Boniface, against whom I took a dislike the first time I saw him! I did not know why, though I know now."

"If you did not desire this marriage, why did you speak to me about it?"

"Because you know well that I am not really your father, that I have no authority over you, that you are free."

"Indeed, am I free?" answered Bathilde, laughing.

"Free as air."

"Well, then, if I am free, I refuse."

"Diable! I am highly satisfied," said Buvat; "but how shall I tell it to Madame Denis?"

"How? Tell her that I am too young, that I do not wish to marry, that I want to stop with you always."

"Come to dinner," said Buvat, "perhaps a bright idea will strike me when I am eating. It is odd! my appetite has come back all of a sudden. Just now I thought I could not swallow a drop of water. Now I could drink the Seine dry."

Buvat drank like a Suisse, and ate like an ogre; but, in spite of this infraction of his ordinary habits, no bright idea came to his aid; so that he was obliged to tell Madame Denis openly that Bathilde was very much honored by her selection, but that she did not wish to marry.

This unexpected response perfectly dumfounded Madame Denis, who had never imagined that a poor little orphan like Bathilde could refuse so brilliant a match as her son; consequently she answered very sharply that every one was free to act for themselves, and that, if[Pg 319] Mademoiselle Bathilde chose to be an old maid, she was perfectly welcome.

But when she reflected on this refusal, which her maternal pride could not understand, all the old calumnies which she had heard about the young girl and her guardian returned to her mind; and as she was in a disposition to believe them, she made no further doubt that they were true, and when she transmitted their beautiful neighbor's answer to Boniface, she said, to console him for this matrimonial disappointment, that it was very lucky that she had refused, since, if she had accepted, in consequence of what she had learned, she could not have allowed such a marriage to be concluded.

Madame Denis thought it unsuited to her dignity that after so humiliating a refusal her son should continue to inhabit the room opposite Bathilde's, so she gave him one on the ground floor, and announced that his old one was to let.

A week after, as M. Boniface, to revenge himself on Bathilde, was teasing Mirza, who was standing in the doorway, not thinking it fine enough to trust her little white feet out of doors, Mirza, whom the habit of being fed had made very petulant, darted out on M. Boniface, and bit him cruelly in the calf.

It was in consequence of this that the poor fellow, whose heart or leg was not very well healed, cautioned D'Harmental to beware of the coquetry of Bathilde, and to throw a sop to Mirza.

CHAPTER XVII.
FIRST LOVE.

M. Boniface's room remained vacant for three or four months, when one day Bathilde, who was accustomed to see the window closed, on raising her eyes found that it was open, and at the window she saw a strange face: it was that of D'Harmental. Few such faces as that of the chevalier were seen in the Rue du Temps-Perdu. Bathilde, admirably situated, behind her curtain, for seeing without being seen, was attracted involuntarily. There was in our hero's features a distinction and an elegance which could not escape Bathilde's eyes. The chevalier's dress, simple as it was, betrayed the elegance of the wearer: then Bathilde had heard him give some orders, and they had been given with that inflection of voice which indicates in him who possesses it the habit of command.

The young girl had discovered at the first glance that this man was very superior in all respects to him whom he succeeded in the possession of this little room, and with that instinct so natural to persons of good birth, she at once recognized him as being of high family. The same day the chevalier had tried his harpsichord. At the first sound of the instrument Bathilde had raised her head. The chevalier, though he did not know that he had a listener, or perhaps because he did not know it, went on with preludes and fantasies, which showed an amateur of no mean talents. At these sounds, which seemed to wake all the musical chords of her own organization, Bathilde had risen and approached the window that she might not lose a note, for such an amusement was unheard of in the Rue du Temps-Perdu. Then it was that D'Harmental had seen against the window the charming little fingers of his neighbor, and had driven them away by turning round so quickly that Bathilde could not doubt she had been seen.

The next day Bathilde thought it was a long time since she had played, and sat down to her instrument. She began nervously, she knew not why; but as she was an excellent musician, her fear soon passed away, and it was then that she executed so brilliantly that piece from Armida, which had been heard with so much astonishment by the chevalier and the Abbe Brigaud.

We have said how the following morning the chevalier had seen Buvat, and become acquainted with Bathilde's name. The appearance of the young girl had made the deeper impression on the chevalier from its being so unexpected in such a place; and he was still under the influence of the charm when Roquefinette entered, and gave a new direction to his thoughts, which, however, soon returned to Bathilde. The next day, Bathilde,[Pg 320] who, profiting by the first ray of the spring sun, was early at her window, noticed in her turn that the eyes of the chevalier were ardently fixed upon her. She had noticed his face, young and handsome, but to which the thought of the responsibility he had taken gave a certain air of sadness; but sadness and youth go so badly together, that this anomaly had struck her—this handsome young man had something to annoy him—perhaps he was unhappy. What could it be? Thus, from the second time she had seen him, Bathilde had very naturally meditated about the chevalier. This had not prevented Bathilde from shutting her window, but, from behind her window, she still saw the outline of the chevalier's sad face. She felt that D'Harmental was sad, and when she sat down to her harpsichord, was it not from a secret feeling that music is the consoler of troubled hearts?

That evening it was D'Harmental who played, and Bathilde listened with all her soul to the melodious voice which spoke of love in the dead of night. Unluckily for the chevalier, who, seeing the shadow of the young girl behind the drapery, began to think that he was making a favorable impression on the other side of the street, he had been interrupted in his concert by the lodger on the third floor; but the most important thing was accomplished—there was already a point of sympathy between the two young people, and they already spoke that language of the heart, the most dangerous of all.

Moreover, Bathilde, who had dreamed all night about music, and a little about the musician, felt that something strange and unknown to her was going on, and, attracted as she was toward the window, she kept it scrupulously closed; from this resulted the movement of impatience, under the influence of which the chevalier had gone to breakfast with Madame Denis.

There he had learned one important piece of news, which

was, that Bathilde was neither the daughter, the wife, nor the niece of Buvat; thus he went upstairs joyfully, and, finding the window open, he had put himself—in spite of the friendly advice of Boniface—in communication with Mirza, by means of bribing her with sugar. The unexpected return of Bathilde had interrupted this amusement; the chevalier, in his egotistical delicacy, had shut his window; but, before the window had been shut, a salute had been exchanged between the two young people. This was more than Bathilde had ever accorded to any man, not that she had not from time to time exchanged salutes with some acquaintance of Buvat's, but this was the first time she had blushed as she did so.

The next day Bathilde had seen the chevalier at his window, and, without being able to understand the action, had seen him nail a crimson ribbon to the outer wall; but what she had particularly remarked was the extraordinary animation visible on the face of the young man. Half an hour afterward she had seen with the chevalier a man perfectly unknown to her, but whose appearance was not re-assuring; this was Captain Roquefinette. Bathilde had also remarked, with a vague uneasiness, that, as soon as the man with the long sword had entered, the chevalier had fastened the door.

The chevalier, as is easy to understand, had a long conference with the captain; for they had to arrange all the preparations for the evening's expedition. The chevalier's window remained thus so long closed that Bathilde, thinking that he had gone out, had thought she might as well open hers.

Hardly was it open, however, when her neighbor's, which had seemed only to wait the moment to put itself in communication with her, opened in turn. Luckily for Bathilde, who would have been much embarrassed by this circumstance, she was in that part of the room where the chevalier could not see her. She determined, therefore, to remain where she was, and sat down near the second half of the window, which was still shut.

Mirza, however, who had not the same scruples as her mistress, hardly saw the chevalier before she ran to the window, placed her front paws on the sill, and[Pg 321] began dancing on her hind ones. These attentions were rewarded, as she expected, by a first, then a second, then a third, lump of sugar; but this third bit, to the no small astonishment of Bathilde, was wrapped up in a piece of paper.

This piece of paper troubled Bathilde a great deal more than it did Mirza, who, accustomed to crackers and sucre de pomme, soon got the sugar out of its envelope by means of her paws; and, as she thought very much of the inside, and very little of the wrapper, she ate the sugar, and, leaving the paper, ran to the window; but the chevalier was gone; satisfied, no doubt, of Mirza's skill, he had retired into his room.

Bathilde was very much embarrassed; she had seen, at the first glance, that the paper contained three or four lines of writing; but, in spite of the sudden friendship which her neighbor seemed to have acquired for Mirza, it was evidently not to Mirza that he was writing letters—it must, therefore, be to her. What should she do? Go and tear it up? That would be noble and proper; but, even if it were possible to do such a thing, the paper in which the sugar had been wrapped might have been written on some time, and then the action would be ridiculous in the highest degree, and it would show, at any rate, that she thought about the letter. Bathilde resolved then, to leave things as they were. The chevalier could not know that she was at home, since he had not seen her; he could not, therefore, draw any deduction from the fact that the paper remained on the floor. She therefore continued to work, or rather to reflect, hidden behind her curtain, as the chevalier, probably, was behind his.

In about an hour, of which it must be confessed Bathilde passed three-quarters with her eyes fixed on the paper, Nanette entered. Bathilde, without moving, told her to shut the window—Nanette obeyed; but in returning she saw the paper.

"What is that?" asked she, stooping down to pick it up.

"Nothing," answered Bathilde quickly, forgetting that Nanette could not read, "only a paper which has fallen out of my pocket." Then, after an instant's pause, and with a visible effort, "and which you may throw on the fire," continued she.——"But perhaps it may be something important; see what it is, at all events, mademoiselle." And Nanette presented the letter to Bathilde.

The temptation was too strong to resist. Bathilde cast her eyes on the paper, affecting an air of indifference as well as she could, and read as follows:

"They say you are an orphan: I have no parents; we are, then, brother and sister before God. This evening I run a great danger; but I hope to come out of it safe and sound if my sister—Bathilde—will pray for her brother Raoul."

"You are right," said Bathilde, in a moved voice, and taking the paper from the hands of Nanette, "that paper is more important than I thought;" and she put D'Harmental's letter in the pocket of her apron. Five minutes after Nanette, who came in twenty times a day without any particular reason, went out as she had entered, and left Bathilde alone.

Bathilde had only just glanced at the letter, and it had seemed to dazzle her. As soon as Nanette was gone she read it a second time.

It would have been impossible to have said more in fewer words. If D'Harmental had taken a whole day to combine every word of the billet, instead of writing on the spur of the moment, he could not have done it better. Indeed, he established a similarity of position between himself and the orphan; he interested Bathilde in her neighbor's fate on account of a menacing danger, a danger which would appear all the greater to the young girl from her not knowing its nature; and, finally, the expression brother and sister, so skillfully glided in at the end, and to ask a simple prayer, excluded from these first advances all idea of love.

It followed, therefore, that, if at this moment Bathilde had found herself vis-a-vis with D'Harmental, instead of being embarrassed and blushing, as a young girl would who had just received her first love-letter, she would have taken him by the hand and said to him, smiling—"Be[Pg 322] satisfied, I will pray for you." There remained, however, on the mind of Bathilde something more dangerous than all the declarations in the world, and that was the idea of the peril which her neighbor ran. By a sort of presentiment with which she had been seized on seeing him, with a face so different from his ordinary expression, nail the crimson ribbon to his window, and withdraw it directly the captain entered, she was almost sure that the danger was somehow connected with this new personage, whom she had never seen before. But how did this danger concern him? What was the nature of the danger itself? This was what she asked herself in vain. She thought of a duel, but to a man such as the chevalier appeared to be, a duel was not one of those dangers for which one asks the prayers of women; besides, the hour named was not suitable to duels. Bathilde lost herself in her conjectures; but, in losing herself, she thought of the chevalier, always of the chevalier, and of nothing but the chevalier; and, if he had calculated upon such an effect, it must be owned that his calculations were wofully true for poor Bathilde.

The day passed; and, whether it was intentional, or whether it was that he was otherwise employed, Bathilde saw him no more, and his window remained closed. When Buvat came home as usual, at ten minutes after four, he found the young girl so much preoccupied that, although his perspicacity was not great in such matters, he asked her three or four times if anything was wrong; each time she answered by one of those smiles which supplied Buvat with enough to do in looking at her; and it followed that, in spite of these repeated questions, Bathilde kept her secret.

After dinner M. Chaulieu's servant entered—he came to ask Buvat to spend the evening with his master. The Abbe Chaulieu was one of Buvat's best patrons, and often came to his house, for he had taken a great liking for Bathilde. The poor abbe became blind, but not so entirely as not to be able to recognize a pretty face; though it is true that he saw it across a cloud. The abbe had told Bathilde, in his sexagenarian gallantry, that his only consolation was that it is thus that one sees the angels.

Bathilde thanked the good abbe from the bottom of her heart for thus getting her an evening's solitude. She knew that when Buvat went to the Abbe Chaulieu he ordinarily stayed some time; she hoped, then, that he would stop late as usual. Poor Buvat went out, without imagining that for the first time she desired his absence.

Buvat was a lounger, as every bourgeois of Paris ought to be. From one end to the other of the Palais Royal, he stared at the shops, stopping for the thousandth time before the things which generally drew his attention. On leaving the colonnade, he heard singing, and saw a group of men and women, who were listening to the songs; he joined them, and listened too. At the moment of the collection he went away, not from a bad heart, nor that he would have wished to refuse the admirable musician the reward which was his due, but that by an old habit, of which time had proved the advantage, he always came out without money, so that by whatever he was tempted he was sure to overcome the temptation. This evening he was much tempted to drop a sou into the singer's bowl, but as he had not a sou in his pocket, he was obliged to go away. He made his way then, as we have seen, toward the Barriere des Sergents, passed up the Rue du Coq, crossed the Pont-Neuf, returned along the quay so far as the Rue Mazarine; it was in the Rue Mazarine that the Abbe Chaulieu lived.

The Abbe Chaulieu recognized Buvat, whose excellent qualities he had appreciated during their two years' acquaintance, and with much pressing on his part, and many difficulties on Buvat's, made him sit down near himself, before a table covered with papers. It is true that at first Buvat sat on the very edge of his chair; gradually, however, he got further and further on—put his hat on the ground—took his cane between his legs, and found himself sitting almost like any one else.

[Pg 323]The work that there was to be done did not promise a short sitting; there were thirty or forty poems on the table to be classified—numbered, and, as the abbe's servant was his amanuensis, corrected; so that it was eleven o'clock before they thought that it had struck nine. They had just finished and Buvat rose, horrified at having to come home at such an hour. It was the first time such a thing had ever happened to him; he rolled up the manuscript, tied it with a red ribbon, which had probably served as a sash to Mademoiselle de Launay, put it in his pocket, took his cane, picked up his hat, and left the house, abridging his leave-taking as much as possible. To add to his misfortunes there was no moonlight, the night was cloudy. Buvat regretted not having two sous in his pocket to cross the ferry which was then where now stands the Pont des Arts; but we have already explained Buvat's theory to our readers, and he was obliged to return as he had come—by the Quai Conti, the Rue Pont-Neuf, the Rue du Coq, and the Rue Saint Honoré.

Everything had gone right so far, and except the statue of Henri IV. of which Buvat had forgotten either the existence or the place, and which had frightened him terribly, and the Samaritaine, which, fifty steps off, had struck the half-hour without any preparation, the noise of which had made poor belated Buvat tremble from head to foot, he had run no real peril, but on arriving at the Rue des Bons Enfants things took a different look. In the first place, the aspect of the street itself, long, narrow, and only lighted by two flickering lanterns in the whole length, was not reassuring, and this evening it had to Buvat a very singular appearance; he did not know whether he was asleep or awake; he fancied that he saw before him some fantastic vision, such as he had heard told of the old Flemish sorceries; the streets seemed alive— the posts seemed to oppose themselves to his passage—the recesses of the doors whispered to each other—men crossed like shadows from one side of the street to the other; at last, when he had arrived at No. 24, he was stopped, as we have seen, by the chevalier and the captain. It was then that D'Harmental had recognized him, and had protected him against the first impulse of Roquefinette, inviting him to continue his route as quickly as possible. There was no need to repeat the request—Buvat set off at a trot, gained the Place des Victoires, the Rue du Mail, the Rue Montmartre, and at last arrived at his own house, No. 4, Rue du Temps-Perdu, where, nevertheless, he did not think himself safe till he had shut the door and bolted it behind him.

There he stopped an instant to breathe and to light his candle—then ascended the stairs, but he felt in his legs the effect of the occurrence, for he trembled so that he could hardly get to the top.

As to Bathilde, she had remained alone, getting more and more uneasy as the evening advanced. Up to seven o'clock she had seen a light in her neighbor's room, but at that time the lamp had been extinguished, and had not been relighted. Then Bathilde's time became divided between two occupations— one of which consisted in standing at her window to see if her neighbor did not return; the other in kneeling before the crucifix, where she said her evening prayers. She heard nine, ten, eleven, and half-past eleven, strike successively. She had heard all the noises in the streets die away one by one, and sink gradually into that vague and heavy sound which seems the breathing of a sleeping town; and all this without bringing her the slightest inkling as to whether he who had called himself her brother had sunk under the danger which hung over his head, or come triumphant through the crisis.

She was then in her own room, without light, so that no one might see that she was watching, and kneeling before her crucifix for the tenth time, when the door opened, and, by the light of his candle she saw Buvat so pale and haggard that she knew in an instant that something must have happened to him, and she rose, in spite of the uneasiness she felt for another, and darted toward him, asking what was the matter. But it was no easy thing to make Buvat speak, in the state[Pg 324] he then was; the shock had reached his mind, and his tongue stammered as much as his legs trembled.

Still, when Buvat was seated in his easy chair, and had wiped his forehead with his handkerchief, when he had made two or three journeys to the door to see that his terrible hosts of the Rue des Bons Enfants had not followed him home, he began to stutter out his adventure. He told how he had been stopped in the Rue des Bons Enfants by a band of robbers, whose lieutenant, a ferocious-looking man nearly six feet high, had wanted to kill him, when the captain had come and saved his life. Bathilde listened with rapt attention, first, because she loved her guardian sincerely, and that his condition showed that—right or wrong—he had been greatly terrified; next, because nothing that happened that night seemed indifferent to her; and, strange as the idea was, it seemed to her that the handsome young man was not wholly unconnected with the scene in which Buvat had just played a part. She asked him if he had time to observe the face of the young man who had come to his aid, and saved his life.

Buvat answered that he had seen him face to face, as he saw her at that moment, and that the proof was that he was a handsome young man of from five to six and twenty, in a large felt hat, and wrapped in a cloak; moreover, in the movement which he had made in stretching out his hand to protect him, the cloak had opened, and shown that, besides his sword, he carried a pair of pistols in his belt. These details were too precise to allow Buvat to be accused of dreaming. Preoccupied as Bathilde was with the danger which the chevalier ran, she was none the less touched by that, smaller no doubt, but still real, which Buvat had just escaped; and as repose is the best remedy for all shocks, physical or moral, after offering him the glass of wine and sugar which he allowed himself on great occasions, and which nevertheless he refused on this one, she reminded him of his bed, where he ought to have been two hours before.

The shock had been violent enough to deprive Buvat of all wish for sleep, and even to convince him that he should sleep badly that night; but he reflected that in sitting up he should force Bathilde to sit up, and should see her in the morning with red eyes and pale cheeks, and, with his usual sacrifice of self, he told Bathilde that she was right—that he felt that sleep would do him good—lit his candle—kissed her forehead—and went up to his own room; not without stopping two or three times on the staircase to hear if there was any noise.

Left alone, Bathilde listened to the steps of Buvat, who went up into his own room; then she heard the creaking of his door, which he double locked; then, almost as trembling as Buvat himself, she ran to the window, forgetting even to pray.

She remained thus for nearly an hour, but without having kept any measure of time. Then she gave a cry of joy, for through the window, which no curtain now obscured, she saw her neighbor's door open, and D'Harmental enter with a candle in his hand.

By a miracle of foresight Bathilde had been right—the man in the felt hat and the cloak, who had protected Buvat, was really the young stranger, for the stranger had on a felt hat and a cloak; and moreover, hardly had he returned and shut the door, with almost as much care as Buvat had his, and thrown his cloak on a chair, than she saw that he had a tight coat of a dark color, and in his belt a sword and pistols. There was no longer any doubt: it was from head to foot the description given by Buvat. Bathilde was the more able to assure herself of this, that D'Harmental, without taking off any of his attire, took two or three turns in his room, his arms crossed, and thinking deeply; then he took his pistols from his belt, assured himself that they were primed, and placed them on the table near his bed, unclasped his sword, took it half out of the scabbard, replaced it, and put it under his pillow; then, shaking his head, as if to shake out the somber ideas that annoyed him, he approached the[Pg 325] window, opened it, and gazed earnestly at that of the young girl, who, forgetting that she could not be seen, stepped back, and let the curtain fall before her, as if the darkness which surrounded her were not a sufficient screen.

She remained thus motionless and silent, her hand on her heart, as if to still its beatings; then she quietly raised the curtain, but that of her neighbor was down, and she saw nothing but his shadow passing and repassing before it.

CHAPTER XVIII.
THE CONSUL DUILIUS.

The morning following the day, or rather the night, on which the events we have just related had occurred, the Duc d'Orleans, who had returned to the Palais Royal without accident, after having slept all night as usual, passed into his study at his accustomed hour—that is to say, about eleven o'clock. Thanks to the sang-froid with which nature had blessed him, and which he owed chiefly to his great courage, to his disdain for danger, and his carelessness of death, not only was it impossible to observe in him any change from his ordinary calm, which ennui only turned to gloom, but he had most probably already forgotten the strange event of which he had so nearly been the victim.

The study into which he had just entered was remarkable as belonging to a man at once a savant, a politician, and an artist. Thus a large table covered with a green cloth, and loaded with papers, inkstand, and pens, occupied the middle of the room; but all round, on desks, on easels, on stands, were an opera commenced, a half-finished drawing, a chemical retort, etc. The regent, with a strange versatility of mind, passed in an instant from the deepest problems of politics to the most capricious fancies of painting, and from the most delicate calculations of chemistry to the somber or joyous inspirations of music. The regent feared nothing but ennui, that enemy against whom he struggled unceasingly, without ever quite succeeding in conquering it, and which,

repulsed by work, study, or pleasure, yet remained in sight—
if one may say so—like one of those clouds on the horizon,
toward which, even in the finest days, the pilot involuntarily
turns his eyes. The regent was never unoccupied, and had the
most opposite amusements always at hand.

On entering his study, where the council were to meet
in two hours, he went toward an unfinished drawing,
representing a scene from "Daphnis and Chloe," and returned
to the work, interrupted two days before by that famous
game of tennis, which had commenced by a racket blow, and
finished by the supper at Madame de Sabran's.

A messenger came to tell him that Madame Elizabeth
Charlotte, his mother, had asked twice if he were up. The
regent, who had the most profound respect for the princess
palatine, sent word that not only was he visible, but that if
madame were ready to receive him, he would pay her a visit
directly. He then returned to his work with all the eagerness
of an artist. Shortly after the door opened, and his mother
herself appeared.

Madame, the wife of Philippe, the first brother of the
king, came to France after the strange and unexpected death
of Madame Henriette of England, to take the place of that
beautiful and gracious princess, who had passed from the
scene like a dream. This comparison, difficult to sustain for
any new-comer, was doubly so to the poor German princess,
who, if we may believe her own portrait, with her little eyes,
her short and thick nose, her long thin lips, her hanging cheeks
and her large face, was far from being pretty. Unfortunately,

the faults of her face were not compensated for by beauty of figure. She was little and fat, with a short body and legs, and such frightful hands that she avows herself that there were none uglier to be found in the world, and that it was the only thing about her to which Louis XIV. could never become accustomed. But Louis XIV. had chosen her, not to increase the beauties of his court, but to extend his influence beyond the Rhine.

By the marriage of his brother with the princess palatine, Louis XIV., who had[Pg 326] already acquired some chance of inheritance in Spain, by marrying Maria Theresa, and by Philippe the First's marriage with the Princess Henriette, only sister of Charles II., would acquire new rights over Bavaria, and probably in the Palatinate. He calculated, and calculated rightly, that her brother, who was delicate, would probably die young, and without children.

Madame, instead of being treated at her husband's death according to her marriage contract, and forced to retire into a convent, or into the old castle of Montargis, was, in spite of Madame de Maintenon's hatred, maintained by Louis XIV. in all the titles and honors which she enjoyed during her husband's lifetime, although the king had not forgotten the blow which she gave to the young Duc de Chartres at Versailles, when he announced his marriage with Mademoiselle de Blois. The proud princess, with her thirty-two quarterings, thought it a humiliation that her son should marry a woman whom the royal legitimation could not prevent from being the fruit of a double adultery, and at the first moment, unable to command her feelings, she revenged herself by this maternal correction, rather exaggerated, when a young man of eighteen was the object, for the affront offered to the honor of her ancestors.

As the young Duc de Chartres had himself only consented unwillingly to this marriage, he easily understood his mother's dislike to it, though he would have preferred, doubtless, that she should have shown it in a rather less Teutonic manner. The result was, that when Monsieur died, and the Duc de Chartres became Duc d'Orleans, his mother, who might have feared that the blow at Versailles had left some disagreeable reminiscence in the mind of the new master of the Palais Royal, found, on the contrary, a more respectful son than ever. This respect increased, and as regent he gave his mother a position equal to that of his wife. When Madame de Berry, his much-loved daughter, asked her father for a company of guards, he granted it, but ordered at the same time that a similar company should be given to his mother.

Madame held thus a high position, and if, in spite of that position, she had no political influence, the reason was that the regent made it a principle of action never to allow women to meddle with state affairs. It may be also, that Philippe the Second, regent of France, was more reserved toward his mother than toward his mistresses, for he knew her epistolary inclinations, and he had no fancy for seeing his projects made the subjects of the daily correspondence which she kept up with the Princess Wilhelmina Charlotte, and the

Duke Anthony Ulric of Brunswick. In exchange for this loss, he left her the management of the house and of his daughters, which, from her overpowering idleness, the Duchesse d'Orleans abandoned willingly to her mother-in-law. In this last particular, however, the poor palatine (if one may believe the memoirs written at the time) was not happy. Madame de Berry lived publicly with Riom, and Mademoiselle de Valois was secretly the mistress of Richelieu, who, without anybody knowing how, and as if he had the enchanted ring of Gyges, appeared to get into her rooms, in spite of the guards who watched the doors, in spite of the spies with whom the regent surrounded him, and though, more than once, he had hidden himself in his daughter's room to watch.

As to Mademoiselle de Chartres, whose character had as yet seemed much more masculine than feminine, she, in making a man of herself, as one may say, seemed to forget that other men existed, when, some days before the time at which we have arrived, being at the opera, and hearing her music master, Cauchereau, the finished and expressive singer of the Academic Royal, who, in a love scene, was prolonging a note full of the most exquisite grace and feeling, the young princess, carried away by artistic enthusiasm, stretched out her arms and cried aloud—"Ah! my dear Cauchereau!" This unexpected exclamation had troubled her mother, who had sent away the beautiful tenor, and, putting aside her habitual apathy, determined to watch over her daughter herself. There remained the[Pg 327] Princess Louise, who was afterward Queen of Spain, and Mademoiselle Elizabeth, who became the Duchesse de Lorraine, but as to them there was nothing said; either they were really wise, or else they understood better than their elders how to restrain the sentiments of their hearts, or the accents of passion. As soon as the prince saw his mother appear, he thought something new was wrong in the rebellious troop of which she had taken the command, and which gave her such trouble; but, as nothing could make him forget the respect which, in public and in private, he paid to his mother, he rose on seeing her, and after having bowed, and taking her hand to lead her to a seat, he remained standing himself.

"Well, my son," said madame, with a strong German accent, "what is this that I hear, and what happened to you last evening?"

"Last evening?" said the regent, recalling his thoughts and questioning himself.

"Yes," answered the palatine, "last evening, in coming home from Madame de Sabran's."

"Oh! it is only that," said the prince.

"How, only that! your friend Simiane goes about everywhere saying that they wanted to carry you off, and that you only escaped by coming across the roofs: a singular road, you will confess, for the regent of the kingdom, and by which, however devoted they may be to you, I doubt your ministers being willing to come to your council."

"Simiane is a fool, mother," answered the regent, not able to help laughing at his mother's still scolding him as if he were a child, "it was not anybody who wanted to carry me away, but some roisterers who had been drinking at some cabaret by the Barriere des Sergents, and who were come to make a row in the Rue des Bons Enfants. As to the road we followed, it was for no sort of flight upon earth that I took it, but simply to gain a wager which that drunken Simiane is furious at having lost."

"My son, my son," said the palatine, shaking her head, "you will never believe in danger, and yet you know what your enemies are capable of. Believe me, my child, those who calumniate the soul would have few scruples about killing the body; and you know that the Duchesse de Maine has said, 'that the very day when she is quite sure that there is really nothing to be made out of her bastard of a husband, she will demand an audience of you, and drive her dagger into your heart.'"

"Bah! my mother," answered the regent, laughing, "have you become a sufficiently good Catholic no longer to believe in predestination? I believe in it, as you know. Would you wish me to plague my mind about a danger which has no existence; or which, if it does exist, has its result already inscribed in the eternal book? No, my mother, no; the only use of all these exaggerated precautions is to sadden life. Let tyrants tremble; but I, who am what St. Simon pretends to be, the most debonnaire man since Louis le Debonnaire, what have I to fear?"

"Oh, mon Dieu! nothing, my dear son," said the palatine, taking the hand of the prince, and looking at him with as much maternal tenderness as her little eyes were capable of expressing, "nothing, if every one knew you as well as I do, and saw you so truly good that you cannot hate even your enemies; but Henry IV., whom unluckily you resemble a little too much on certain points, was as good, and that did not prevent the existence of a Ravaillac. Alas! mein Gott," continued the princess, mixing up French and German in her agitation, "it is always the best kings that they do assassinate; tyrants take precautions, and the poniard never reaches them. You must never go out without a guard; it is you, and not I, my son, who require a regiment of soldiers."

"My mother," answered the regent, "will you listen to a story?"

"Yes, certainly, for you relate them exquisitely."

"Well, you know that there was in Rome, I forget in what precise year of the republic, a very brave consul, who[Pg 328] had the misfortune, shared by Henry IV. and myself, of going out of a night. It happened that this consul was sent against the Carthaginians, and having invented an implement of war called a crow, he gained the first naval battle in which the Romans had been victors, so that when he returned to Rome, congratulating himself beforehand, no doubt, on the increase of fortune which would follow his increase of reputation, he was not deceived; all the population awaited him at the city gates, and conducted him in triumph to the capitol, where the senate expected him.

"The senate announced to him that, in reward for his victory, they were going to bestow on him something which must be highly pleasing to him, which was, that whenever

249

he went out he should be preceded by a musician, who should announce to every one, by playing on the flute, that he was followed by the famous Duilius, the conqueror of the Carthaginians. Duilius, you will understand, my mother, was at the height of joy at such an honor. He returned home with a proud bearing, and preceded by his flute-player, who played his best, amid the acclamations of the multitude, who cried at the top of their voices, 'Long live, Duilius; long live the conqueror of the Carthaginians; long live the savior of Rome!' This was so intoxicating that the poor consul nearly went crazy with joy. Twice during the day he went out, although he had nothing to do in the town, only to enjoy the senatorial privilege, and to hear the triumphal music and the cries which accompanied it. This occupation had raised him by the evening into a state of glorification such as it is not easy to explain. The evening came. The conqueror had a mistress whom he loved, and whom he was eager to see again—a sort of Madame de Sabran—with the exception that the husband thought proper to be jealous, while ours, as you know, is not so absurd.

"The consul therefore had his bath, dressed and perfumed himself with the greatest care, and when eleven o'clock arrived he set out on tiptoe for the Suburranian Road. But he had reckoned without his host; or, rather, without his musician. Hardly had he gone four steps when the flute-player, who was attached to his service by night as well as day, darted from a post on which he was seated and went before, playing with all his might and main. The consequence of this was, that those who were in the streets turned round, those who were at home came to the door, and those who were in bed got up and opened their windows, all repeating in chorus—'Here is the Consul Duilius; long live Duilius; long live the conqueror of the Carthaginians; long live the savior of Rome!' This was highly flattering, but inopportune. The consul wished to silence his instrumentalist, but he declared that the orders he had received from the senate were precise—not to be quiet a minute—that he had ten thousand sesterces a year to blow his flute, and that blow he would as long as he had any breath left.

"The consul saw that it was useless to discuss with a man who had the dictate of the senate on his side, so he began to run, hoping to escape from his melodious companion, but he copied his actions from those of Duilius with such exactitude, that all the consul could gain was to get before the flute-player instead of behind him. He doubled like a hare, sprang like a roebuck, rushed madly forward like a wild boar—the cursed flute-player did not lose his track for an instant, so that all Rome, understanding nothing about the object of this nocturnal race, but knowing that it was the victor who performed it, came to their windows, shouting, 'Long live Duilius; long live the conqueror of the Carthaginians; long live the savior of Rome!' The poor man had one last hope; that of finding the people at his mistress's house asleep and the door half-open, as she had promised to leave it. But no; as soon as he arrived at that hospitable and gracious house, at whose door he had so often poured perfumes and hung garlands, he found that they were awake like all the rest, and at the window he saw the husband, who, as soon he saw him, began to cry, 'Long live, Duilius;[Pg 329] long live the conqueror of the Carthaginians; long live the savior of Rome!' The hero returned home despairing.

"The next day he hoped to escape his musician; but this hope was fallacious; and it was the same the day after, and all following days, so that the consul, seeing that it was impossible to keep his incognito, left for Sicily, where, out of anger, he beat the Carthaginians again; but this time so unmercifully, that every one thought that must be the end of all Punic wars, past, present, or to come. Rome was so convulsed with joy that it gave public rejoicings like those on the anniversary of the foundation of the city, and proposed to give the conqueror a triumph more splendid even than the last. As to the senate, it assembled before the arrival of Duilius, to determine what reward should be conferred upon him. They were all in favor of a public statue, when suddenly they heard shouts of triumph and the sound of a flute. It was the consul who had freed himself from the triumph, thanks to his haste, but who could not free himself from public gratitude, thanks to his flute-player. Suspecting that they were preparing something new, he came to take part in the deliberations. He found the senate ready to vote, with their balls in their hands.

"He advanced to the tribune. 'Conscript fathers,' said he, 'is it not your intention to give me a reward which will be agreeable to me?' 'Our intention,' replied the president, 'is to make you the happiest man on earth.' 'Good,' said Duilius; 'will you allow me to ask from you that which I desire most?' 'Speak,' cried all the senators at once. 'And you will confer it on me?' asked he, with all the timidity of doubt. 'By Jupiter we will!' answered the president in the name of the assembly. 'Then, Conscript fathers,' said Duilius, 'if you think that I have deserved well of the country, take away from me, in recompense for this second victory, this cursed flute-player, whom you gave me for the first.' The senate thought the request strange, but they had pledged their word, and at that period people kept their promises. The flute-player was allowed to retire on half-pay, and the Consul Duilius, having got rid of his musician, recovered his incognito, and, without noise, found the door of that little house in the Suburranian Road, which one victory had closed against him, and which another had reopened."

"Well," asked the palatine, "what has this story to do with the fear I have of your being assassinated?"

"What has it to do with it, my mother?" said the prince, laughing. "It is, that if, instead of the one musician which the Consul Duilius had, and which caused him such disappointment, I had a regiment of guards, you may fancy what would happen to me."

"Ah! Philippe, Philippe," answered the princess, laughing and sighing at the same time, "will you always treat serious matters so lightly!"

"No, mother," said the regent; "and the proof is, that as I presume you did not come here solely to read me a lecture on my nocturnal courses, but to speak on business, I am ready to listen to you, and to reply seriously."

"Yes, you are right," said the princess; "I did come to speak to you of other things. I came to speak of Mademoiselle de Chartres."

"Yes, of your favorite, mother; for it is useless to deny it, Louise is your favorite. Can it be because she does not love her uncles much, whom you do not love at all?"

"No, it is not that, but I confess it is pleasing to me to see that she has no better opinion of bastards than I have; but it is because, except as to beauty, which she has and I never had, she is exactly what I was at her age, having true boy's tastes, loving dogs, horses, and cavalcades, managing powder like an artilleryman, and making squibs like a workman; well, guess what has happened to her."——"She wants a commission in the guards?"

"No, no; she wants to be a nun."

"A nun! Louise! Impossible; it must be some joke of her sisters!"

[Pg 330]"Not at all," replied the palatine; "there is no joke about it, I swear to you."

"How has she got this passion for the cloister?" asked the regent, beginning to believe in the truth of what his mother told him, accustomed as he was to live at a time when the most extravagant things were always the most probable.

"Where did she get it?" replied madame; "why, from the devil, I suppose; I do not know where else she could have got it. The day before yesterday she passed with her sister, riding, shooting, laughing; in fact, I had never seen her so gay; but this evening Madame d'Orleans sent for me. I found Mademoiselle de Chartres at her mother's knees, in tears, and begging permission to retire to the Abbey des Chelles. Her mother turned to me, and said, 'What do you think of this, madame?' 'I think,' I replied, 'that we can perform our devotions equally well in any place and that all depends on our own preparations;' but hearing my words, Mademoiselle de Chartres redoubled her prayers, and with so much earnestness that I said to her mother, 'It is for you to decide.' 'Oh,' replied the duchess, 'we cannot prevent this poor child from performing her devotions.' 'Let her go then,' I replied, 'and may God grant that she goes in that intention.' 'I swear to you, madame,' said Mademoiselle de Chartres, 'that I go for God alone, and that I am influenced by no worldly idea.' Then she embraced us, and yesterday morning at seven o'clock she set out."

"I know all that, since I was to have taken her there," replied the regent. "Has nothing happened since then?"

"Yes, yesterday evening she sent back the carriage, giving the coachman a letter addressed to you, to her mother, and to me, in which she says that finding in the cloister that tranquillity and peace which she cannot hope for in the world, she does not wish to leave it."

"And what does her mother say to this resolution?"

"Her mother!" replied madame. "To tell you the truth, I believe her mother is very glad, for she likes convents, and thinks it a great piece of good-luck to have a daughter a nun;

but I say there is no happiness where there is no vocation."

The regent read and re-read the letter of Mademoiselle de Chartres, trying to discover, by the expression of her desire to remain at Chelles, the secret causes which had given rise to it. Then, after an instant of meditation, as deep as if the fate of empires depended on it:

"There is some love pique here," said he; "do you know if Louise loves any one?"

Madame told the regent the adventure of the opera, and the exclamation of the princess, in her admiration for the handsome tenor.

"Diable!" cried the regent, "and what did you and the Duchesse d'Orleans do in your maternal council?"

"We showed Cauchereau the door, and forbade the opera to Mademoiselle de Chartres; we could not do less."

"Well!" replied the regent, "there is no need to seek further. We must cure her at once of this fancy."

"And how will you do that, my son?"

"I will go to-day to the Abbey des Chelles, and interrogate Louise. If the thing is but a caprice, I will give it time to pass off. I will appear to adopt her views, and, in a year hence, when she is to take the veil, she herself will come and beg us to free her from the difficulty she has got herself into. If, on the contrary, the thing is serious, then it will be different."

"Mon Dieu!" said madame, rising, "remember that poor Cauchereau has, perhaps, nothing to do with it, and that he is even ignorant of the passion he has inspired."

"Do not be afraid," replied the prince, laughing at the

tragic interpretation which the princess, with her German ideas, had given to his words. "I shall not renew the lamentable history of the lovers of the Paraclete; Cauchereau's voice shall neither lose nor gain a single note in this adventure, and we do not treat a princess of the blood in the same manner as a little bourgeoise."

[Pg 331]"But, on the other hand," said madame, almost as much afraid of the regent's real indulgence as of his apparent severity, "no weakness either."

"My mother," said the regent, "if she must deceive some one, I would rather that it was her husband than God." And kissing his mother's hand respectfully, he led her to the door, quite scandalized at those easy manners, among which she died, without ever having accustomed herself to them. Then the Duc d'Orleans returned to his drawing, humming an air from his opera of Porthée.

In crossing the antechamber, madame saw a little man in great riding-boots coming toward her, his head sunk in the immense collar of a coat lined with fur. When he reached her he poked out of his surtout a little face with a pointed nose, and bearing a resemblance at once to a polecat and a fox.

"Oh!" said the palatine, "is it you, abbe?"

"Myself, your highness. I have just saved France—nothing but that." And bowing to madame, without waiting for her to dismiss him, as etiquette required, he turned on his heel, and entered the regent's study without being announced.

CHAPTER XIX.
THE ABBE DUBOIS.

All the world knows the commencement of the Abbe Dubois. We will not enlarge on the history of his youth, which may be found in the memoirs of the time, and particularly in those of the implacable Saint-Simon. Dubois has not been calumniated—it was impossible; but all the evil has been told of him, and not quite all the good.

There was in his antecedents, and in those of Alberoni, his rival, a great resemblance, but the genius was on the side of Dubois; and in the long struggle with Spain, which the nature of our subject does not allow us to do more than indicate, all the advantage was with the son of the apothecary over the son of the gardener. Dubois preceded Figaro, to whom he probably served as type; but, more fortunate than he, he passed from the office to the drawing-room, and from the drawing-room to the court. All these successive advantages were the rewards of various services, private or public.

His last negotiation was his chef-d'oeuvre; it was more than the ratification of the treaty of Utrecht; it was a treaty more advantageous still for France. The emperor not only renounced all right to the crown of Spain, as Philip V. had renounced all his to the crown of France, but he entered, with England and Holland, into a league, formed at once against Spain on the south, and against Sweden and Russia on the north. The division of the five or six great states of Europe was established by this treaty on so solid and just a basis that, after a hundred years of wars and revolutions, all these states, except the empire, remain in the same situation that they then were.

On his part, the regent, not very particular by nature, loved this man, who had educated him, and whose fortune he had made. The regent appreciated in Dubois the talents he had, and was not too severe on the vices from which he was not exempt. There was, however, between the regent and Dubois an abyss. The regent's vices and virtues were those of a gentleman, Dubois' those of a lackey. In vain the regent said to him, at each new favor that he granted, "Dubois, take care, it is only a livery-coat that I am putting on your back." Dubois, who cared about the gift, and not about the manner in which it was given, replied, with that apish grimace which belonged to him, "I am your valet, monseigneur, dress me always the same."

Dubois, however, loved the regent, and was devoted to him. He felt that this powerful hand alone had raised him from the sink in which he had been found, and to which, hated and despised as he was by all, a sign from the master might restore him. He watched with a personal interest the hatreds and plots which might reach the prince; and more than once, by the aid of a police often better managed than that of the lieutenant-general, and which extended, by means of Madame de[Pg 332] Tencin, into the highest aristocracy, and, by means of La Fillon, to the lowest grades of society, he had defeated conspiracies of which Messire Voyer d'Argenson had not even heard a whisper.

Therefore the regent, who appreciated the services which Dubois had rendered him, and could still render him, received the ambassador with open arms. As soon as he saw him appear, he rose, and, contrary to the custom of most princes, who depreciate the service in order to diminish the reward—

"Dubois," said he, joyously, "you are my best friend, and the treaty of the quadruple alliance will be more profitable to King Louis XV. than all the victories of his ancestor, Louis XIV."

"Bravo!" said Dubois, "you do me justice, monseigneur, but, unluckily, every one is not equally grateful."

"Ah! ah!" said the regent, "have you met my mother? She has just left the room."

"And how is his majesty?" asked Dubois, with a smile full of a detestable hope. "He was very poorly when I left."

"Well, abbe, very well," answered the prince, gravely. "God will preserve him to us, I hope, for the happiness of France, and the shame of our calumniators."

"And monseigneur sees him every day as usual?"

"I saw him yesterday, and I even spoke to him of you."

"Bah! and what did you tell him?"

"I told him that in all probability you had just secured the tranquillity of his reign."

"And what did the king answer?"

"What did he answer! He answered, my friend, that he did not think abbes were so useful."

"His majesty is very witty; and old Villeroy was there,

without doubt?"

"As he always is."

"With your permission, I must send that old fellow to look for me at the other end of France some fine morning. His insolence to you begins to tire my patience."

"Leave him alone, Dubois, leave him alone, everything will come in time."

"Even my archbishopric."

"Ha! What is this new folly?"

"New folly, monseigneur! on my honor nothing can be more serious."

"Oh! this letter from the king of England, which asks me for an archbishopric for you—"

"Did your highness not recognize the style?"

"You dictated it, you rascal!"

"To Nericault Destouches, who got the king to sign it."

"And the king signed it as it is, without saying anything?"

"Exactly. 'You wish,' said he to our poet, 'that a Protestant prince should interfere to make an archbishop in France. The regent will read my recommendation, will laugh at it, and pay no attention to it.' 'Yes, yes, sire,' replied Destouches, who has more wit than he puts into his verses, 'the regent will laugh at it, but after all will do what your majesty asks.'"

"Destouches lied."

"Destouches never spoke more truly, monseigneur."

"You an archbishop! King George would deserve that, in return, I should point out to him some rascal like you for the archbishopric of York when it becomes vacant."

"I defy you to find my equal—I know but one man."

"And who is he? I should like to know him."

"Oh, it is useless, he is already placed, and, as his place is good, he would not change it for all the archbishoprics in the world."

"Insolent!"

"With whom are you angry, monseigneur?"

"With a fellow who wants to be an archbishop, and who has never yet officiated at the communion table."

"I shall be all the better prepared."

"But the archdeaconship, the deaconship, the priesthood."

"Bah! We will find somebody; some second Jean des Entomeures, who will dispatch all that in an hour."

"I defy you to find him."

[Pg 333]"It is already done."

"And who is that?"

"Your first almoner, the bishop of Nantes, Tressan."

"The fellow has an answer for everything.—But your marriage?"

"My marriage!"

"Yes, Madame Dubois."

"Madame Dubois! Who is that?"

"What, fellow, have you assassinated her?"

"Monseigneur forgets that it is only three days since he gave her her quarter's pension."

"And if she should oppose your archbishopric?"

"I defy her; she has no proofs."

"She may get a copy of the marriage certificate."

"There is no copy without an original."

"And the original?"

"Here it is," said Dubois, drawing from his pocket a little paper, containing a pinch of ashes.

"What! and are you not afraid that I shall send you to the galleys?"

"If you wish to do so, now is the time, for I hear the lieutenant of police speaking in the antechamber."

"Who sent for him?"

"I did."

"What for?"

"To find fault with him."

"For what reason?"

"You will hear. It is understood then—I am an archbishop."

"And have you already chosen your archbishopric?"

"Yes, I take Cambray."

"Peste! you are not modest."

"Oh, mon Dieu! it is not for the profit, it is for the honor of succeeding Fenelon."

"Shall we have a new Telemachus?"

"Yes, if your highness will find me a Penelope in the kingdom."

"Apropos of Penelope, you know that Madame de Sabran—"

"I know all."

"Ah, abbe; your police, then, is as good as ever!"

"You shall judge."

Dubois stretched out his hand, rang the bell, and a

messenger appeared.

"Send the lieutenant-general," said Dubois.

"But, abbe, it seems to me that it is you who give orders here now."

"It is for your good, monseigneur.—Let me do it."

"Well, well!" said the regent, "one must be indulgent to new-comers."

Messire Voyer d'Argenson entered—he was as ugly as Dubois, but his ugliness was of a very different kind. He was tall, thick, and heavy; wore an immense wig, had great bushy eyebrows, and was invariably taken for the devil by children who saw him for the first time. But with all this, he was supple, active, skillful, intriguing, and fulfilled his office conscientiously, when he was not turned from his nocturnal duties by other occupations.

"Messire d'Argenson," said Dubois, without even leaving the lieutenant-general time to finish his bow, "monseigneur, who has no secrets from me, has sent for you, that you may tell me in what costume he went out last night, in whose house he passed the evening, and what happened to him on leaving it. I should not need to ask these questions if I had not just arrived from London; you understand, that as I traveled post from Calais, I can know nothing of them."

"But," said D'Argenson, who thought these questions concealed some snare, "did anything extraordinary happen last evening? I confess I received no report; I hope no accident happened to monseigneur?"

"Oh, no, none; only monseigneur, who went out at eight

o'clock in the evening, as a French guard, to sup with Madame de Sabran, was nearly carried off on leaving her house."

"Carried off!" cried D'Argenson, turning pale, while the regent could not restrain a cry of astonishment, "carried off! and by whom?"

"Ah!" said Dubois, "that is what we do not know, and what you ought to know, Messire d'Argenson, if you had not passed your time at the convent of the Madeleine de Traisnel."

"What, D'Argenson! you, a great magistrate, give such an example!"[Pg 334] said the regent, laughing. "Never mind, I will receive you well, if you come, as you have already done in the time of the late king, to bring me, at the end of the year, a journal of my acts."

"Monseigneur," said the lieutenant, stammering, "I hope your highness does not believe a word of what the Abbe Dubois says."

"What! instead of being humiliated by your ignorance, you give me the lie. Monseigneur, I will take you to D'Argenson's seraglio; an abbess of twenty-six, and novices of fifteen; a boudoir in India chintz, and cells hung with tapestry. Oh, Monsieur le Lieutenant de Police knows how to do things well."

The regent held his sides with laughing, seeing D'Argenson's disturbed face.

"But," replied the lieutenant of police, trying to bring back the conversation to the less disagreeable, though more humiliating subject, "there is not much merit, abbe, in your knowing the details of an event, which, doubtless, monseigneur himself told you."

"On my honor," said the regent, "I did not tell him a single word."

"Listen, lieutenant; is it monseigneur also who told me the story of the novice of the Faubourg Saint-Marceau, whom you so nearly carried off over the convent walls? Is it monseigneur who told me of that house which you have had built under a false name, against the wall of the convent of the Madeleine, so that you can enter at all hours by a door hidden in a closet, and which opens on to the sacristy of the chapel of Saint Mark, your patron? No, no, all that, my dear lieutenant, is the infancy of the art, and he who only knew this, would not, I hope, be worthy to hold a candle to you."

"Listen, abbe," replied the lieutenant of police with a grave air, "if all you have told me about monseigneur is true, the thing is serious and I am in the wrong not to know it, if any one does—but there is no time lost. We will find the culprits, and punish them as they deserve."

"But," said the regent, "you must not attach too much importance to this; they were, probably, some drunken officers who wished to amuse their companions."

"It is a conspiracy, monseigneur," replied Dubois, "which emanates from the Spanish embassy, passing through the Arsenal before it arrives at the Palais Royal."

"Again, Dubois?"

"Always, monseigneur."

"And you, D'Argenson, what is your opinion?"

"That your enemies are capable of anything, monseigneur; but that we will mar their plots, whatever they may be, I give you my word."

At this moment the door opened, and the Duc de Maine was announced, who came to attend the council, and whose privilege it was, as prince of the blood, not to be kept waiting. He advanced with that timid and uneasy air which was natural to him, casting a side-glance over the three persons in whose presence he found himself, as though to discover what subject occupied them at his entrance. The regent understood his thought.

"Welcome, my cousin," said he; "these two bad fellows—whom you know—have just been assuring me that you are conspiring against me."

The Duc de Maine turned as pale as death, and was obliged to lean for support on the crutch-shaped stick which he carried.

"And I hope, monseigneur," replied he, in a voice which he vainly endeavored to render firm, "that you did not give ear to such a calumny."

"Oh, mon Dieu! no!" replied the regent negligently; "but they are obstinate, and declare that they will take you one day in the fact. I do not believe it, but at any rate I give you warning; be on your guard against them, for they are clever fellows, I warrant you."

The Duc de Maine opened his mouth to give some contemptible excuse, when the door opened again, and the groom announced successively the Duc de Bourbon,[Pg

335] the Prince de Conti, the Duc de St. Simon, the Duc de Guiche, captain of the guards; the Duc Noailles, president of the council of finance; the Duc d'Antin, superintendent of ships; the Marshal d'Uxelles, president of the council of foreign affairs; the Archbishop of Troyes; the Marquis de Lavrilliere; the Marquis d'Efflat; the Duc de Laforce; the Marquis de Torcy; and the Marshals de Villeroy, d'Estrées, de Villars, and de Bezons.

As these grave personages were gathered together to deliberate upon the treaty of the quadruple alliance, brought from London by Dubois, and as the treaty of the quadruple alliance only figures secondarily in this history, our readers will excuse our leaving the sumptuous reception-room in the Palais Royal, to lead them back to the attic in the Rue du Temps-Perdu.

CHAPTER XX.
THE CONSPIRACY.

D'Harmental, after having placed his hat and cloak on a chair, after having placed his pistols on his table, and his sword under his pillow, threw himself dressed on to his bed, and, more happy than Damocles, he slept, though, like Damocles, a sword hung over his head by a thread.

When he awoke it was broad daylight, and as the evening before he had forgotten to close his shutters, the first thing he saw was a ray of sunshine playing joyously across his room. D'Harmental thought that he had been dreaming, when he found himself again calm and tranquil in his little room, so neat and clean, while he might have been at that hour in some gloomy and somber prison. For a moment he doubted of its reality, remembering all that had passed the evening before; but all was there—the red ribbon, the hat and cloak on the chair, the pistols on the table, and the sword under the pillow; and, as a last proof, he himself in the costume of the day before, which he had not taken off, for fear of being surprised by some nocturnal visit.

D'Harmental jumped from his bed. His first look was for his neighbor's window: it was already open, and he saw Bathilde passing and repassing in her room; the second was for his glass, which told him that conspiracies suited him— indeed, his face was paler than usual, and therefore more interesting; his eyes were rather feverish, and therefore more expressive: so that it was evident that, when he had smoothed

269

his hair and arranged his collar and cravat, he would be a most interesting person to Bathilde. D'Harmental did not say this, even to himself; but the bad instinct which always impels our poor souls to evil whispered these thoughts to him, so that when he went to his toilet he suited his dress to the expression of his face—that is to say, that he dressed entirely in black, that his hair was arranged with a charming negligence, and that he left his waistcoat more than usually open, to give place to his shirt-frill, which fell with an ease full of coquetry. All this was done in the most preoccupied and careless manner in the world; for D'Harmental, brave as he was, could not help remembering that at any minute he might be arrested; but it was by instinct that, when the chevalier gave the last look in the glass, before leaving his little dressing-room, he smiled at himself with a melancholy which doubled the charm of his countenance. There was no mistake as to the meaning of this smile, for he went directly to the window.

Perhaps Bathilde had also her projects for the moment when her neighbor should reappear, perhaps she had arranged a defense which should consist in not looking toward him, or in closing her window after a simple recognition; but at the noise her neighbor's window made in opening, all was forgotten, and she ran to the window, crying out:

"Ah! there you are. Mon Dieu! monsieur, how anxious you have made me!"

This exclamation was ten times more than D'Harmental had hoped for. If he, on his part, had prepared some well-turned and eloquent phrases, they were all forgotten, and clasping his hands:

"Bathilde! Bathilde!" he cried, "you are, then, as good as you are beautiful!"

"Why good?" asked Bathilde. "Did[Pg 336] you not tell me that if I was an orphan, you also were without parents? Did you not say that I was your sister, and you were my brother?"

"Then, Bathilde, you prayed for me?"

"All night," replied the young girl blushing.

"And I thanked chance for having saved me, when I owed all to an angel's prayers!"

"The danger is then past?" cried Bathilde.

"The night was dark and gloomy," replied D'Harmental. "This morning, however, I was awakened by a ray of sunshine which a cloud may again conceal: so it is with the danger I have run; it has passed to give place to a great happiness— that of knowing you have thought of me, yet it may return. But stay," continued he, hearing steps on the staircase, "there it is, perhaps, approaching my door."

As he spoke, some one knocked three times at the chevalier's door.

"Who is there?" asked D'Harmental from the window, in a voice which, in spite of all his firmness, betrayed some emotion.

"A friend," answered a voice.

"Well?" asked Bathilde, with anxiety.

"Thanks to you, God still continues to protect me: it is

a friend who knocks. Once again, thanks, Bathilde." And the chevalier closed his window, sending the young girl a last salute which was very like a kiss; then he opened to the Abbe Brigaud, who, beginning to be impatient, had knocked a second time.

"Well," said the abbe, on whose face it was impossible to see the smallest change, "what has happened, then, my dear pupil, that you are shut in thus by bolts and bars? Is it as a foretaste of the Bastille?"

"Holla! abbe," said D'Harmental, in a cheerful voice, "no such jokes, I beg; they might bring misfortune."

"But look! look!" said Brigaud, throwing his eyes round him, "would not any one suppose they were visiting a conspirator? Pistols on the table, a sword on the pillow, and a hat and cloak on the chair. Ah! my dear pupil, you are discomposed, it appears to me! Come, put all this in order, that I may not be able to perceive, when I pay my paternal visit, what passes during my absence."

D'Harmental obeyed, admiring, in this man of the Church, the sang-froid which he himself found it difficult to attain.

"Very good," said Brigaud, watching him, "and this shoulder-knot which you have forgotten, and which was never made for you (for it dates from the time when you were in jackets), put it away too; who knows?—you may want it."

"And what for, abbe?" asked D'Harmental, laughing; "to attend the regent's levée in?"

"Oh, no, but for a signal to some good fellow who is

passing; come, put it away."

"My dear abbe," said D'Harmental, "if you are not the devil in person, you are at least one of his most intimate acquaintances."

"Oh, no! I am a poor fellow who goes his own quiet way, and who, as he goes, looks high and low, right and left, that is all. Look, there is a ray of spring, the first, which knocks humbly at your window, and you do not open it: one would suppose you were afraid of being seen. Ah, pardon! I did not know that, when your window opened, another must close."

"My dear abbe, you are full of wit," replied D'Harmental, "but terribly indiscreet; so much so, that, if you were a musketeer instead of an abbe, I should quarrel with you."

"And why? Because I wish to open you a path to glory, fortune, and, perhaps, love? It would be monstrous ingratitude."

"Well, let us be friends, abbe," said D'Harmental, offering his hand, "and I shall not be sorry to have some news."

"Of what?"

"How do I know? Of the Rue des Bons Enfants, where there has been a great deal going on, I believe; of the Arsenal, where, I believe, Madame de Maine has given a soirée; and even of the regent, who, if I may believe a dream I had, came back to the Palais Royal very late and rather agitated."

[Pg 337]"All has gone well. The noise of the Rue des Bons Enfants, if there were any, is quite calm this morning; Madame de Maine has as much gratitude for those whom important affairs kept away from the Arsenal as she has contempt for those who were there; finally, the regent, dreaming last night, as usual, that he was king of France, has already forgotten that he was nearly the prisoner of the king of Spain. Now we must begin again."

"Ah, pardon, abbe," said D'Harmental; "but, with your permission, it is the turn of the others. I shall not be sorry to rest a little, myself."

"Ah, that goes badly with the news I bring you."

"What news?"

"It was decided last night that you should leave for Brittany this morning."

"For Brittany!—and what to do there?"

"You will know when you are there."

"And if I do not wish to go?"

"You will reflect, and go just the same."

"And on what shall I reflect?"

"That it would be the act of a madman to interrupt an enterprise near its end for a love only at its beginning. To abandon the interests of a princess of the blood to gain the good graces of a grisette."

"Abbe!" said D'Harmental.

"Oh, we must not get angry, my dear chevalier; we must reason! You engaged voluntarily in the affair we have in hand, and you promised to aid us in it. Would it be loyal to abandon us now for a repulse? No, no, my dear pupil; you must have a little more connection in your ideas if you mix in a conspiracy."

"It is just because I have connection in my ideas," replied

D'Harmental, "that this time, as at first, before undertaking anything new, I wish to know what it is. I offered myself to be the arm, it is true; but, before striking, the arm must know what the head has decided. I risk my liberty. I risk my life. I risk something perhaps dearer to me still. I will risk all this in my own manner, with my eyes open, and not closed. Tell me first what I am to do in Brittany, and then perhaps I will go there."

"Your orders are that you should go to Rennes. There you will unseal this letter, and find your instructions."

"My orders! my instructions!"

"Are not these the terms which a general uses to his officers? And are they in the habit of disputing the commands they receive?"

"Not when they are in the service; but you know I am in it no longer."

"It is true. I forgot to tell you that you had re-entered it."——"I!"

"Yes, you. I have your brevet in my pocket." And Brigaud drew from his pocket a parchment, which he presented to D'Harmental, who unfolded it slowly, questioning Brigaud with his looks.

"A brevet!" cried the chevalier; "a brevet as colonel in one of the four regiments of carabineers! Whence comes this brevet?"

"Look at the signature."

"Louis-Auguste, Duc de Maine!"

"Well, what is there astonishing in that? As grand master

of artillery, he has the nomination of twelve regiments. He gives you one to replace that which was taken from you, and, as your general, he sends you on a mission. Is it customary for soldiers in such a case to refuse the honor their chief does them in thinking of them? I am a churchman, and do not know."

"No, no, my dear abbe. It is, on the contrary, the duty of every officer of the king to obey his chief."

"Besides which," replied Brigaud, negligently, "in case the conspiracy failed, you would only have obeyed orders, and might throw the whole responsibility of your actions on another."

"Abbe!" cried D'Harmental, a second time.

"Well, if you do not go, I shall make you feel the spur."

"Yes, I am going. Excuse me, but there are some moments when I am half mad. I am now at the orders of Monsieur de Maine, or, rather, at those of Madame. May I not see her before I go, to fall at her feet, and tell her that I am ready to sacrifice my life at a word from her?"

[Pg 338]"There, now, you are going into the opposite extreme; but no, you must not die; you must live—live to triumph over our enemies, and wear a beautiful uniform, with which you will turn all the women's heads."

"Oh, my dear Brigaud, there is but one I wish to please."

"Well, you shall please her first, and the others afterward."

"When must I go?"

"This instant."

"You will give me half an hour?"

276

"Not a second."

"But I have not breakfasted."

"You shall come and breakfast with me."

"I have only two or three thousand francs here, and that is not enough."

"You will find a year's pay in your carriage."

"And clothes?"

"Your trunks are full. Had I not your measure? You will not be discontented with my tailor."

"But at least, abbe, tell me when I may return."

"In six weeks to a day, the Duchesse de Maine will expect you at Sceaux."

"But at least you will permit me to write a couple of lines."

"Well, I will not be too exacting."

The chevalier sat down and wrote:

"Dear Bathilde—To-day it is more than a danger which threatens me; it is a misfortune which overtakes me. I am forced to leave this instant, without seeing you, without bidding you adieu. I shall be six weeks absent. In the name of Heaven, Bathilde, do not forget him who will not pass an hour without thinking of you.

Raoul."

This letter written, folded, and sealed, the chevalier rose and went to the window; but as we have said, that of his neighbor was closed when Brigaud appeared. There was then no means of sending to Bathilde the dispatch destined for her. D'Harmental made an impatient gesture. At this moment they heard a scratching at the door. The abbe opened it, and

Mirza appeared, guided by her instinct, and her greediness, to the giver of the bon-bons, and making lively demonstrations of joy.

"Well," said Brigaud, "who shall say God is not good to lovers? You wanted a messenger, and here is one."

"Abbe, abbe," said D'Harmental, shaking his head, "do not enter into my secrets before I wish it."

"Oh," replied Brigaud, "a confessor, you know, is an abyss."

"Then not a word will pass your lips?"

"On my honor, chevalier."

D'Harmental tied the letter to Mirza's neck, gave her a piece of sugar as a reward for the commission she was about to accomplish; and, half sad at having lost his beautiful neighbor for six weeks, half glad at having regained forever his beautiful uniform, he took his money, put his pistols into his pockets, fastened on his sword, took his hat and cloak, and followed the Abbe Brigaud.

CHAPTER XXI.
THE ORDER OF THE HONEY-BEE.

At the appointed day and hour, that is to say, six weeks after his departure from the capital, and at four o'clock in the afternoon, D'Harmental, returning from Brittany, entered the courtyard of the Palace of Sceaux, with his post horses going at full gallop. Servants in full livery waited on the door-step, and everything announced preparations for a fete. D'Harmental entered, crossed the hall, and found himself in a large room, where about twenty people were assembled, standing in groups talking, while waiting for the mistress of the house.

There were, among others, the Comte de Laval, the Marquis de Pompadour, the poet St. Genest, the old Abbe Chaulieu, St. Aulaire, Madame de Rohan, Madame de Croissy, Madame de Charost, and Madame de Brissac.

D'Harmental went straight to the Marquis de Pompadour, the one out of all this noble and intelligent society with whom he was best acquainted. They shook hands. Then D'Harmental, drawing him aside, said:

[Pg 339]"My dear marquis, can you tell me how it is that where I expected to find only a dull political assembly I find preparations for a fete?"

"Ma foi! I do not know, my dear chevalier," replied Pompadour, "and I am as astonished as you are. I have just returned from Normandy myself."

"Ah! you also have just arrived?"

279

"This instant I asked the same question of Laval, but he has just arrived from Switzerland, and knows no more than we do."

At this moment the Baron de Valef was announced.

"Ah, pardieu! now we shall know," continued Pompadour. "Valef is so intimate with the duchesse he will be able to tell us."

Valef, recognizing them, came toward them.

D'Harmental and Valef had not seen each other since the day of the duel with which this story opened, so that they met with pleasure; then, after exchanging compliments—

"My dear Valef," said D'Harmental, "can you tell me what is the meaning of this great assembly, when I expected to find only a select committee?"

"Ma foi! I do not know anything of it," said Valef, "I have just come from Madrid."

"Every one has just arrived from somewhere," said Pompadour, laughing. "Ah! here is Malezieux, I hope he has been no further than Dombes or Chatenay; and as at any rate he has certainly passed through Madame de Maine's room we shall have some news at last."

At these words Pompadour made a sign to Malezieux, but the worthy chancellor was so gallant that he must first acquit himself of his duty toward the ladies. After he had bowed to them, he came toward the group, among which were Pompadour, D'Harmental, and Valef.

"Come, my dear Malezieux," said Pompadour, "we are waiting for you most impatiently. We have just arrived from the four quarters of the globe, it appears. Valef from the south, D'Harmental from the west, Laval from the east, I from the north, you from I do not know where; so that we confess that we are very curious to know what we are going to do here at Sceaux."

"You have come to assist at a great solemnity, at the reception of a new knight of the order of the honey-bee."

"Peste!" said D'Harmental, a little piqued that they should not have left him time to go to the Rue du Temps-Perdu before coming to Sceaux; "I understand now why Madame de Maine told us to be so exact to the rendezvous; as to myself, I am very grateful to her highness."

"First of all you must know, young man," interrupted Malezieux, "that there is no Madame de Maine nor highness in the question. There is only the beautiful fairy Ludovic, the queen of the bees, whom every one must obey blindly. Our queen is all-wise and all-powerful, and when you know who is the knight we are to receive you will not regret your diligence."

"And who is it?" asked Valef, who, arriving from the greatest distance, was naturally the most anxious to know why he had been brought home.

"His excellency the Prince de Cellamare."

"Ah!" said Pompadour, "I begin to understand."——"And I," said Valef.

"And I," said D'Harmental.

"Very well," said Malezieux, smiling; "and before the end of the evening you will understand still better; meanwhile, do not try to see further. It is not the first time you have entered with your eyes bandaged, Monsieur d'Harmental?"

At these words, Malezieux advanced toward a little man, with a flat face, flowing hair, and a discontented expression. D'Harmental inquired who it was, and Pompadour replied that it was the poet Lagrange-Chancel. The young men looked at the new-comer with a curiosity mixed with disgust; then, turning away, and leaving Pompadour to advance toward the Cardinal de Polignac, who entered at this moment, they went into the embrasure of a window to talk over the occurrences of the evening.

[Pg 340]The order of the honey-bee had been founded by Madame de Maine, apropos of the Italian motto which she had adopted at her marriage: "Little insects inflict large stings."

This order had, like others, its decorations, its officers, and its grand-master. The decoration was a medal, representing on one side a hive, and on the other the queen-bee: it was hung by a lemon-colored ribbon, and was worn by every knight whenever he came to Sceaux. The officers were Malezieux, St. Aulaire, the Abbe Chaulieu, and St. Genest. Madame de Maine was grand-master.

It was composed of thirty-nine members, and could not exceed this number. The death of Monsieur de Nevers had left a vacancy which was to be filled by the nomination of the Prince de Cellamare. The fact was, that Madame de Maine had thought it safer to cover this political meeting with a frivolous pretext, feeling sure that a fete in the gardens at

Sceaux would appear less suspicious in the eyes of Dubois and Messire Voyer d'Argenson than an assembly at the Arsenal. Thus, as will be seen, nothing had been forgotten to give its old splendor to the order of the honey-bee.

At four o'clock precisely, the time fixed for the ceremony, the doors of the room opened, and they perceived, in a salon hung with crimson satin, spangled with silver bees, the beautiful fairy Ludovic seated on a throne raised on three steps. She made a gesture with her golden wand, and all her court, passing into the salon, arranged themselves in a half circle round her throne, on the steps of which the dignitaries of the order placed themselves.

After the initiation of the Prince de Cellamare as a knight of the honey-bee, a second door was opened, displaying a room brilliantly lighted, where a splendid supper was laid. The new knight of the order offered his hand to the fairy, and conducted her to the supper-room followed by the assistants.

The entertainment was worthy of the occasion, and the flow of wit which so peculiarly characterized the epoch was well sustained. As the hour began to draw late, the Duchesse de Maine rose and announced that having received an excellent telescope from the author of "The Worlds," she invited her company to study astronomy in the garden.

CHAPTER XXII.
THE QUEEN OF THE GREENLANDERS.

As might have been expected, new surprises awaited the guests in the garden. These gardens, designed by Le Notre for Colbert, and sold by him to the Duc de Maine, had now really the appearance of a fairy abode. They were bounded only by a large sheet of water, in the midst of which was the pavilion of Aurora—so called because from this pavilion was generally given the signal that the night was finished, and that it was time to retire—and had, with their games of tennis, football, and tilting at the ring, an aspect truly royal. Every one was astonished on arriving to find all the old trees and graceful paths linked together by garlands of light which changed the night into brilliant day.

At the approach of Madame de Maine a strange party, consisting of seven individuals, advanced gravely toward her. They were dressed entirely in fur, and wore hairy caps, which hid their faces. They had with them a sledge drawn by two reindeer, and their deputation was headed by a chief wearing a long robe lined with fur, with a cap of fox-skin, on which were three tails. This chief, kneeling before Madame de Maine, addressed her.

"Madame! the Greenlanders have chosen me, as one of the chief among them, to offer you, on their parts, the sovereignty of their state."

This allusion was so evident, and yet so safe, that a murmur of approbation ran through the whole assembly, and the ambassador, visibly encouraged by this reception, continued—

"Fame has told us, even in the midst of our snows, in our little corner of the world, of the charms, the virtues, and the inclinations of your highness. We know that you abhor the sun."

This allusion was as quickly seized on[Pg 341] as the first, for the sun was the regent's device, and as we have said, Madame de Maine was well known for her predilection in favor of night.

"Consequently, madame," continued the ambassador, "as in our geographical position God has blessed us with six months of night and six months of twilight, we come to propose to you to take refuge in our land from the sun which you so much dislike; and in recompense for that which you leave here, we offer you the title of Queen of the Greenlanders. We are certain that your presence will cause our arid plains to flower, and that the wisdom of your laws will conquer our stubborn spirit, and that, thanks to the gentleness of your reign, we shall renounce a liberty less sweet than your rule."

"But," said Madame de Maine, "it seems to me that the kingdom you offer me is rather distant, and I confess I do not like long voyages."

"We foresaw your reply, madame," replied the ambassador, "and, thanks to the enchantments of a powerful magician, have so arranged, that if you would not go to the mountain, the mountain should come to you. Hola, genii!" continued the chief, describing some cabalistic circles in the air with his wand, "display the palace of your new sovereign."

At this moment some fanciful music was heard; the veil which covered the pavilion of Aurora was raised as if by magic, and the water showed the reflection of a light so skillfully placed that it might have been taken for the moon. By this light was seen an island of ice at the foot of a snowy peak, on which was the palace of the Queen of the Greenlanders, to which led a bridge so light that it seemed to be made of a floating cloud. Then, in the midst of general acclamation, the ambassador took from the hands of one of his suite a crown, which he placed on the duchess's head, and which she received with as haughty a gesture as though it had been a real crown. Then, getting into the sledge, she went toward the marine palace; and, while the guards prevented the crowd from following her into her new domain, she crossed the bridge and entered, with the seven ambassadors. At the same instant the bridge disappeared, as if, by an illusion not less visible than the others, the skillful machinist had wished to separate the past from the future, and fireworks expressed the joy of the Greenlanders at seeing their new sovereign. Meanwhile Madame de Maine was introduced by an usher into the most retired part of the palace, and the seven ambassadors having thrown off caps and cloaks, she found herself surrounded by the Prince de Cellamare, Cardinal Polignac, the Marquis de Pompadour, the Comte de Laval, the Baron de Valef, the Chevalier d'Harmental, and Malezieux. As to the usher, who, after having carefully closed all the doors, came and mixed familiarly with all this noble assembly, he was no other than our old friend the Abbe Brigaud. Things now began to take their true form, and the fete, as the ambassadors had done, threw off mask and costume, and turned openly to conspiracy.

"Gentlemen," said the duchess, with her habitual vivacity, "we have not an instant to lose, as too long an absence would be suspicious. Let every one tell quickly what he has done, and we shall know what we are about."

"Pardon, madame," said the prince, "but you had spoken to me, as being one of ourselves, of a man whom I do not see here, and whom I am distressed not to count among our numbers."

"You mean the Duc de Richelieu?" replied Madame de Maine; "it is true he promised to come; he must have been detained by some adventure; we must do without him."

"Yes, certainly," replied the prince, "if he does not come we must do without him; but I confess that I deeply regret his absence. The regiment which he commands is at Bayonne, and for that reason might be very useful to us. Give orders, I beg, madame, that if he should come he should be admitted directly."

"Abbe," said Madame de Maine, turning to Brigaud, "you heard; tell D'Avranches."

[Pg 342]The abbe went out to execute this order.

"Pardon, monsieur," said D'Harmental to Malezieux, "but I thought six weeks ago that the Duc de Richelieu positively refused to be one of us."

"Yes," answered Malezieux, "because he knew that he

was intended to take the cordon bleu to the Prince of the Asturias, and he would not quarrel with the regent just when he expected the Golden Fleece as the reward of his embassy; but now the regent has changed his mind and deferred sending the order, so that the Duc de Richelieu, seeing his Golden Fleece put off till the Greek kalends, has come back to us."

"I have given the order," said the Abbe Brigaud, returning.

"Well," said the duchess, "now let us go to business. Laval, you begin."

"I, madame," said Laval, "as you know, have been in Switzerland, where, with the king of Spain's name and money, I raised a regiment in the Grisons. This regiment is ready to enter France at any moment, armed and equipped, and only waits the order to march."

"Very good, my dear count," said the duchess; "and if you do not think it below a Montmorency to be colonel of a regiment while waiting for something better, take the command of this one. It is a surer way of getting the Golden Fleece than taking the Saint Esprit into Spain."

"Madame," said Laval, "it is for you to appoint each one his place, and whatever you may appoint will be gratefully accepted by the most humble of your servants."

"And you, Pompadour," said Madame de Maine, thanking Laval by a gesture of the hand, "what have you done?"

"According to your highness's instructions," replied the marquis, "I went to Normandy, where I got the protestation signed by the nobility. I bring you thirty-eight good signatures" (he drew a paper from his pocket). "Here is the request to the king, and here the signatures."

The duchess snatched the paper so quickly that she almost tore it, and throwing her eyes rapidly over it:

"Yes, yes," said she, "you have done well to put them so, without distinction or difference of rank, so that there may be no question of precedence. Guillaume-Alexandre de Vieux-Pont, Pierre-Anne-Marie de la Pailleterie, De Beaufremont, De Latour-Dupin, De Chatillon. Yes, you are right; these are the best and most faithful names in France. Thanks, Pompadour; you are a worthy messenger; your skill shall not be forgotten. And you, chevalier?" continued she, turning to D'Harmental with her irresistible smile.

"I, madame," said the chevalier, "according to your orders left for Brittany, and at Nantes I opened my dispatches and took my instructions."

"Well?" asked the duchess quickly.

"Well, madame," replied D'Harmental, "I have been as successful as Messieurs de Laval and Pompadour. I have the promises of Messieurs de Mont-Louis, De Bonamour, De Pont-Callet, and De Rohan Soldue. As soon as Spain shows a squadron in sight of the coasts, Brittany will rise."

"You see, prince," cried the duchess, addressing Cellamare, with an accent full of ambitious joy, "everything favors us."

"Yes," replied the prince; "but these four gentlemen, influential as they are, are not all that we must have. There are Laguerche-Saint-Amant, Les Bois-Davy, De Larochefoucault-Gondral, Les Decourt, and Les d'Erée, whom it would be important to gain."

"It is done, prince," said D'Harmental; "here are their letters;" and taking several from his pocket, he opened two or three by chance and read their contents.

"Well, prince," cried Madame de Maine, "what do you think now? Besides these three letters, here is one from Lavauguyon, one from Bois-Davy, one from Fumée. Stay, chevalier, here is our right hand; 'tis that which holds the pen—let it be a pledge to you that, if ever its signature should be royal, it would have nothing to refuse to you."

"Thanks, madame," said D'Harmental, kissing her hand respectfully, "but you have already given me more than I deserve, and success itself would recompense me so highly, by placing your highness in[Pg 343] your proper position, that I should have nothing left to desire."

"And now, Valef, it is your turn," continued the duchess; "we kept you till the last, for you were the most important. If I understood rightly your signs during dinner, you are not displeased with their Catholic majesties."

"What would your highness say to a letter written by his highness Philippe himself?"

"Oh! it is more than I ever dared to hope for," cried Madame de Maine.

"Prince," said Valef, passing a paper to Cellamare, "you know his majesty's writing. Assure her royal highness, who does not dare to believe it, that this is from his own hand."

"It is," said Cellamare.

"And to whom is it addressed?" asked Madame de Maine,

taking it from the prince's hands.

"To the king, Louis XV., madame," said the latter.

"Good!" said the duchess; "we will get it presented by the Marshal de Villeroy. Let us see what it says." And she read as rapidly as the writing permitted:

"'The Escurial, 16th March, 1718.

"'Since Providence has placed me on the throne of Spain, I have never for an instant lost sight of the obligations of my birth. Louis XIV., of eternal memory, is always present to my mind. I seem always to hear that great prince, at the moment of our separation, saying to me, 'The Pyrenees exist no longer.' Your majesty is the only descendant of my elder brother, whose loss I feel daily. God has called you to the succession of this great monarchy, whose glory and interests will be precious to me till my death. I can never forget what I owe to your majesty, to my country, and to the memory of my ancestor.

"'My dear Spaniards (who love me tenderly, and who are well assured of my love for them, and not jealous of the sentiments which I hold for you) are well assured that our union is the base of public tranquillity. I flatter myself that my personal interests are still dear to a nation which has nourished me in its bosom, and that a nobility who has shed so much blood to support them will always look with love on a king who feels it an honor to be obliged to them, and to have been born among them.'

"This is addressed to you, gentlemen," said the duchess, interrupting herself; and, looking round her, she continued, impatient to know the rest of the letter:

"'What, then, can your faithful subjects think of a treaty signed against me, or rather against yourself?

"'Since your exhausted finances can no longer support the current expenses of peace, it is desired that you should unite with my most mortal enemy, and should make war on me, if I do not consent to give up Sicily to the archduke. I will never subscribe to these conditions: they are insupportable to me.

"'I do not enter into the fatal, consequences of this alliance. I only beg your majesty to convoke the States-General directly, to deliberate on an affair of such great consequence.'"

"The States-General!" murmured the Cardinal de Polignac.

"Well, what does your eminence say to the States-General?" interrupted Madame de Maine, impatiently. "Has this measure the misfortune not to meet with your approbation?"

"I neither blame nor approve, madame," replied the cardinal; "I only remember that this convocation was made during the league, and that Philip came off badly."

"Men and times are changed, cardinal," replied the duchess; "we are not in 1594, but in 1718. Philip II. was Flemish, and Philip V. is French. The same results cannot take place, since the causes are different." And she went on with the letter:

"'I ask this in the name of the blood which unites us—in

the name of the great king from whom we have our origin—in the name of your people and mine. If[Pg 344] ever there was a necessity to listen to the voice of the French nation, it is now. It is indispensable to learn what they think: whether they wish to declare war on us. As I am ready to expose my life to maintain its glory and interests, I hope you will reply quickly to the propositions I make to you. The Assembly will prevent the unfortunate results which threaten us, and the forces of Spain will only be employed to sustain the greatness of France, and to fight her enemies, as I shall never employ them but to show your majesty my sincere regard and affection.'

"What do you think of that, gentlemen? Can his majesty say more?"

"He might have joined to this an epistle addressed directly to the States-General," answered the Cardinal de Polignac. "This letter, if the king had deigned to send it, would have had a great influence on their deliberations."

"Here it is," said the Prince de Cellamare, taking a paper from his pocket.

"What, prince!" cried the cardinal.

"I say that his majesty is of the same opinion as your eminence, and has sent me this letter, which is the complement of the letter which the Baron de Valef has."

"Then nothing is wanting," cried Madame de Maine.

"We want Bayonne," said the Prince de Cellamare;—"Bayonne, the door of France."

At this moment D'Avranches entered, announcing the

Duc de Richelieu.

"And now, prince, there is nothing wanting," said the Marquis de Pompadour, laughing: "for here is he who holds the key."

CHAPTER XXIII.
THE DUC DE RICHELIEU.

"At last!" cried the duchess, seeing Richelieu enter. "Are you, then, always the same? Your friends cannot count on you any more than your mistresses."

"On the contrary, madame," said Richelieu, approaching the duchess, "for to-day, more than ever, I prove to your highness that I can reconcile everything."

"Then you have made a sacrifice for us, duke," said Madame de Maine, laughing.

"Ten thousand times greater than you can imagine. Who do you think I have left?"

"Madame de Villars?" asked the duchess.

"Oh no! better than that."

"Madame de Duras?"

"No."

"Madame de Nésle?"

"Bah!"

"Madame de Polignac? Ah! pardon, cardinal."

"Go on. It does not concern his eminence."

"Madame de Soubise, Madame de Gabriant, Madame de Gacé?"

"No, no, no."

"Mademoiselle de Charolais?"

"I have not seen her since my last trip to the Bastille."

"Mademoiselle de Valois?"

"Oh! I intend her for my wife, when we have succeeded,

and I am a Spanish prince. No, madame; I have left, for your highness, the two most charming grisettes."

"Grisettes! Ah! fie!" cried the duchess, with a movement of contempt, "I did not think that you descended to such creatures."

"Creatures! two charming women! Madame Michelin and Madame Rénaud. Do you not know them? Madame Michelin, a beautiful blonde; her husband is a carpet manufacturer; I recommend him to you, duchesse. Madame Rénaud, an adorable brunette, with blue eyes and black lashes, and whose husband is—. Ma foi! I do not remember exactly—"

"What M. Michelin is, probably," said Pompadour, laughing.

"Pardon, duke," replied Madame de Maine, who had lost all curiosity for Richelieu's love adventures as soon as they traveled from a certain set, "may I venture to remind you that we met here on important business!"

"Oh, yes! we are conspiring, are we not?"

[Pg 345]"Had you forgotten it?"

"Ma foi! a conspiracy is not one of the gayest thing's in the world, therefore I forget it whenever I can; but that is nothing—whenever it is necessary I can come back to it. Now let us see: how does the conspiracy go on?"

"Here, duke, look at these letters, and you will know as much as we do."

"Oh! your highness must excuse me," said Richelieu; "but really I do not read those which are addressed to me, and I have seven or eight hundred, in the most charming writings, which I am keeping to amuse my old days. Here, Malezieux, you, who are clearness itself, give me a report."

"Well, these letters are the engagements of the Breton nobles to sustain the rights of her highness."

"Very good."

"This paper is the protestation of the nobility."

"Oh! give it me. I protest."

"But you do not know against what."

"Never mind, I protest all the same."

And, taking the paper, he wrote his name after that of Guillaume Antoine de Chastellux, which was the last signature.

"Let him alone," said Cellamare to the duchess, "Richelieu's name is useful everywhere."

"And this letter?" asked the duke, pointing to the missive of Philip V.

"That letter," continued Malezieux, "is written by King Philip himself."

"Then his Catholic majesty writes worse than I do," answered Richelieu. "That pleases me. Raffé always says it is impossible."

"If the letter is badly written, the news it contains is none the less good," said Madame de Maine, "for it is a letter begging the king of France to assemble the States-General to oppose the treaty of the quadruple alliance."

"And is your highness sure of the States-General?"

"Here is the protestation which engages the nobility. The

cardinal answers for the clergy, and there only remains the army."

"The army," said Laval, "is my affair. I have the signs-manual of twenty-two colonels."

"First," said Richelieu, "I answer for my regiment, which is at Bayonne, and which, consequently, is able to be of great service to us."

"Yes," said Cellamare, "and we reckon on it, but I heard that there was a question of changing the garrison."

"Seriously?"

"Very seriously. You understand, duke? We must be beforehand."

"Instantly—paper—ink; I will write to the Duc de Berwick. At the moment of commencing a campaign, no one will be astonished at my begging not to be removed from the theater of war."

The duchess hastened to give Richelieu what he asked, and taking a pen, presented it to him herself. The duke bowed, took the pen, and wrote a letter to the Duc de Berwick, begging that his regiment should not be removed till May.

"Now read, madame," continued the duke, passing the paper to Madame de Maine. The duchess took the letter, read it, and passed it to her neighbor, who passed it on, so that it made the round of the table. Malezieux, who had it the last, could not repress a slight smile.

"Ah! poet," said Richelieu, "you are laughing; I suppose I have had the misfortune to offend that ridiculous prude called orthography. You know I am a gentleman, and they forgot to teach me French; thinking, I suppose, that for fifteen hundred francs a year I can always have a valet-de-chambre, who could write my letters and make my verses. This will not prevent me, my dear Malezieux, from being in the Academy, not only before you, but before Voltaire."

"In which case, will your valet-de-chambre write your discourse?"

"He is working at it, and you will see that it will not be worse than those that some academicians of my acquaintance have done themselves."

"Duke," said Madame de Maine, "it will doubtless be a curious thing to see your reception into the illustrious body of which you speak, and I promise you to employ myself to-morrow in procuring a[Pg 346] seat for that day; but this evening we are occupied with other things."

"Well," said Richelieu, "speak, I listen. What have you resolved?"

"To obtain from the king, by means of these two letters, the convocation of the States-General; then, sure as we are of the three orders, we depose the regent, and name Philip V. in his place."

"And as Philip V. cannot leave Madrid, he gives us full powers, and we govern France in his stead. Well, it is not badly arranged, all that, but to convoke the States-General you must have an order from the king."

"The king will sign it."

"Without the regent's knowledge?"

"Without the regent's knowledge."

"Then you have promised the bishop of Frejus to make him a cardinal."

"No; but I will promise Villeroy a title and the Golden Fleece."

"I am afraid, madame," said the Prince of Cellamare, "that all this will not determine the marshal to undertake so grave a responsibility."

"It is not the marshal we want; it is his wife."

"Ah! you remind me," said Richelieu, "I undertake it."

"You!" said the duchess with astonishment.

"Yes, madame," replied Richelieu, "you have your correspondence, I have mine. I have seen seven or eight letters that you have received to-day. Will your highness have the goodness to look at one I received yesterday?"

"Is this letter for me only, or may it be read aloud?"

"We are among discreet people, are we not?" said Richelieu, looking round him.

"I think so," replied the duchess, "besides, the gravity of the situation."

The duchess took the letter, and read:

"'Monsieur le Duc—I am a woman of my word. My husband is on the eve of setting out for the little journey you know of. To-morrow, at eleven o'clock, I shall be at home for you only. Do not think that I decide on this step without having put all the blame on the shoulders of Monsieur de Villeroy. I begin to fear for him, as you may have undertaken to punish him. Come, then, at the appointed hour, to prove to me that I am not too much to blame in conspiring with you against my lord and master.'"

"Ah! pardon, this is not the one I intended to show you, that is the one of the day before yesterday. Here is yesterday's."

The duchess took the second letter, and read as follows:

"'My dear Armand,'

—"Is this it, or are you mistaken again?" said the duchess to Richelieu.

"No, no; this time it is right."

The duchess went on.

"'My dear Armand—You are a dangerous advocate when you plead against Monsieur de Villeroy. I need to exaggerate your talents to diminish my weakness. You had, in my heart, a judge, interested in your gaining your cause. Come to-morrow to plead again, and I will give you an audience.'

"And have you been there?"

"Certainly, madame."

"And the duchess?"

"Will do, I hope, all we desire; and, as she makes her husband do whatever she likes, we shall have our order for the convocation of the States-General on his return."

"And when will he return?"

"In a week."

"And can you be faithful all that time?"

"Madame, when I have undertaken a cause, I am capable of the greatest sacrifices to forward it."

"Then we may count on your word?"

"I pledge myself."

"You hear, gentlemen?" said the Duchesse de Maine.

"Let us continue to work. You, Laval, act on the army. You, Pompadour, on the nobility. You, cardinal, on the clergy, and let us leave the Duc de Richelieu to act on Madame de Villeroy."

"And for what day is our next meeting fixed?" asked Cellamare.

[Pg 347]"All depends on circumstances, prince," replied the duchess. "At any rate, if I have not time to give you notice, I will send the same carriage and coachman to fetch you who took you to the Arsenal the first time you came there." Then, turning toward Richelieu, "You give us the rest of the evening, duke?"

"I ask your pardon," replied Richelieu, "but it is absolutely impossible; I am expected in the Rue des Bons Enfants."

"What! have you made it up with Madame de Sabran?"

"We never quarreled, madame."

"Take care, duke; that looks like constancy."

"No, madame, it is calculation."

"Ah! I see that you are on the road toward becoming devoted."

"I never do things by halves, madame."

"Well, we will follow your example, Monsieur le Duc. And now we have been an hour and a half away, and should, I think, return to the gardens, that our absence may not be too much noticed; besides, I think the Goddess of Night is on the shore, waiting to thank us for the preference we have given her over the sun."

"With your permission, however, madame," said Laval,

"I must keep you an instant longer, to tell you the trouble I am in."

"Speak, count," replied the duchess; "what is the matter?"

"It is about our requests and our protestations. It was agreed, if you remember, that they should be printed by workmen who cannot read."

"Well."

"I bought a press, and established it in the cellar of a house behind the Val-de-Grace. I enlisted the necessary workmen, and, up to the present time, have had the most satisfactory results; but the noise of our machine has given rise to the suspicion that we were coining false money, and yesterday the police made a descent on the house; fortunately, there was time to stop the work and roll a bed over the trap, so that they discovered nothing. But as the visit might be renewed, and with a less fortunate result, as soon as they were gone I dismissed the workmen, buried the press, and had all the proofs taken to my own house."

"And you did well, count," cried the Cardinal de Polignac.

"But what are we to do now?" asked Madame de Maine.

"Have the press taken to my house," said Pompadour.

"Or mine," said Valef.

"No, no," said Malezieux; "a press is too dangerous a means. One of the police may easily slip in among the workmen, and all will be lost. Besides, there cannot be much left to print."

"The greater part is done," said Laval.

"Well," continued Malezieux, "my advice is, as before, to

employ some intelligent copyist, whose silence we can buy."

"Yes, this will be much safer," said Polignac.

"But where can we find such a man?" said the prince. "It is not a thing for which we can take the first comer."

"If I dared," said the Abbe Brigaud.

"Dare, abbe! dare!" said the duchess.

"I should say that I know the man you want."

"Did I not tell you," said Pompadour, "that the abbe was a precious man?"

"But is he really what we want?" said Polignac.

"Oh, if your eminence had him made on purpose he could not do better," said Brigaud. "A true machine, who will write everything and see nothing."

"But as a still greater precaution," said the prince, "we might put the most important papers into Spanish."

"Then, prince," said Brigaud, "I will send him to you."

"No, no," said Cellamare; "he must not set his foot within the Spanish embassy. It must be done through some third party."

"Yes, yes, we will arrange all that," said the duchess. "The man is found—that is the principal thing. You answer for him, Brigaud?"

"I do, madame."

"That is all we require. And now there is nothing to keep us any longer,"[Pg 348] continued the duchess. "Monsieur d'Harmental, give me your arm, I beg."

The chevalier hastened to obey Madame de Maine, who seized this opportunity to express her gratitude for the courage he had shown in the Rue des Bons Enfants, and his skill in Brittany. At the door of the pavilion, the Greenland envoys—now dressed simply as guests—found a little galley waiting to take them to the shore. Madame de Maine entered first, seated D'Harmental by her, leaving Malezieux to do the honors to Cellamare and Richelieu. As the duchess had said, the Goddess of Night, dressed in black gauze spangled with golden stars, was waiting on the other side of the lake, accompanied by the twelve Hours; and, as the duchess approached, they began to sing a cantata appropriate to the subject. At the first notes of the solo D'Harmental started, for the voice of the singer had so strong a resemblance to another voice, well known to him and dear to his recollection, that he rose involuntarily to look for the person whose accents had so singularly moved him; unfortunately, in spite of the torches which the Hours, her subjects, held, he could not distinguish the goddess's features, which were covered with a long veil, similar to her dress. He could only hear that pure, flexible, sonorous voice, and that easy and skillful execution, which he had so much admired when he heard it for the first time in the Rue du Temps-Perdu; and each accent of that voice, becoming more distinct as he approached the shore, made him tremble from head to foot. At length the solo ceased, and the chorus recommenced; but D'Harmental, insensible to all other thoughts, continued to follow the vanished notes.

"Well, Monsieur d'Harmental," said the duchess, "are you so accessible to the charms of music that you forget that you are my cavalier?"

"Oh, pardon, madame," said D'Harmental, leaping to the shore, and holding out his hand to the duchess, "but I thought I recognized that voice, and I confess it brought back such memories!"

"That proves that you are an habitué of the opera, my dear chevalier, and that you appreciate, as it deserves, Mademoiselle Berry's talent."

"What, is that voice Mademoiselle Berry's?" asked D'Harmental, with astonishment.

"It is, monsieur; and if you do not believe me," replied the duchess, "permit me to take Laval's arm, that you may go and assure yourself of it."

"Oh, madame," said D'Harmental, respectfully retaining the hand she was about to withdraw, "pray excuse me. We are in the gardens of Armida, and a moment of error may be permitted among so many enchantments;" and, presenting his arm again to the duchess, he conducted her toward the chateau. At this instant a feeble cry was heard, and feeble as it was, it reached D'Harmental's heart, and he turned involuntarily.

"What is it?" asked the duchess, with an uneasiness mixed with impatience.

"Nothing, nothing," said Richelieu; "it is little Berry, who has the vapors. Make yourself easy, madame. I know the disease; it is not dangerous. If you particularly wish it, I would even go to-morrow to learn how she is."

Two hours after this little accident—which was not sufficient to disturb the fete in any way—D'Harmental was brought back to Paris by the Abbe Brigaud, and re-entered his little attic in the Rue du Temps-Perdu, from which he had been absent six weeks.

CHAPTER XXIV.
JEALOUSY.

The first sensation D'Harmental experienced on returning was one of inexpressible satisfaction at finding himself again in that little room so filled with recollections. Though he had been absent six weeks, one might have supposed that he had only quitted it the day before, as, thanks to the almost maternal care of Madame Denis, everything was in its accustomed place. D'Harmental remained an instant, his candle in his hand, looking around him with a look almost of ecstasy. All the other impressions of his life were effaced by those which he had experi[Pg 349]enced in this little corner of the world. Then he ran to the window, opened it, and threw an indescribable look of love over the darkened windows of his neighbor. Doubtless Bathilde slept the sleep of an angel, unconscious that D'Harmental was there, trembling with love and hope.

He remained thus for more than half an hour, breathing the night air, which had never seemed to him so pure and fresh, and began to feel that Bathilde had become one of the necessities of his life; but as he could not pass the whole night at his window, he then closed it, and came into his room, although only to follow up the recollections with which it was filled. He opened his piano, and passed his fingers over the keys, at the risk of re-exacting the anger of the lodger on the third floor. From the piano he passed to the unfinished portrait of Bathilde. At length he slept, listening again in his mind to the air sung by Mademoiselle Berry, whom he finished by believing to be one and the same person as Bathilde. When he awoke, D'Harmental jumped from his bed and ran to the window. The day appeared already advanced; the sun was shining brilliantly; yet Bathilde's window remain hermetically closed.

The chevalier looked at his watch; it was ten o'clock, and he began to dress. We have already confessed that he was not free from a certain almost feminine coquetry; but this was the fault of the time, when everything was mannered—even passion. At this time it was not a melancholy expression on which he reckoned. The joy of return had given to his face a charming expression of happiness, and it was evident that a glance from Bathilde would crown him king of the creation. This glance he came to the window to seek, but Bathilde's remained closed. D'Harmental opened his, hoping that the noise would attract her attention; nothing stirred. He remained there an hour: during this hour there was not even a breath of wind to stir the curtains: the young girl's room must be abandoned. He coughed, opened and closed the window, detached little pieces of plaster from the wall, and threw them against the window—all in vain.

To surprise succeeded uneasiness; this window, so obstinately closed, must indicate absence, if not misfortune. Bathilde absent!—where could she be? What had happened to disturb her calm, regular life? Who could he ask? No one but Madame Denis could know. It was quite natural that D'Harmental should pay a visit to his landlady on his return, and he accordingly went down. Madame Denis had not seen him since the day of the breakfast. She had not forgotten his attention when she fainted. She received him like the prodigal son. Fortunately for D'Harmental, the young ladies were occupied with a drawing lesson, and Boniface was at his office, so that he saw no one but his hostess. The conversation fell naturally on the order and neatness of his room during his absence; from this the transition was easy to the question if the opposite lodging had changed tenants. Madame Denis replied that she had seen Bathilde at the window the morning before; and that in the evening her son had met Buvat returning from his office, but had noticed in him a singular air of pride and hauteur. This was all D'Harmental wished to know. Bathilde was in Paris, and at home; chance had not yet directed her looks toward that window so long closed, and that room so long empty. He took leave of Madame Denis with an effusion of gratitude which she was far from attributing to its true cause; and on the landing he met the Abbe Brigaud, who was coming to pay his daily visit to Madame Denis.

The abbe asked if he was going home, and promised to pay him a visit. On entering his room D'Harmental went straight to the window. Nothing was changed; it was evidently a plan, and he resolved to employ the last means which he had reserved. He sat down to the piano, and after a brilliant prelude sang the air of the cantata of Night which he had heard the evening before, and of which he had retained every note in his memory. Meanwhile he did not lose sight for an[Pg 350] instant of the inexorable window; but there was no sign. The opposite room had no echo.

But D'Harmental had produced an effect which he did not expect. Hearing applause, he turned round, and saw the Abbe Brigaud behind him.

"Ah! it is you, abbe?" said D'Harmental; "I did not know that you were so great a lover of music."

"Nor you so good a musician. Peste! my dear pupil, an air you only heard once. It is wonderful."

"I thought it very beautiful, abbe, and as I have a very good memory for sounds, I retained it."

"And then it was so admirably sung. Was it not?"

"Yes," said D'Harmental; "Mademoiselle Berry has an exquisite voice, and the first time she sings I shall go incognito to the opera."

"Is it that voice you want to hear?" asked Brigaud.——"Yes."

"Then you must not go to the opera for that."

"And where must I go?"

"Nowhere. Stay here. You are in the boxes."

"What! The Goddess of Night?"

"Is your neighbor."

"Bathilde!" cried D'Harmental. "Then I was not deceived; I recognized her. But it is impossible! How could she have been there?"

"First of all," said the abbe, "nothing is impossible; remember that, before you deny or undertake anything. Believe that everything is possible; it is the way to succeed in everything."

"But Bathilde?"

"Yes, does it not appear strange at first? Well, nothing is more simple. But it does not interest you, chevalier; let us talk of something else."

"Yes, yes, abbe; you are strangely mistaken—I am deeply interested."

"Well, my dear pupil, since you are so curious, this is the whole affair. The Abbe Chaulieu knows Mademoiselle Bathilde; is not that your neighbor's name?"

"Yes. How does the Abbe Chaulieu know her?"

"Oh! it is very simple. The guardian of this charming child is, as you know, or do not know, one of the best writers and copyists in the capital. The Abbe Chaulieu wants some one to copy his poetry, since, being blind, he is obliged to dictate in the first instance to a little lackey who cannot spell, and he has confided this important task to Buvat. By this means he has become acquainted with Mademoiselle Bathilde."

"But all this does not explain how Mademoiselle Bathilde came to Sceaux."

"Stop; every history has its commencement, its middle, and its termination."

"Abbe, you will make me swear."

"Patience, patience."

"Go on; I listen to you."

"Well, having made Mademoiselle Bathilde's acquaintance, the Abbe Chaulieu, like the rest, has felt the influence of her charms, for there is a species of magic attached to the young person in question; no one can see her without loving her."

"I know it," murmured D'Harmental.

"Then, as Mademoiselle Bathilde is full of talent, and not only sings like a nightingale, but draws like an angel, Chaulieu spoke of her so enthusiastically to Mademoiselle de Launay that she thought of employing her for the costumes of the different personages in the fete."

"This does not tell me that it was Bathilde and not Mademoiselle Berry who sang lost night."

"We are coming to it."

"Well?"

"It happened that Mademoiselle de Launay, like the rest of the world, took a violent fancy to the little witch. Instead of sending her away after the costumes were finished, she kept her three days at Sceaux. She was still there the day before yesterday, closeted with Mademoiselle de Launay, when some one entered with a bewildered air to announce that the director of the opera wished to speak to her on a matter of importance. Mademoiselle de Launay went out, leaving Bathilde alone. Bathilde, to amuse herself, went to the piano and finding both[Pg 351] the instrument and her voice in good order, began to sing a great scene from some opera, and with such perfection that Mademoiselle de Launay, returning and hearing this unexpected song, opened the door softly, listened to the air, and threw her arms round the beautiful singer's neck, crying out that she could save her life. Bathilde, astonished, asked how, and in what manner, she could render her so great a service. Then Mademoiselle de Launay told her how she had engaged Mademoiselle Berry of the opera to sing the cantata of Night on the succeeding evening, and she had fallen ill and sent to say that to her great regret her Royal Highness the Duchesse de Maine could not rely upon her, so that there would be no 'Night,' and, consequently, no fete, if Bathilde would not have the extreme goodness to undertake the aforesaid cantata.

"Bathilde, as you may suppose, defended herself with all her might, and declared that it was impossible that she should thus sing music which she did not know. Mademoiselle de Launay put the cantata before her. Bathilde said that the music seemed terribly difficult. Mademoiselle de Launay answered that for a musician of her powers nothing was difficult. Bathilde got up. Mademoiselle de Launay made her sit down again. Bathilde clasped her hands. Mademoiselle de Launay unclasped them and placed them on the piano. The piano being touched gave out a sound. Bathilde, in spite of herself, played the first bar; then the second; then the whole cantata. Then she attacked the song, and sang it to the end with an admirable justness of intonation and beauty of expression. Mademoiselle de Launay was enchanted. Madame de Maine arrived in despair at what she had heard of Mademoiselle Berry. Mademoiselle de Launay begged Bathilde to recommence the cantata. Bathilde did not dare to refuse; she played and sang like an angel. Madame de Maine joined her prayers to those of Mademoiselle de Launay. You know, chevalier, that it is impossible to refuse Madame de

Maine anything.

"Poor Bathilde was obliged to give way, and half laughing, half crying, she consented, on two conditions. The first, that she might go herself to her friend Buvat to explain her absence; the second, that she might remain at home all that evening and the next morning in order to study the unfortunate cantata. These clauses, after a long discussion, were granted, with reciprocal promises, on Bathilde's part that she would return at seven o'clock the next evening, on the part of Mademoiselle de Launay and Madame de Maine that every one should continue to believe that it was Mademoiselle Berry who sung."

"But then," asked D'Harmental, "how was the secret betrayed?"

"Oh! by an unforeseen circumstance," replied Brigaud, in that strange manner which caused one to doubt if he was in jest or earnest. "All went off capitally, as you know, till the end of the cantata, and the proof is, that having only heard it once, you are able to remember it from one end to the other. At the moment the galley which brought us from the pavilion of Aurora touched the shore, whether from emotion at having sung for the first time in public, or that she recognized among Madame de Maine's suite some one she had not expected to see there, for some unknown reason, however, the poor Goddess of Night uttered a cry and fainted in the arms of the Hours, her companions. All promises and oaths were at once forgotten; her veil was removed to throw water in her face, so that when I came up, while you were going away with her highness, I was much astonished to find, instead of Mademoiselle Berry, your pretty neighbor. I questioned Mademoiselle de Launay, and as it was impossible any longer to keep the incognito, she told me what had passed, under the seal of secrecy, which I have betrayed for you only, my dear pupil, because, I do not know why, I can refuse you nothing."

"And this indisposition?" asked D'Harmental with uneasiness.

"Oh! it was nothing; a mere momentary emotion which had no bad conse[Pg 352]quences, since, in spite of all they could say to the contrary, Bathilde would not remain another hour at Sceaux, but insisted on returning, so that they put a carriage at her disposal, and she ought to have been home an hour before us."

"Then you are sure she is at home? Thanks, abbe, that is all I wished to know."

"And now," said Brigaud, "I may go, may I not? You have no more need of me, now that you know all you wish to know."

"I do not say so, my dear Brigaud; on the contrary, stop, you will give me great pleasure."

"No, I thank you; I have got some business of my own to transact in the town, and will leave you to your reflections, my dear pupil."

"When shall I see you again?" asked D'Harmental, mechanically.

"Most likely to-morrow," answered the abbe.

"Adieu till to-morrow, then."

"Till to-morrow."

So saying, the abbe turned round, laughing his peculiar laugh, and reached the door while D'Harmental was reopening his window, determined to remain there till the next day, if necessary, and only desiring, as a reward for this long watch, to catch a single glimpse of Bathilde.

The poor gentleman was in love over head and ears.

CHAPTER XXV.
A PRETEXT.

At a few minutes past four D'Harmental saw Buvat turning the corner of the Rue du Temps-Perdu. The chevalier thought he could recognize in the worthy writer an air of greater haste than usual, and instead of holding his stick perpendicularly, as a bourgeois always does when he is walking, he held it horizontally, like a runner. As to that air of majesty which had so struck Monsieur Boniface, it had entirely vanished, and had given place to a slight expression of uneasiness. He could not be mistaken. Buvat would not return so quickly if he was not uneasy about Bathilde. Bathilde, then, was suffering.

The chevalier followed Buvat with his eyes till the moment when he disappeared in his own door. D'Harmental, with reason, imagined that Buvat would go into Bathilde's room, instead of mounting to his own, and he hoped that Buvat would open the window to admit the last rays of the sun, which had been caressing it all day.

But D'Harmental was wrong; Buvat contented himself with raising the curtain, and pressing his good round face against the window, and drumming on the panes with his hands; but even this apparition was of short duration, for he turned round suddenly, as a man does when any one calls him, and let fall the muslin curtain behind him and disappeared. D'Harmental presumed that his disappearance was caused by some appeal to his appetite, and this reminded him, that in his preoccupation about the obstinacy of that unlucky window in refusing to open, he had forgotten his own breakfast, which, it must be confessed, to the shame of his sensibility, was a very great infraction on his habits. Now, however, as there was no chance that the window would open while his neighbors were at dinner, the chevalier determined to profit by the interval by dining himself; consequently he rang for the porter, and ordered him to get from the confectioner the fattest pullet, and from the fruiterer the finest fruit that he could find. As to wine, he had still got some bottles of that which the Abbe Brigaud had sent him.

D'Harmental ate with a certain remorse. He could not understand how he could be at the same time so tormented, and have such a good appetite. Luckily he remembered reading in the works of some moralist or other that sorrow sharpened hunger wonderfully. This maxim set his conscience at rest, and the result was, that the unfortunate pullet was eaten up to the very bones.

Although the act of dining was very natural, and by no means reprehensible, D'Harmental shut the window, leaving, however, a corner of the curtain raised;[Pg 353] and, thanks to this precaution, he saw Buvat—who had doubtless finished his repast—appear at the window of his terrace. As we have said, the weather was splendid, and Buvat seemed disposed to profit by it; but as he belonged to that class of beings who enjoy nothing alone, he turned round, with a gesture, which D'Harmental took to be an invitation to Bathilde—who had doubtless followed him into his room—to come on to the terrace to him; consequently he hoped for an instant that Bathilde would appear, and he rose with a beating heart; but he was mistaken. However tempting might be the beautiful evening, and however pressing the invitations of Buvat, both were useless; but it was not thus with Mirza, who, jumping out of the window without being invited, began to bound joyously about the terrace, holding in her mouth a purple ribbon, which she caused to flutter like a streamer, and which D'Harmental recognized as the one which had fastened his neighbor's veil on the preceding night. Apparently, Buvat recognized it also, for he started off in pursuit of Mirza as fast as his little legs would allow him; a pursuit which would doubtless have been indefinitely prolonged, if Mirza had not had the imprudence to take refuge in the arbor. Buvat pursued, and an instant afterward D'Harmental saw him return with the ribbon in his hand, and after smoothing it on his knee, he folded it up, and went in, probably to deposit it in a place of safety.

The Chevalier set Mirza to eat sugar.

The Chevalier set Mirza to eat sugar.—*Page* 353.

Link to larger image

This was the moment that the chevalier had waited for; he opened his window and watched. In a minute he saw Mirza put her head out of the arbor, look about her, and jump on to the terrace; then D'Harmental called her in the most caressing and seductive tone possible. Mirza trembled at the sound of his voice, then directed her eyes toward him. At the first look she recognized the man of the bits of sugar—gave a little growl of joy—then, with a rapid gastronomic instinct, she darted through Buvat's window with a single bound, and disappeared.

D'Harmental lowered his head, and, almost at the same instant, saw Mirza coming across the street like a flash of lightning; and before he had time to shut his window, she was already scratching at the door. Luckily for D'Harmental, Mirza had the memory of sugar as strongly developed as he had that of sounds.

It will be easily understood that the chevalier did not make the charming little creature wait; and she darted into the room, bounding, and giving the most unequivocal signs of her joy at his unexpected return. As to D'Harmental, he was almost as happy as if he had seen Bathilde. Mirza was something to the young girl; she was her dearly loved greyhound, so caressed and kissed by her—who laid his head on her knees during the day, and slept on the foot of her bed during the night. The chevalier set Mirza to eat sugar, and sat down; and letting his heart speak, and his pen flow, wrote the following letter:

"Dearest Bathilde—You believe me very guilty, do you not? But you cannot know the strange circumstances in which I find myself, and which are my excuse; if I could be happy enough to see you for an instant—even for an instant—you would understand that there are in me two different persons—the young student of the attic, and the gentleman of the fetes at Sceaux. Open your window then, so that I may see you—or your door, so that I may speak to you. Let me come and sue for your pardon on my knees. I am certain that when you know how unfortunate I am, and how devotedly I love you, you will have pity on me.

"Adieu, once more; I love you more than I can express!—more than you can believe—more than you can ever imagine.

"Raoul."

This billet, which would have appeared very cold to a woman of these days, because it only said just what the writer intended, seemed sufficient to the chevalier, and was really impassioned for the epoch; thus D'Harmental folded it up, and attached it, as he had the first, to Mirza's collar; then, taking up the sugar, which the greedy little animal[Pg 354] followed with her eyes to the cupboard, where D'Harmental shut it up, the chevalier opened the door of his room, and showed Mirza, with a gesture, what there remained for her to do. Whether it was pride or intelligence, the little creature did not wait to be told twice; darted out on the staircase as if she had wings, and only stopped on the way to bite Monsieur Boniface, whom she met coming home from his office; crossed the road, and disappeared in Bathilde's house. D'Harmental remained at the window for a minute, fearing that Mirza would take his note to Buvat instead of Bathilde, but she was too intelligent for that, and he soon saw her appear in Bathilde's room. Consequently, in order not to frighten poor Bathilde too much, he shut his window, hoping that by this concession he should obtain some sign, which would indicate to him that he was pardoned.

But it did not turn out so. D'Harmental waited in vain all

the evening, and a great part of the night. At eleven o'clock, the light scarcely seen through the double curtains, still hermetically closed, went out altogether, and D'Harmental was obliged to renounce the hope of seeing Bathilde till the next day.

The next day brought the same rigor; it was a settled plan of defense, which, with a man less in love than D'Harmental, would simply have indicated fear of defeat; but the chevalier, with a simplicity worthy of the age of gold, saw nothing but a coldness, in the eternity of which he began to believe, and it is true that it had lasted four and twenty hours.

D'Harmental passed the morning in turning in his mind a thousand projects, each more absurd than the preceding one. The only one which had common sense was to cross the street, mount boldly to Bathilde's room, and tell her everything. It came to his mind like all the rest; and as it was the only reasonable one, D'Harmental did well to stop at it. However, it would be a great boldness to present himself thus before Bathilde, without being authorized by the least sign, and without having any pretext to give. Such a course of conduct could but wound Bathilde, who was only too much irritated already; it was better to wait then, and D'Harmental waited. At two o'clock Brigaud returned, and found D'Harmental in a very savage state of mind. The abbe threw a glance toward the window, still hermetically closed, and divined everything. He took a chair, and sat down opposite D'Harmental, twisting his thumbs round one another, as he saw the chevalier doing.

"My dear pupil," said he, after an instant's silence, "either I am a bad physiognomist, or I read on your face that something profoundly sad has happened to you."

"And you read right, my dear abbe," said the chevalier; "I am ennuied."

"Ah, indeed!"

"So much so," said D'Harmental, "that I am ready to send your conspiracy to the devil."

"Oh, chevalier, one must not throw the helve after the hatchet! What! send the conspiracy to the devil, when it is going on wheels! Nonsense; and what will the others say?"

"Oh, you are charming, you and your others. The others, my dear abbe, have society, balls, the opera, duels, mistresses, amusements in fact, and they are not shut up like me in a nasty garret."

"Yes; but the piano, the drawing?"

"Even with this, it is not amusing."

"Ah, it is not amusing when one sings or draws alone; but when one sings or draws in company, it begins to do better."

"And with whom, in the devil's name, should I sing or draw?"

"In the first place there are the Demoiselles Denis."

"Oh, yes, they sing beautifully and draw well, do they not?"

"Mon Dieu! I do not propose them to you as virtuosos and artists; they have not the talents of your neighbor. But, by-the-by, there is your neighbor."

"Well, my neighbor?"

"Why do you not sing with her, since she sings so well? That will amuse you."

"Do I know her? Does she even open her window? Look, since yesterday she[Pg 355] has barricaded herself in her own room. Ah, yes, my neighbor is amiable."

"Yes, they told me that she was charming."

"Besides, it seems to me, that both singing in our own rooms, we should have a singular duet."

"Then go to her room."

"To her room! Have I been introduced to her? Do I know her?"

"Well, make a pretext."

"I have been searching for one since yesterday."

"And you have not found one, a man of imagination like you? My dear pupil, I do not recognize you there."

"Listen, abbe! A truce to your pleasantries—I am not in the humor for them to-day: every one has his stupid days."

"Well, on those days one addresses one's self to one's friends."

"To one's friends—and what for?"

"To find the pretext which one has sought for vainly one's self."

"Well, then, abbe, you are my friend; find the pretext; I wait for it."

"Nothing is easier."

"Really!"

"Do you want it?"

"Take care what you engage to do."

"I engage to open your neighbor's door to you."

"In a proper manner?"

"How! do I know any others?"

"Abbe, I will strangle you if your pretext is bad."

"But it is good."

"Then you are an adorable man."

"You remember what the Comte de Laval said about the descent which the police have made upon the house in the Val-de-Grace, and the necessity he was under of sending away his workmen and burying his press?"

"Perfectly."

"You remember the determination which was come to in consequence?"

"To employ a copyist."

"Finally, you remember that I undertook to find that copyist?"

"I do."

"Well, this copyist on whom I had cast my eyes, this honest man whom I promised to discover, is discovered, and is no other than the guardian of Bathilde."

"Buvat?"

"Himself! Well, I give you full powers, you go to his house, you offer him gold, the door is opened to you on the instant, and you can sing as much as you like with Bathilde."

"My dear abbe," cried D'Harmental, "you have saved my life!"

D'Harmental took his hat, and darted toward the door; now that he had a pretext he doubted of nothing.

"Stop, stop," said Brigaud; "you do not even ask me where the good man must go for the papers in question."

"To your house, pardieu!"

"Certainly not, young man, certainly not."

"Where then?"

"At the Prince de Listhnay's, Rue du Bac, 110."

"The Prince de Listhnay! And who is he?"

"One of our own making—D'Avranches, the valet-de-chambre to Madame de Maine."

"And you think that he will play his part well?"

"Not for you, perhaps, who are accustomed to see princes, but for Buvat."

"You are right. Au revoir, abbe!"

"You find the pretext good?"

"Capital."

"Go, then, and good luck go with you."

D'Harmental descended the stairs four at a time; then, having arrived at the middle of the street, and seeing the abbe watching him from the window, he made a parting sign to him with his hand, and disappeared through the door of Bathilde's house.

CHAPTER XXVI.
COUNTERPLOTS.

On her part, as may be easily understood, Bathilde had not made such an effort without suffering from it; the poor child loved D'Harmental with all the strength of a love at seventeen, a first love. During the first month of his absence she had counted the days; during[Pg 356] the fifth week she had counted the hours; during the last week she had counted the minutes. Then it was that the Abbe Chaulieu fetched her, to take her to Mademoiselle de Launay; and as he had taken care, not only to speak of her talents, but also to tell who she was, Bathilde was received with all the consideration which was due to her, and which poor De Launay paid all the more readily from its having been so long forgotten toward herself.

This removal, which had rendered Buvat so proud, was received by Bathilde as an amusement, which might help her to pass these last moments of suspense; but when she found that Mademoiselle de Launay wished to retain her longer, when, according to her calculation, Raoul would return, she cursed the instant when the abbe had taken her to Sceaux, and would certainly have refused, if Madame de Maine herself had not interposed. It was impossible to refuse a person who, according to the ideas of the time, from the supremacy of her rank, had almost a right to command this service; but as she would have reproached herself eternally if Raoul had returned in her absence, and in returning had found her window closed, she had, as we have seen, insisted

328

on returning to study the cantata, and to explain to Buvat what had passed. Poor Bathilde! she had invented two false pretexts, to hide, under a double veil, the true motive of her return.

If Buvat had been proud when Bathilde was employed to draw the costumes for the fete, he was doubly so when he found that she was destined to play a part in it. Buvat had constantly dreamed of Bathilde's return to fortune, and to that social position of which her parents' death had deprived her, and all that brought her among the world in which she was born appeared to him a step toward this inevitable and happy result. However, the three days which he had passed without seeing her appeared to him like three centuries. At the office it was not so bad, though every one could see that some extraordinary event had happened; but it was when he came home that poor Buvat found himself so miserable.

The first day he could not eat, when he sat down to that table where, for thirteen years, he had been accustomed to see Bathilde sitting opposite to him. The next day, when Nanette reproached him, and told him that he was injuring his health, he made an effort to eat; but he had hardly finished his meal when he felt as if he had been swallowing lead, and was obliged to have recourse to the most powerful digestives to help down this unfortunate dinner. The third day Buvat did not sit down to table at all, and Nanette had the greatest trouble to persuade him to take some broth, into which she declared she saw two great tears fall. In the evening Bathilde returned, and brought back his sleep and his appetite.

Buvat, who for three nights had hardly slept, and for three days had hardly eaten, now slept like a top and ate like an ogre. Bathilde also was very joyous; she calculated that this must be the last day of Raoul's absence. He had said he should be away six weeks. She had already counted forty-one long days, and Bathilde would not admit that there could be an instant's delay; thus the next day she watched her neighbor's window constantly while studying the cantata. Carriages were rare in the Rue du Temps-Perdu, but it happened that three passed between ten and four; each time she ran breathless to the window, and each time was disappointed. At four o'clock Buvat returned, and this time it was Bathilde who could not swallow a single morsel. The time to set out for Sceaux at length arrived, and Bathilde set out deploring the fate which prevented her following her watch through the night.

When she arrived at Sceaux, however, the lights, the noise, the music, and above all the excitement of singing for the first time in public, made her—for the time—almost forget Raoul. Now and then the idea crossed her mind that he might return during her absence, and finding her window closed, would think her indifferent; but then she remembered that[Pg 357] Mademoiselle de Launay had promised her that she should be home before daylight, and she determined that Raoul should see her standing at her window directly he opened his—then she would explain to him how she had been obliged to be absent that evening, she would allow him to suspect what she had suffered, and he would be so happy

330

that he would forgive her.

All this passed through Bathilde's mind while waiting for Madame de Maine on the border of the lake, and it was in the midst of the discourse she was preparing for Raoul that the approach of the little galley surprised her. At first— in her fear of singing before such a great company—she thought her voice would fail, but she was too good an artiste not to be encouraged by the admirable instrumentation which supported her. She resolved not to allow herself to be intimidated, and abandoning herself to the inspiration of the music and the scene, she went through her part with such perfection that every one continued to take her for the singer whom she replaced, although that singer was the first at the opera, and was supposed to have no rival. But Bathilde's astonishment was great, when, after the solo was finished, she looked toward the group which was approaching her, and saw, seated by Madame de Maine, a young cavalier, so much like Raoul, that, if this apparition had presented itself to her in the midst of the song, her voice must have failed her. For an instant she doubted; but as the galley touched the shore she could do so no longer. Two such likenesses could not exist—even between brothers; and it was certain that the young cavalier of Sceaux and the young student of the attic were one and the same person.

This was not, however, what wounded Bathilde; the rank which Raoul appeared to hold, instead of removing him from the daughter of Albert du Rocher, only brought him nearer to her, and she had recognized in him, at first sight, as he had in her, the marks of high birth. What wounded her—as a betrayal of her good faith and an insult to her love—was this pretended absence, during which Raoul, forgetting the Rue du Temps-Perdu, had left his little room solitary, to mix in the fetes at Sceaux. Thus Raoul had had but an instant's caprice for her, sufficient to induce him to pass a week or two in an attic, but he had soon got tired of this life: then he had invented the pretext of a journey, declaring that it was a misfortune; but none of this was true. Raoul had never quitted Paris—or, if he had, his first visit had not been to the Rue du Temps-Perdu.

When Raoul touched the shore, and she found herself only four steps from him, and saw him whom she had supposed to be a young provincial offering his arm, in that elegant and easy manner, to the proud Madame de Maine herself, her strength abandoned her, and with that cry which had gone to D'Harmental's heart, she fainted. On opening her eyes she found near her Mademoiselle de Launay, who lavished on her every possible attention. She wished that instead of returning to Paris Bathilde should remain at Sceaux, but she was in haste to leave this place where she had suffered so much, and begged, with an accent that could not be refused, to be allowed to return, and as a carriage was in readiness to take her, she went directly. On arriving, Bathilde found Nanette waiting for her; Buvat also had wished to do so, but by twelve o'clock he was so sleepy that it was in vain he rubbed his eyes, and tried to sing his favorite song; he could not keep awake, and at length he went to bed, telling Nanette to let him know the next morning as soon as Bathilde was visible.

Bathilde was delighted to find Nanette alone; Buvat's presence would have been very irksome to her, but as soon as she found that there was no one but Nanette, Bathilde burst into tears. Nanette had expected to see her young mistress return proud and joyous at the triumph which she could not fail to obtain, and was distressed to see her in this state, but to all her questions Bathilde replied that it was nothing, absolutely nothing. Nanette saw that it was no use to insist, and went to[Pg 358] her room, which was next to Bathilde's, but could not resist the impulse of curiosity, and looking through the key-hole, she saw her young mistress kneel down before her little crucifix, and then, as by a sudden impulse, run to the window, open it, and look opposite. Nanette doubted no longer, Bathilde's grief was somehow connected with her love, and it was caused by the young man who lived opposite. Nanette was more easy; women pity these griefs, but they also know that they may come to a good end. Nanette went to sleep much more easy than if she had not been able to find out the cause of Bathilde's tears.

Bathilde slept badly; the first griefs and the first joys of love have the same results. She woke therefore with sunken eyes and pale cheeks. Bathilde would have dispensed with seeing Buvat, but he had already asked for her twice, so she took courage, and went smiling to speak to him. Buvat, however, was not deceived; he could not fail to notice her pale cheeks, and Bathilde's grief was revealed to him. She

333

denied that there was anything the matter. Buvat pretended to believe her, but went to the office very uneasy and anxious to know what could have happened to her.

When he was gone, Nanette approached Bathilde, who was sitting in her chair with her head leaning on her hand, and stood an instant before her, contemplating her with an almost maternal love; then, finding that Bathilde did not speak, she herself broke silence.

"Are you suffering still, mademoiselle?" said she.

"Yes, my good Nanette."

"If you would open the window, I think it would do you good."

"Oh! no, Nanette, thank you, the window must remain closed."

"You do not know perhaps, mademoiselle?"

"Yes, yes, Nanette, I know."

"That the young man opposite returned this morning—"

"Well, Nanette?" said Bathilde, raising her head and looking at her with severity, "what is that to me?"

"Pardon, mademoiselle," said Nanette, "but I thought—"

"What did you think?"

"That you regretted his absence, and would be glad of his return."

"You were wrong."

"Pardon, mademoiselle, but he appears so distinguished."

"Too much so, Nanette; a great deal too much so for poor Bathilde."

"Too distinguished for you, Mademoiselle!" cried

Nanette, "as if you were not worth all the noblemen in the world! besides, you are noble!"

"I know what I appear to be, Nanette—that is to say, a poor girl, with whose peace, honor, and love, every nobleman thinks he may play with impunity. You see, Nanette, that this window must be closed. I must not see this young man again."

"Mon Dieu! Mademoiselle Bathilde, you wish then to kill this poor young man with grief? This whole morning he has not moved from his window, and looks so sad that it is enough to break one's heart."

"What does his looking sad matter to me? What has he to do with me? I do not know him. I do not even know his name. He is a stranger, who has come here to stay for a few days, and who to-morrow may go away again. If I had thought anything of him I should have been wrong, Nanette; and, instead of encouraging me in a love which would be folly, you ought, on the contrary—supposing that it existed—to show me the absurdity and the danger of it."

"Mon Dieu! mademoiselle, why so? you must love some day, and you may as well love a handsome young man who looks like a king, and who must be rich, since he does not do anything."

"Well, Nanette, what would you say if this young man who appears to you so simple, so loyal, and so good, were nothing but a wicked traitor, a liar!"

"Ah, mon Dieu! mademoiselle, I should say it was impossible."

"If I told you that this young man who lives in an attic, and who shows himself at the window dressed so simply, was yester[Pg 359]day at Sceaux, giving his arm to Madame de Maine, dressed as a colonel?"

"I should say, mademoiselle, that at last God is just in sending you some one worthy of you. Holy Virgin! a colonel! a friend of the Duchesse de Maine! Oh, Mademoiselle Bathilde, you will be a countess, I tell you! and it is not too much for you. If Providence gave every one what they deserve, you would be a duchess, a princess, a queen, yes, queen of France; Madame de Maintenon was—"

"I would not be like her, Nanette."

"I do not say like her; besides, it is not the king you love, mademoiselle."

"I do not love any one, Nanette."

"I am too polite to contradict you; but never mind, you are ill; and the first remedy for a young person who is ill, is air and sun. Look at the poor flowers, when they are shut up, they turn pale. Let me open the window, mademoiselle."

"Nanette, I forbid you; go to your work and leave me."

"Very well, mademoiselle, I will go, since you drive me away," said Nanette, lifting the corner of her apron to her eye; "but if I were in that young man's place I know very well what I would do."

"And what would you do?"

"I would come and explain myself, and I am sure that even if he were wrong you would excuse him."

"Nanette," said Bathilde, "if he comes, I forbid you to

admit him; do you hear?"

"Very well, mademoiselle; he shall not be admitted, though it is not very polite to turn people away from the door."

"Polite or not, you will do as I tell you," said Bathilde, to whom contradiction gave strength; "and now go. I wish to be alone."

Nanette went out.

When she was alone, Bathilde burst into tears, for her strength was but pride. She believed herself the most unfortunate woman in the world, as D'Harmental thought himself the most unfortunate man. At four o'clock Buvat returned. Bathilde, seeing the traces of uneasiness on his good-natured face, tried all she could to tranquilize him. She smiled, she joked, she kept him company at table; but all was in vain. After dinner he proposed to Bathilde, as an amusement which nothing could resist—to take a walk on the terrace. Bathilde, thinking that if she refused Buvat would remain with her, accepted, and went up with him into his room, but when there, she remembered that she must write a letter of thanks to the Abbe Chaulieu, for his kindness in presenting her to Madame de Maine; and, leaving her guardian with Mirza, she went down. Shortly after she heard Mirza scratching at the door, and went to open it. Mirza entered with such demonstrations of joy that Bathilde understood that something extraordinary must have happened, but on looking attentively she saw the letter tied to her collar. As this was the second she had brought, Bathilde had no difficulty in guessing the writer. The temptation was too strong to be resisted, so she detached the paper with one hand, which trembled as she remembered that it probably contained the destiny of her life, while with the other she caressed Mirza, who, standing on her hind legs, appeared delighted to become so important a personage. Bathilde opened the letter, and looked at it twice without being able to decipher a single line. There was a mist before her eyes.

The letter, while it said a great deal, did not say quite enough. It protested innocence and asked for pardon; it spoke of strange circumstances requiring secrecy; but, above all, it said that the writer was madly in love. The result was, that, without completely reassuring her, it yet did her good. Bathilde, however, with a remnant of pride, determined not to relent till the next day. Since Raoul confessed himself guilty, he should be punished. Bathilde did not remember that half of this punishment recoiled upon herself. The effect of the letter, incomplete as it was, was such that when Buvat returned from the terrace he thought Bathilde looked infinitely better, and began to believe what she herself had told him in the morning, that her agitation was only caused by the emotion of the day before. Buvat went to his own room at eight o'clock, leaving Bathilde free to[Pg 360] retire at any hour she liked, but she had not the least inclination to sleep; for a long time she watched, contented and happy, for she knew that her neighbor's window was open, and by this she guessed his anxiety. Bathilde at length dreamed that Raoul was at her feet, and that he gave her such good reasons that it was she, in her turn, who asked for pardon.

Thus in the morning she awoke convinced that she had been dreadfully severe, and wondering how she could have had the courage to do so. It followed that her first movement was to run to the window and open it; but perceiving, through an almost imperceptible opening, the young man at his window, she stopped short. Would not this be too complete an avowal? It would be better to wait for Nanette; she would open the window naturally, and in this way her neighbor would not be so able to pride himself on his conquest. Nanette arrived, but she had been too much scolded the day before about this window to risk a second representation of the same scene. She took the greatest pains to avoid even touching the curtains. Bathilde was ready to cry. Buvat came down as usual to take his coffee with Bathilde, and she hoped that he at least would ask why she kept herself so shut up, and give her an opportunity to open the window. Buvat, however, had received a new order for the classification of some manuscripts, and was so preoccupied, that he finished his coffee and left the room without once remarking that the curtains were closed.

For the first time Bathilde felt almost angry with him, and thought he must have paid her very little attention not to discover that she must be half-stifled in such a close room. What was she to do? Tell Nanette to open the window? She would not do it. Open it herself she could not. She must then wait; but till when? Till the next day, or the day after perhaps, and what would Raoul think? Would he not become impatient at this exaggerated severity? Suppose he should again leave for a fortnight, for a month, for six weeks— forever; Bathilde would die, she could not live without Raoul. Two hours passed thus; Bathilde tried everything, her embroidery, her harpsichord, her drawing, but she could do nothing. Nanette came in—a slight hope returned to her, but it was only to ask leave to go out. Bathilde signed to her that she could go. Nanette was going to the Faubourg St. Antoine; she would be away two hours. What was she to do during these two hours? It would have been so delightful to pass them at the window.

Bathilde sat down and drew out the letter; she knew it by heart, but yet she read it again. It was so tender, so passionate, so evidently from the heart. Oh! if she could receive a second letter. This was an idea; she looked at Mirza, the graceful little messenger; she took her in her arms, and then, trembling as if she were about to commit a crime, she went to open the outer door. A young man was standing before this door, reaching out his hand toward the bell. Bathilde uttered a cry of joy, and the young man a cry of love—it was Raoul.

CHAPTER XXVII.
THE SEVENTH HEAVEN.

Bathilde made some steps backward, for she had nearly fallen into Raoul's arms. Raoul, having shut the door, followed Bathilde into the room. Their two names, exchanged in a double cry, escaped their lips. Their hands met in an electric clasp, and all was forgotten. These two, who had so much to say to each other, yet remained for a long time silent; at length Bathilde exclaimed—

"Oh, Raoul, how I have suffered!"

"And I," said D'Harmental, "who have appeared to you guilty, and am yet innocent!"

"Innocent!" cried Bathilde, to whom, by a natural reaction, all her doubts returned.

"Yes, innocent," replied the chevalier.

And then he told Bathilde all of his life that he dared to tell her—his duel with Lafare; how he had, after that, hidden in the Rue du Temps-Perdu; how he had seen Bathilde, and loved her; his astonishment at discovering successively in her[Pg 361] the elegant woman, the skillful painter, the accomplished musician; his joy when he began to think that she was not indifferent to him; then he told her how he had received, as colonel of carabineers, the order to go to Brittany, and on his return was obliged to render an account of his mission to the Duchesse de Maine before returning to Paris. He had gone directly to Sceaux, expecting only to leave his dispatches in passing, when he had found himself in the midst of the fete, in which he had been obliged unwillingly to take a part. This recital was finished by expressions of regret, and such protestations of fidelity and love that Bathilde almost forgot the beginning of his discourse in listening to the end.

It was now her turn. She also had a long history to tell D'Harmental; it was the history of her life. With a certain pride in proving to her lover that she was worthy of him, she showed herself as a child with her father and mother, then an orphan and abandoned; then appeared Buvat with his plain face and his sublime heart, and she told all his kindness, all his love to his pupil; she passed in review her careless childhood, and her pensive youth; then she arrived at the time when she first saw D'Harmental, and here she stopped and smiled, for she felt that he had nothing more to learn. Yet D'Harmental insisted on hearing it all from her own lips, and would not spare her a single detail. Two hours passed thus like two seconds, and they were still there when some one rang at the door. Bathilde looked at the clock which was in the corner of the room; it was six minutes past four; there was no mistake, it was Buvat. Bathilde's first movement was one of fear, but Raoul reassured her, smiling, for he had the pretext with which the Abbe Brigaud had furnished him. The two lovers exchanged a last grasp of the hand, then Bathilde went to open the door to her guardian, who, as usual, kissed her on the forehead, then, on entering the room, perceived D'Harmental. Buvat was astonished; he had never before found any man with his pupil. Buvat fixed on him his astonished eyes and waited; he fancied he had seen the young man before. D'Harmental advanced toward him with that ease of which people of a certain class have not even an idea.

"It is to Monsieur Buvat," he said, "that I have the honor of speaking?"

"To myself, sir," said Buvat, starting at the sound of a voice which he thought he recognized; "but the honor is on my side."

"You know the Abbe Brigaud?" continued D'Harmental.

"Yes, perfectly, monsieur—the—that—the—of Madame Denis, is he not?"

"Yes," replied D'Harmental, smiling; "the confessor to Madame Denis."

"Yes, I know him. A clever man."

"Did you not once apply to him to get some copies to make?"

"Yes, monsieur, for I am a copyist, at your service."

"Well," said D'Harmental, "this dear Abbe Brigaud, who is my guardian (that you may know who you are speaking to), has found an excellent customer for you."

"Ah! truly; pray take a seat, monsieur."

"Thank you."

"And who is the customer?"

"The Prince de Listhnay, Rue du Bac, 110."

"A prince, monsieur, a prince!"

"Yes; a Spaniard, who is in correspondence with the 'Madrid Mercury,' and sends all the news from Paris."

"Oh! that is a great honor."

"It will give you some trouble, however, for all the dispatches are in Spanish."

"Diable!" said Buvat.

"Do you know Spanish?" asked D'Harmental.

"No, monsieur; I do not think so, at least."

"Never mind," continued the chevalier, smiling; "one need not know a language to copy it."

"I could copy Chinese, monsieur; caligraphy, like drawing, is an imitative art."

"And I know that in this respect, Monsieur Buvat," replied D'Harmental, "you are a great artist."

[Pg 362]"Monsieur," said Buvat, "you embarrass me. May I ask, without indiscretion, at what time I shall find his highness?"

"What highness?"

"His highness the prince—I do not remember the name you said," replied Buvat.

"Ah! the Prince de Listhnay."

"Himself."

"He is not highness, my dear Monsieur Buvat."

"Oh! I thought all princes—"

"This is only a prince of the third order, and he will be quite satisfied if you call him monseigneur."

"You think so?"

"I am sure of it."

"And when shall I find him?"

"After your dinner; from five to half-past five. You remember the address?"

"Yes; Rue du Bac, 110. I will be there, monsieur."

"Now," said D'Harmental, "au revoir! And you, mademoiselle," said he, turning to Bathilde, "receive my thanks for your kindness in keeping me company while I waited for M. Buvat—a kindness for which I shall be eternally grateful."

And D'Harmental took his leave, while Bathilde remained astonished at his ease and assurance in such a situation.

"This young man is really very amiable," said Buvat.

"Yes, very," said Bathilde, mechanically.

"But it is an extraordinary thing; I think I have seen him before."

"It is possible," said Bathilde.

"And his voice—I am sure I know his voice."

Bathilde started; for she remembered the evening when Buvat had returned frightened from the adventure in the Rue des Bons Enfants, and D'Harmental had not spoken of that adventure. At this moment Nanette entered, announcing dinner. Buvat instantly went into the other room.

"Well, mademoiselle," said Nanette softly, "the handsome young man came, then, after all?"

"Yes, Nanette, yes," answered Bathilde, raising her eyes to heaven with an expression of infinite gratitude, "and I am very happy."

She passed in to the dining-room, where Buvat, who had put down his hat and stick on a chair, was waiting for her, and slapping his thighs with his hands, as was his custom in his moments of extreme satisfaction.

As to D'Harmental, he was no less happy than Bathilde; he was loved—he was sure of it; Bathilde had told him so, with the same pleasure she had felt on hearing him make the same declaration. He was loved; not by a poor orphan, not by a little grisette, but by a young girl of rank, whose father and mother had occupied an honorable position at court. There were, then, no obstacles to their union, there was no social interval between them. It is true that D'Harmental forgot the conspiracy, which might at any time open an abyss under his feet and engulf him. Bathilde had no doubts for the future; and when Buvat, after dinner, took his hat and cane to go to the Prince de Listhnay's, she first fell on her knees to thank God, and then, without hesitation, went to open the window so long closed. D'Harmental was still at his. They had very soon settled their plans, and taken Nanette into their confidence. Every day, when Buvat was gone, D'Harmental was to come and stay two hours with Bathilde. The rest of the time would be passed at the windows, or, if by chance these must be closed, they could write to each other. Toward seven o'clock they saw Buvat turning the corner of the Rue Montmartre; he carried a roll of paper in one hand, and his cane in the other, and by his important air, it was easy to see that he had spoken to the prince himself. D'Harmental closed his window. Bathilde had seen Buvat set out with some uneasiness, for she feared that this story of the Prince de Listhnay was only an invention to explain D'Harmental's presence. The joyous expression of Buvat's face, however, quite reassured her.

"Well!" said she.

"Well! I have seen his highness."

"But, you know," answered Bathilde, "that M. Raoul said the Prince de Listh[Pg 363]nay had no right to that title, and was only a prince of the third order."

"I guarantee him of the first," said Buvat, "sabre de bois! a man of five feet ten, who throws his money about, and pays for copies at fifteen francs the page, and has given twenty-five louis in advance!"

Then another fear began to come into Bathilde's mind, that this pretended customer, whom Raoul had found for Buvat, was only a pretext to induce him to accept money. This fear had in it something humiliating; Bathilde turned her eyes toward D'Harmental's window, but she saw D'Harmental looking at her with so much love through the glass, that she thought of nothing but looking at him in return, which she did for so long, that Buvat came forward to see what was attracting her attention; but D'Harmental, seeing him, let fall the curtain.

"Well, then," said Bathilde, wishing to turn off his attention, "you are content?"

"Quite; but I must tell you one thing."

"What is it?"

"You remember that I told you that I thought I recognized the face and voice of this young man, but could not tell you where I had seen or heard them?"

"Yes, you told me so."

"Well, it suddenly struck me to-day, as I was crossing the Rue des Bons Enfants, that it was the same young man whom I saw on that terrible night, of which I cannot think without trembling."

"What folly!" said Bathilde, trembling, however, herself.

"I was on the point of returning, however, for I thought this prince might be some brigand chief, and that they were going to entice me into a cavern; but as I never carry any money, I thought that my fears were exaggerated, and so I went on."

"And now you are convinced, I suppose," replied Bathilde, "that this poor young man, who came from the Abbe Brigaud, has no connection with him of the Rue des Bons Enfants."

"Certainly, a captain of thieves could have no connection with his highness; and now," continued Buvat, "you must excuse me if I do not stay with you this evening. I promised his highness to begin the copies directly, and I must do so." Buvat went into his room, leaving Bathilde free to resume the interrupted conversation. Heaven only knows at what hour the windows were closed.

CHAPTER XXVIII.
FENELON'S SUCCESSOR.

The events which were to rouse our lovers from their happy idleness were preparing in silence. The Duc de Richelieu had kept his promise. The Marshal Villeroy, who had intended to remain a week away from the Tuileries, was recalled on the fourth day by a letter from his wife, who wrote to him that his presence was more than ever necessary near the king, the measles having declared itself at Paris, and having already attacked several persons in the Palais Royal. Monsieur de Villeroy came back directly, for, it will be remembered, that all those successive deaths which three or four years before had afflicted the kingdom, had been attributed to the measles, and the marshal would not lose this opportunity of parading his vigilance. It was his privilege, as governor of the king, never to leave him except by an order from himself, and to remain with him whoever entered, even though it was the regent himself. It was especially with regard to the regent that the marshal affected such extraordinary precaution; and as this suited the hatred of Madame de Maine and her party, they praised Monsieur de Villeroy highly, and spread abroad a report that he had found on the chimney piece of Louis XV. some poisoned bon-bons which had been placed there.

The result of all this was an increase of calumny against the Duc d'Orleans, and of importance on the part of the marshal, who persuaded the young king that he owed him his life. By this means he acquired great influence over the king, who, indeed, had confidence in no one but M. de Villeroy and M. de Frejus. M. de Villeroy was then the man they wanted for the message; and it was agreed that[Pg 364] the following Monday, a day when the regent rarely saw the king, the two letters of Philip V. should be given to him, and M. de Villeroy should profit by his solitude with the king to make him sign the convocation of the States-General, and that it should be made public the next day before the hour of the regent's visit, so that there should be no means of drawing back.

While all these things were plotting against him, the regent was leading his ordinary life in the midst of his work, his studies, and his pleasures, and above all, of his family bickerings. As we have said, three of his daughters gave him serious trouble. Madame de Berry, whom he loved the best, because he had saved her when the most celebrated doctors had given her up, throwing off all restraint, lived publicly with Riom, whom she threatened to marry at every observation her father made. A strange threat, but which, if carried out, would at that time have caused far more scandal than the amours, which, at any other time, such a marriage would have sanctified.

Mademoiselle de Chartres persisted in her resolution of becoming a nun, although she still, under her novitiate, continued to enjoy all the pleasures she could manage to introduce into the cloister. She had got in her cell her guns and pistols, and a magnificent assortment of fireworks, with which she amused her young friends every evening; but she would not leave the convent, where her father went every Wednesday to visit her.

The third person of the family who gave him uneasiness was Mademoiselle de Valois, whom he suspected of being Richelieu's mistress, but without ever being able to obtain certain proof—although he had put his police on the watch, and had himself more than once paid her visits at hours when he thought it most probable he should meet him. These suspicions were also increased by her refusal to marry the Prince de Dombe, an excellent match, enriched as he was by the spoils of La Grande Mademoiselle. The regent had seized a new opportunity of assuring himself whether this refusal were caused by her antipathy to the young prince, or her love for the duke, by welcoming the overtures which Pleneuf, his ambassador at Turin, had made for a marriage between the beautiful Charlotte Aglaë and the Prince de Piedmont. Mademoiselle de Valois rebelled again, but this time in vain; the regent, contrary to his usual easy goodness, insisted, and the lovers had no hope, when an unexpected event broke it off. Madame, the mother of the regent, with her German frankness, had written to the queen of Sicily, one of her most constant correspondents, that she loved her too much not to warn her that the princess, who was destined for the young prince, had a lover, and that that lover was the Duc de Richelieu. It may be supposed that this declaration put an end to the scheme.

The regent was at first excessively angry at this result of his mother's mania for writing letters, but he soon began to laugh at this epistolary escapade, and his attention was called off for the time by an important subject, namely that of Dubois, who was determined to become an archbishop. We have seen how on Dubois's return from London, the thing had first been broached under the form of a joke, and how the regent had received the recommendation of King George; but Dubois was not a man to be beaten by a first refusal. Cambray was vacant by the death of the Cardinal la Tremouille, and was one of the richest archbishoprics in the Church. A hundred and fifty thousand francs a year were attached to it, and it was difficult to say whether Dubois was most tempted by the title of successor to Fenelon, or by the rich benefice.

Dubois, on the first opportunity, brought it again on the tapis. The regent again tried to turn it off with a joke, but Dubois became more positive, and more pressing. The regent, thinking to settle it, defied Dubois to find a prelate who would consecrate him.

"Is it only that?" cried Dubois, joyously, "then I have the man at hand."

"Impossible!" said the regent.

"You will see," said Dubois; and he ran out.

[Pg 365]In five minutes he returned.

"Well?" asked the regent.

"Well," answered Dubois, "I have got him."

"And who is the scoundrel who is willing to consecrate such another scoundrel as you?"

"Your first almoner, monseigneur."

"The bishop of Nantes!"

"Neither more nor less."

"Tressan!"

"Himself."

"Impossible!"

"Here he is."

And at this moment the door was opened, and the bishop of Nantes was announced.

"Come," cried Dubois, running to him, "his royal highness honors us both in naming me archbishop of Cambray, and in choosing you to consecrate me."

"M. de Nantes," asked the regent, "is it true that you consent to make the abbe an archbishop?"

"Your highness's wishes are commands for me."

"Do you know that he is neither deacon, archdeacon, nor priest?"

"Never mind, monseigneur," cried Dubois, "here is M. de Tressan, who will tell you all these orders may be conferred in a day."

"But there is no example of such a thing."

"Yes, Saint Ambloise."

"Then, my dear abbe," said the regent, laughing, "if you have all the fathers of the Church with you, I have nothing more to say, and I abandon you to M. de Tressan."

"I will give him back to you with the cross and miter, monseigneur."

"But you must have the grade of licentiate," continued the regent, who began to be amused at the discussion.

"I have a promise from the University of Orleans."

"But you must have attestations."

"Is there not Besons?"

"A certificate of good life and manners."

"I will have one signed by Noailles."

"No, there I defy you, abbe."

"Then your highness will give me one. The signature of the regent of France must have as much weight at Rome as that of a wicked cardinal."

"Dubois," said the regent, "a little more respect, if you please, for the princes of the Church."

"You are right, monseigneur. There is no saying what one may become."

"You, a cardinal!" cried the regent, laughing.

"Certainly. I do not see why I should not be pope some day."

"Well! Borgia was one."

"May God give us both a long life, monseigneur, and you will see that, and many other things."

"Pardieu!" said the regent, "you know that I laugh at death."

"Alas, too much."

"Well, you will make a poltroon of me by curiosity."

"It would be none the worse; and to commence, monseigneur would do well to discontinue his nocturnal excursions."

"Why?"

"In the first place because they endanger his life."

"What does that matter?"

"Then for another reason."

"What?"

"Because," said Dubois, assuming a hypocritical air, "they are a subject of scandal for the Church!"

"Go to the devil."

"You see, monsieur," said Dubois, turning to Tressan, "in the midst of what libertines and hardened sinners I am obliged to live. I hope that your eminence will consider my position, and will not be too severe upon me."

"We will do our best, monsieur," said Tressan.

"And when?" asked Dubois, who was unwilling to lose an hour.

"As soon as you are ready."

"I ask for three days."

"Very well; on the fourth I shall be at your orders."

"To-day is Saturday. On Wednesday then."

"On Wednesday," answered Tressan.

"Only I warn you beforehand, abbe,"[Pg 366] answered the regent, "that one person of some importance will be absent at your consecration."

"And who will dare to do me that injury?"

"I shall."

"You, monseigneur! You will be there, and in your official gallery."

"I say not."

"I bet a thousand louis."

"And I give you my word of honor."

355

"I double my bet."——"Insolent!"

"On Wednesday, M. de Tressan. At my consecration, monseigneur."

And Dubois left the room highly delighted, and spread about everywhere the news of his nomination. Still Dubois was wrong on one point, namely, the adhesion of the Cardinal de Noailles. No menace or promise could draw from him the attestation to good life and morals which Dubois flattered himself he should obtain at his hands. It is true that he was the only one who dared to make this holy and noble opposition to the scandal with which the Church was menaced. The University of Orleans gave the licenses, and everything was ready on the appointed day. Dubois left at five o'clock in the morning, in a hunting-dress, for Pautoix, where he found M. de Tressan, who, according to his promise, bestowed on him the deaconship, the archdeaconship, and the priesthood. At twelve all was finished; and at four, after having attended the regent's council, which was held at the old Louvre in consequence of the measles having, as we have said, attacked the Tuileries, Dubois returned home in the dress of an archbishop.

The first person whom he saw in his room was La Fillon. In her double quality of attachée to his secret police and to his public loves, she had admittance to his room at all hours; and in spite of the solemnity of the day, as she had said that she had business of importance to communicate, they had not dared to refuse her.

"Ah!" cried Dubois, on perceiving his old friend, "a lucky

meeting."

"Pardieu! my dear gossip," answered La Fillon, "if you are ungrateful enough to forget your old friends I am not stupid enough to forget mine, particularly when they rise in the world."

"Ah! tell me," said Dubois, beginning to pull off his sacerdotal ornaments, "do you count on continuing to call me your gossip now that I am an archbishop?"

"More than ever. And I count on it so strongly that the first time the regent enters my house I shall ask him for an abbey, that we may still be on an equality one with the other."

"He comes to your house then? the libertine!"

"Alas! no more, my dear gossip. Ah! the good time is passed. But I hope that, thanks to you, it will return, and that the house will feel your elevation."

"Oh! my poor gossip," said Dubois, stooping down in order that La Fillon might unclasp his frock, "you see that now things are much changed, and that I can no longer visit you as I used to."

"You are proud. Philippe comes there."

"Philippe is only regent of France, and I am an archbishop. Do you understand? I want a mistress at a house where I can go without scandal; like Madame de Tencin, for example."

"Yes, who will deceive you for Richelieu."

"And how, on the contrary, do you know that she will not deceive Richelieu for me?"

"Hey-day! and will she manage your police and your love at the same time?"

"Perhaps. But apropos of police," answered Dubois, continuing to undress, "do you know that yours have slept infernally during three or four months, and that if this continues I shall be obliged to withdraw you from the superintendence?"

"Ah! diable!" cried La Fillon; "this is the way you treat your old friends. I come to make a revelation; well, you shall not know it."

"A revelation! and what about?"

"Pshaw! take away my superintendence; scoundrel that you are."

"Is it relating to Spain?" asked the archbishop, frowning, and feeling instinctively that the danger came from thence.

"It relates to nothing at all. Good-evening."

[Pg 367]And La Fillon made toward the door.

"Come here," said Dubois, stepping toward his desk; and the two old friends, who understood each other so well, looked toward each other and laughed.

"Come, come," said La Fillon, "I see that all is not lost, and that there is yet some good in you. Come, open this little desk and show me what it contains, and I will open my mouth and show you what I have in my heart."

Dubois took out a rouleau of a hundred louis, and showed it to La Fillon.

"How much is it?" said she; "come, tell the truth; however, I shall count after you, to be sure."

"Two thousand four hundred francs; that is a pretty penny, it seems to me."

"Yes, for an abbe, but not for an archbishop."

"Do you not know to what an extent the finances are involved?"

"Well, what does that matter, you humbug, when Law is going to make millions for us?"

"Would you like in exchange ten thousand francs in Mississippi bonds?"

"Thanks, my dear, I prefer the hundred louis; give them to me; I am a good woman, and another day you will be more generous."

"Well, what have you to tell me? Come."—"First promise me one thing."

"What is it?"

"That as it is about an old friend, he shall come to no harm."

"But if your old friend is a beggar who deserves to be hanged, why should you cheat him of his due?"

"I have my own reasons."

"Go along; I promise nothing."

"Well, good-evening then. Here are the hundred louis."

"Ah! you are getting scrupulous all at once."

"Not at all; but I am under obligations to this man; he started me in the world."

"He may boast of having done a good thing for society that day."

"Rather, my friend; and he shall never have cause to repent it, for I will not speak a word to-day unless his life is safe."

"Well, safe it shall be, I promise you; are you content?"

"By what do you promise it me?"

"On the faith of an honest man."

"Ah! you are going to deceive me."

"Do you know that you are very tiresome?"

"Oh! I am very tiresome. Well, good-by."

"Gossip, I will have you arrested."

"What do I care?"

"You shall be sent to prison."

"That is a good joke."

"I will leave you to die there."

"Till you do it yourself. It will not be long."

"Well, what do you want?"

"My captain's life."

"You shall have it."

"On what faith?"

"On the faith of an archbishop."

"I want a better."

"On the faith of an abbe."

"Better still."

"On the faith of Dubois."

"That will do."

"First, I must tell you that my captain is the most out at elbows of any in the kingdom."

"Diable! he has a rival."

"Still, he will have the prize."

"Continue."

"Well, you must know that lately he has become as rich

as Crœsus."

"He must have robbed some millionaire."

"Incapable. Killed maybe—but robbed! What do you take him for?"

"Do you know where the money comes from?"

"Do you know the different coinages?"

"Yes."

"Where does this come from, then?"

"Ah! a Spanish doubloon."

"And without alloy, with the effigy of King Charles II. Doubloons which are worth forty-eight francs if they are worth a penny, and which run from his pockets like a stream, poor dear fellow."

"And when did he begin to sweat gold?"

"The day after the regent was nearly carried off in the Rue des Bons Enfants.[Pg 368] Do you understand the apologue, gossip?"

"Yes; and why have you not told me before to-day?"

"Because his pockets were full then; they are now nearly empty, which is the time to find out where he will fill them again."

"And you wished to give him time to empty them?"

"Well, all the world must live."

"And so they shall; even your captain. But you understand that I must know what he does?"

"Day by day."

"And which of your girls does he love?"

"All when he has money."

"And when he has none?"

"La Normande."

"I know her; she is as sharp as a needle."

"Yes, but you must not reckon on her."

"Why not?"

"She loves him, the little fool."

"Ah! he is a lucky fellow."

"And he merits it. He has got the heart of a prince, not like you, old miser."

"Oh! you know that sometimes I am worse than the prodigal son, and it depends on you to make me so."

"I will do my best."

"Then day by day I shall know what your captain does?"

"You shall."

"On what faith?"

"On the faith of an honest woman."

"Something better."

"On the faith of Fillon."

"That will do."

"Adieu, monseigneur the archbishop."

"Adieu, gossip."

La Fillon was going toward the door, when at that moment an usher entered.

"Monseigneur," said he, "here is a man who wants to speak to your eminence."

"And who is he, idiot?"

"An employé of the royal library, who, in his spare time, makes copies."

"And what does he want?"

"He says that he has an important revelation to make to your eminence."

"Oh! it is some poor fellow begging."

"No, monseigneur; he says that it is a political affair."

"Diable! about what?"

"Relative to Spain."

"Send him in; and you, gossip, go into this closet."

"What for?"

"Suppose my writer and your captain should know each other?"

"Ah, that would be droll."

"Come, get in quickly."

La Fillon entered the closet which Dubois showed her.

An instant afterward, the usher opened the door and announced Monsieur Jean Buvat.

We must now show how this important personage came to be received in private audience by the archbishop of Cambray.

CHAPTER XXIX.
THE PRINCE DE LISTHNAY'S ACCOMPLICE.

We left Buvat going up to his own room, with his papers in his hand, to fulfill his promise to the Prince de Listhnay, and this promise was so scrupulously kept, that by seven o'clock the next evening the copy was finished and taken to the Rue du Bac. He then received from the same august hands some more work, which he returned with the same punctuality; so that the Prince de Listhnay, feeling confidence in a man who had given such proofs of exactitude, gave him at once sufficient papers to necessitate an interval of three or four days between this interview and the next. Buvat was delighted with this mark of confidence, and, on his return, set himself gayly to his work; and, although he found that he did not understand a word of Spanish, he could now read it fluently, and had become so accustomed to it, that he felt quite disappointed when he found among the copies one all in French. It had no number, and almost appeared to have slipped in by mistake; but he resolved, nevertheless, to copy it. He began with these lines:

"Confidential.

"For his Excellency Monsieur Alberoni in person.

"Nothing is more important than to[Pg 369] make sure of the places near the Pyrenees, and of the noblemen who reside in these cantons."

"In these cantons!" repeated Buvat, after having written it; then, taking a hair from his pen, he continued:

"To gain or master the garrison of Bayonne."

"What is that?" said Buvat. "Is not Bayonne a French town? Let us see—let us see;" and he continued:

"The Marquis de P—— is governor of D——. One knows the intentions of that nobleman; when it is decided, it will be necessary for him to triple his expenditure, in order to attract the aristocracy: he ought to scatter rewards.

"In Normandy, Charenton is an important post. Pursue the same course with the governor of that town as with the Marquis of P——; go further—promise his officers suitable rewards.

"Do the same in all the provinces."

"Hallo!" cried Buvat, re-reading what he had just written; "what does this mean? It seems to me that it would be prudent to read it all before going further."

"He read:

"To supply this expenditure one ought to be able to reckon on at least three hundred thousand francs the first month, and afterward a hundred thousand per month, paid to the day."

"Paid to the day!" murmured Buvat, breaking off. "It is evidently not by France that these payments are to be made, since France is so poor that she has not paid me my nine hundred francs' salary for five years. Let us see—let us see;" and he recommenced:

"That expenditure, which will cease at the peace, will enable his Catholic majesty to act with certainty in case of war.

"Spain will only be an auxiliary. The army of Philip V. is in France."

"What! what! what!" cried Buvat; "and I did not even know that it had crossed the frontier."

"The army of Philip V. is in France. A body of about ten thousand Spaniards is more than sufficient, with the presence of the king.

"But we must be able to count on being able to seduce over at least half of the Duc d'Orleans' army (Buvat trembled). This is the most important, and cannot be done without money. A present of one hundred thousand francs is necessary for each battalion or squadron.

"Twenty battalions would be two millions; with that sum one might form a trustworthy army, and destroy that of the enemy.

"It is almost certain, that the subjects most devoted to the king of Spain will not be employed in the army which will march against him. Let them disperse themselves through the provinces; there they will act usefully. To resupply them with a character—if they have none—it will be necessary for his Catholic majesty to send his orders in blank, for his minister in Paris to fill up.

"In consequence of the multiplicity of orders, it would be better if the ambassador had the power to sign for the king of Spain.

"It would be well, moreover, if his majesty were to sign his orders as a French prince; the title is his own.

"Prepare funds for an army of thirty thousand men,

whom his majesty will find brave, skillful, and disciplined.

"This money should arrive in France at the end of May, or the commencement of June, and be distributed directly in the capitals of provinces, such as Nantes, Bayonne, etc.

"Do not allow the French ambassador to leave Spain. His presence will answer for the safety of those who declare themselves."

"Sabre de bois!" cried Buvat, rubbing his eyes; "but this is a conspiracy—a conspiracy against the person of the regent, and against the safety of the kingdom. Oh! oh!"

Buvat fell into profound meditation.

Indeed the position was critical. Buvat mixed up in a conspiracy—Buvat charged with a state secret—Buvat holding in his hands, perhaps, the fate of nations: a smaller thing would have thrown him into a state of strange perplexity.

Thus seconds, minutes, hours flowed[Pg 370] away, and Buvat remained on his chair, his head drooping, his eyes fixed on the floor, and perfectly still. From time to time, however, a deep breath—like an expression of astonishment—escaped his breast.

Ten o'clock, eleven—midnight sounded. Buvat thought that the night would bring him aid, and he determined to go to bed. It is needless to say that his copying came to an end, when he saw that the original was assuming an illegal character.

Buvat could not sleep; the poor fellow tossed from side to side, but scarcely had he shut his eyes, before he saw this horrible plan of the conspiracy written upon the wall in letters of fire. Once or twice, overcome by fatigue, he fell asleep; but he had no sooner lost consciousness, than he dreamed, the first time that he was arrested by the watch as a conspirator; the second that he was stabbed by the conspirators themselves. The first time Buvat awoke trembling; the second time bathed in perspiration. These two impressions had been so terrible, that he lighted his candle, and determined to wait for day, without another attempt to sleep.

The day came, but, far from dispelling the phantoms of the night, it only gave a more terrific reality. At the least noise Buvat trembled. Some one knocked at the street-door. Buvat thought he should faint. Nanette opened his room door, and he uttered a cry. Nanette ran to him, and asked what was the matter, but he contented himself with shaking his head, and answering, with a sigh—

"Ah, my poor Nanette, we live in very sad times."

He stopped directly, fearing he had said too much. He was too preoccupied to go down to breakfast with Bathilde; besides, he feared lest the young girl should perceive his uneasiness, and ask the cause; and as he did not know how to keep anything from her, he would have told her all, and she would then have become his accomplice. He had his coffee sent up to him, under pretext of having an overwhelming amount of work to do, and that he was going to work during breakfast. As Bathilde's love profited by this absence, she was rather pleased at it than otherwise.

A few minutes before ten, Buvat left for his office; his fears had been strong in his own house, but once in the street, they changed into terrors. At every crossing, at the end of every court, behind every angle, he thought that he saw the police-officers waiting for him. At the corner of the Place des Victoires a musketeer appeared, coming from the Rue Pagevin, and Buvat gave such a start on seeing him, that he almost fell under the wheels of a carriage. At last, after many alarms, he reached the library, bowed almost to the ground before the sentinel, darted up the stairs, gained his office, and falling exhausted on his seat, he shut up in his drawer all the papers of the Prince de Listhnay, which he had brought with him, for fear the police should search his house during his absence; and finding himself in safety, heaved a sigh, which would not have failed in denouncing him to his colleagues as being a prey to the greatest agitation, if he had not, as usual, arrived the first.

Buvat had a principle, which was, that no personal preoccupation, whether grave or gay, ought to disturb a clerk in the execution of his duty. Therefore he set himself to his work, apparently as if nothing had happened, but really in a state of moral perturbation impossible to describe.

This work consisted, as usual, in classifying and arranging books. There having been an alarm of fire three or four days before, the books had been thrown on the floor, or carried out of the reach of the flames, and there were consequently four or five thousand volumes to be reinstated in their proper places; and, as it was a particularly tedious business, Buvat had been selected for it, and had hitherto acquitted himself with an intelligence and assiduity which had merited the commendations of his superiors, and the raillery of his colleagues.

In spite of the urgency of the work, Buvat rested some minutes to recover himself; but as soon as he saw the door open, he rose instinctively, took a pen,[Pg 371] dipped it in the ink, took a handful of parchment labels, and went toward the remaining books, took the first which came to hand, and continued his classification, murmuring between his teeth, as was his habit under similar circumstances.

"The 'Breviary of Lovers,' printed at Liege in 1712; no printer's name. Ah, mon Dieu! what amusement can Christians possibly find in reading such books? It would be better if they were all burned in the Place de Grève by the hand of the public hangman! Chut! What name have I been pronouncing there! I wonder who this Prince de Listhnay, who has made me copy such things, is; and the young man who, under pretense of doing me a service, introduced me to such a scoundrel. Come, come, this is not the place to think about that. How pleasant it is writing on parchment; the pen glides as if over silk. What is the next?"

"Well, monsieur," said the head clerk, "and what have you been doing for the last five minutes, with your arms crossed and your eyes fixed?"

"Nothing, M. Ducoudray, nothing. I was planning a new mode of classification."

"A new mode of classification! Are you turned reformer? Do you wish to commence a revolution, M. Buvat?"

"I! a revolution!" cried Buvat, with terror. "A revolution,

monsieur!—never, oh, never! Good heavens, my devotion to monseigneur the regent is known; a disinterested devotion, since he has not paid me for five years, as you know."

"Well, go on with your work."

Buvat continued:—"'Conspiracy of Monsieur de Cinq Mars'—diable! diable! I have heard of that. He was a gallant gentleman, who was in correspondence with Spain; that cursed Spain. What business has it to mix itself up eternally with our affairs? It is true that this time it is said that Spain will only be an auxiliary; but an ally who takes possession of our towns, and who debauches our soldiers, appears to me very much like an enemy. 'Conspiracy of Monsieur de Cinq-Mars, followed by a History of his Death, and that of Monsieur de Thou, condemned for not revealing it. By an Eye-Witness.' For not revealing! It is true, no doubt, for the law is positive. Whoever does not reveal is an accomplice—myself, for instance. I am the accomplice of the Prince de Listhnay; and if they cut off his head, they will cut off mine too. No, they will only hang me—I am not noble. Hanged!—it is impossible; they would never go to such extremities in my case: besides, I will declare all. But then I shall be an informer: never! But then I shall be hanged—oh, oh!"

"What is the matter, Buvat?" said a clerk: "you are strangling yourself by twisting your cravat."

"I beg your pardon, gentlemen," said Buvat, "I did it mechanically; I did not mean to offend you."

Buvat stretched out his hand for another book. "'Conspiracy of the Chevalier Louis de Rohan.' Oh, I come to nothing but conspiracies! 'Copy of a Plan of Government found among the Papers of Monsieur de Rohan, and entirely written by Van der Enden.' Ah, mon Dieu! yes. That is just my case. He was hanged for having copied a plan. Oh, I shall die! 'Procès-verbal of the Torture of Francis-Affinius Van der Enden.' If they read one day, at the end of the conspiracy of the Prince de Listhnay, 'Procès-verbal of the Torture of Jean Buvat!'" Buvat began to read.

"Well, well, what is the matter, Buvat?" said Ducoudray, seeing the good man shake and grow pale: "are you ill?"

"Ah, M. Ducoudray," said Buvat, dropping the book, and dragging himself to a seat, "ah, M. Ducoudray, I feel I am going to faint."

"That comes of reading instead of working," said an employé.

"Well, Buvat, are you better?" asked Ducoudray.

"Yes, monsieur, for my resolution is taken, taken irrevocably. It would not be just, by Heaven, that I should bear the punishment for a crime which I never committed. I owe it to society, to my ward, to myself. M. Ducoudray, if the[Pg 372] curator asks for me, you will tell him that I am gone out on pressing business."

And Buvat drew the roll of paper from the drawer, pressed his hat on to his head, took his stick, and went out with the majesty of despair.

"Do you know where he has gone?" asked the employé.

"No," answered Ducoudray.

"I will tell you;—to play at bowls at the Champs-Elysées,

or at Porcherons."

The employé was wrong; he had neither gone to the Champs-Elysées nor to Porcherons. He had gone to Dubois.

CHAPTER XXX.
THE FOX AND THE GOOSE.

"M. Jean Buvat," said the usher. Dubois stretched out his viper's head, darted a look at the opening which was left between the usher and the door, and, behind the official introducer, perceived a little fat man, pale, and whose legs shook under him, and who coughed to give himself assurance. A glance sufficed to inform Dubois the sort of person he had to deal with.

"Let him come in," said Dubois.

The usher went out, and Jean Buvat appeared at the door.

"Come in, come in," said Dubois.

"You do me honor, monsieur," murmured Buvat, without moving from his place.

"Shut the door, and leave us," said Dubois to the usher.

The usher obeyed, and the door striking the posterior part of Buvat, made him bound a little way forward. Buvat, shaken for an instant, steadied himself on his legs, and became once more immovable, looking at Dubois with an astounded expression.

In truth, Dubois was a curious sight. Of his episcopal costume he had retained the inferior part; so that he was in his shirt, with black breeches and violet stockings. This disagreed with all Buvat's preconceived notions. What he had before his eyes was neither a minister nor an archbishop, but seemed much more like an orang-outang than a man.

"Well, monsieur," said Dubois, sitting down and crossing

his legs, and taking his foot in his hand, "you have asked to speak to me. Here I am."

"That is to say," said Buvat, "I asked to speak to Monseigneur the Archbishop of Cambray."

"Well, I am he."

"How! you, monseigneur?" cried Buvat, taking his hat in both hands, and bowing almost to the ground: "excuse me, but I did not recognize your eminence. It is true that this is the first time I have had the honor of seeing you. Still—hum! at that air of majesty—hum, hum—I ought to have understood—"

"Your name?" asked Dubois, interrupting the good man's compliments.

"Jean Buvat, at your service."

"You are—?"

"An employé at the library."

"And you have some revelations to make to me concerning Spain?"

"That is to say, monseigneur—This is how it is. As my office work leaves me six hours in the evening and four in the morning, and as Heaven has blessed me with a very good handwriting, I make copies."

"Yes, I understand," said Dubois; "and some one has given you suspicious papers to copy, so you have brought these suspicious papers to me, have you not?"

"In this roll, monseigneur, in this roll," said Buvat, extending it toward Dubois.

Dubois made a single bound from his chair to Buvat,

took the roll, and sat down at a desk, and in a turn of the hand, having torn off the string and the wrapper, found the papers in question. The first on which he lighted were in Spanish; but as Dubois had been sent twice to Spain, and knew something of the language of Calderon and Lopez de Vega, he saw at the first glance how important these papers were. Indeed, they were neither more nor less than the protestation of the nobility, the list of officers who requested commissions under the king of Spain, and the manifesto prepared by the Cardinal de Polignac and the Marquis de Pompadour to rouse the kingdom. These different documents were addressed direct[Pg 373]ly to Philip V.; and a little note—which Dubois recognized as Cellamare's hand writing—announced that the denouement of the conspiracy was near at hand; he informed his Catholic majesty, from day to day, of all the important events which could advance or retard the scheme. Then came, finally, that famous plan of the conspirators which we have already given to our readers, and which—left by an oversight among the papers which had been translated into Spanish—had opened Buvat's eyes. Near the plan, in the good man's best writing, was the copy which he had begun to make, and which was broken off at the words, "Act thus in all the provinces."

Buvat had followed all the working of Dubois's face with a certain anxiety; he had seen it pass from astonishment to joy, then from joy to impassibility. Dubois, as he continued to read, had passed, successively, one leg over the other, had bitten his lips, pinched the end of his nose, but all had been utterly untranslatable to Buvat, and at the end of the reading he understood no more from the face of the archbishop than he had understood at the end of the copy from the Spanish original. As to Dubois, he saw that this man had come to furnish him with the beginning of a most important secret, and he was meditating on the best means of making him furnish the end also. This was the signification of the crossed legs, the bitten lips, and the pinched nose. At last he appeared to have taken his resolution. A charming benevolence overspread his countenance, and turning toward the good man, who had remained standing respectfully—

"Take a seat, my dear M. Buvat," said he.

"Thank you, monseigneur," answered Buvat, trembling; "I am not fatigued."

"Pardon, pardon," said Dubois, "but your legs shake."

Indeed, since he had read the procès-verbal of the question of Van der Enden, Buvat had retained in his legs a nervous trembling, like that which may be observed in dogs that have just had the distemper.

"The fact is, monseigneur," said Buvat, "that I do not know what has come to me the last two hours, but I find a great difficulty in standing upright."

"Sit down, then, and let us talk like two friends."

Buvat looked at Dubois with an air of stupefaction, which, at any other time, would have had the effect of making him burst out laughing, but now he did not seem to notice it, and taking a chair himself, he repeated with his hand the invitation which he had given with his voice. There was no means of drawing back; the good man approached trembling, and sat down on the edge of his chair; put his hat on the ground, took his cane between his legs, and waited. All this, however, was not executed without a violent internal struggle as his face testified, which, from being white as a lily when he came in, had now become as red as a peony.

"My dear M. Buvat, you say that you make copies?"

"Yes, monseigneur."

"And that brings you in—?"

"Very little, monseigneur, very little."

"You have, nevertheless, a superb handwriting, M. Buvat."

"Yes, but all the world does not appreciate the value of that talent as your eminence does."

"That is true, but you are employed at the library?"——"I have that honor."

"And your place brings you—?"

"Oh, my place—that is another thing, monseigneur; it brings me in nothing at all, seeing that for five years the cashier has told us at the end of each month that the king was too poor to pay us."

"And you still remained in the service of his majesty? that was well done, M. Buvat; that was well done."

Buvat rose, saluted Dubois, and reseated himself.

"And, perhaps, all the while you have a family to support—a wife, children?"

"No, monseigneur; I am a bachelor."

"But you have parents, at all events?"

"No, monseigneur; but I have a ward, a charming young

person, full of talent, who sings like Mademoiselle Berry, and who draws like Greuze."

"Ah, ah! and what is the name of your ward, M. Buvat?"

[Pg 374]"Bathilde—Bathilde du Rocher, monseigneur; she is a young person of noble family, her father was squire to Monsieur the Regent, when he was still Duc de Chartres, and had the misfortune to be killed at the battle of Almanza."

"Thus I see you have your charges, my dear Buvat."

"Is it of Bathilde that you speak, monseigneur? Oh no, Bathilde is not a charge; on the contrary, poor dear girl, she brings in more than she costs. Bathilde a charge! Firstly, every month M. Papillon, the colorman at the corner of the Rue Clery, you know, monseigneur, gives her eighty francs for two drawings; then—"

"I should say, my dear Buvat, that you are not rich."

"Oh! rich, no, monseigneur, I am not, but I wish I was, for poor Bathilde's sake; and if you could obtain from monseigneur, that out of the first money which comes into the State coffers he would pay me my arrears, or at least something on account—"

"And to how much do your arrears amount?"

"To four thousand seven hundred francs, two sous, and eight centimes, monseigneur."

"Is that all?" said Dubois.

"How! is that all, monseigneur?"

"Yes, that is nothing."

"Indeed, monseigneur, it is a great deal, and the proof is that the king cannot pay it."

"But that will not make you rich."

"It will make me comfortable, and I do not conceal from you, monseigneur, that if, from the first money which comes into the treasury—"

"My dear Buvat," said Dubois, "I have something better than that to offer you."

"Offer it, monseigneur."

"You have your fortune at your fingers' ends."

"My mother always told me so, monseigneur."

"That proves," said Dubois, "what a sensible woman your mother was."

"Well, monseigneur! I am ready; what must I do?"

"Ah! mon Dieu! the thing is very simple, you will make me, now, and here, copies of all these."

"But, monseigneur—"

"That is not all, my dear Monsieur Buvat. You will take back to the person who gave you these papers, the copies and the originals, you will take all that that person gives you; you will bring them to me directly, so that I may read them, then you will do the same with other papers as with these, and so on indefinitely, till I say enough."

"But, monseigneur, it seems to me that in acting thus I should betray the confidence of the prince."

"Ah! it is with a prince that you have business, Monsieur Buvat! and what may this prince be called?"

"Oh, monseigneur, it appears to me that in telling you his name I denounce—"

"Well, and what have you come here for, then?"

"Monseigneur, I have come here to inform you of the danger which his highness runs, that is all."

"Indeed," said Dubois, in a bantering tone, "and you imagine you are going to stop there?"

"I wish to do so, monseigneur."

"There is only one misfortune, that it is impossible, my dear Monsieur Buvat."

"Why impossible?"

"Entirely."

"Monseigneur, I am an honest man."

"M. Buvat, you are a fool."

"Monseigneur, I still wish to keep silence."

"My dear monsieur, you will speak."

"And if I speak I shall be the informer against the prince."

"If you do not speak you are his accomplice."

"His accomplice, monseigneur! and of what crime?"

"Of the crime of high treason. Ah! the police have had their eyes on you this long time, M. Buvat!"

"On me, monseigneur?"

"Yes, on you; under the pretext that they do not pay you your salary, you entertain seditious proposals against the State."

[Pg 375]"Oh! monseigneur, how can they say so?"

"Under the pretext of their not paying you your salary, you have been making copies of incendiary documents for the last four days."

"Monseigneur, I only found it out yesterday; I do not understand Spanish."

381

"You do understand it, monsieur?"

"I swear, monseigneur."

"I tell you you do understand it, and the proof is that there is not a mistake in your copies. But that is not all."

"How, not all?"

"No, that is not all. Is this Spanish? Look, monsieur," and he read:

"'Nothing is more important than to make sure of the places in the neighborhood of the Pyrenees, and the noblemen who reside in the cantons.'"

"But, monseigneur, it was just by that that I made the discovery."

"M. Buvat, they have sent men to the galleys for less than you have done."

"Monseigneur!"

"M. Buvat, men have been hanged who were less guilty than you."

"Monseigneur! monseigneur!"

"M. Buvat, they have been broken on the wheel."

"Mercy, monseigneur, mercy!"

"Mercy to a criminal like you, M. Buvat! I shall send you to the Bastille, and Mademoiselle Bathilde to Saint Lazare."

"To Saint Lazare! Bathilde at Saint Lazare, monseigneur! Bathilde at Saint Lazare! and who has the right to do that?"——"I, M. Buvat."

"No, monseigneur, you have not the right!" cried Buvat, who could fear and suffer everything for himself, but who, at the thought of such infamy, from a worm became a serpent.

"Bathilde is not a daughter of the people, monseigneur! Bathilde is a lady of noble birth, the daughter of a man who saved the life of the regent, and when I represent to his highness—"

"You will go first to the Bastille, M. Buvat," said Dubois, pulling the bell so as nearly to break it, "and then we shall see about Mademoiselle Bathilde."

"Monseigneur, what are you doing?"

"You will see." (The usher entered.) "An officer of police, and a carriage."

"Monseigneur!" cried Buvat, "all that you wish—"

"Do as I have bid you," said Dubois.

The usher went out.

"Monseigneur!" said Buvat, joining his hands; "monseigneur, I will obey."

"No, M. Buvat. Ah! you wish a trial, you shall have one. You want a rope, you shall not be disappointed."

"Monseigneur," cried Buvat, falling on his knees, "what must I do?"

"Hang, hang, hang!" continued Dubois.

"Monseigneur," said the usher, returning, "the carriage is at the door, and the officer in the anteroom."

"Monseigneur," said Buvat, twisting his little legs, and tearing out the few yellow hairs which he had left, "monseigneur, will you be pitiless!"

"Ah! you will not tell me the name of the prince?"

"It is the Prince de Listhnay, monseigneur."

"Ah! you will not tell me his address?"

"He lives at No. 110, Rue du Bac, monseigneur."

"You will not make me copies of those papers?"

"I will do it, I will do it this instant," said Buvat; and he went and sat down before the desk, took a pen, dipped it in the ink, and taking some paper, began the first page with a superb capital. "I will do it, I will do it, monseigneur; only you will allow me to write to Bathilde that I shall not be home to dinner. Bathilde at the Saint Lazare?" murmured Buvat between his teeth, "Sabre de bois! he would have done as he said."

"Yes, monsieur, I would have done that, and more too, for the safety of the State, as you will find out to your cost, if you do not return these papers, and if you do not take the others, and if you do not bring a copy here every evening."

"But, monseigneur," cried Buvat, in despair, "I cannot then go to my office."

"Well then, do not go to your office."

"Not go to my office! but I have not[Pg 376] missed a day for twelve years, monseigneur."

"Well, I give you a month's leave."

"But I shall lose my place, monseigneur."

"What will that matter to you, since they do not pay you?"

"But the honor of being a public functionary, monseigneur; and, moreover, I love my books, I love my table, I love my hair seat," cried Buvat, ready to cry; "and to think that I shall lose it all!"

"Well, then, if you wish to keep your books, your table, and your chair, I should advise you to obey me."

"Have I not already put myself at your service?"

"Then you will do what I wish?"

"Everything."

"Without breathing a word to any one?"

"I will be dumb."

"Not even to Mademoiselle Bathilde?"

"To her less than any one, monseigneur."

"That is well. On that condition I pardon you."

"Oh, monseigneur!"

"I shall forget your fault."

"Monseigneur is too good."

"And, perhaps, I will even reward you."

"Oh, monseigneur, what magnanimity!"

"Well, well, set to work."

"I am ready, monseigneur. I am ready."

And Buvat began to write in his most flowing hand, and never moving his eyes, except from the original to the copy, and staying from time to time to wipe his forehead, which was covered with perspiration. Dubois profited by his industry to open the closet for La Fillon, and signing to her to be silent, he led her toward the door.

"Well, gossip," whispered she, for in spite of his caution she could not restrain her curiosity; "where is your writer?"

"There he is," said Dubois, showing Buvat, who, leaning over his paper, was working away industriously.

"What is he doing?"

"Guess."

"How should I know?"

"Then you want me to tell you?"

"Yes."

"Well, he is making my cardinal's hat."

La Fillon uttered such an exclamation of surprise that Buvat started and turned round; but Dubois had already pushed her out of the room, again recommending her to send him daily news of the captain.

But the reader will ask what Bathilde and D'Harmental were doing all this time. Nothing—they were happy.

CHAPTER XXXI.
A CHAPTER OF SAINT-SIMON.

Four days passed thus, during which Buvat—remaining absent from the office on pretext of indisposition—succeeded in completing the two copies, one for the Prince de Listhnay, the other for Dubois. During these four days—certainly the most agitated of his life—he was so taciturn and gloomy that Bathilde several times asked him what was the matter; but as he always answered nothing, and began to sing his little song, Bathilde was easily deceived, particularly as he still left every morning as if to go to the office—so that she saw no material alteration from his ordinary habits.

As to D'Harmental, he received every morning a visit from the Abbe Brigaud, announcing that everything was going on right; and as his own love affairs were quite as prosperous, D'Harmental began to think that to be a conspirator was the happiest thing on the earth.

As to the Duc d'Orleans, suspecting nothing, he continued his ordinary life, and had invited the customary guests to his Sunday's supper, when in the afternoon Dubois entered his room.

"All, it is you, abbe! I was going to send to you to know if you were going to make one of us to-night."

"You are going to have a supper then, monseigneur?" asked Dubois.

"Where do you come from with your fast-day face? Is not to-day Sunday?"

"Yes, monseigneur."

"Well, then, come back to us; here is the list of the guests. Nocé, Lafare, Fargy, Ravanne, Broglie; I do not invite[Pg 377] Brancas: he has been wearisome for some days. I think he must be conspiring. Then La Phalaris, and D'Averne, they cannot bear each other; they will tear out each other's eyes, and that will amuse us. Then we shall have La Souris, and perhaps Madame de Sabran, if she has no appointment with Richelieu."

"This is your list, monseigneur?"

"Yes."

"Well, will your highness look at mine now?"———"Have you made one, too?"

"No, it was brought to me ready made."

"What is this?" asked the regent, looking at a paper which Dubois presented to him.

"'Nominal list of the officers who request commissions in the Spanish army: Claude Francois de Ferrette, Knight of Saint Louis, field marshal and colonel of cavalry; Boschet, Knight of Saint Louis, and colonel of infantry, De Sabran, De Larochefoucault-Gondrel, De Villeneuve, De Lescure, De Laval.' Well, what next?"

"Here is another;" and he presented a second letter to the duke.

"'Protestation of the nobility.'"

"Make your lists, monseigneur, you are not the only one, you see—the Prince de Cellamare has his also."

"Signed without distinction of ranks, so that there may

be no dissatisfaction:—De Vieux-Pont, De la Pailleterie, De Beaufremont, De Latour-du-Pin, De Montauban, Louis de Caumont, Claude de Polignac, Charles de Laval, Antoine de Chastellux, Armand de Richelieu.' Where did you fish up all this, you old fox?"

"Wait, monseigneur, we have not done yet. Look at this."

"'Plan of the conspirators: Nothing is more important than to make sure of the strong places near the Pyrenees, to gain the garrison of Bayonne.' Surrender our towns! give the keys of France into the hands of the Spanish! What does this mean, Dubois?"

"Patience, monseigneur; we have better than that to show you; we have here the letters from his majesty Philip V. himself."

"'To the king of France—' But these are only copies."

"I will tell you soon where the originals are."

"Let us see, my dear abbe, let us see. 'Since Providence has placed me on the throne of Spain,' etc., etc. 'In what light can your faithful subjects regard the treaty which is signed against me?' etc., etc. 'I beg your majesty to convoke the States-General of the kingdom.' Convoke the States-General! In whose name?"

"In the name of Philip V."

"Philip V. is king of Spain and not of France. Let him keep to his own character. I crossed the Pyrenees once to secure him on his throne; I might cross them a second time to remove him from it."

"We will think of that later—I do not say no; but for the

present we have the fifth piece to read—and not the least important as you will see."

And Dubois presented another paper to the regent, which he opened with such impatience that he tore it in opening it.

"Never mind," said Dubois, "the pieces are good; put them together and read them."

The regent did so, and read—

"'Dearly and well beloved.'

"Ah!" said the regent, "it is a question of my deposition, and these letters, I suppose, were to be given to the king?"

"To-morrow, monseigneur."

"By whom?"——"The marshal."

"Villeroy?"

"Himself."

"How did he determine on such a thing?"

"It was not he; it was his wife, monseigneur."

"Another of Richelieu's tricks?"

"You are right, monseigneur."

"And from whom do you get these papers?"

"From a poor writer to whom they have been given to be copied, since, thanks to a descent made on Laval's house, a press which he had hidden in the cellar has ceased to work."

"And this writer is in direct communication with Cellamare? The idiots!"

[Pg 378]"Not at all, monseigneur; their measures are better taken. The good man has only had to deal with the Prince de Listhnay."

"Prince de Listhnay! Who is he?"

"Rue du Bac, 110."

"I do not know him."

"Yes, you do, monseigneur."

"Where have I seen him?"

"In your antechamber."

"What! this pretended Prince de Listhnay?"

"Is no other than that scoundrel D'Avranches, Madame de Maine's valet-de-chambre."

"Ah! I was astonished that she was not in it."

"Oh! she is at the head, and if monseigneur would like to be rid of her and her clique, we have them all."

"Let us attend to the most pressing."

"Yes, let us think of Villeroy. Have you decided on a bold stroke?"

"Certainly. So long as you confine yourself to parading about like a man at a theater or a tournament, very well; so long as you confine yourself to calumnies and impertinences against me, very good; but when it becomes a question of the peace and tranquillity of France, you will find, Monsieur le Marechal, that you have already compromised them sufficiently by your military inaptitude, and we shall not give you an opportunity of doing so again by your political follies."

"Then," said Dubois, "we must lay hold of him?"

"Yes; but with certain precautions. We must take him in the act."

"Nothing easier. He goes every morning at eight o'clock to the king."

"Yes."

"Be to-morrow at half-past seven at Versailles."

"Well?"

"You will go to his majesty before him."———"Very well."

The regent and Dubois talked for some little time longer, after which Dubois took his leave.

"There is no supper this evening," said Dubois to the usher, "give notice to the guests; the regent is ill."

That evening at nine o'clock the regent left the Palais Royal, and, contrary to his ordinary habit, slept at Versailles.

CHAPTER XXXII.
A SNARE.

The next day, about seven o'clock in the morning, at the time when the king rose, an usher entered his majesty's room and announced that his royal highness, Monseigneur le Duc d'Orleans, solicited the honor of assisting at his toilet. Louis XV., who was not yet accustomed to decide anything for himself, turned toward Monsieur de Frejus, who was seated in the least conspicuous corner of the room, as if to ask what he should say; and to this mute question Monsieur de Frejus not only made a sign with his head signifying that it was necessary to receive his royal highness, but rose and went himself to open the door. The regent stopped a minute on the doorstep to thank Fleury, then having assured himself by a rapid glance round the room that the Marshal de Villeroy had not yet arrived, he advanced toward the king.

Louis XV. was at this time a pretty child of nine or ten years of age, with long chestnut hair, jet-black eyes, and a mouth like a cherry, and a rosy complexion like that of his mother, Mary of Savoy, duchesse de Burgundy, but which was liable to sudden paleness. Although his character was already very irresolute, thanks to the contradictory influences of the double government of the Marshal de Villeroy and Monsieur de Frejus, he had something ardent in his face which stamped him as the great-grandson of Louis XIV.; and he had a trick of putting on his hat like him. At first, warned against the Duc d'Orleans as the man in all France from whom he had most to fear, he had felt that prejudice yield little by little during the interviews which they had had together, in which, with that juvenile instinct which so rarely deceives children, he had recognized a friend.

On his part, it must be said that the Duc d'Orleans had for the king, beside the respect which was his due, a love the most attentive and the most tender. The[Pg 379] little business which could be submitted to his young mind he always presented to him with so much clearness and talent, that politics, which would have been wearisome with any one else, became a recreation when pursued with him, so that the royal child always saw his arrival with pleasure. It must be confessed that this work was almost always rewarded by the most beautiful toys which could be found, and which Dubois, in order to pay his court to the king, imported from Germany and England. His majesty therefore received the regent with his sweetest smile, and gave him his little hand to kiss with a peculiar grace, while the archbishop of Frejus, faithful to his system of humility, had sat down in the same corner where he had been surprised by the arrival of the regent.

"I am very glad to see you, monsieur," said Louis XV. in a sweet little voice, from which even the etiquette which they imposed upon him could not entirely take away all grace; "and all the more glad to see you from its not being your usual hour. I presume that you have some good news to tell me."

"Two pieces, sire," answered the regent; "the first is, that

I have just received from Nuremberg a chest which seems to me to contain—"

"Oh, toys! lots of toys! does it not, Monsieur le Regent?" cried the king, dancing joyously, and clapping his hands, regardless of his valet-de-chambre who was waiting for him, and holding the little sword with a cut-steel handle which he was going to hang in the king's belt. "Oh, the dear toys! the beautiful toys! how kind you are! Oh! how I love you, Monsieur le Regent!"

"Sire, I only do my duty," answered the Duc d'Orleans, bowing respectfully, "and you owe me no thanks for that."

"And where is it, monsieur? Where is this pretty chest?"

"In my apartments, sire; and if your majesty wishes it brought here, I will send it during the course of the day, or to-morrow morning."

"Oh! no; now, monsieur; now, I beg."

"But it is at my apartments."

"Well, let us go to your apartments," cried the child, running to the door, and forgetting that he wanted, in order to complete his toilet, his little sword, his little satin jacket, and his cordon-bleu.

"Sire," said Frejus, advancing, "I would remark that your majesty abandons yourself too entirely to the pleasure caused by the possession of things that you should already regard as trifles."

"Yes, monsieur; yes, you are right," said Louis XV., making an effort to control himself; "but you must pardon me; I am only ten years old, and I worked hard yesterday."

"That is true," said Monsieur de Frejus; "and so your majesty will employ yourself with the toys when you have asked Monsieur le Regent what the other piece of news which he came to bring you is."

"Ah! yes. By-the-by, what is the second affair?"

"A work which will be profitable to France, and which is of so much importance that I think it most necessary to submit it to your majesty."

"Have you it here?" asked the king.

"No, sire; I did not expect to find your majesty so well inclined to work, and I left it in my study."

"Well," said Louis XV., turning half toward Monsieur de Frejus, half toward the regent, and looking at both of them with an imploring eye, "cannot we reconcile all that? Instead of taking my morning walk, I will go and see these beautiful Nuremberg toys, and when we have seen them we will pass into your study and work."

"It is against etiquette, sire," answered the regent, "but if your majesty wishes it—"

"Oh, I do wish it! That is," added he, turning and looking at Frejus so sweetly that there was no resisting it, "if my good preceptor permits it."

"Does Monsieur de Frejus see anything wrong in it?" said the regent, turning toward Fleury, and pronouncing these words with an accent which showed that the preceptor would wound him deeply by[Pg 380] refusing the request which his royal pupil made him.

"No, monseigneur," said Frejus; "quite the contrary. It

is well that his majesty should accustom himself to work; and if the laws of etiquette are a little violated, that violation will bring about a happy result for the people. I only ask of monseigneur the permission to accompany his majesty."

"Certainly, monsieur," said the regent, "with the greatest pleasure."

"Oh, how good! how kind!" cried Louis XV. "Quick! my sword, my jacket, my cordon-bleu. Here I am, Monsieur le Regent;" and he advanced to take the regent's hand. But instead of allowing that familiarity, the regent bowed, and, opening the door, signed to the king to precede him, following three or four paces behind, hat in hand, together with Frejus.

The king's apartments, situated on the ground floor, were level with those of the Duc d'Orleans, and were only separated by an antechamber, opening into the king's rooms, and a gallery leading from thence to the antechamber of the regent. The distance was short, therefore, and—as the king was in haste to arrive—they found themselves in an instant in a large study, lighted by four windows, all forming doors, which opened into the garden. This large study led to a smaller one, where the regent generally worked, and where he brought his most intimate friends and his favorites. All his highness's court was in attendance—a very natural circumstance, since it was the hour for rising. The king, however, did not notice either Monsieur d'Artagnan, captain of the Gray Musketeers, or the Marquis de Lafare, captain of the Guards, or a very considerable number of the Light

Horse, who were drawn up outside the windows. It is true that on a table in the middle of the room, he had seen the welcome chest, whose monstrous size had, in spite of the chilling exhortation of Monsieur de Frejus, caused him to give a cry of joy.

However, he was obliged to contain himself, and receive the homage of Monsieur d'Artagnan and Monsieur de Lafare; meanwhile the regent had called two valets-de-chambre, who quickly opened the lid, and displayed the most splendid collection of toys which had ever dazzled the eyes of a king of nine years old. At this tempting sight, the king forgot alike perceptor, guards, and Gray Musketeers. He hastened toward this paradise which was opened to him, and, as from an inexhaustible mine, he drew out successively locks, three-deckers, squadrons of cavalry, battalions of infantry, pedlars with their packs, jugglers with their cups; in fact, all those wonders, which, on Christmas eve, turn the heads of all children beyond the Rhine; and that, with such undisguised transports of joy, that Monsieur de Frejus himself respected his royal pupil's happiness. The assistants watched him with that religious silence which surrounds great griefs or great joys. While this silence was the most profound, a violent noise was heard in the antechamber, the door was opened, an usher announced the Duke de Villeroy, and the marshal appeared, loudly demanding to see the king. As they were, however, accustomed to such proceedings, the regent merely pointed to his majesty, who was still continuing to empty the chest, covering the furniture and floor with the splendid toys.

The marshal had nothing to say; he was nearly an hour late; the king was with Monsieur Frejus, but he approached him, grumbling, and throwing round him glances, which appeared to say that he was there ready to protect his majesty from all danger.

The regent exchanged glances with D'Artagnan and Lafare; every thing went well.

The chest was emptied—and, after having allowed the king to enjoy for an instant the sight of all his treasures—the regent approached him, and, still hat in hand, recalled to his mind the promise he had made to devote an hour to the consideration of State affairs.

Louis XV., with that scrupulousness which afterward led him to declare that punctuality was the politeness of kings,[Pg 381] threw a last glance over his toys; and then merely asking permission to have them removed to his apartments, advanced toward the little study, and the regent opened the door. Then, according to their different characters, Monsieur de Fleury, under pretext of his dislike of politics, drew back, and sat down in a corner, while the marshal darted forward, and, seeing the king enter the study tried to follow him. This was the moment that the regent had impatiently expected.

"Pardon, marshal," said he, barring the passage; "but I wish to speak to his majesty on affairs which demand the most absolute secrecy, and therefore I beg for a short tete-à-tete."

"Tete-à-tete!" cried Villeroy; "you know, monseigneur, that it is impossible."

"And why impossible?" asked the regent, calmly.

"Because, as governor to his majesty, I have the right of accompanying him everywhere."

"In the first place, monsieur," replied the regent, "this right does not appear to me to rest on any very positive proof, and if I have till now tolerated—not this right, but this pretension—it is because the age of the king has hitherto rendered it unimportant; but now that his majesty has nearly completed his tenth year, and that I am permitted to commence instructing him on the science of government, in which I am his appointed preceptor, you will see that it is quite right that I, as well as Monsieur de Frejus and yourself, should be allowed some hours of tete-à-tete with his majesty. This will be less painful to you to grant, marshal," added the regent, with a smile, the expression of which it was impossible to mistake, "because, having studied these matters so much yourself, it is impossible that you can have anything left to learn."

"But, monsieur," said the marshal, as usual forgetting his politeness as he became warm, "I beg to remind you that the king is my pupil."

"I know it, monsieur," said the regent, in the same tone; "make of his majesty a great captain, I do not wish to prevent you. Your campaigns in Italy and Flanders prove that he could not have a better master; but, at this moment it is not a question of military science, but of a State secret, which can only be confided to his majesty; therefore, again I beg to speak to the king in private."

"Impossible, monseigneur!" cried the marshal.

"Impossible!" replied the regent; "and why?"

"Why?" continued the marshal; "because my duty is not to lose sight of the king for a moment, and because I will not permit it."

"Take care, marshal," interrupted the Duc d'Orleans, haughtily: "you are forgetting your proper respect toward me."

"Monseigneur," continued the marshal, becoming more and more angry, "I know the respect which I owe to your royal highness, and I also know what I owe to my charge, and to the king, and for that reason I will not lose sight of his majesty for an instant, inasmuch as—"

The duke hesitated.

"Well, finish," said the regent.

"Inasmuch as I answer for his person," said the marshal.

At this want of all restraint, there was a moment's silence, during which nothing was heard but the grumblings of the marshal, and the stifled sighs of Monsieur de Fleury.

As to the Duc d'Orleans, he raised his head with a sovereign air of contempt, and, taking that air of dignity which made him, when he chose, one of the most imposing princes in the world:

"Monsieur de Villeroy," said he, "you mistake me strangely, it appears, and imagine that you are speaking to some one else; but since you forget who I am, I must endeavor to remind you. Marquis de Lafare," continued he, addressing his captain of the guards, "do your duty."

Then the Marshal de Villeroy, seeing on what a precipice he stood, opened his mouth to attempt an excuse, but the regent left him no time to finish his sentence, and shut the door in his face.

The Marquis de Lafare instantly approached the marshal, and demanded his[Pg 382] sword. The marshal remained for an instant as if thunderstruck. He had for so long a time been left undisturbed in his impertinence that he had begun to think himself invincible. He tried to speak, but his voice failed him, and, on the second, and still more imperative demand, he gave up his sword. At the same moment a door opens, and a chair appears; two musketeers push the marshal into it—it is closed. D'Artagnan and Lafare place themselves at each side, and the prisoner is carried off through the gardens. The Light Horse follow, and, at a considerable and increasing speed they descend the staircase, turn to the left, and enter the orangery. There the suite remain, and the chair, its porters, and tenant, enter a second room, accompanied only by Lafare and D'Artagnan. The marshal, who had never been remarkable for sang-froid, thought himself lost.

"Gentlemen," cried he, turning pale, while perspiration and powder ran down his face, "I hope I am not going to be assassinated!"

"No, no, make yourself easy," said Lafare, while D'Artagnan could not help laughing at his ridiculous figure—"something much more simple, and infinitely less tragic."

"What is it, then?" asked the marshal, whom this assurance rendered a little more easy.

"There are two letters, monsieur, which you were to have given to the king this morning, and which you must have in one of your pockets."

The marshal, who, till that moment, in his anxiety about himself, had forgotten Madame de Maine's affairs, started, and raised his hands to the pocket where the letters were.

"Your pardon," said D'Artagnan, stopping his hand, "but we are authorized to inform you—in case you should feel inclined to remove these letters—that the regent has copies of them."

"I may add," said Lafare, "that we are authorized to take them by force, and are absolved in advance from all accidents that may happen in such a struggle."

"And you assure me," said the marshal, "that the regent has copies of these letters?"

"On my word of honor," said D'Artagnan.

"In this case," replied Villeroy, "I do not see why I should prevent you from taking these letters, which do not regard me in the least, and which I undertook to deliver to oblige others."

"We know it," said Lafare.

"But," added the marshal, "I hope you will inform his royal highness of the ease with which I submitted to his orders, and of my regret for having offended him."

"Do not doubt it; all will be reported as it has passed. But these letters?"

"Here they are, monsieur," said the marshal, giving two letters to Lafare.

Lafare assured himself by the seals that they were really the letters he was in search of. "My dear D'Artagnan," said he, "now conduct the marshal to his destination, and give orders, in the name of the regent, that he is to be treated with every respect."

The chair was closed, and the porters carried it off. At the gate of the gardens a carriage with six horses was waiting, in which they placed the marshal, who now began to suspect the trap which had been laid for him. D'Artagnan seated himself by him, an officer of musketeers and Du Libois, one of the king's gentlemen, opposite; and with twenty musketeers at each side, and twelve following, the carriage set off at a gallop. Meanwhile, the Marquis of Lafare returned to the chateau with the two letters in his hand.

CHAPTER XXXIII.
THE BEGINNING OF THE END.

The same day, toward two o'clock in the afternoon, while D'Harmental, profiting by Buvat's absence, was repeating to Bathilde for the thousandth time that he loved her, Nanette entered, and announced that some one was waiting in his own room on important business. D'Harmental, anxious to know who this inopportune visitor could be, went to the window, and saw the Abbe Brigaud walk[Pg 383]ing up and down his room. D'Harmental instantly took leave of Bathilde, and went up to his own apartments.

"Well," said the abbe, "while you are quietly making love to your neighbor, fine things are happening."

"What things?" asked D'Harmental.

"Do you not know?"

"I know absolutely nothing, except that—unless what you have to tell me is of the greatest importance—I should like to strangle you for having disturbed me; so take care, and if you have not any news worthy of the occasion, invent some."

"Unfortunately," replied the abbe, "the reality leaves little to the imagination."

"Indeed, my dear abbe," said D'Harmental, "you look in a terrible fright. What has happened? Tell me."

"Oh, only that we have been betrayed by some one. That the Marshal de Villeroy was arrested this morning at Versailles, and that the two letters from Philip V. are in the hands of the regent."

D'Harmental perfectly understood the gravity of the situation, but his face exhibited the calmness which was habitual to him in moments of danger.

"Is that all?" he asked, quietly.

"All for the present; and, if you do not think it enough, you are difficult to satisfy."

"My dear abbe," said D'Harmental, "when we entered on this conspiracy, it was with almost equal chances of success and failure. Yesterday, our chances were ninety to a hundred; to-day they are only thirty; that is all."

"I am glad to see that you do not easily allow yourself to be discouraged," said Brigaud.

"My dear abbe," said D'Harmental, "at this moment I am a happy man, and I see everything on the bright side. If you had taken me in a moment of sadness, it would have been quite the reverse, and I should have replied 'Amen' to your 'De Profundis.'"

"And your opinion?"

"Is that the game is becoming perplexed, but is not yet lost. The Marshal de Villeroy is not of the conspiracy, does not even know the names of the conspirators. Philip V.'s letters—as far as I remember them—do not name anybody; and the only person really compromised is the Prince de Cellamare. The inviolability of his character protects him from any real danger. Besides, if our plan has reached the Cardinal Alberoni, Monsieur de Saint-Aignan must serve as hostage."

"There is truth in what you say."

"And from whom have you this news?" asked the chevalier.

"From Valef, who had it from Madame de Maine; who, on receipt of the news, went to the Prince of Cellamare himself."

"We must see Valef."

"I have appointed him to meet me here, and on my way I stopped at the Marquis de Pompadour's. I am astonished that he is not here before me."

"Raoul," said a voice on the staircase.

"Stay, it is he," cried D'Harmental, running to the door and opening it.

"Thank you," said Valef, "for your assistance, which is very seasonable, for I was just going away, convinced that Brigaud must have made a mistake, and that no Christian could live at such a height, and in such a pigeon-hole. I must certainly bring Madame de Maine here, that she may know what she owes you."

"God grant," said the Abbe Brigaud, "that we may not all be worse lodged a few days hence!"

"Ah! you mean the Bastille! It is possible, abbe; but at least one does not go to the Bastille of one's own accord; moreover, it is a royal lodging, which raises it a little, and makes it a place where a gentleman may live without degradation; but a place like this—fie, abbe!"

"If you knew what I have found here," said D'Harmental, a little piqued, "you would be as unwilling to leave it as I am."

"Ah, some little bourgeoise; some Madame Michelin,

perhaps. Take care, D'Harmental; these things are only allowed to Richelieu. With you and me, who are perhaps worth as much as he is, but are unfortunately not quite so much in fashion, it will not do."

"Well," said the Abbe Brigaud, "al[Pg 384]though your conversation is somewhat frivolous, I hear it with pleasure, since it assures me that our affairs are not so bad as I thought."

"On the contrary, the conspiracy is gone to the devil."

"How so?"

"I scarcely thought they would leave me time to bring you the news."

"Were you nearly arrested then, Valef?" asked D'Harmental.

"I only escaped by a hair's breadth."

"How did it happen, baron?"

"You remember, abbe, that I left you to go to the Prince de Cellamare?"

"Yes."

"Well, I was there when they came to seize his papers."

"Have they seized the prince's papers?"

"All except what we burned, which unfortunately were the smaller number."

"Then we are all lost," said the abbe.

"Why, my dear abbe, how you throw the helve after the hatchet!"

"But, Valef, you have not told us how it happened," said D'Harmental.

"My dear chevalier, imagine the most ridiculous thing

in the world. I wish you had been there: we should have laughed fit to kill ourselves. It would have enraged that fellow Dubois."

"What! was Dubois himself at the ambassador's?"

"In person, abbe. Imagine the Prince de Cellamare and I quietly sitting by the corner of the fire, taking out letters from a little casket, and burning those which seemed to deserve the honors of an auto-da-fé, when all at once his valet-de-chambre enters, and announces that the hotel of the embassy is invested by a body of musketeers, and that Dubois and Leblanc wish to speak to him. The object of this visit is not difficult to guess. The prince—without taking the trouble to choose—empties the caskets into the fire, pushes me into a dressing closet, and orders that they shall be admitted. The order was useless. Dubois and Leblanc were at the door. Fortunately, neither one nor the other had seen me."

"Well, I see nothing droll as yet," said Brigaud.

"This is just where it begins," replied Valef. "Remember that I was in the closet, seeing and hearing everything. Dubois entered, and stretching out his weasel's head to watch the Prince de Cellamare, who, wrapped in his dressing-gown, stood before the fire to give the papers time to burn.

"'Monsieur,' said the prince, in that phlegmatic manner you know he has, 'may I know to what event I owe the honor of this visit?'

"'Oh, mon Dieu, monseigneur!' said Dubois, 'to a very simple thing—a desire which Monsieur Leblanc and I had to learn a little of your papers, of which,' added he, showing the letters of Philip V., 'these two patterns have given us a foretaste.'"

"How!" said Brigaud, "these letters seized at ten o'clock at Versailles are in Dubois's hands at one o'clock!"

"As you say, abbe. You see that they traveled faster than if they had been put in the post."

"And what did the prince say then?" asked D'Harmental.

"Oh! the prince wished to carry it off with a high hand, by appealing to his rights as an envoy; but Dubois, who is not wanting in a certain logic, showed him that he had himself somewhat violated these rights, by covering the conspiracy with his ambassador's cloak. In short, as he was the weakest, he was obliged to submit to what he could not prevent. Besides, Leblanc, without asking permission, had already opened the desk, and examined its contents, while Dubois drew out the drawers of a bureau and rummaged in them. All at once Cellamare left his place, and stopping Leblanc, who had just taken a packet of papers tied with red ribbon—

"'Pardon, monsieur,' said he, 'to each one his prerogatives. These are ladies' letters.'

"'Thanks for your confidence,' said Dubois, not in the least disconcerted, but rising and taking the papers from the hand of Leblanc, 'I am accustomed to these sort of secrets, and yours shall be well kept.'

Buvat found himself in a sort of laboratory, situated onthe ground-floor.

Buvat found himself in a sort of laboratory, situated on the ground-floor.—*Page 406.*

Link to larger image

[Pg 385]"At this moment, looking toward the fire, he saw—in the midst of the burned letters—a paper still untouched, and darting toward it, he seized it just as the flames were reaching it. The movement was so rapid that the ambassador could not prevent it, and the paper was in Dubois's hands.

"'Peste!' said the prince, seeing Dubois shaking his fingers, 'I knew that the regent had skillful spies, but I did not know that they were brave enough to go in the fire.'

"'Ma foi! prince,' said Dubois, unfolding the paper, 'they are well rewarded for their bravery, see.'

"The prince cast his eyes over the paper; I do not know what it contained, but I know that the prince turned pale as death; and that, as Dubois burst out laughing, Cellamare broke in pieces a little marble statue which was near his hand.

"'I am glad it was not I,' said Dubois, coldly, and putting the paper in his pocket.

"'Every one in turn, monsieur; Heaven is just!' said the ambassador.

"'Meanwhile,' said Dubois, 'as we have got what we wanted, and have not much time to lose to-day, we will set about affixing the seals.'

"'The seals here!' cried the ambassador, exasperated.

"'With your permission,' replied Dubois; 'proceed, Monsieur Leblanc.'

"'Leblanc drew out from a bag bands and wax, all ready prepared. They began operations with the desk and the

411

bureau, then they advanced toward the door of my closet.

"'No,' cried the prince, 'I will not permit—'

"'Gentlemen,' said Dubois, opening the door, and introducing into the room two officers of musketeers, 'the ambassador of Spain is accused of high treason against the State. Have the kindness to accompany him to the carriage which is waiting, and take him—you know where; if he resists, call eight men, and take him by force.'"

"Well, and what did the prince do then?" asked Brigaud.

"What you would have done in his place, I presume, my dear abbe. He followed the two officers, and five minutes afterward your humble servant found himself under seal."

"How the devil did you get out?" cried D'Harmental.

"That is the beauty of it. Hardly was the prince gone, when Dubois called the valet-de-chambre.

"'What are you called?' asked Dubois.

"'Lapierre, at your service, monseigneur.'

"'My dear Leblanc,' said Dubois, 'explain, if you please, to Monsieur Lapierre, what are the penalties for breaking seals.'

"'The galleys,' replied Leblanc.

"'My dear Monsieur Lapierre,' continued Dubois, in a mild tone, 'you hear. If you like to spend a few years rowing on one of his majesty's vessels, touch one of these seals and the affair is done. If, on the contrary, a hundred louis are agreeable to you, keep them faithfully, and in three days the money shall be given you.'

"'I prefer the hundred louis,' said the scoundrel.

"'Well, then, sign this paper. We constitute you guardian

of the prince's cabinet.'

"'I am at your orders, monseigneur,' replied Lapierre; and he signed.

"'Now,' said Dubois, 'you understand all the responsibility you have undertaken?'

"'Yes, monseigneur.'

"'And submit to it.'

"'I do.'

"'Now, Leblanc,' said Dubois, 'we have nothing further to do here, and,' added he, showing the paper which he had snatched from the fire, 'I have all I wanted.'

"And at these words he left, followed by Leblanc.

"Lapierre, as soon as he had seen them off, ran to the cabinet, and exclaimed, 'Quick, baron, we must profit by our being alone for you to leave.'

"'Did you know I was here then, fellow?'

"'Pardieu! I should not have accepted the office of guardian if I had not. I saw[Pg 386] you go in, and I thought you would not like to stay there for three days.'

"'And you were right; a hundred louis for your good idea.'

"'Mon Dieu! what are you doing?' cried Lapierre.

"'I am trying to get out.'

"'Oh, not by the door! You would not send a poor fellow to the galleys; besides, they have taken the key with them.'

"'And where am I to get out, then?'

"'Raise your head.'

"'It is raised.'

"'Look in the air.'

413

"'I am looking.'

"'To your right. Do you not see anything?'

"'Yes, a little window.'

"'Well, get on a chair, on anything you find; it opens into the alcove, let yourself slip now, you will fall on the bed—that is it. You have not hurt yourself, monsieur?'

"'No, I hope the prince will have as comfortable a bed where they are taking him.'

"'And I hope monsieur will not forget the service I have rendered him.'

"'Oh, the hundred louis? Well, as I do not want to part with money at this moment, take this ring, it is worth three hundred pistoles—you gain six hundred francs on the bargain.'

"'Monsieur is the most generous gentleman I know.'

"'Now, tell me how I must go.'

"'By this little staircase; you will find yourself in the pantry; you must then go through the kitchen into the garden, and go out by the little door.'

"'Thanks for the itinerary.'

"I followed the instructions of Monsieur Lapierre exactly, and here I am."

"And the prince; where is he?" asked the chevalier.

"How do I know? In prison probably."

"Diable! diable! diable!" said Brigaud.

"Well, what do you say to my Odyssey, abbe?"

"I say that it would be very droll if it was not for that cursed paper which Dubois picked out of the cinders."

"Yes," said Valef, "that spoils it."

"And you have not any idea what it could be?"

"Not the least; but never mind, it is not lost, we shall know some day."

At this moment they heard some one coming up the staircase. The door opened, and Boniface appeared.

"Pardon, Monsieur Raoul," said he, "but it is not you I seek, it is Father Brigaud."

"Never mind, my dear Boniface, you are welcome. Baron, allow me to present you to my predecessor in my room. The son of our worthy landlady, and godson of the Abbe Brigaud."

"Oh, you have friends barons, Monsieur Raoul! what an honor for our house!"

"Well," said the abbe, "you were looking for me you said. What do you want?"

"I want nothing. It was my mother who sent for you."

"What does she want? Do you know?"

"She wants to know why the parliament is to assemble to-morrow."

"The parliament assemble to-morrow!" cried Valef and D'Harmental together.

"And how did your mother know?"

"I told her."

"And how did you know?"

"At the office. Maitre Joullu was with the president when the order arrived."

"Well, tell your mother I will come to her directly."

"She will expect you. Adieu, Monsieur Raoul."

And Monsieur Boniface went out, far from suspecting the effect he had produced on his listeners.

"It is some coup-d'état which is preparing," murmured D'Harmental.

"I will go to Madame de Maine to warn her," said Valef.

"And I to Pompadour for news," said Brigaud.

"And I," said D'Harmental, "remain here; if I am wanted, abbe, you know where I am."

"But if you were not at home, chevalier?"

"Oh! I should not be far off. Open the window, clap your hands, and I should come."

[Pg 387]Valef and Brigaud went away together, and D'Harmental went back to Bathilde, whom he found very uneasy. It was five o'clock in the afternoon, and Buvat had not returned—it was the first time such a thing had ever happened.

CHAPTER XXXIV.
PARLIAMENTARY JUSTICE.

The following day, about seven o'clock in the morning, Brigaud came to fetch D'Harmental, and found the young man ready and waiting. They both wrapped themselves in their cloaks, drew down their hats over their eyes, and proceeded through the Rue de Cléry, the Place des Victoires, and the garden of the Palais Royal.

On reaching the Rue de l'Echelle they began to perceive an unusual stir. All the avenues leading toward the Tuileries were guarded by detachments of musketeers and light horse, and the people, expelled from the court and gardens of the Tuileries, crowded into the Place du Carrousel. D'Harmental and Brigaud mixed with the mob.

Having arrived at the place where the triumphal arch now stands, they were accosted by an officer of Gray Musketeers, wrapped in a large cloak like themselves. It was Valef.

"Well, baron," asked Brigaud, "what news?"

"Ah! it is you, abbe," said Valef; "we have been looking for you, Laval, Malezieux, and myself. I have just left them; they must be somewhere near. Let us stop here; it will not be long before they find us. Do you know anything yourself?"

"No, nothing. I called at Malezieux's, but he had already gone out."

"Say that he was not yet come home. We remained at the Arsenal all night."

"And no hostile demonstration has been made?" asked

D'Harmental.

"None. Monsieur le Duc de Maine, and Monsieur le Comte de Toulouse were summoned for the regent's council, which is to be held before the sitting of the parliament. At half-past six they were both at the Tuileries, so Madame de Maine, in order to get the news as soon as possible, has come and installed herself in her superintendent's apartments."

"Is it known what has become of the Prince de Cellamare?" asked D'Harmental.

"He is sent to Orleans, in a chaise and four, in the company of a gentleman of the king's household, and an escort of a dozen light horse."

"And is nothing known about the paper which Dubois picked out of the cinders?" asked Brigaud.——"Nothing."

"What does Madame de Maine think?"

"That he is brewing something against the legitimated princes, and that he will profit by this to take away some more of their privileges. This morning she lectured her husband sharply, and he promised to remain firm, but she does not rely upon him."

"And Monsieur de Toulouse?"

"We saw him yesterday evening, but, you know, my dear abbe, there is nothing to be done with his modesty, or rather his humility. He always thinks that they have done too much for him, and is ready to abandon to the regent anything that is asked of him."

"By-the-by, the king?"

"Well, the king—"

"Yes, how has he taken the arrest of his tutor?"

"Ah! do you not know? It seems that there was a compact between the marshal and Monsieur de Frejus, that if one of them left his majesty, the other should leave immediately—yesterday morning Monsieur de Frejus disappeared."

"And where is he?"

"God knows! And so the king, who had taken the loss of his marshal very well, was inconsolable at that of his bishop."

"And how do you know all that?"

"Through the Duc de Richelieu, who went yesterday, about two o'clock, to Versailles, to pay his respects to the king, and who found his majesty in despair in the midst of the china and ornaments which he had broken. Unfortunately, Richelieu, instead of encouraging[Pg 388] the king's grief, made him laugh by telling him a hundred stories, and almost consoled him by helping him to break the rest of the china and ornaments."

At this moment an individual clothed in a long advocate's robe, and with a square cap, passed near the group which was formed by Brigaud, D'Harmental, and Valef, humming the burden of a song made on the marshal after the battle of Ramillies. Brigaud turned round, and, under the disguise, thought he recognized Pompadour. On his part the advocate stopped, and approached the group in question. The abbe had no longer any doubt. It was really the marquis.

"Well, Maitre Clement," said he, "what news from the palace?"

"Oh!" answered Pompadour, "good news, particularly if it

be true; they say that the parliament refuses to come to the Tuileries."

"Vive Dieu!" cried Valef, "that will reconcile me with the red robes. But they will not dare."

"Why not? You know that Monsieur de Mesme is for us, and has been named president through the influence of Monsieur de Maine."

"Yes, that is true, but that is long since," said Brigaud; "and if you have nothing better to rely upon, Maitre Clement, I should advise you not to count upon him."

"Particularly," answered Valef, "as he has just obtained from the regent the payment of five hundred thousand francs of his salary."

"Oh, oh!" said D'Harmental, "see, it appears to me that something new is going on. Are they not coming out of the regent's council?"

Indeed, a great movement was taking place in the court of the Tuileries, and the two carriages of the Duc de Maine and the Comte de Toulouse left their post, and approached the clock pavilion. At the same instant they saw the two brothers appear. They exchanged few words, each got into his own carriage, and the two vehicles departed at a rapid pace by the waterside wicket.

For ten minutes Brigaud, D'Harmental, Pompadour, and Valef were lost in conjectures regarding this event, which, having been remarked by others as well as by them, had made a sensation among the crowd, but without being able to assign it to its proper cause. Then they noticed Malezieux, who appeared to be looking for them: they went to him, and by his discomposed face they judged that the information which he had to bring was not comforting.

"Well," asked Pompadour, "have you any idea of what has been going on?"

"Alas!" answered Malezieux, "I am afraid that all is lost."

"You know that the Duc de Maine and the Comte de Toulouse have left the council?" asked Valef.

"I was on the quay when he passed in his carriage, and he recognized me, and stopped the carriage, and sent me this little pencil note by his valet-de-chambre."

"Let us see," said Brigaud, and he read:

"I do not know what is plotting against us, but the regent invited us—Toulouse and me—to leave the council. That invitation appeared to me an order, and, as all resistance would have been useless, seeing that we have in the council only four or five voices, upon which we cannot count, I was obliged to obey. Try and see the duchesse, who must be at the Tuileries, and tell her that I am retiring to Rambouillet, where I shall wait for the turn of events.

"Your affectionate,

"Louis Auguste."

"The coward," said Valef.

"And these are the men for whom we risk our heads," murmured Pompadour.

"You are mistaken, my dear marquis," said Brigaud, "we risk our heads on our own account I hope, and not for others. Is not that true, chevalier? Well, what the devil are you about now?"

"Wait, abbe," answered D'Harmental; "I seem to recognize—yes, by[Pg 389] Heaven, it is he! You will not go away from this place, gentlemen!"

"No, I answer for myself at least," said Pompadour.

"Nor I," said Valef.

"Nor I," said Malezieux.

"Nor I," said the abbe.

"Well, then, I will rejoin you in an instant."

"Where are you going?" asked Brigaud.

"Do not look, abbe," said D'Harmental, "it is on private business."

Dropping Valef's arm, D'Harmental began to traverse the crowd in the direction of an individual whom he had been following with his eyes for some time, and who, thanks to his personal strength, had approached the gate.

"Captain," said the chevalier, tapping Roquefinette on the shoulder, and hoping that, thanks to the movement occasioned by the approach of the parliament, they should be able to talk without being observed, "can I say a few words to you in private?"

"Yes, chevalier, with the greatest pleasure. What is it?" continued he, drawing back. "I have recognized you for the last five minutes, but it was not my business to speak first."

"And I see with pleasure," said D'Harmental, "that Captain Roquefinette is still prudent."

"Prudentissimo, chevalier; so if you have any new overture to make, out with it."

"No, captain, no; not at present, at least. Besides, the place is not suitable for a conference of that nature. Only I wish to know, in case of my having need of you, whether you still live in the same place?"

"Still, chevalier; I am like a briar—I die where I grow; only, instead of your finding me, as you did the first time, on the first or second floor, you will have to look for me on the fifth or sixth, seeing that, by a very natural see-saw movement, as my funds lower I go up."

"How, captain," said D'Harmental, laughing, and putting his hand in his pocket, "you are in want of money, and you do not address yourself to your friends?"

"I, borrow money!" cried the captain, stopping D'Harmental's liberal intentions with a sign; "no; when I do you a service you make me a present; well and good. When I conclude a bargain you execute the conditions. But I to ask without having a right to ask! It may do for a church rat, but not for a soldier; although I am only a simple gentleman, I am as proud as a duke or a peer; but, pardon me, if you want me, you know where to find me. Au revoir, chevalier! au revoir!"

And, without waiting for D'Harmental's answer, Roquefinette left him, not thinking it safe that they should be seen talking together.

As it was only eleven o'clock in the morning, however, and as in all probability the parliament would not break up till four in the afternoon, and as, no doubt, there was nothing determined on yet, the chevalier thought that, instead of remaining on the Place du Carrousel, he would do better to turn the four hours which he had before him to the profit of his love. Moreover, the nearer he approached to the catastrophe, the more need he felt of seeing Bathilde. Bathilde had become one of the elements of his life; one of the organs necessary to his existence; and, at the moment when he might perhaps be separated from her forever, he did not understand how he could live a single day away from her. Consequently, pressed by the eternal craving for the presence of the loved object, the chevalier, instead of going to look for his companions, went toward the Rue du Temps-Perdu.

D'Harmental found the poor child very uneasy. Buvat had not come home since half-past nine the morning before. Nanette had been to inquire at the library, and to her great astonishment, and the scandal of his fellow-clerks, she had learned that he had not been there for five or six days. Such a derangement in Buvat's habits indicated serious events. On the other hand, the young girl had noticed in Raoul, the day before, a sort[Pg 390] of nervous agitation, which, although kept down by determination, gave warning of an important crisis. Thus, joining her old fears to her new agonies, Bathilde felt instinctively that a misfortune, invisible but inevitable, hung above her, and that at any moment it might fall on her devoted head.

But when Bathilde saw Raoul, all fear, past or future, was lost in the happiness of the present. On his part, Raoul, whether it was self-command, or a similar feeling to her own, thought of nothing but Bathilde. Nevertheless, this time the preoccupations on both sides were so powerful that Bathilde could not help expressing her uneasiness to Raoul; he made but little answer, for the absence of Buvat became connected in his mind with some suspicions which he had entertained for a minute, and then cast from him. The time, nevertheless, flowed away with its accustomed rapidity, and four o'clock struck, when the lovers fancied that they had only been together a few minutes. It was the hour at which he generally took his leave.

If Buvat returned, he would probably return at this time. After exchanging a hundred vows, the two young people separated, agreeing, that if anything new happened to either of them, whatever hour of the day or night it might be, they should let the other know directly.

At the door of Madame Denis's house D'Harmental met Brigaud. The sitting was over, and nothing positive was yet known, but vague rumors were afloat that terrible measures had been taken. The information must soon arrive, and Brigaud had fixed a rendezvous with Pompadour and Malezieux at D'Harmental's lodgings, which, as they were the least known, must be the least watched.

In about an hour the Marquis de Pompadour arrived. The parliament had at first wished to make opposition, but everything had given way before the will of the regent. The king of Spain's letters had been read and condemned. It had been decided that the dukes and peers should rank immediately after the princes of the blood. The honors of the legitimated princes were restricted to the simple rank of their peerages.

Finally, the Duc de Maine lost the superintendence of the king's education, which was given to the Duc de Bourbon. The Comte de Toulouse alone was maintained, during his lifetime, in his privileges and prerogatives. Malezieux arrived in his turn; he had recently left the duchess. They had just given her notice to quit her apartments in the Tuileries, which belonged henceforward to Monsieur le Duc. Such an affront had, as may easily be understood, exasperated the granddaughter of the great Condé. She had flown into a violent passion, broken all the looking-glasses with her own hands, and had all the furniture thrown out of the window; then, this performance finished, she had got into her carriage, sending Laval to Rambouillet, in order to urge Monsieur de Maine to some vigorous action, and charging Malezieux to assemble all her friends that evening at the Arsenal.

Pompadour and Brigaud cried out against the imprudence of such a meeting. Madame de Maine was evidently watched. To go to the Arsenal the day when they must know that she was the most irritated would be to compromise themselves openly. Pompadour and Brigaud were therefore in favor of going and begging her highness to appoint some other time or place for the rendezvous. Malezieux and D'Harmental were of the same opinion regarding the danger of the step; but they both declared—the first from devotion, the second from a sense of duty—that the more perilous the order was, the more honorable it would be to obey it.

The discussion, as always happens in similar circumstances, began to degenerate into a pretty sharp altercation, when they heard the steps of two persons mounting the stairs. As the three individuals who had appointed a meeting at D'Harmental's were all assembled, Brigaud, who, with his ear always on the qui-vive had heard the sound first, put his finger to his mouth, to impose silence on the disputants. They could plainly hear the steps approaching; then a low whis[Pg 391]pering, as of two people questioning; finally, the door opened, and gave entrance to a soldier of the French guard, and a little grisette.

The guardsman was the Baron de Valef.

As to the grisette, she threw off the little black veil which hid her face, and they recognized Madame de Maine.

CHAPTER XXXV.
MAN PROPOSES.

"Your highness! your highness at my lodging!" cried D'Harmental. "What have I done to merit such an honor?"

"The hour is come, chevalier," said the duchess, "when it is right that we should show people the opinion we hold of their merits. It shall never be said that the friends of Madame de Maine expose themselves for her, and that she does not expose herself with them. Thank God, I am the granddaughter of the great Conde, and I feel that I am worthy of my ancestor."

"Your highness is most welcome," said Pompadour; "for your arrival will get us out of a difficulty. Decided, as we were, to obey your orders, we nevertheless hesitated at the idea of the danger incurred by an assembly at the Arsenal, at such a moment as the present, when the police have their eyes upon it."

"And I thought with you, marquis; so, instead of waiting for you, I resolved to come and seek you. The baron accompanied me. I went to the house of the Comtesse de Chavigny, a friend of De Launay's, who lives in the Rue du Mail. We had clothes brought there; and, as we were only a few steps off, we came here on foot, and here we are. On my honor, Messire Voyer d'Argenson would be clever, indeed, if he recognized us in this disguise."

"I see, with pleasure," said Malezieux, "that your highness is not cast down by the events of this horrible day."

"Cast down! I! Malezieux, I hope you know me too well to have feared it for a single instant. Cast down! On the contrary, I never felt more vigor, or more determination. Oh, if I only were a man!"

"Let your highness command," said D'Harmental, "and everything that you could do if you could act yourself, we will do—we, who stand in your stead."

"No, no; it is impossible that any other should do that which I should have done."

"Nothing is impossible, madame, to five men as devoted as we are. Moreover, our interest demands a prompt and energetic course of action. It is not reasonable to believe that the regent will stop there. The day after to-morrow—to-morrow evening, perhaps—we shall all be arrested. Dubois gives out that the paper which he saved from the flames at the Prince of Cellamare's is nothing less than the list of the conspirators. In that case he knows all our names. We have, then, at this very moment, a sword hanging over each of our heads; do not let us wait tamely till the thread which suspends it snaps; let us seize it, and strike!"

"Strike! What—where—and how?" asked Brigaud. "That abominable parliament has destroyed all our schemes. Have we measures taken, or a plot made out?"

"The best plan which has been conceived," said Pompadour, "and the one which offered the greatest chance of success, was the first; and the proof is, that it was only overthrown by an unheard-of circumstance."

"Well, if the plan was good then, it is so still," said Valef;

"let us return to it!"

"Yes, but in failing," said Malezieux, "this plan put the regent on his guard."

"On the contrary," said Pompadour; "in consequence of that very failure, it will be supposed that we have abandoned it."

"And the proof is," said Valef, "that the regent, on this head, takes fewer precautions than ever. For example—since his daughter, Mademoiselle de Chartres, has become abbess of Chelles, he goes to see her every week, and he goes through the wood of Vincennes without guards, and with only a coachman and two lackeys, and that at eight or nine o'clock at night."

[Pg 392]"And what day does he pay this visit?" asked Brigaud.

"Wednesday."

"That is to-morrow," said the duchess.

"Brigaud," said Valef, "have you still the passport for Spain?"

"Yes."

"And the same facilities for the route?"

"The same. The postmaster is with us, and we shall have only to explain to him."

"Well," said Valef, "if her royal highness will allow me, I will to-morrow call together seven or eight friends, wait for the regent in the Bois de Vincennes, carry him off; and in three days I am at Pampeluna."

"An instant, my dear baron," said D'Harmental. "I would

observe to you that you are stepping into my shoes, and that this undertaking belongs to me of right."

"You, my dear chevalier! you have already done what you had to do: now it is our turn."

"Not at all, if you please, Valef. My honor is concerned in it, for I have revenge to take. You would annoy me infinitely by insisting on this subject."

"All that I can do for you, my dear D'Harmental," said Valef, "is to leave it to her highness's choice. She knows that we are equally devoted to her; let her decide."

"Will you accept my arbitration, chevalier," said the duchess.

"Yes, for I trust to your justice, madame," said D'Harmental.

"And you are right; yes, the honor of the undertaking belongs to you. I place in your hands the fate of the son of Louis the Fourteenth, and the granddaughter of the great Conde. I trust entirely to your devotion and courage, and I have the greater hope of your success, that fortune owes you a compensation. To you, my dear D'Harmental, all the honor, and all the peril."

"I accept both with gratitude," said D'Harmental, kissing the duchess's hand; "and to-morrow, at this hour, I shall be dead, or the regent will be on the way to Spain."

"Very good," said Pompadour, "that is what I call speaking; and if you want any one to give you a helping hand, my dear chevalier, count on me."

"And on me," said Valef.

"And are we good for nothing?" said Malezieux.

"My dear chancellor," said the duchess, "to each one his share. To poets, churchmen, and magistrates, advice; to soldiers, execution. Chevalier, are you sure of finding the men who assisted you before?"

"I am sure of their chief, at least."

"When shall you see him?"

"This evening."——"At what time?"

"Directly, if your highness wishes it."

"The sooner the better."

"In a quarter of an hour I will be ready."

"Where can we learn the result of the interview?"

"I will come to your highness, wheresoever you may be."

"Not at the Arsenal," said Brigaud, "it is too dangerous."

"Can we not wait here?" asked the duchess.

"Remember," said Brigaud, "that my pupil is a steady fellow, receiving scarcely any one, and that a long visit might arouse suspicion."

"Can we not fix a rendezvous where there would be no such fear?" asked Pompadour.

"Certainly," said the duchess, "at the stone in the Champs-Elysées, for instance. Malezieux and I will come there in a carriage without livery, and without arms. Pompadour, Valef, and Brigaud will meet us there, each one separately; there we will wait for D'Harmental, and settle the last measure."

"That will suit well," said D'Harmental, "for my man lives in the Rue Saint Honore."

"You know, chevalier," replied the duchess, "that you may

promise as much money as you like."

"I undertake to fill the purse," said Brigaud.

"That is well, abbe, for I know who will undertake to empty it," said D'Harmental.

[Pg 393]"Then all is agreed," said the duchess. "In an hour, in the Champs-Elysées."

Then the duchess—having readjusted her mantle so as to hide her face—took Valef's arm, and went out. Malezieux followed at a little distance, taking care not to lose sight of her. Brigaud and Pompadour went out together, and D'Harmental went directly to the Rue Saint Honore.

Whether it were chance, or calculation on the part of the duchess, who appreciated D'Harmental, and understood how fully she might rely upon him, the chevalier found himself more than ever put forward in the conspiracy: but his honor was engaged; and although he foresaw the terrible consequences of the step which he was about to take, he went boldly forward, resolved to sacrifice everything, even his life and his love, to the fulfillment of his promise.

He presented himself at La Fillon's with the same tranquillity as before, although many things were altered in his life since then, and having been, as before, received by the mistress of the house in person he inquired if Captain Roquefinette were visible.

Without doubt La Fillon had expected a much less moral demand; for on recognizing D'Harmental, she could not repress a movement of surprise. However, she asked if he were not the same person, who—two months before—had come there to inquire for the captain. D'Harmental replied in the affirmative. As soon as she was informed on this point, she called a servant, and ordered her to conduct the chevalier to No. 72. The girl obeyed, taking a candle, and going before D'Harmental, who followed her. This time, no songs guided him in his ascent; all was silent in the house; and as the chevalier himself was occupied with grave thoughts, he mounted the six flights, and knocked at once at the door.

"Enter," said Roquefinette.

The chevalier slipped a louis into the servant's hand, opened the door, and went in.

The same change was observable in the interior as in the exterior. Roquefinette was no longer, as on the first occasion, sitting among the debris of a feast, surrounded by slaves, smoking his long pipe. He was alone, in a little dark attic, lighted by a single candle, which, nearly burned out, gave more smoke than flame, and whose flickering light gave a strange expression to the harsh face of the brave captain, who was standing leaning against the chimney-piece.

"Ah!" said Roquefinette in a slightly ironical tone, "it is you, chevalier; I expected you."

"You expected me, captain! and what induced you to do so?"

"Events, chevalier; events."

"What do you mean?"

"I mean that you thought you could make open war, and consequently put poor Captain Roquefinette aside, as a bandit, who is good for nothing but a nocturnal blow at a street corner, or in a wood; and now Dubois knows all; the parliament, on whom we thought we might count, have failed us, and has said yes, instead of no. Now we come back to the captain. My dear captain here! my good captain there! Is not this exactly as it has happened, chevalier? Well, here is the captain, what do you want of him? Speak."

"Really, my dear captain," said D'Harmental, not knowing exactly how to take this speech, "there is some truth in what you say. Only you are mistaken if you think we had forgotten you. If our plan had succeeded, you would have had proof that my memory was better, and I should have come to offer you my credit, as I now come to ask your assistance."

"Hum!" said the captain; "for the last three days, since I have inhabited this new apartment, I have made many reflections on the vanity of human things, and have more than once felt inclined to retire altogether from these affairs, or—if I did undertake one—to take care that it should be sufficiently brilliant to insure my future."

"What I come to propose to you is just the thing. Without preamble, it is—"

"What?" asked the captain, after waiting two or three minutes in vain for the end of the speech.

[Pg 394]"Oh captain, I thought—"

"What did you think, chevalier?"

"I thought I heard steps—a sort of creaking in the wall."

"Ah!" said the captain, "there are not a few rats in this establishment, I can tell you."

"Oh, that must be it!" said D'Harmental. "Well! my dear

435

Roquefinette, we wish to profit by the regent's returning unguarded from Chelles to carry him off and take him to Spain."

"Before going any further," said Roquefinette, "I must warn you that this is a new treaty, and that every new treaty implies new conditions."

"No need of discussions on that point. You shall fix them yourself; but can you still dispose of your men?"

"I can."

"Will they be ready at two o'clock to-morrow?"

"They will."

"That is all that is necessary."

"Something else is necessary—money to buy a horse and arms."

"There are a hundred louis in that purse; take it."

"It is well. You shall have an account of it."

"Then to-morrow at my house at two o'clock."

"It is agreed, chevalier; you are not to be astonished if I am a little exacting."

"You know that last time I only complained of your being too modest."

"Very well, that will do," said the captain, "you are easily satisfied. Let me light you; it would be a pity that a brave fellow like you should break his neck."

And the captain took the candle, which, now burned down to the paper, threw a splendid light over the staircase.

D'Harmental had not forgotten that Madame de Maine waited with anxiety for the result of the interview. He did not trouble himself, therefore, about what had become of La Fillon, whom he did not see on leaving; and having gone down the Rue des Feuillons, he passed along the Champs-Elysées, which, without being altogether deserted, was nevertheless almost solitary. Having arrived at the stone, he noticed a carriage standing on the opposite side of the road, while two men were walking at a little distance off in the cross-road. He approached the carriage; a woman, seeing him, put her head impatiently out of the window. The chevalier recognized Madame de Maine; Malezieux and Valef were with her. As to the walkers, who, seeing D'Harmental, approached the vehicle, it is needless to say that they were Brigaud and Pompadour.

The chevalier, without naming Roquefinette, or enlarging on the character of the illustrious captain, told them in a few words what had passed. This recital was welcomed by a general exclamation of joy. The duchess gave D'Harmental her hand to kiss; the men pressed his. It was agreed that the next day at two o'clock the duchess, Pompadour, Laval, Valef, Malezieux, and Brigaud, should meet at No. 15, Faubourg Saint Antoine, a house occupied by D'Avranches' mother, and that they should there await the event.

The result was to be announced to them by D'Avranches himself, who, at three o'clock, should be at the Barrière du Trône with two horses, one for himself, the other for the chevalier. He was to follow D'Harmental at a distance, and return to announce what had passed. Five other horses, saddled and bridled, were to be ready in the stables of the house in the Faubourg Saint Antoine, so that the conspirators might fly at once in case of the chevalier's failure.

These plans settled, the duchess forced the chevalier to seat himself beside her. The duchess wished to drive him home, but he told her that the appearance of a carriage at Madame Denis's door would produce too much sensation, and that, flattering as it would be to him, it would be too dangerous for all. In consequence, the duchess set D'Harmental down in the Place des Victoires, after repeatedly expressing her gratitude for his devotion. It was ten o'clock in the evening. D'Harmental had scarcely seen Bathilde during the day; he wished to see her again; he[Pg 395] was sure to find her at her window, but that was not sufficient, for what he had to say was too serious to be thus spoken from one side to the other of the street.

He was thinking under what pretext he could present himself at such a late hour, when he thought he saw a woman at the door of her house. He advanced and recognized Nanette, who was there by Bathilde's order. The poor girl was dreadfully uneasy, Buvat not having returned. All the evening she had remained at the window to watch for D'Harmental, but had not seen him. It seemed to Bathilde that there must be some connection between Buvat's strange disappearance and the melancholy which she had remarked the day before in D'Harmental's face. Nanette was waiting at the door for Buvat and D'Harmental; she now waited for Buvat, and D'Harmental went up to Bathilde.

Bathilde had heard and recognized his step, and ran to

open the door. At the first glance she noticed the pensive expression of his face.

"Oh! mon Dieu, Raoul!" she exclaimed, "has anything happened to you?"

"Bathilde," said D'Harmental, with a melancholy smile, "you have often told me that there is in me something mysterious which frightens you."

"Yes," cried Bathilde; "it is the only torment of my life; my only fear for the future."

"And you are right; for before I knew you, Bathilde, I had abandoned a part of my free-will; this portion of myself no longer belongs to me, but submits to a supreme law, and to unforeseen events. It is a black point in a clear sky. According to the way the wind blows, it may disappear as a vapor or increase into a storm. The hand which holds and guides mine may lead me to the highest favor or to the most complete disgrace. Tell me, Bathilde, are you disposed to share my good and evil fortune; the calm and the tempest?"

"Everything with you, Raoul."

"Think of what you are undertaking, Bathilde. It may be a happy and a brilliant life which is reserved for you; it may be exile; it may be captivity; it may be that you will be a widow before you are a wife."

Bathilde turned so pale that Raoul thought she would fall; but she quickly regained her self-command, and, holding out her hand to D'Harmental—

"Raoul," said she, "have I not already told you that I love you; that I never have and never can love any other? It seems to me that all these promises you ask are included in those words; but since you wish them renewed, I do so. Your life shall be my life, and your death my death; both are in the hands of God."

"And I, Bathilde," said D'Harmental, leading her before the crucifix, "I swear that from this moment you are my wife before God and before men; and since the events which may dispose of my life leave me nothing but my love to offer to you, that love is yours—profound, unalterable, eternal;" and the young people exchanged their first kiss with the renewal of their vows.

When D'Harmental left Bathilde, Buvat had not returned.

CHAPTER XXXVI.
DAVID AND GOLIATH.

Toward ten o'clock in the morning the Abbe Brigaud entered D'Harmental's room; he brought him 20,000 francs, partly in gold, partly in Spanish paper. The duchess had passed the night at the Comtesse de Chavigny's, in the Rue du Mail. The plans of the preceding day were in no degree changed, and they had ascertained that the regent would pay his accustomed visit to Chelles. At ten o'clock Brigaud and D'Harmental went down, Brigaud to join Pompadour and Valef on the Boulevard du Temple, and D'Harmental to visit Bathilde.

Uneasiness was at its height in the little household; Buvat was still absent, and it was easy to see by Bathilde's eyes that she had had but little sleep. As soon as she saw D'Harmental, she understood that some expedition was preparing. D'Harmental again wore that dark costume in which she had never seen him but on[Pg 396] that evening when, on returning, he had thrown his mantle on a chair, and displayed to her sight the pistols in his belt. Moreover, she saw by his spurs that he expected to ride during the day. All these things would have appeared insignificant at any other time, but, after the nocturnal betrothal we have described, they took a new and grave importance. Bathilde tried at first to make the chevalier speak, but he told her that the secret she asked did not belong to himself, and she desisted. An hour after, Nanette appeared, with a distressed face. She

441

came from the library; Buvat had not been there, and no one had heard anything of him.

Bathilde could contain herself no longer; she fell into Raoul's arms, and burst into tears. Then Raoul confessed to her his fears, and that the papers which the pretended Prince de Listhnay had given Buvat to copy were politically important, by which he might have been compromised and arrested, but had nothing to fear, and that the passive part which he had played in this affair did not endanger him in the least.

Bathilde, having feared some much greater misfortune, eagerly seized on this idea. She did not confess to herself that the greater part of her uneasiness was not for Buvat, and that all the tears she shed were not for the absent.

When D'Harmental was near Bathilde, time appeared to fly; he was astonished when he found that he had been with her an hour and a half, and remembering that at two o'clock he had to arrange his new treaty with Roquefinette, he rose to go. Bathilde turned pale. D'Harmental, to reassure her, promised to come to her again after the departure of the person he expected.

The chevalier had only been a few minutes at his window when he saw Roquefinette appear at the corner of the Rue Montmartre. He was mounted on a dapple-gray horse, both swift and strong, and evidently chosen by a connoisseur. He came along leisurely, like a man to whom it is equally indifferent whether he is seen or not. On arriving at the door he dismounted, fastened up his horse, and ascended the stairs. As on the day before, his face was grave and pensive, his compressed lips indicated some fixed determination, and D'Harmental received him with a smile, which met with no answer on the captain's face. D'Harmental at a glance took in all these different signs.

"Well, captain," said he, "I see that you are still punctuality itself."

"It is a military habit, chevalier, and is not astonishing in an old soldier."

"I did not doubt you, but you might not have been able to meet your men."

"I told you I knew where to find them."

"And where are they?"

"In the horse-market at the Porte Saint Martin."

"Are you not afraid they will be noticed?"

"How should twelve or fifteen men dressed as peasants be noticed among three hundred other peasants, buying and selling horses? It is like a needle in a bottle of hay, which none but myself can find."

"But how can these men accompany you, captain?"

"The simplest thing in the world. Each one has bargained for the horse which suits him. Each one has offered a price, to which the vendor replies by another. I arrive, give to each twenty-five or thirty louis. Every one pays for his horse, has it saddled, mounts, slips into the holsters the pistols which he has in his belt, and, by a different route, arrives at a given place in the Bois de Vincennes at four o'clock. Then only I explain to them for what they are wanted. I again distribute money, put myself at the head of my squadron, and go to the work—supposing that you and I agree on the conditions."

"Well, these conditions, captain," said D'Harmental, "let us discuss them, and I think I have arranged so that you will be satisfied with what I have to offer you."

"Let us hear them," said Roquefinette, sitting down by the table.

"First, double the sum you received last time," said the chevalier.

[Pg 397]"Ah!" said Roquefinette, "I do not care for money."

"What! you do not care for money, captain?"—"Not the least in the world."

"What do you care for, then?"

"A position."

"What do you mean?"

"I mean, chevalier, that every day I am four-and-twenty hours older, and that with age comes philosophy."

"Well, captain," said D'Harmental, beginning to be seriously uneasy, "what is the ambition of your philosophy?"

"I have told you, chevalier, a position suitable to my long services—not in France, you understand. In France I have too many enemies, beginning with the lieutenant of police; but in Spain, for instance. Ah! that would suit me well. A fine country—beautiful women—plenty of doubloons! Decidedly, I should like a rank in Spain."

"The thing is possible; it depends on the rank you desire."

"Well, you know, chevalier, when one is wishing, it is as

well to wish for something worth the trouble."

"You make me uneasy, monsieur," said D'Harmental, "for I have not the seals of King Philip, to sign brevets in his name. But never mind; speak."

"Well," said Roquefinette, "I see so many greenhorns at the heads of regiments, that I also have thought of being a colonel."

"Colonel? Impossible!"

"Why so?"

"Because, if they make you a colonel, you who only hold a secondary position in the affair, what am I to ask, I, who am at the head?"

"That is the very thing: I wish to change positions for the moment. You remember what I said to you on a certain evening in the Rue du Valois?"

"Aid my memory, captain. I have unfortunately forgotten."

"I told you that if I had an affair like this to manage, things would go better. I added that I would speak to you of it again. I do so now."

"What the devil are you talking about, captain?"

"A simple matter, chevalier. We made a first attempt together, which failed. Then you changed batteries: you thought you could do without me, and you failed again. The first time you failed at night, and without noise: we each went our own way, and there was nothing known about it. The second time, on the contrary, you failed in broad daylight, and with an éclat which has compromised all; so that if you do not save yourselves by a bold stroke, you are all lost, as Dubois has your names; and to-morrow—to-night perhaps—you may be all arrested, knights, barons, dukes, and princes. Now, there is in the world one man, and one only, who can free you from your troubles—that man is Captain Roquefinette, and you offer him the same place he held before! Fie, chevalier!—you wish to bargain with him. Remember, pretensions increase with the services to be rendered. I am now an important personage. Treat me as such, or I put my hands in my pockets, and leave Dubois to do as he likes."

D'Harmental bit his lips, but he understood that he had to treat with a man who was accustomed to sell his services as dear as possible; and as what the captain said of their necessity was literally true, he restrained his impatience and his pride.

"Then you wish to be a colonel?"

"That is my idea."

"But suppose I make you this promise, who can answer that I have influence enough to ratify it?"

"Oh, chevalier, I reckon on managing my little affairs myself."

"Where?"

"At Madrid."

"Who told you that I shall take you there?"

"I do not know if you will take me there, but I know that I shall go there."

"You, to Madrid! What for?"

"To take the regent."

"You are mad."

"Come, come, chevalier, no big words. You ask my conditions; I tell them you. They do not suit you: good-evening. We are not the worst friends for that."

[Pg 398]And Roquefinette rose, took his hat, and was going toward the door.

"What, are you going?"

"Certainly."

"But you forget, captain."

"Ah! it is true," said Roquefinette, intentionally mistaking D'Harmental's meaning: "you gave me a hundred louis; I must give you an account of them."

He took his purse from his pocket.

"A horse, thirty louis; a pair of double-barreled pistols, ten louis; a saddle, bridle, etc., two louis; total, forty-two louis. There are fifty-eight louis in this purse; the horse, pistols, saddle, and bridle, are yours. Count, we are quits."

And he threw the purse on the table.

"But that is not what I have to say to you, captain."

"What is it, then?"

"That it is impossible to confide to you a mission of such importance."

"It must be so, nevertheless, or not at all. I must take the regent to Madrid, and I alone, or he remains at the Palais Royal."

"And you think yourself worthy to take from the hands of Philippe d'Orleans the sword which conquered at Lérida La Pucelle, and which rested by the scepter of Louis XIV., on the velvet cushion with the golden tassels?"

"I heard in Italy that Francis I., at the battle of Pavia, gave up his to a butcher."

And the captain pressed his hat on his head, and once more approached the door.

"Listen, captain," said D'Harmental, in his most conciliating tone; "a truce to arguments and quotations; let us split the difference. I will conduct the regent to Spain, and you shall accompany me."

"Yes, so that the poor captain may be lost in the dust which the dashing chevalier excites, and that the brilliant colonel may throw the old bandit into the shade! Impossible, chevalier, impossible! I will have the management of the affair, or I will have nothing to do with it."

"But this is treason!" cried D'Harmental.

"Treason, chevalier! And where have you seen, if you please, that Captain Roquefinette was a traitor? Where are the agreements which I have made and not kept? Where are the secrets which I have divulged? I, a traitor! Good heavens, chevalier, it was only the day before yesterday that I was offered gold to betray you, and I refused! No, no! Yesterday you came and asked me to aid you a second time. I told you that I was ready, but on new conditions. Well, I have just told you those conditions. Accept them or refuse them. Where do you see treason in all this?"

"And if I was weak enough to accept these conditions, monsieur, do you imagine that the confidence which her royal highness the Duchesse de Maine reposes in the Chevalier d'Harmental can be transferred to Captain Roquefinette?"

"And what has the Duchesse de Maine to remark upon in this? You undertake a piece of business. There are material hindrances in the way of your executing it yourself. You hand it over to me. That is all."

"That is to say," answered D'Harmental, shaking his head, "that you wish to be free to loose the regent, if the regent offers you, for leaving him in France, twice as much as I offer you for taking him to Spain."

"Perhaps," replied Roquefinette.

"Hearken, captain." said D'Harmental, making a new effort to retain his sang-froid, and endeavoring to renew the negotiations, "I will give you twenty thousand francs down."

"Trash," answered the captain.

"I will take you with me to Spain."

"Fiddlesticks."

"And I engage on my honor to obtain you a regiment."

Roquefinette began to hum a tune.

"Take care," said D'Harmental; "it is more dangerous for you now, at the point at which we have arrived, and with the terrible secrets which you know, to refuse than to accept."

"And what will happen, then, if I refuse?" asked Roquefinette.

"It will happen, captain, that you will not leave this room."

"And who will prevent me?"

[Pg 399]"I!" cried D'Harmental, bounding before the door, a pistol in each hand.

"You?" said Roquefinette, making a step toward the

chevalier, and then crossing his arms and regarding him fixedly.

"One step more, captain," said the chevalier, "and I give you my word I will blow your brains out."

"You blow my brains out—you! In the first place, it is necessary for that, that you should not tremble like an old woman. Do you know what you will do? You will miss me; the noise will alarm the neighbors, who will call the guard, and they will question me as to the reasons of your shooting at me, and I shall be obliged to tell them."

"Yes, you are right, captain," cried the chevalier, uncocking his pistols, and replacing them in his belt, "and I shall be obliged to kill you more honorably than you deserve. Draw, monsieur, draw."

And D'Harmental, leaning his left foot against the door, drew his sword, and placed himself on guard. It was a court sword, a thin ribbon of steel, set in a gold handle. Roquefinette began to laugh.

"With what shall I defend myself, chevalier? Do you happen to have one of your mistress's knitting needles here?"

"Defend yourself with your own sword, monsieur; long as it is, you see that I am placed so that I cannot make a step to avoid it."

"What do you think of that, my dear?" said the captain, addressing his blade.

"It thinks that you are a coward, captain," cried D'Harmental, "since it is necessary to strike you in the face to make you fight." And with a movement as quick as lightning,

D'Harmental cut the captain across the face with his rapier, leaving on the cheek a long blue mark like the mark of a whip.

Roquefinette gave a cry which might have been taken for the roaring of a lion, and bounding back a step, threw himself on guard, his sword in his hand. Then began between these two men a duel, terrible, hidden, silent, for both were intent on their work, and each understood what sort of an adversary he had to contend with. By a reaction, very easy to be understood, it was now D'Harmental who was calm, and Roquefinette who was excited. Every instant he menaced D'Harmental with his long sword, but the frail rapier followed it as iron follows the loadstone, twisting and spinning round it like a viper. At the end of about five minutes the chevalier had not made a single lunge, but he had parried all those of his adversary. At last, on a more rapid thrust than the others, he came too late to the parry, and felt the point of his adversary's sword at his breast. At the same time a red spot spread from his shirt to his lace frill. D'Harmental saw it, and with a spring engaged so near to Roquefinette that the hilts almost touched. The captain instantly saw the disadvantage of his long sword in such a position. A thrust "sur les armes" and he was lost; he made a spring backward, his foot slipped on the newly-waxed floor, and his sword-hand rose in spite of himself. Almost by instinct D'Harmental profited by it, lunged within, and pierced the captain's chest, where the blade disappeared to the hilt. D'Harmental recovered to parry in return, but the precaution was needless; the captain stood still an instant, opened his eyes wildly, the sword dropped from his grasp, and pressing his two hands to the wound, he fell at full length on the floor.

"Curse the rapier!" murmured he, and expired; the strip of steel had pierced his heart.

Still D'Harmental remained on guard, with his eyes fixed on the captain, only lowering his sword as the dead man let his slip. Finally, he found himself face to face with a corpse, but this corpse had its eyes open, and continued to look at him. Leaning against the door, the chevalier remained an instant thunderstruck; his hair bristled, his forehead became covered with perspiration, he did not dare to move, he did not dare to speak, his victory seemed to him a dream. Suddenly the mouth of the dying man set in a last convulsion—the partisan was dead, and his secret had died with him.

How to recognize, in the midst of three hundred peasants, buying and selling[Pg 400] horses, the twelve or fifteen pretended ones who were to carry off the regent?

D'Harmental gave a low cry; he would have given ten years of his own life to add ten minutes to that of the captain. He took the body in his arms, raised it, called it, and, seeing his reddened hands, let it fall into a sea of blood, which, following the inclination of the boards down a channel in the floor, reached the door, and began to spread over the threshold.

At that moment, the horse, which was tied to the shutter, neighed violently.

D'Harmental made three steps toward the door,

then he remembered that Roquefinette might have some memorandum about him which might serve as a guide. In spite of his repugnance, he searched the pockets of the corpse, one after another, but the only papers he found were two or three old bills of restaurateurs, and a love-letter from La Normande.

Then, as he had nothing more to do in that room, he filled his pockets with gold and notes, closed the door after him, descended the stairs rapidly, left at a gallop toward the Rue Gros Chenet, and disappeared round the angle nearest to the Boulevard.

CHAPTER XXXVII.
THE SAVIOR OF FRANCE.

While these terrible events were going forward in the attic of Madame Denis's house, Bathilde, uneasy at seeing her neighbor's window so long shut, had opened hers, and the first thing she saw, was the dappled gray horse attached to the shutter; but as she had not seen the captain go in, she thought that the steed was for Raoul, and that reflection immediately recalled both her former and present fears.

Bathilde consequently remained at the window, looking on all sides, and trying to read in the physiognomy of every passer-by whether that individual was an actor in the mysterious drama which was preparing, and in which she instinctively understood that Raoul was to play the chief part. She remained, then, with a beating heart, her neck stretched out, and her eyes wandering hither and thither, when all at once her unquiet glances concentrated on a point. The young girl gave a cry of joy, for she saw Buvat coming round the corner from the Rue Montmartre. Indeed, it was the worthy caligraphist in person, who, looking behind him from time to time—as if he feared pursuit—advanced with his cane horizontal, and at as swift a run as his little legs permitted.

While he enters, and embraces his ward, let us look back and relate the causes of that absence, which, doubtless, caused as much uneasiness to our readers as to Nanette and Bathilde.

It will be remembered how Buvat—driven by fear

of torture to the revelation of the conspiracy—had been forced by Dubois to make every day, at his house, a copy of the documents which the pretended Prince de Listhnay had given him. It was thus that the minister of the regent had successively learned all the projects of the conspirators, which he had defeated by the arrest of Marshal Villeroy, and by the convocation of parliament.

Buvat had been at work as usual, but about four o'clock, as he rose, and took his hat in one hand and his cane in the other, Dubois came in and took him into a little room above that where he had been working, and, having arrived there, asked him what he thought of the apartment. Flattered by this deference of the prime minister's to his judgment, Buvat hastened to reply that he thought it very agreeable.

"So much the better," answered Dubois, "and I am very glad that it is to your taste, for it is yours."

"Mine!" cried Buvat, astonished.

"Certainly; is it astonishing that I should wish to have under my hand, or rather, under my eyes, a personage as important as yourself?"

"But," asked Buvat, "am I then going to live in the Palais Royal?"

"For some days, at least," answered Dubois.

"Monseigneur, let me at all events inform Bathilde."

"That is just the thing. Bathilde must not be informed."

The body of the captain lay stretched on the floor, swimming in a sea of blood.

The body of the captain lay stretched on the floor,

swimming in a sea of blood.—*Page* 408.

Link to larger image

[Pg 401]"But you will permit that the first time I go out—"

"As long as you remain here you will not go out."

"But," cried Buvat, with terror, "but I am then a prisoner?"

"A State prisoner, as you have said, my dear Buvat: but calm yourself; your captivity will not be long, and while it lasts we will take of you all the care which is the due of the savior of France, for you have saved France, Monsieur Buvat."

"I have saved France, and here I am a prisoner under bolts and bars!"

"And where on earth do you see bolts and bars, my dear Buvat?" said Dubois, laughing; "the door shuts with a latch, and has not even a lock: as to the window, yours looks on the gardens of the Palais Royal, and has not even a lattice to intercept the view, a superb view—you are lodged here like the regent himself."

"Oh, my little room! Oh, my terrace!" cried Buvat, letting himself sink exhausted on a seat.

Dubois, who had no other consolation to bestow upon Buvat, went out, and placed a sentinel at the door. The explanation of this step is easy. Dubois feared that, seeing the arrest of Villeroy, they would suspect from whence the information came, and would question Buvat, and that he would confess all. This confession would, doubtless, have arrested the conspirators in the midst of their schemes, which, on the contrary, Dubois, informed beforehand of all their plans, wished to see carried to a point, so that in crushing one monster rebellion he might put an end to all lesser ones.

Toward eight o'clock, as daylight began to fade, Buvat heard a great noise at his door, and a sort of metallic clashing, which did not tend to reassure him. He had heard plenty of lamentable stories of State prisoners who had been assassinated in their prisons, and he rose trembling and ran to the window. The court and gardens of the Palais Royal were full of people, the galleries began to be lighted up, the whole scene was full of gayety and light. He heaved a profound sigh, thinking perhaps that he might be bidding a last adieu to that life and animation. At that instant the door was opened; Buvat turned round shuddering, and saw two tall footmen in red livery bringing in a well-supplied table. The metallic noise which had so much disturbed him had been the clattering of the silver plates and dishes.

Buvat's first impression was one of thankfulness to Heaven, that so imminent a danger as that which he had feared had changed into such a satisfactory event. But immediately the idea struck him that the deadly intentions held toward him were still the same, and that only the mode of their execution were changed—instead of being assassinated, like Jeansans-Peur, or the Duc de Guise, he was going to be poisoned, like the Dauphin, or the Duc de Burgundy. He threw a rapid glance on the two footmen, and thought he remarked something somber which denoted the agents of a secret vengeance. From this instant his determination was taken, and, in spite of the scent of the dishes, which appeared to him an additional proof, he refused all sustenance, saying majestically that he was neither hungry nor thirsty.

The footmen looked at each other knowingly. They were two sharp fellows, and had understood Buvat's character at a glance, and not understanding a man not being hungry when before a pheasant stuffed with truffles, or not thirsty before a bottle of Chambertin, had penetrated the prisoner's fears pretty quickly. They exchanged a few words in a low tone, and the boldest of the two, seeing that there was a means of drawing some profit from the circumstances, advanced toward Buvat, who recoiled before him as far as the room would allow.

"Monsieur," said he, in a reassuring tone, "we understand your fears, and, as we are honest servants, we will show you that we are incapable of lending ourselves to the dealings which you suspect; consequently, during the whole time that you remain here, my comrade and I, each in our turn, will taste all the dishes which are brought you, and all the wines which[Pg 402] are sent in, happy if by our devotion we can restore your tranquillity."

"Monsieur," answered Buvat, ashamed that his secret sentiments had been discovered thus, "monsieur, you are very polite, but in truth I am neither hungry nor thirsty."

"Never mind, monsieur," said the man, "as my comrade and myself desire not to leave the smallest doubt on your mind, we will execute what we have offered. Comtois, my friend," continued the fellow, sitting down in the place which had been intended for Buvat, "do me the favor to help me to a little of that soup, a wing of that pullet in rice, a glass of that Chambertin, there—to your health, monsieur."

"Monsieur," said Buvat, opening his eyes, and looking at the footman who was dining so impudently in his stead, "monsieur, it is I who am your servant, and I should wish to know your name, in order to preserve it in my memory by the side of that of the good jailer who gave to Comte l'Ancien a similar proof of devotion to that which you give me."

"Monsieur," answered the footman modestly, "I am called Bourguignon, and here is my comrade Comtois, whose turn for devotion will come to-morrow, and who, when the moment shall have arrived, will not be behindhand. Comtois, my friend, a slice of that pheasant, and a glass of champagne. Do you not see that, in order to reassure monsieur completely, I must taste everything; it is a severe test, I know, but where would be the merit of being an honest man if it did not sometimes bring trials like the present? To your health, Monsieur Buvat."

"Heaven preserve yours, Monsieur Bourguignon."

"Now, Comtois, hand me the dessert, so that I may leave no doubt on Monsieur Buvat's mind."

"Monsieur Bourguignon, I beg you to believe that, if I had any, they are completely dissipated."

"No, monsieur, no, I beg your pardon, you still have some. Comtois, my friend, now the hot coffee, very hot; I wish to drink it exactly as monsieur would have done, and I presume it is thus that monsieur likes it."

"Boiling, monsieur, boiling," answered Buvat, bowing.

"Oh!" said Bourguignon, sipping his coffee, and raising his eyes blissfully to the ceiling, "you are right, monsieur. It is only so that coffee is good—half-cold it is a very second-rate beverage. This, I may say, is excellent. Comtois, my friend, receive my compliments, you wait admirably; now help me to take away the table. You ought to know that there is nothing more unpleasant than the smell of wines and viands to those who are not hungry nor thirsty. Monsieur," continued Bourguignon, stepping toward the door, which he had carefully shut during the repast, and which he opened while his companion pushed the table before him, "monsieur, if you have need of anything, you have three bells, one at the head of your bed, and two at the mantelpiece. Those at the fireplace are for us, that at the bed for your valet-de-chambre."

"Thank you, monsieur," said Buvat, "you are too good. I do not wish to disturb any one."

"Do not trouble yourself about that, monsieur—monseigneur desires that you should make yourself at home."

"Monseigneur is very polite."

"Does monsieur require anything else?"

"Nothing more, my friend, nothing more," said Buvat, touched by so much devotion; "nothing, except to express my gratitude."

"I have only done my duty, monsieur," answered Bourguignon, modestly, bowing for the last time, and shutting the door.

"Ma foi!" said Buvat, following Bourguignon with his eyes, "it must be allowed that some proverbs are great liars. One says, 'As insolent as a lackey,' and yet here is an individual practicing that calling, who nevertheless could not possibly be more polite. I shall never believe in proverbs again, or rather, I shall make a difference between them."

And making himself this promise, Buvat found himself alone.

[Pg 403]Nothing makes a man so hungry as the sight of a good dinner; that which had just been eaten under the good man's very eyes surpassed in luxury everything that he had ever dreamed of, and he began—influenced by the decided calls of his stomach—to reproach himself for his too great defiance of his persecutors; but it was too late. Buvat, it is true, might have rung for Monsieur Bourguignon, and requested a second dinner, but he was of too timid a character for that, and the result was, that he had to search among his stock of proverbs for the most consoling, and having found, between his situation and the proverb, "He who sleeps dines," an analogy which seemed to him most direct, he resolved to make use of it, and, as he could not dine, to endeavor at least to sleep.

But, at the moment of taking this resolution, Buvat found himself assailed by new fears. Could they not profit by his sleep to dispatch him? The night is the time of ambushes— he had often heard his mother tell of beds which, by the lowering of their canopies, smothered the unfortunate sleeper; of beds which sank through a trap, so softly as not to wake the occupant; finally, of secret doors opening in panels, and even in furniture, to give entrance to assassins. This luxuriant dinner, these rich wines, had they not been sent him to insure a sounder sleep? All this was possible, nay, probable, and Buvat, who felt the instinct of self-preservation in the highest degree, took his candle, and commenced a most minute investigation. After having opened the doors of all the cupboards, sounded all the paneling, Buvat had gone down on his hands and feet, and was stretching his head timidly under the bed, when he thought he heard steps behind him. The position in which he found himself did not permit him to act on the defensive; he therefore remained motionless, and waited with a beating heart. After a few seconds of solemn silence, which filled Buvat with vague alarms, a voice said:

"Your pardon; but is not monsieur looking for his nightcap?"

Buvat was discovered—there was no means of escaping the danger, if danger there was. He therefore drew his head from under the bed, took his candle, and remaining on his knees, as a humble and beseeching posture, he turned toward the individual who had just addressed him, and found himself face to face with a man dressed in black, and carrying, folded up on his arm, many articles, which Buvat recognized as human clothes.

"Yes, monsieur," said Buvat, seizing the opening which was offered to him, with a presence of mind on which he secretly congratulated himself; "is that search forbidden?"

"Why did not monsieur, instead of troubling himself, ring the bell? I have the honor to be appointed monsieur's valet-de-chambre, and I have brought him a night-cap and night-shirt."

And with these words the valet-de-chambre spread out on the bed a night-shirt, embroidered with flowers, a cap of the finest lawn, and a rose-colored ribbon. Buvat, still on his knees, regarded him with the greatest astonishment.

"Now," said the valet-de-chambre, "will monsieur allow me to help him to undress?"

"No, monsieur, no," said Buvat, accompanying the refusal with the sweetest smile he could assume. "No, I am accustomed to undress myself. I thank you, monsieur."

The valet-de-chambre retired, and Buvat remained alone.

As the inspection of the room was completed, and as his increasing hunger rendered sleep more necessary, Buvat began to undress, sighing; placed—in order not to be left in the dark—a candle on the corner of the chimney-piece, and sprang, with a groan, into the softest and warmest bed he had ever slept on.

"The bed is not sleep," is an axiom which Buvat might, from experience, have added to the list of his true proverbs. Either from fear or hunger, Buvat passed a very disturbed night, and it was not till near morning that he fell asleep; even then his slumbers were peopled with the most terrible visions and nightmares. He was just waking from a dream that[Pg 404] he had been poisoned by a leg of mutton, when the valet-de-chambre entered, and asked at what time he would like breakfast.

Buvat was not in the habit of breakfasting in bed, so he rose quickly, and dressed in haste; he had just finished, when Messieurs Bourguignon and Comtois entered, bringing the breakfast, as the day before they had brought the dinner.

Then took place a second rehearsal of the scene which we have before related, with the exception that now it was Monsieur Comtois who ate and Monsieur Bourguignon who waited; but when it came to the coffee, and Buvat, who had taken nothing for twenty-four hours, saw his dearly-loved beverage, after having passed from the silver coffee-pot into the porcelain cup, pass into the cavernous mouth of Monsieur Comtois, he could hold out no longer, and declared that his stomach demanded to be amused with something, and that, consequently, he desired that they would leave him the coffee and a roll. This declaration appeared to disturb the devotion of Monsieur Comtois, who was nevertheless obliged to satisfy himself with one cup of the odoriferous liquid, which, together with a roll and the sugar, was placed on a little table, while the two scamps carried off the rest of the feast, laughing in their sleeves.

Scarcely was the door closed, when Buvat darted toward the little table, and, without even waiting to dip one into the other, ate the bread and drank the coffee; then, a little comforted by that repast, insufficient as it was, began to look at things in a less gloomy point of view.

In truth, Buvat was not wanting in a certain kind of good sense, and, as he had passed the preceding evening and night, and entered on the present morning, without interference, he began to understand that, though from some political motive they had deprived him of his liberty, they were far from wishing to shorten his days, and surrounded him, on the contrary, with cares, of which he had never before been the object. He had seen that the dinner of the day before was better than his ordinary dinner—that the bed was softer than his ordinary bed—that the coffee he had just drunk possessed an aroma which the mixture of chicory took away from his, and he could not conceal from himself that the elastic couches and stuffed chairs which he had sat upon for the last twenty-four hours were much preferable to the hair sofa and cane chairs of his own establishment. The only thing, then, which remained to trouble him, was the uneasiness which Bathilde would feel at his not returning. He had for an instant the idea—not daring to renew the request which he had made the day before, to have news of him sent to his ward—of imitating the man with the iron mask, who had thrown a silver plate from the window of his prison on to the shore, by throwing a letter from his balcony into the courtyard of the Palais Royal; but he knew what a fatal result this infraction of the will of Monsieur de Saint-Mars had had for the unfortunate prisoner, so that he feared, by such an action, to increase the rigors of his captivity, which at present seemed to him tolerable.

The result of all these reflections was, that Buvat passed the morning in a much less agitated manner than he had the evening and the night; moreover, his hunger—appeased by the roll and the coffee—only existed in the form of that appetite which is an enjoyment when one is sure of a good dinner. Add to all this the particularly cheerful look-out which the prisoner had from his window, and it will be easily understood that mid-day arrived without too many sorrows, or too much ennui.

Exactly at one o'clock the door opened, and the table reappeared ready laid, and brought, like the day before and that morning, by the two valets. But this time, it was neither Monsieur Bourguignon nor Monsieur Comtois who sat down to it. Buvat declared himself perfectly reassured concerning the intentions of his august host; he thanked Messieurs Comtois and Bourguignon for the devotion of which each in turn had given him[Pg 405] a proof, and begged them to wait upon him in their turn. The two servants made wry faces, but obeyed. It will be understood that the happy disposition in which Buvat now was became more blissful under the influence of a good dinner. Buvat ate all the eatables, drank all the drinkables, and at last, after having sipped his coffee—a luxury which he usually only allowed himself on Sundays—and having capped the Arabian nectar with a glass of Madame Anfoux' liquor, was, it must be confessed, in a state bordering upon ecstasy.

That evening the supper was equally successful; but as Buvat had abandoned himself at dinner rather freely to the consumption of Chambertin and Sillery, about eight o'clock in the evening he found himself in a state of glorification impossible to describe. The consequence was, that when the valet-de-chambre entered, instead of finding him like the evening before, with his head under the bed, he found Buvat seated on a comfortable sofa, his feet on the hobs, his head leaning back, his eyes winking, and singing between his teeth, with an expression of infinite tenderness:

"Then let me go, And let me play, Beneath the hazel-tree."

Which, as may be seen, was a great improvement on the state of the worthy writer twenty-four hours before. Moreover, when the valet-de-chambre offered to help him to undress, Buvat, who found a slight difficulty in expressing his thoughts, contented himself with smiling in sign of approbation; then extended his arms to have his coat taken off, then his legs to have his slippers removed; but, in spite of his state of exaltation, it is only just to Buvat to say, that it was only when he found himself alone that he laid aside the rest of his garments.

This time, contrary to what he had done the day before, he stretched himself out luxuriously in his bed, and fell asleep in five minutes, and dreamed that he was the Grand Turk.

He awoke as fresh as a rose, having only one trouble— the uneasiness that Bathilde must experience, but otherwise perfectly happy.

It may easily be imagined that the breakfast did not lessen his good spirits; on the contrary, being informed that he might write to Monsieur the Archbishop of Cambray, he asked for paper and ink, which were brought him, took from his pocket his penknife, which never left him, cut his pen with the greatest care, and commenced, in his finest writing, a most touching request, that if his captivity was to last, Bathilde might be sent for, or, at least, that she might be informed, that, except his liberty, he was in want of nothing, thanks to the kindness of the prime minister.

This request, to the caligraphy of which Buvat had devoted no little care, and whose capital letters represented different plants, trees, or animals, occupied the worthy writer from breakfast till dinner. On sitting down to table he gave the note to Bourguignon, who charged himself with carrying it to the prime minister, saying that Comtois would wait during his absence. In a quarter of an hour Bourguignon returned, and informed Buvat that monseigneur had gone out, but that—in his absence—the petition had been given to the person who aided him in his public affairs, and that person had requested that Monsieur Buvat would come and see him as soon as he had finished his dinner, but hoped that monsieur would not in any degree hurry himself, since he who made the request was dining himself. In accordance with this permission Buvat took his time, feasted on the best cookery, imbibed the most generous wines, sipped his coffee, played with his glass of liquor, and then—the last operation completed—declared in a resolute tone, that he was ready to appear before the substitute of the prime minister.

The sentinel had received orders to let him pass, so Buvat, conducted by Bourguignon, passed proudly by him. For some time they followed a long corridor, then descended a staircase; at last the footman opened a door, and announced

Monsieur Buvat.

[Pg 406]Buvat found himself in a sort of laboratory, situated on the ground-floor, with a man of from forty to forty-two, who was entirely unknown to him, and who was very simply dressed, and occupied in following—at a blazing furnace—some chemical experiment, to which he appeared to attach great importance. This man, seeing Buvat, raised his head, and having looked at him curiously—

"Monsieur," said he, "are you Jean Buvat?"——"At your service, monsieur," answered Buvat, bowing.

"The request which you have just sent to the abbé is your handwriting?"

"My own, monsieur."

"You write a fine hand."

Buvat bowed, with a proudly modest smile.

"The abbé," continued the unknown, "has informed me of the services which you have rendered us."

"Monseigneur is too good," murmured Buvat, "it was not worth the trouble."

"How! not worth the trouble? Indeed, Monsieur Buvat, it was, on the contrary, well worth the trouble, and the proof is, that if you have any favor to ask from the regent, I will charge myself with the message."

"Monsieur," said Buvat, "since you are so good as to offer to interpret my sentiments to his royal highness, have the kindness to request him, when he is less pressed, if it is not too inconvenient, to pay me my arrears."

"How! your arrears, Monsieur Buvat? What do you

mean?"

"I mean, monsieur, that I have the honor to be employed at the royal library, but that for six years I have received no salary."

"And how much do your arrears amount to?"

"Monsieur, I must have a pen and ink to calculate exactly."

"Oh, but something near the mark—calculate from memory."

"To five thousand three hundred and odd francs, besides the fractions of sous and deniers."

"And you wish for payment, Monsieur Buvat?"

"I do not deny it, monsieur; it would give me great pleasure."

"And is this all you ask?"

"All."

"But do you not ask anything for the service which you have just rendered France?"

"Indeed, monsieur, I should like permission to let my ward Bathilde know that she may be easy on my account, and that I am a prisoner at the Palais Royal. I would also ask—if it would not be imposing upon your kindness too much—that she might be allowed to pay me a little visit, but, if this second request is indiscreet, I will confine myself to the first."

"We will do better than that; the causes for which you were retained exist no more, and we are going to set you at liberty; so you can go yourself to carry the news to Bathilde."

"What, monsieur, what!" cried Buvat; "am I, then, no

longer a prisoner?"

"You can go when you like."

"Monsieur, I am your very humble servant, and I have the honor of presenting you my respects."

"Pardon, Monsieur Buvat, one word more."——"Two, monsieur."

"I repeat to you that France is under obligations to you, which she will acquit. Write, then, to the regent, inform him of what is due to you, show him your situation, and if you have a particular desire for anything, say so boldly. I guarantee that he will grant your request."

"Monsieur, you are too good, and I shall not fail. I hope, then, that out of the first money which comes into the treasury—"

"You will be paid. I give you my word."

"Monsieur, this very day my petition shall be addressed to the regent."

"And to-morrow you will be paid."

"Ah, monsieur, what goodness!"

"Go, Monsieur Buvat, go; your ward expects you."

"You are right, monsieur, but she will lose nothing by having waited for me, since I bring her such good news. I may have the honor of seeing you again, monsieur. Ah! pardon, would it be an indiscretion to ask your name?"

[Pg 407]"Monsieur Philippe."

"Au revoir! Monsieur Philippe!"

"Adieu! Monsieur Buvat. One instant—I must give orders that they are to allow you to pass."

471

At these words he rang: an usher appeared. "Send Ravanne."

The usher went out; a few seconds afterward a young officer of guards entered.

"Ravanne," said Monsieur Philippe, "conduct this gentleman to the gate of the Palais Royal. There he is free to go where he wishes."

"Yes, monseigneur," answered the young officer.

A cloud passed over Buvat's eyes, and he opened his mouth to ask who it was that was being called monseigneur, but Ravanne did not leave him time.

"Come, monsieur," said he, "I await you."

Buvat looked at Monsieur Philippe and the page with a stupefied air; but the latter—not understanding his hesitation—renewed his invitation to follow. Buvat obeyed, drawing out his handkerchief, and wiping his forehead.

At the door, the sentinel wished to stop Buvat.

"By the order of his royal highness Monseigneur the Regent, monsieur is free," said Ravanne.

The soldier presented arms, and allowed him to pass.

Buvat thought he should faint, he felt his legs fail him, and leaned against a wall.

"What is the matter, monsieur?" asked his guide.

"Pardon, monsieur," murmured Buvat, "but who is the person to whom I have just had the honor of speaking?"

"Monseigneur the Regent in person."

"Not possible!"

"Not only possible, but true."

"What! it was the regent himself who promised to pay me my arrears?"

"I do not know what he promised you, but I know that the person who gave me the order to accompany you was the regent."

"But he told me he was called Philippe."

"Well, he is—Philippe d'Orleans."

"That is true, monsieur, that is true, Philippe is his Christian name. The regent is a brave man, and when I remember that there exist scoundrels who conspire against him—against a man who has promised to pay me my arrears—but they deserve to be hanged, all of them, to be broken on the wheel, drawn and quartered, burned alive; do not you think so, monsieur?"

"Monsieur," said Ravanne, laughing, "I have no opinion on matters of such importance. We are at the gate; I should be happy to accompany you further, but monseigneur leaves in half an hour for the Abbey of Chelles, and, as he has some orders to give me before his departure, I am—to my great regret—obliged to quit you."

"All the regret is on my side, monsieur," said Buvat, graciously, and answering by a profound bow to the slight nod of the young man, who, when Buvat raised his head, had already disappeared. This departure left Buvat perfectly free in his movements, and he profited thereby to take his way down the Place des Victoires toward the Rue du Temps-Perdu, round the corner of which he turned at the very moment when D'Harmental ran his sword through the body of Roquefinette. It was at this moment that poor Bathilde—who was far from suspecting what was passing in her neighbor's room—had seen her guardian, and had rushed to meet him on the stairs, where Buvat and she had met at the third flight.

"Oh, my dear, dear father," cried Bathilde, remounting the staircase in Buvat's arms, and stopping to embrace him at every step, "where have you been? What has happened? How is it that we have not seen you since Monday? What uneasiness you have caused us, mon Dieu! But something extraordinary must have occurred."

"Yes, most extraordinary," answered Buvat.

"Ah, mon Dieu! tell then me, first, where do you come from?"

"From the Palais Royal."

"What! from the Palais Royal; and[Pg 408] with whom were you stopping at the Palais Royal?"

"The regent."

"You with the regent! and what about?"

"I was a prisoner."

"A prisoner—you!"

"A State prisoner."

"And why were you a prisoner?"

"Because I have saved France."

"Oh, father! are you mad?" cried Bathilde, terrified.

"No, but there has been enough to make me so if I had not had a pretty strong head."

"Oh, explain, for God's sake!"

"Fancy that there was a conspiracy against the regent."

"Oh, mon Dieu!"

"And that I belonged to it."

"You?"

"Yes, I, without being—that is to say, you know that Prince de Listhnay?"

"Well!"

"A sham prince, my child, a sham prince!"

"But the copies which you made for him?"

"Manifestoes, proclamations, incendiary papers, a general revolt, Brittany—Normandy—the States-General—king of Spain—I have discovered all this."

"You?" cried Bathilde, horrified.

"Yes, I; and the regent has called me the savior of France—me; and is going to pay me my arrears."

"My father, my father, you talk of conspirators, do you remember the name of any of them?"

"Firstly, Monsieur the Duc de Maine; fancy that miserable bastard conspiring against a man like Monseigneur the Regent. Then a Count de Laval, a Marquis de Pompadour, a Baron de Valef, the Prince de Cellamare, the Abbe Brigaud, that abominable Abbe Brigaud! Think of my having copied the list."

"My father," said Bathilde, shuddering with fear, "my father, among all those names, did you not see the name— the name—of—Chevalier—Raoul d'Harmental?"

"That I did," cried Buvat, "the Chevalier Raoul d'Harmental—why he is the head of the company: but the regent knows them all, and this very evening they will all be arrested, and to-morrow hanged, drawn, quartered, broken on the wheel."

"Oh, luckless, shameful, that you are!" cried Bathilde, wringing her hands wildly; "you have killed the man whom I love—but, I swear to you, by the memory of my mother, that if he dies, I will die also!"

And thinking that she might still be in time to warn D'Harmental of the danger which threatened him, Bathilde left Buvat confounded, darted to the door, flew down the staircase, cleared the street at two bounds, rushed up the stairs, and, breathless, terrified, dying, hurled herself against the door of D'Harmental's room, which, badly closed by the chevalier, yielded before her, exposing to her view the body of the captain stretched on the floor, and swimming in a sea of blood.

At this sight, so widely different from what she expected, Bathilde, not thinking that she might perhaps be compromising her lover, sprang toward the door, calling for help, but on reaching the threshold, either from weakness, or from the blood, her foot slipped, and she fell backward with a terrible cry.

The neighbors came running in the direction of the cry, and found that Bathilde had fainted, and that her head, in falling against the angle of the door, had been badly wounded.

They carried Bathilde to Madame Denis's room, and the good woman hastened to offer her hospitality.

As to Captain Roquefinette, as he had torn off the

address of the letter which he had in his pocket to light his pipe with, and had no other paper to indicate his name or residence, they carried his body to the Morgue, where, three days afterward, it was recognized by La Normande.

CHAPTER XXXVIII.
GOD DISPOSES.

D'Harmental, as we have seen, had set off at a gallop, feeling that he had not an instant to lose in bringing about the[Pg 409] changes which the death of Captain Roquefinette rendered necessary in his hazardous enterprise. In the hope of recognizing by some sign the individuals who were destined to play the part of supernumeraries in this great drama, he followed the boulevards as far as the Porte Saint Martin, and having arrived there, turned to the left, and was in the midst of the horse market: it was there, it will be remembered, that the twelve or fifteen sham peasants enlisted by Roquefinette waited the orders of their captain. But, as the deceased had said, no sign pointed out to the eye of the stranger who were the men, clothed like the rest, and scarcely known to each other. D'Harmental, therefore, sought vainly; all the faces were unknown to him; buyers and sellers appeared equally indifferent to everything except the bargains which they were concluding. Twice or thrice, after having approached persons whom he fancied he recognized as false bargainers, he went away without even speaking to them, so great was the probability, that, among the five or six hundred individuals who were on the ground, the chevalier would make some mistake which might be not only useless, but even dangerous.

The situation was pitiable: D'Harmental unquestionably had there, ready to his hand, all the means necessary to the happy completion of his plot, but he had, in killing the captain, broken with his own hand the thread which should have served him as a clew to them, and, the center link broken, the whole chain had become useless.

D'Harmental bit his lips till the blood came, and wandered to and fro, from end to end of the market, still hoping that some unforeseen event would get him out of his difficulty. Time, however, flowed away, the market presented the same aspect, no one spoke to him, and two peasants to whom despair had caused him to address some ambiguous words, had opened their eyes and mouths in such profound astonishment that he had instantly broken off the conversation, convinced that he was mistaken.

Five o'clock struck.

At eight or nine the regent would repair to Chelles, there was therefore no time to be lost, particularly as this ambuscade was the last resource for the conspirators, who might be arrested at any moment, and who staked their remaining hopes on this last throw. D'Harmental did not conceal from himself the difficulties of the situation; he had claimed for himself the honor of the enterprise; on him therefore rested all the responsibility—and that responsibility was terrible. On the other hand, he found himself in one of those situations where courage is useless, and where human will shatters itself against an impossibility, and where the last chance is to confess one's weakness, and ask aid from those who expect it of us. But D'Harmental was a man of determination; his resolution was soon taken—he took a last turn round the market to see if some conspirator would not betray himself by his impatience; but, seeing that all faces retained their expression of unconcern, he put his horse to the gallop, rode down the Boulevards, gained the Faubourg Saint Antoine, dismounted at No. 15, went up the staircase, opened the door of a little room, and found himself in the company of Madame de Maine, Laval, Valef, Pompadour, Malezieux and Brigaud.

A general cry arose on seeing him.

D'Harmental related everything: the pretensions of Roquefinette, the discussion which had followed, the duel which had terminated that discussion. He opened his cloak and showed his shirt saturated with blood; then he passed to the hopes which he had entertained of recognizing the sham peasants, and putting himself at their head in place of the captain. He showed his hopes destroyed, his investigations useless, and wound up by an appeal to Laval, Pompadour, and Valef, who answered that they were ready to follow the chevalier to the end of the earth, and to obey his orders.

Nothing was lost, then—four resolute men, acting on their own account, were well worth twelve or fifteen hired vagabonds, who were not influenced by any motive beyond that of gaining some hun[Pg 410]dred louis a-piece. The horses were ready in the stable, every one had come armed; D'Avranches was not yet gone, which re-enforced the little troop by another devoted man. They sent for masks of black velvet, so as to hide from the regent as long as possible who his enemies were, left with Madame de Maine Malezieux, who from his age, and Brigaud, who from his profession, were naturally excluded from such an expedition, fixed a rendezvous at Saint Mande, and left, each one separately, so as not to arouse suspicions. An hour afterward the five friends were reunited, and ambushed on the road to Chelles, between Vincennes and Nogent-sur-Marne.

Half-past six struck on the chateau clock.

D'Avranches had been in search of information. The regent had passed at about half-past three; he had neither guards nor suite, he was in a carriage and four, ridden by two jockeys, and preceded by a single outrider. There was no resistance to be feared; on arresting the prince they would turn his course toward Charenton, where the postmaster was, as we have said, in the interest of Madame de Maine, take him into the courtyard, whose door would close upon him, force him to enter a traveling carriage, which would be waiting with the postilion in his saddle; D'Harmental and Valef would seat themselves by him, they would cross the Marne at Alfort, the Seine at Villeneuve-Saint-Georges, reach Grand-Vaux, then Monthéry, and find themselves on the road to Spain. If at any of the villages where they changed horses the regent endeavored to call out, D'Harmental and Valef would threaten him, and, if he called out in spite of the menaces, they had that famous passport to prove that he who claimed assistance was not the prince, but only a madman who thought himself the regent, and whom they were conducting to his family, who lived at Saragossa. All this was a little dangerous, it is true, but, as is well known, these are the very enterprises which succeed, so much the easier from their unforeseen audacity.

Seven o'clock, eight o'clock, struck successively. D'Harmental and his companions saw with pleasure the night approaching, and the darkness falling more and more dense and black around them; two or three carriages had already given false alarms, but had had no other effect than preparing them for the real attack. At half-past eight the night was pitch-dark, and a sort of natural fear, which the conspirators had felt at first, began to change into impatience.

At nine o'clock they thought they could distinguish sounds. D'Avranches lay down, with his ear to the ground, and distinctly heard the rolling of a carriage. At that instant they saw, at about a thousand paces from the angle of the road, a point of light like a star; the conspirators trembled with excitement, it was evidently the outrider with his torch. There was soon no doubt—they saw the carriage with its two lanterns. D'Harmental, Pompadour, Valef, and Laval, grasped one another's hands, put on their masks, and each one took the place assigned to him. The carriage advanced rapidly—it was really that of the duke. By the light of the torch which he carried they could distinguish the red dress of the outrider, some five-and-twenty paces before the horses. The road was silent and deserted, everything was favorable. D'Harmental threw a last glance on his companions. D'Avranches was in the middle of the road pretending to be drunk, Laval and Pompadour on each side of the path, and opposite him Valef, who was cocking his pistols. As to the outrider, the two jockeys and the prince, it was evident that they were all in a state of perfect security, and would fall quietly into the trap. The carriage still advanced; already the outrider had passed D'Harmental and Valef, suddenly he struck against D'Avranches, who sprang up, seized the bridle, snatched the torch from his hand, and extinguished it. At this sight the jockeys tried to turn the carriage, but it was too late; Pompadour and Laval sprang upon them pistol in hand, while D'Harmental and Valef presented themselves at the two doors, extin[Pg 411]guished the lanterns, and intimated to the prince that if he did not make any resistance his life would be spared, but that if, on the contrary, he defended himself, or cried out, they were determined to proceed to extremities.

Contrary to the expectation of D'Harmental and Valef, who knew the courage of the regent, the prince only said:

"Well, gentlemen, do not harm me. I will go wherever you wish."

D'Harmental and Valef threw a glance at the road; they saw Pompadour and D'Avranches leading into the depth of the wood the outrider, the two jockeys, the outrider's horse, and two of the carriage horses which they had unharnessed. The chevalier sprang from his horse, mounted that of the first postilion; Laval and Valef placed themselves before the doors, the carriage set off at a gallop, and taking the first turn to the left, began to roll, without noise and without light, in the direction of Charenton. All the arrangements had been so perfect, that the seizure had not occupied more than five minutes; no resistance had been made, not a cry had been uttered. Most assuredly, this time fortune was on the side of the conspirators.

But having arrived at the end of the cross-road, D'Harmental encountered a first obstacle; the barrier—either by accident or design—was closed, and they were obliged to retrace their steps and take another road. The chevalier turned his horses, took a lateral alley, and the journey, interrupted for an instant, recommenced at an increased speed.

The new route which the chevalier had taken led him to a four-cross road; one of the roads led straight to Charenton. There was no time to lose, and in any event he must traverse this square. For an instant he thought he distinguished men in the darkness before him, but this vision disappeared like a mist, and the carriage continued its progress without interruption. On approaching the cross-roads D'Harmental fancied he heard the neighing of a horse, and a sort of ringing of iron, like sabers being drawn from their sheaths, but either taking it for the wind among the leaves, or for some other noise for which he need not stop, he continued with the same swiftness, the same silence, and in the midst of the same darkness. But, having arrived at the cross-roads, D'Harmental noticed a singular circumstance, a sort of wall seemed to close all the roads; something was happening. D'Harmental stopped the carriage, and wished to return by the road he had come down, but a similar wall had closed behind him. At that instant he heard the voices of Laval and Valef crying:

"We are surrounded, save yourself!"

And both left the doors, leaped their horses over the ditch, darted into the forest, and disappeared among the trees.

But it was impossible for D'Harmental, who was mounted on the postilion's horse, to follow his companions, and, not being able to escape the living wall, which the chevalier recognized as a regiment of musketeers, he tried to break through it, and with his head lowered, and a pistol in each hand, spurred his horse up the nearest road, without considering whether it was the right one. He had scarcely gone ten steps, however, when a musket-ball entered the head of his horse, which fell, entangling D'Harmental's leg. Instantly eight or ten cavaliers sprang upon him; he fired one pistol by hazard, and put the other to his head, to blow his brains out, but he had not time, for two musketeers seized him by the arms, and four others dragged him from beneath the horse. The pretended prince descended from the carriage, and turned out to be a valet in disguise; they placed D'Harmental with two officers inside the carriage, and harnessed another horse in the place of the one which had been shot. The carriage once more moved forward, taking a new direction, and escorted by a squadron of musketeers. A quarter of an hour afterward it rolled over a drawbridge, a heavy door grated upon its hinges, and D'Harmental passed under a somber and vaulted gateway, on the inner side of which, an officer in the uniform of a colonel was waiting for him. It was Monsieur de Launay, the governor of the Bastille.

[Pg 412]If our readers desire to know how the plot had been discovered, they must recall the conversation between Dubois and La Fillon. The gossip of the prime minister, it will be remembered, suspected Roquefinette of being mixed up in some illicit proceeding, and had denounced him on condition of his life being spared. A few days afterward D'Harmental came to her house, and she recognized him as the young man who had held the former conference with Roquefinette. She had consequently mounted the stairs behind him, and, going into the next room, had, by aid of a hole bored in the partition, heard everything.

What she had heard was the project for carrying off the regent on his return from Chelles. Dubois had been informed the same evening, and, in order to take the conspirators in the act, had put a suit of the regent's clothes on Monsieur Bourguignon, and, having surrounded the Bois de Vincennes with a regiment of Gray Musketeers, besides light-horse and dragoons, had produced the result we have just related. The head of the plot had been taken in the fact, and as the prime minister knew the names of all the conspirators, there was little chance remaining for them of escape from the meshes of the vast net which was hourly closing around them.

CHAPTER XXXIX.
A PRIME MINISTER'S MEMORY.

When Bathilde reopened her eyes, she found herself in Mademoiselle Emilie's room. Mirza was lying on the end of the bed; the two sisters were one at each side of her pillow, and Buvat, overcome by grief, was sitting in a corner, his head bent, and his hands resting on his knees.

At first all her thoughts were confused, and her sensation was one of bodily pain; she raised her hand to her head; the wound was behind the temple. A doctor, who had been called in, had arranged the first dressing, and left orders that he was to be sent for if fever declared itself.

Astonished to find herself—on waking from a sleep which had appeared to her heavy and painful—in bed in a strange room, the young girl turned an inquiring glance on each person present, but Emilie and Athenais shunned her eyes, and Buvat heaved a mournful sigh. Mirza alone stretched out her little head for a caress. Unluckily for the coaxing little creature, Bathilde began to recover her memory; the veil which was drawn before the late events rose little by little, and soon she began to connect the broken threads which might guide her in the past. She recalled the return of Buvat, what he had told her of the conspiracy, the danger which would result to D'Harmental from the revelation he had made. Then she remembered her hope of being in time to save him, the rapidity with which she had crossed the street and mounted the staircase; lastly, her entry into Raoul's room returned to her memory, and once more she found herself before the corpse of Roquefinette.

"And he," she cried, "what has become of him?"

No one answered, for neither of the three persons who were in the room knew what reply to give; only Buvat, choking with tears, rose, and went toward the door. Bathilde understood the grief and remorse expressed in that mute withdrawal; she stopped him by a look, and extending her arms toward him—

"My father," said she, "do you no longer love your poor Bathilde?"

"I no longer love you, my darling child!" cried Buvat, falling on his knees, and kissing her hand, "I love you no longer! My God! it will be you who will not love me now, and you will be right, for I am worthless; I ought to have known that that young man loved you, and ought to have risked all, suffered all, rather than—. But you told me nothing, you had no confidence in me, and I—with the best intentions in the world—made nothing but mistakes; oh, unlucky, unhappy, that I am, you will never forgive me, and then—how shall I live?"

"Father," cried Bathilde, "for Heaven's sake try and find out what has happened."

"Well, my child, well, I will discover; will not you forgive me if I bring you good news? If the news is bad, you will hate[Pg 413] me even more; that will but be just, but you will not die, Bathilde?"

"Go, go," said Bathilde, throwing her arms round his

neck, and giving him a kiss in which fifteen years of gratitude struggled with one day of pain; "go, my existence is in the hands of God, He only can decide whether I shall live or die."

Buvat understood nothing of all this but the kiss, and—having inquired of Madame Denis how the chevalier had been dressed—he set out on his quest.

It was no easy matter for a detective so simple as Buvat to trace Raoul's progress; he had learned from a neighbor that he had been seen to spring upon a gray horse which had remained some half hour fastened to the shutter, and that he had turned round the Rue Gros Chenet. A grocer, who lived at the corner of the Rue des Jeuneurs, remembered having seen a cavalier, whose person and horse agreed perfectly with the description given by Buvat, pass by at full gallop; and, lastly, a fruit woman, who kept a little shop at the corner of the Boulevards, swore positively that she had seen the man, and that he had disappeared by the Porte Saint Denis; but from this point all the information was vague, unsatisfactory, and uncertain, so that, after two hours of useless inquiry, Buvat returned to Madame Denis's house without any more definite information to give Bathilde than that, wherever D'Harmental might be gone, he had passed along the Boulevard Bonne-Nouvelle. Buvat found his ward much agitated; during his absence she had grown rapidly worse, and the crisis foreseen by the doctor was fast approaching. Bathilde's eyes flashed; her skin seemed to glow; her words were short and firm. Madame Denis had just sent for the doctor.

The poor woman was not without her own anxieties; for some time she had suspected that the Abbe Brigaud was mixed up in some plot, and what she had just learned, that D'Harmental was not a poor student but a rich colonel, confirmed her conjectures, since it had been Brigaud who had introduced him to her. This similarity of position had not a little contributed to soften her heart—always kind— toward Bathilde. She listened, then, with eagerness to the little information which Buvat had been able to collect for the sufferer, and, as it was far from being sufficiently positive to calm the patient, she promised, if she heard anything herself, to report it directly.

In the meantime the doctor arrived. Great as was his command over himself, it was easy to see that he thought Bathilde in some danger—he bled her abundantly, ordered refreshing drinks, and advised that some one should watch at the bedside. Emilie and Athenais, who, their little absurdities excepted, were excellent girls, declared directly that that was their business, and that they would pass the night with Bathilde alternately; Emilie, as eldest, claimed the first watch, which was given her without contest. As to Buvat, since he could not remain in the room, they asked him to return home; a thing to which he would not consent till Bathilde herself had begged it. The bleeding had somewhat calmed her, and she seemed to feel better; Madame Denis had left the room; Mademoiselle Athenais also had retired; Monsieur Boniface, after returning from the Morgue, where he had been to pay a visit to the body of Roquefinette, had mounted to his own room, and Emilie watched by the fireplace, and read a little book which she took from her pocket. She shortly heard a movement in the bed, and ran toward it; then, after an instant's silence, during which she heard the opening and shutting of two or three doors, and before she had time to say—"That is not the voice of Monsieur Raoul, it is the Abbe Brigaud," Bathilde had fallen back on her pillow.

An instant afterward Madame Denis half opened the door, and in a trembling voice called Emilie, who kissed Bathilde and went out.

Suddenly Bathilde was aroused; the abbe was in the room next to hers, and she thought that she heard him pronounce Raoul's name. She now remembered having several times seen the abbe at D'Har[Pg 414]mental's rooms; she knew that he was one of the most intimate friends of Madame de Maine; she thought, then, that the abbe must bring news of him. Her first idea was to slip from the bed, put on a dressing-gown, and go and ask what had happened; but she considered that if the news was bad they would not tell it, and that it would be better to overhear the conversation, which appeared animated. Consequently she pressed her ear to the panel, and listened as if her whole life had been spent in cultivating that single sense.

Brigaud was relating to Madame Denis what had happened. Valef had made his way to the Faubourg Saint Antoine, and given warning to Madame de Maine of the failure of the expedition. Madame de Maine had immediately

491

freed the conspirators from their oaths, advised Malezieux and Brigaud to save themselves, and retired to the Arsenal. Brigaud came therefore to bid adieu to Madame Denis; he was going to attempt to reach Spain in the disguise of a peddler. In the midst of his recital, interrupted by the exclamation of poor Madame Denis and of Mesdemoiselles Athenais and Emilie, the abbe thought that he heard a cry in the next room, just at the time when he was relating D'Harmental's catastrophe; but as no one had paid any attention to the cry, and as he was not aware of Bathilde's being there, he had attached no importance to this noise, regarding the nature of which he might easily have been mistaken; moreover, Boniface, summoned in his turn, had entered at the moment, and, as the abbe had a particular fancy for Boniface, his entrance had naturally turned Brigaud's thoughts into a different channel.

Still, this was not the time for long leave-takings; Brigaud desired that daylight should find him as far as possible from Paris. He took leave of the Denis family, and set out with Boniface, who declared that he would accompany friend Brigaud as far as the barrier.

As they opened the staircase-door they heard the voice of the portress, who appeared to be opposing the passage of some one; they descended to discover the cause of the discussion, and found Bathilde, with streaming hair, naked feet, and wrapped in a long white robe, standing on the staircase, and endeavoring to go out in spite of the efforts of the portress. The poor girl had heard everything; the fever had changed into delirium; she would join Raoul; she would see him again; she would die with him.

The three women took her in their arms. For a minute she struggled against them, murmuring incoherent words; her cheeks were flushed with fever, while her limbs trembled, and her teeth chattered; but soon her strength failed her, her head sank back, and, calling on the name of Raoul, she fainted a second time.

They sent once more for the doctor. What he had feared was now no longer doubtful—brain fever had declared itself. At this moment some one knocked; it was Buvat, whom Brigaud and Boniface had found wandering to and fro before the house like a ghost; and who, not able to keep up any longer, had come to beg a seat in some corner, he did not care where, so long as from time to time he had news of Bathilde. The poor family were too sad themselves not to feel for the grief of others. Madame signed to Buvat to seat himself in a corner, and retired into her own room with Athenais, leaving Emilie once more with the sufferer. About daybreak Boniface returned: he had gone with Brigaud as far as the Barriere d'Enfer, where the abbe had left him, hoping—thanks to his good steed, and to his disguise—to reach the Spanish frontier.

Bathilde's delirium continued. All night she talked of Raoul; she often mentioned Buvat's name, and always accused him of having killed her lover. Buvat heard it, and, without daring to defend himself, to reply, or even to groan, had silently burst into tears, and, pondering on what means existed of repairing the evil he had caused, he at last arrived at a desperate resolution. He approached the bed, kissed the feverish hand of Bathilde, who did not recognize him, and went out.

Buvat had, in fact, determined on a[Pg 415] bold course. It was to go himself to Dubois, tell him everything, and ask, as his recompense—not the payment of his arrears—not advancement at the library—but pardon for D'Harmental. It was the least that could be accorded to the man whom the regent himself had called the savior of France. Buvat did not doubt that he should soon return bearing good news, and that it would restore Bathilde to health.

Consequently Buvat went home to arrange his disordered dress, which bore the marks of the events of the day and the emotions of the night; and, moreover, he did not dare to present himself at the minister's house so early, for fear of disturbing him. His toilet finished, and as it was still only nine o'clock, he returned for a few minutes to Bathilde's room—it was that which the young girl had left the day before. Buvat sat down in the chair which she had quitted, touched the articles which she liked to touch, kissed the feet of the crucifix, which she kissed each night—one would have thought him a lover following the steps of his mistress.

Ten o'clock struck; it was the hour at which Buvat had often before repaired to the Palais Royal. The fear of being importunate gave place to the hope of being received as he had always been. He took his hat and cane, and called at Madame Denis's to ask how Bathilde had been during his absence; he found that she had never ceased to call for Raoul. The doctor had bled her for the third time. He raised his eyes to heaven, heaved a profound sigh, and set out for the Palais Royal.

The moment was unlucky. Dubois, who had been constantly on his feet for four or five days, suffered horribly from the malady which was to cause his death in a few months; moreover, he was beyond measure annoyed that only D'Harmental had been taken, and had just given orders to Leblanc and D'Argenson to press on the trial with all possible speed, when his valet-de-chambre, who was accustomed to see the worthy writer arrive every morning, announced M. Buvat.

"And who the devil is M. Buvat?"

"It is I, monseigneur," said the poor fellow, venturing to slip between the valet and the door, and bowing his honest head before the prime minister.

"Well, who are you?" asked Dubois, as if he had never seen him before.

"What, monseigneur!" exclaimed the astonished Buvat; "do you not recognize me? I come to congratulate you on the discovery of the conspiracy."

"I get congratulations enough of that kind—thanks for yours, M. Buvat," said Dubois, quietly.

"But, monseigneur, I come also to ask a favor."

"A favor! and on what grounds?"

"Monseigneur," stammered Buvat, "but—monseigneur—do you not remember that you promised me a—a recompense?"

"A recompense to you, you double idiot."

"What! monseigneur," continued poor Buvat, getting more and more frightened, "do you not recollect that you told me, here, in this very room, that I had my fortune at my fingers' ends?"

"And now," said Dubois, "I tell you that you have your life in your legs, for unless you decamp pretty quick—"

"But, monseigneur—"

"Ah! you reason with me, scoundrel," shouted Dubois, raising himself with one hand on the arm of his chair, and the other on his archbishop's crook, "wait, then, you shall see—"

Buvat had seen quite enough; at the threatening gesture of the premier he understood what was to follow, and turning round, he fled at full speed; but, quick as he was, he had still time to hear Dubois—with the most horrible oaths and curses—order his valet to beat him to death if ever again he put his foot inside the door of the Palais Royal.

Buvat understood that there was no hope in that direction, and that, not only must he renounce the idea of being of service to D'Harmental, but also of the payment of his arrears, in which he had fondly trusted. This chain of thought naturally reminded him that for eight days he had[Pg 416] not been to the library—he was near there—he resolved to go to his office, if it was only to excuse himself to his superior, and relate to him the causes of his absence; but here a grief, not less terrible than the rest, was in store for Buvat; on opening the door of his office, he saw his seat occupied—a stranger had been appointed to his place!

As he had never before—during the whole fifteen years—been an hour late, the curator had imagined him dead, and had replaced him. Buvat had lost his situation for having saved France!

This last stroke was more than he could bear, and Buvat returned home almost as ill as Bathilde.

CHAPTER XL.
BONIFACE.

As we have seen, Dubois urged on the trial of D'Harmental, hoping that his revelations would furnish him with weapons against those whom he wished to attack, but D'Harmental took refuge in a total denial with respect to others. As to what concerned himself personally, he confessed everything, saying, that his attempt on the regent was the result of private revenge, a revenge which had arisen from the injustice which had been done him in depriving him of his regiment. As to the men who had accompanied him, and who had lent him their aid in the execution of his plans, he declared that they were poor devils of peasants, who did not even know whom they were escorting. All this was not highly probable, but there was no means of bringing anything beyond the answers of the accused to bear on the matter; the consequence was, that to the infinite annoyance of Dubois, the real criminals escaped his vengeance, under cover of the eternal denials of the chevalier, who denied having seen Monsieur or Madame de Maine more than once or twice in his life, or ever having been trusted with any political mission by either of them.

They had arrested successively Laval, Pompadour, and Valef, and had taken them to the Bastille, but they knew that they might rely upon the chevalier; and, as the situation in which they found themselves had been foreseen, and it had been agreed what each should say, they all entirely denied any knowledge of the affair, confessing associations with

Monsieur and Madame de Maine, but saying that those associations were confined to a respectful friendship. As to D'Harmental, they knew him, they said, for a man of honor, who complained of a great injustice which had been done to him. They were confronted, one after the other, with the chevalier; but these interviews had no other result than that of confirming each in his system of defense, and showing each that the system was religiously adhered to by his companion.

Dubois was furious—he reopened the proofs for the affair of the States-General, but that had been settled by the special parliament, which had condemned the king of Spain's letters, and degraded the legitimated princes from their rank; everyone regarded them as sufficiently punished by this judgment, without raising a second prosecution against them on the same grounds. Dubois had hoped, by the revelations of D'Harmental, to entangle Monsieur and Madame de Maine in a new trial, more serious than the first; for this time it was a question of a direct attempt, if not on the life, at least on the liberty of the regent; but the obstinacy of the chevalier destroyed all his hopes. His anger had therefore turned solely on D'Harmental, and, as we have said, he had ordered Leblanc and D'Argenson to expedite the prosecution—an order which the two magistrates had obeyed with their ordinary punctuality.

During this time the illness of Bathilde had progressed in a manner which had brought the poor girl to death's door; but at last youth and vigor had triumphed; to the excitement of delirium had succeeded a complete and utter prostration;

one would have said that the fever alone had sustained her, and that, in departing, it had taken life along with it.

Still every day brought improvement—slight, it is true, but decided—to the eyes of the good people who surrounded the bed[Pg 417] of sickness. Little by little Bathilde began to recognize those who were about her, then she had stretched out her hand to them, and then spoken to them. As yet, to the astonishment of every one, they had remarked that Bathilde had not mentioned the name of D'Harmental; this was a great relief to those who watched her, for, as they had none but sad news to give her about him, they preferred, as will easily be understood, that she should remain silent on the subject; every one believed, and the doctor most of all, that the young girl had completely forgotten the past, or, if she remembered it, that she confounded the reality with the dreams of her delirium. They were all wrong, even the doctor: this was what had occurred:

One morning when they had thought Bathilde sleeping, and had left her alone for a minute, Boniface, who, in spite of the severity of his neighbor, still preserved a great fund of tenderness toward her, had, as was his custom every morning since she had been ill, half opened the door to ask news of her. The growling of Mirza aroused Bathilde, who turned round and saw Boniface, and having before conjectured that she might probably know from him that which she should ask in vain from the others, namely, what had become of D'Harmental, she had, while quieting Mirza, extended her pale and emaciated hand to Boniface. Boniface took it between his own two great red hands, then, looking at the young girl, and shaking his head:

"Yes, Mademoiselle Bathilde, yes," said he, "you were right; you are a lady, and I am only a coarse peasant. You deserved a nobleman, and it was impossible that you should love me."

"As you wished, true, Boniface, but I can love you in another manner."

"True, Mademoiselle Bathilde, very true; well, love me as you will, so that you love me a little."

"I can love you as a brother."

"As a brother! You could love poor Boniface as a brother, and he might love you as a sister; he might sometimes hold your hand as he holds it now, and embrace you as he sometimes embraces Mélie and Naïs? Oh! speak, Mademoiselle Bathilde, what must I do for that?"

"My friend—" said Bathilde.

"She has called me her friend," said Boniface, "she has called me her friend—I, who have said such things about her. Listen, Mademoiselle Bathilde: do not call me your friend, I am not worthy of the name. You do not know what I have said—I said that you lived with an old man; but I did not believe it, Mademoiselle Bathilde, on my honor I did not—it was anger, it was rage. Mademoiselle Bathilde, call me beggar, rascal; it will give me less pain than to hear you term me your friend."

"My friend," recommended Bathilde, "if you have said all that, I pardon you, for now not only can you make up for it, but also acquire eternal claims upon my gratitude."

"And what shall I do? Speak! Let me see! Must I go through the fire? Shall I jump out of the second-floor window? Shall I—What shall I do? Tell me! Everything is alike."

"No, no, my friend, something much easier."

"Speak, Mademoiselle Bathilde, speak!"

"First it is necessary that you should swear to do it."

"I swear by Heaven!"

"Whatever they may say to hinder you?"

"Hinder me from doing what you ask?—never!"

"Whatever may be the grief that it may cause me?"

"No, that is a different thing; if it is to give you pain I would rather be cut in half."

"But if I beg you, my friend, my brother," said Bathilde, in her most persuasive voice.

"Oh, if you speak like that I shall cry like the Fountain of the Innocents!"

And Boniface began to sob.

"You will tell me all then, my dear Boniface?"

"Everything."

"Well, tell me first—"

Bathilde stopped.

[Pg 418]"What?"

"Can you not imagine, Boniface?"

"Yes, I think so; you want to know what has become of M. Raoul, do you not?"

"Oh yes," cried Bathilde, "in Heaven's name, what has

502

become of him?"

"Poor fellow!" murmured Boniface.

"Mon Dieu! is he dead?" exclaimed Bathilde, sitting up in the bed.

"No, happily not; but he is a prisoner."

"Where?"

"In the Bastille."

"I feared it," said Bathilde, sinking down in the bed; "in the Bastille! oh, mon Dieu! mon Dieu!"

"Oh, now you are crying, Mademoiselle Bathilde."

"And I am here in this bed, chained, dying!" cried Bathilde.

"Oh, do not cry like that, mademoiselle; it is your poor Boniface who begs you."

"No, I will be firm, I will have courage; see, Boniface, I weep no longer; but you understand that I must know everything from hour to hour, so that when he dies I may die."

"You die, Mademoiselle Bathilde! oh, never, never!"

"You have promised, you have sworn it. Boniface, you will keep me informed of all?"

"Oh, wretch that I am, what have I promised!"

"And, if it must be, at the moment—the terrible moment—you will aid me, you will conduct me, will you not, Boniface? I must see him again—once—once more—if it be on the scaffold."

"I will do all you desire, mademoiselle," said Boniface, falling on his knees, and trying vainly to restrain his sobs.

"You promise me?"

"I swear."

"Silence! some one is coming—not a word of this, it is a secret between us two. Rise, wipe your eyes, do as I do, and leave me."

And Bathilde began to laugh with a feverish nervousness that was frightful to see. Luckily it was only Buvat, and Boniface profited by his entrance to depart.

"Well, how are you?" asked the good man.

"Better, father—much better; I feel my strength returning; in a few days I shall be able to rise; but you, father, why do you not go to the office?"—Buvat sighed deeply.—"It was kind not to leave me when I was ill, but now I am getting better, you must return to the library, father."

"Yes, my child, yes," said Buvat, swallowing his sobs. "Yes, I am going."

"Are you going without kissing me?"

"No, my child, on the contrary."

"Why, father, you are crying, and yet you see that I am better!"

"I cry!" said Buvat, wiping his eyes with his handkerchief. "I, crying! If I am crying, it is only joy. Yes, I am going, my child—to my office—I am going."

And Buvat, after having embraced Bathilde, returned home, for he would not tell his poor child that he had lost his place, and the young girl was left alone.

Then she breathed more freely now that she was tranquil; Boniface, in his quality of clerk to the procureur at Chatelet, was in the very place to know everything, and Bathilde was sure that Boniface would tell her everything. Indeed, from that time she knew all: that Raoul had been interrogated, and that he had taken everything on himself; then the day following she learned that he had been confronted with Laval, Valef, and Pompadour, but that interview had produced nothing. Faithful to his promise, Boniface every evening brought her the day's news, and every evening Bathilde, at this recital, alarming as it was, felt inspired with new resolution. A fortnight passed thus, at the end of which time Bathilde began to get up and walk a little about the room, to the great joy of Buvat, Nanette, and the whole Denis family.

One day Boniface, contrary to his usual habit, returned home from Joullu's at three o'clock, and entered the room of the sufferer. The poor boy was so pale and so cast down, that Bathilde understood that he brought some terrible informa[Pg 419]tion, and giving a cry, she rose upright, with her eyes fixed on him.

"All is finished, then?" asked Bathilde.

"Alas!" answered Boniface, "it is all through his own obstinacy. They offered him pardon—do you understand, Mademoiselle Bathilde?—his pardon if he would—and he would not speak a word."

"Then," cried Bathilde, "no more hope; he is condemned."

"This morning, Mademoiselle Bathilde, this morning."

"To death?"

Boniface bowed his head.

"And when is he to be executed?"

"To-morrow morning at eight o'clock."

505

"Very well," said Bathilde.

"But perhaps there is still hope," said Boniface.

"What?" asked Bathilde.

"If even now he would denounce his accomplices."

The young girl began to laugh, but so strangely that Boniface shuddered from head to foot.

"Well," said Boniface, "who knows? I, if I was in his place, for example, should not fail to do so; I should say, 'It was not I, on my honor it was not I; it was such a one, and such another, and so on.'"

"Boniface, I must go out."

"You, Mademoiselle Bathilde!" cried Boniface, terrified. "You go out! why, it would kill you."

"I say I must go out."

"But you cannot stand upright."

"You are wrong, Boniface, I am strong—see."

And Bathilde began to walk up and down the room with a firm step.

"Moreover," added Bathilde, "you will go and fetch a coach."

"But, Mademoiselle Bathilde—"

"Boniface," said the young girl, "you have promised to obey me; till this minute you have kept your word; are you getting lax in your devotion?"

"I, Mademoiselle Bathilde! I lax in my devotion to you? You ask for a coach, I will fetch two."

"Go, my friend, my brother," said Bathilde.

"Oh! Mademoiselle Bathilde, with such words you could

make me do what you liked. In five minutes the coach will be here."

And Boniface ran out.

Bathilde had on a loose white robe; she tied it in with a girdle, threw a cloak over her shoulders, and got ready. As she was advancing to the door Madame Denis entered.

"Oh, my dear child, what in Heaven's name are you going to do?"

"Madame," said Bathilde, "it is necessary that I should go out."

"Go out! you are mad?"

"No, madame," said Bathilde, "I am in perfect possession of my senses, but you would drive me mad by retaining me."

"But at least where are you going, my dear child?"

"Do you not know that he is condemned?"

"Oh! mon Dieu! mon Dieu! who told you that? I had asked every one to keep it from you."

"Yes, and to-morrow you would have told me that he was dead, and I should have answered, 'You have killed him, for I had a means of saving him, perhaps.'"

"You, you, my child! you have a means of saving him?"

"I said, perhaps; let me try the means, it is the only one remaining."

"Go, my child," said Madame Denis, struck by the inspired tone of Bathilde's voice, "go, and may God guide you!"

Bathilde went out, descended the staircase with a slow but firm step, crossed the street, ascended the four stories without resting, opened the door of her room, which she had not entered since the day of the catastrophe. At the noise which she made, Nanette came out of the inner room, and gave a cry at seeing her young mistress.

"Well," asked Bathilde, in a grave tone, "what is it, my good Nanette?"

"Oh, mon Dieu!" cried the poor woman, trembling, "is that really you, or is it your shadow?"

"It is I, Nanette; I am not yet dead."

"And why have you left the Denis's[Pg 420] house? Have they said anything to wound you?"

"No, Nanette, but I have something to do which is necessary—indispensable."

"You, go out in your present state! You will kill yourself. M. Buvat! M. Buvat! here is our young lady going out; come and tell her that it must not be."

Bathilde turned toward Buvat, with the intention of employing her ascendency over him, if he endeavored to stop her, but she saw him with so sorrowful a face that she did not doubt that he knew the fatal news. On his part, Buvat burst into tears on seeing her.

"My father," said Bathilde, "what has been done to-day has been the work of men, what remains is in the hands of God, and he will have pity on us."

"Oh!" cried Buvat, sinking into a chair, "it is I who have killed him! it is I who have killed him!"

Bathilde went up to him solemnly and kissed him.

"But what are you going to do, my child?"

"My duty," answered Bathilde.

She opened a little cupboard in the prie-Dieu, took out a black pocket-book, opened it, and drew out a letter.

"You are right, you are right, my child, I had forgotten that letter."

"I remembered it," answered Bathilde, kissing the letter, and placing it next her heart, "for it was the sole inheritance my mother left me."

At that moment they heard the noise of a coach at the door.

"Adieu, father! adieu, Nanette! Pray for my success."

And Bathilde went away, with a solemn gravity which made her, in the eyes of those who watched her, almost a saint.

At the door she found Boniface waiting with a coach.

"Shall I go with you, Mademoiselle Bathilde?" asked he.

"No, no, my friend," said Bathilde, "not now; to-morrow, perhaps."

She entered the coach.

"Where to?" asked the coachman.

"To the Arsenal."

CHAPTER XLI.
THE THREE VISITS.

On arriving at the Arsenal Bathilde asked for Mademoiselle de Launay, who—at her request—led her at once to Madame de Maine.

"Ah, it is you, my child!" said the duchess, with a distracted air and voice; "it is well to remember one's friends when they are in misfortune."

"Alas, madame!" replied Bathilde, "I come to your royal highness to speak of one still more unfortunate. Doubtless you may have lost some of your titles, some of your dignities, but their vengeance will stop, for no one would dare to attack the life, or even the liberty, of the son of Louis XIV., or the granddaughter of the great Conde."

"The life, no; but the liberty, I will not answer for it. Do you know that that idiot of an Abbe Brigaud has got arrested three days ago at Orleans, dressed as a peddler, and—on false revelations, which they represented to him as coming from me—has confessed all, and compromised us terribly, so that I should not be astonished at being arrested this very day?"

"He for whom I come to implore your pity, madame, has revealed nothing, but, on the contrary, is condemned to death for having kept silence."

"Ah! my dear child," cried the duchess, "you speak of poor D'Harmental; he is a gentleman; you know him, then?"

"Alas!" said Mademoiselle de Launay, "not only Bathilde knows him, but she loves him."

510

"Poor child! but what can I do? I can do nothing: I have no influence. For me to attempt anything in his favor would be to take away from him the last hope remaining."

"I know it, madame," said Bathilde, "and I only ask of your highness one thing; it is, that, through some of your friends or acquaintances, I may gain admission to Monseigneur the Regent. The rest lies with me."

"My child, do you know what you are asking?" inquired the duchess. "Do you know that the regent respects no one?[Pg 421] Do you know—that you are beautiful as an angel, and still more so from your present paleness? Do you know—"

"Madame," said Bathilde, with dignity, "I know that my father saved his life, and died in his service."

"Ah, that is another thing," said the duchess; "stay, De Launay, call Malezieux."

Mademoiselle de Launay obeyed, and a moment afterward the faithful chancellor entered.

"Malezieux," said the duchess, "you must take this child to the Duchesse de Berry, with a recommendation from me. She must see the regent, and at once; the life of a man depends upon it—it is that of D'Harmental, whom I would myself give so much to save."

"I go, madame," said Malezieux.

"You see, my child," said the duchess, "I do all I can for you; if I can be useful to you in any other way—if, to prepare his flight, or to seduce a jailer, money is needed, I have still some diamonds, which cannot be better employed than in saving the life of so brave a gentleman. Come, lose no time, go at once to my niece; you know that she is her father's favorite."

"I know, madame," said Bathilde, "that you are an angel, and, if I succeed, I shall owe you more than my life."

"Come, De Launay," continued Madame de Maine, when Bathilde was gone, "let us return to our trunks."

Bathilde, accompanied by Malezieux, arrived at the Luxembourg in twenty minutes. Thanks to Malezieux, Bathilde entered without difficulty; she was conducted into a little boudoir, where she was told to wait while the chancellor should see her royal highness, and inform her of the favor they came to ask.

Malezieux acquitted himself of the commission with zeal, and Bathilde had not waited ten minutes when she saw him return with the Duchesse de Berry. The duchess had an excellent heart, and she had been greatly moved by Malezieux' recital, so that, when she appeared, there was no mistaking the interest she already felt in the young girl who came to solicit her protection. Bathilde came to her, and would have fallen at her feet, but the duchess took her by the hand, and kissing her on the forehead—

"My poor child," said she, "why did you not come to me a week ago?"

"And why a week ago rather than to-day, madame?" asked Bathilde, with anxiety.

"Because a week ago I should have yielded to none the pleasure of taking you to my father, and that now is impossible."

"Impossible! and why?" cried Bathilde.

"Do you not know that I am in complete disgrace since the day before yesterday? Alas! princess as I am, I am a woman like you, and like you I have had the misfortune to love. We daughters of the royal race, you know, may not dispose of our hearts without the authority of the king and his ministers. I have disposed of my heart, and I have nothing to say, for I was pardoned; but I disposed of my hand, and I am punished. See, what a strange thing! They make a crime of what in any one else would have been praised. For three days my lover has been my husband, and for three days, that is to say, from the moment when I could present myself before my father without blushing, I am forbidden his presence. Yesterday my guard was taken from me; this morning I presented myself at the Palais Royal and was refused admittance."

"Alas!" said Bathilde, "I am unhappy, for I had no hope but in you, madame, and I know no one who can introduce me to the regent. And it is to-morrow, madame, at eight o'clock, that they will kill him whom I love as you love M. de Riom. Oh, madame, take pity on me, for if you do not, I am lost!"

"Mon Dieu! Riom, come to our aid," said the duchess, turning to her husband, who entered at this moment; "here is a poor child who wants to see my father directly, without delay; her life depends on the interview. Her life! What am I saying? More than her life—the life of a man she loves. Lauzun's nephew should never be at a loss; find us a[Pg 422] means, and, if it be possible, I will love you more than ever."

"I have one," said Riom, smiling.

"Oh, monsieur," cried Bathilde, "tell it me, and I will be eternally grateful."

"Oh, speak!" said the Duchesse de Berry, in a voice almost as pressing as Bathilde's.

"But it compromises your sister singularly."

"Which one?"

"Mademoiselle de Valois."

"Aglaé! how so?"

"Do you not know that there exists a kind of sorcerer, who has the power of appearing before her day or night, no one knows how?"

"Richelieu? it is true!" cried the Duchesse de Berry; "but—"

"But what, madame?"

"He will not, perhaps—"

"I will beg him so that he will take pity on me," said Bathilde; "besides, you will speak a word for me, will you not? He will not dare to refuse what your highness asks."

"We will do better than that," said the duchess. "Riom, call Madame de Mouchy, beg her to take mademoiselle herself to the duke. Madame de Mouchy is my first lady-in-waiting," said the duchess, turning to Bathilde, "and it is supposed that the Duc de Richelieu owes her some gratitude. You see, I could not choose you a better introductress."

"Oh, thanks, madame," cried Bathilde, kissing the duchess's hands, "you are right, and all hope is not yet lost.

And you say that the Duc de Richelieu has a means of entering the Palais Royal?"

"Stay, let us understand each other. I do not say so, report says so."

"Oh!" cried Bathilde, "if we only find him at home!"

"That is a chance; but yet, let me see, what time is it? scarcely eight o'clock. He will probably sup in town, and return to dress. I will tell Madame de Mouchy to wait for him with you. Will you not," said she, turning to the lady-in-waiting, who now entered, "wait for the duke till he returns?"

"I will do whatever your highness orders," said Madame de Mouchy.

"Well, I order you to obtain from the Duc de Richelieu a promise that mademoiselle shall see the regent, and I authorize you to use, for this purpose, whatever influence you may possess over him."

"Madame goes a long way," said Madame de Mouchy, smiling.

"Never mind, go and do what I tell you; and you, my child, take courage, follow madame, and if, on your road in life, you hear much harm of the Duchesse de Berry, whom they anathematize, tell them that I have a good heart, and that, in spite of all these excommunications, I hope that much will be forgiven me, because I have loved much. Is it not so, Riom?"

"I do not know, madame," said Bathilde, "whether you are well or ill spoken of, but I know that to me you seem so good and great that I could kiss the trace of your footsteps."

"Now go, my child; if you miss M. de Richelieu you may not know where to find him, and may wait for him uselessly."

"Since her highness permits it, come, then, madame," said Bathilde, "for every minute seems to me an age."

A quarter of an hour afterward, Bathilde and Madame de Mouchy were at Richelieu's hotel. Contrary to all expectation, he was at home. Madame de Mouchy entered at once, followed by Bathilde. They found Richelieu occupied with Raffe, his secretary, in burning a number of useless letters, and putting some others aside.

"Well, madame," said Richelieu, coming forward with a smile on his lips, "what good wind blows you here? And to what event do I owe the happiness of receiving you at my house at half-past eight in the evening?"

"To my wish to enable you to do a good action, duke."

"In that case, make haste, madame."

"Do you leave Paris this evening?"

"No, but I am going to-morrow morning—to the Bastille."

"What joke is this?"

"I assure you it is no joke at all to[Pg 423] leave my hotel, where I am very comfortable, for that of the king, where I shall be just the reverse. I know it, for this will be my third visit."

"What makes you think you will be arrested to-morrow?"

"I have been warned."

"By a sure person?"

"Judge for yourself."

And he handed a letter to Madame de Mouchy, who took it and read—

"Innocent or guilty you have only time to fly. The regent has just said aloud before me that at last he has got the Duc de Richelieu. To-morrow you will be arrested."

"Do you think the person in a position to be well informed?"

"Yes, for I think I recognize the writing."

"You see, then, that I was right in telling you to make haste. Now, if it is a thing which may be done in the space of a night, speak, I am at your orders."

"An hour will suffice."

"Speak, then; you know I can refuse you nothing."

"Well," said Madame de Mouchy, "the thing is told in a few words. Do you intend this evening to go and thank the person who gave you this advice?"

"Probably," said the duke, laughing.

"Well, you must present mademoiselle to her."

"Mademoiselle!" cried the duke, astonished, and turning toward Bathilde, who till then had remained hidden in the darkness, "and who is mademoiselle?"

"A young girl who loves the Chevalier d'Harmental— who is to be executed to-morrow, as you know, and whose pardon she wishes to ask from the regent."

"You love the Chevalier d'Harmental, mademoiselle?" said the duke, addressing Bathilde.

"Oh, monsieur!" stammered Bathilde, blushing.

"Do not conceal it, mademoiselle. He is a noble young

man, and I would give ten years of my own life to save him. And do you think you have any means of interesting the regent in his favor?"

"I believe so."

"It is well. I only hope it may be so. Madame," continued the duke, turning to Madame de Mouchy, "return to her royal highness and tell her that mademoiselle shall see the regent in an hour."

"Oh, M. le Duc!" cried Bathilde.

"Decidedly, my dear Richelieu, I begin to think, as people say, that you have made a compact with the devil; that you may pass through key-holes, and I confess I shall be less uneasy now, in seeing you go to the Bastille."

"At any rate, you know, madame, that charity teaches us to visit prisoners, and if you retain any recollection of poor Armand—"

"Silence, duke, be discreet, and we will see what can be done for you. Meanwhile, you promise that mademoiselle shall see the regent?"

"It is a settled thing."

"Adieu, duke, and may the Bastille be easy to you."

"Is it adieu you say?"

"Au revoir!"

"That is right."

And having kissed Madame de Mouchy's hand he led her to the door; then, returning to Bathilde:

"Mademoiselle," said he, "what I am about to do for you compromises the reputation and honor of a princess of the blood, but the gravity of the occasion demands some sacrifice. Swear to me, then, that you will never tell, but to one person (for I know there are persons for whom you have no secrets), swear that you will never tell any but him, and that no other shall ever know in what manner you came to the regent.”

“Monsieur, I swear it by all I hold most sacred in the world—by my mother’s memory.”

“That will suffice,” said the duke, ringing a bell. A valet-de-chambre entered.

“Lafosse,” said the duke, “the bay horses and the carriage without arms.”

“Monsieur,” said Bathilde, “if you would save time, I have a hired carriage below.”

“That is still better. I am at your orders, mademoiselle.”

[Pg 424]”Am I to go with monsieur?” asked the servant.

“No, stay and help Raffe to put these papers in order. There are several which it is quite unnecessary for Dubois to see.”

And the duke offered his arm to Bathilde, went down, handed her into the carriage, and after telling the coachman to stop at the corner of the Rue Saint Honore and the Rue de Richelieu, placed himself by her side, as thoughtless as though the fate from which he was about to save the chevalier might not also await himself.

CHAPTER XLII.
THE CLOSET.

The carriage stopped at its destination, and Richelieu, getting out and taking a key from his pocket, opened the door of a house at the corner of the Rue de Richelieu.

"I must ask your pardon, mademoiselle," said the duke, offering his arm to Bathilde, "for leading you by badly-lighted staircases and passages; but I am anxious not to be recognized, should any one meet me here. We have not far to go."

Bathilde had counted about twenty steps, when the duke stopped, drew a second key from his pocket, and opened a door, then entered an antechamber, and lighted a candle at a lamp on the staircase.

"Once again I must ask pardon, mademoiselle," said the duke, "but you will soon understand why I chose to dispense with a servant here."

It mattered little to Bathilde whether the duke had a servant or not; she entered the antechamber without replying, and the duke locked the door behind her.

"Now follow me," said the duke; and he walked before the young girl, lighting her with the candle which he held in his hand. They crossed a dining-room and drawing-room, then entered a bedroom, where the duke stopped.

"Mademoiselle," said Richelieu, placing the candle on the chimney-piece, "I have your word that you will reveal nothing of what you are about to see."

"I have given you my promise, and I now renew it; I should be ungrateful indeed if I were to fail."

"Well, then, be the third in our secret, which is one of love; we put it under the safeguard of love."

And the Duc de Richelieu, sliding away a panel in the woodwork, discovered an opening in the wall, beyond which was the back of a closet, and he knocked softly three times. Presently they heard a key turn in the lock, then saw a light between the planks, then a low voice asked, "Is it you?" On the duke's replying in the affirmative, three of these planks were quietly detached, opening a means of communication from one room to the other, and the duke and Bathilde found themselves in the presence of Mademoiselle de Valois, who uttered a cry on seeing her lover accompanied by a woman.

"Fear nothing, dear Aglaé," said the duke, passing into the room where she was, and taking her hand, while Bathilde remained motionless in her place, not daring to move a step till her presence was explained.

"But will you tell me?" began Mademoiselle de Valois, looking at Bathilde uneasily.

"Directly. You have heard me speak of the Chevalier d'Harmental, have you not?"

"The day before yesterday you told me that by a word he might save his own life and compromise you all, but that he would never speak this word."

"Well, he has not spoken, and he is condemned to death, and is to be executed to-morrow. This young girl loves him, and his pardon depends on the regent. Do you understand?"

"Oh, yes!" said Mademoiselle de Valois.

"Come, mademoiselle," said the duke to Bathilde, taking her by the hand; then, turning again to the princess, "She did not know how to reach your father, my dear Aglaé, and came to me just as I had received your letter. I had to thank you for the good advice you gave me; and, as I know your heart, I thought I should please you by showing my grati[Pg 425]tude, in offering you an opportunity to save the life of a man to whose silence you probably owe my own."

"And you were right, duke. You are welcome, mademoiselle. What can I do for you?"

"I wish to see the regent," said Bathilde, "and your highness can take me to him."

"Will you wait for me, duke?" asked Mademoiselle de Valois uneasily.

"Can you doubt it?"

"Then go into the closet, lest any one should surprise you here. I will take mademoiselle to my father, and return directly."

"I will wait," said the duke, following the instructions of the princess and entering the closet. Mademoiselle de Valois exchanged some low words with her lover, locked the closet, put the key in her pocket, and holding out her hand to Bathilde—

"Mademoiselle," said she, "all women who love are sisters; Armand and you did well to rely upon me; come."

Bathilde kissed the hand she held out, and followed her. They passed through all the rooms facing the Palais Royal, and then, turning to the left, entered those which looked on the Rue de Valois, among which was the regent's bedroom.

"We have arrived," said Mademoiselle de Valois, stopping before a door, and turning to Bathilde, who at this news trembled and turned pale; for all the strength which had sustained her for the last three or four hours was ready to disappear just as she needed it the most.

"Oh, mon Dieu! I shall never dare to speak," said Bathilde.

"Courage, mademoiselle! enter, fall at his feet, God and his own heart will do the rest."

At these words, seeing that the young girl still hesitated, she opened the door, pushed Bathilde in, and closed it behind her. She then ran down with a light step to rejoin Richelieu, leaving Bathilde to plead her cause tete-à-tete with the regent.

At this unforeseen action, Bathilde uttered a low cry, and the regent, who was walking to and fro with his head bent down, raised it, and turned toward Bathilde, who, incapable of making a step in advance, fell on her knees, drew out her letter, and held it toward the regent. The regent had bad sight; he did not understand what was going on, and advanced toward this woman, who appeared to him in the shade as a white and indistinct form; but soon in that form he recognized a woman, and, in that woman, a young, beautiful, and kneeling girl.

As to the poor child, in vain she attempted to articulate a prayer. Voice and strength failing her together, she would have fallen if the regent had not held her in his arms.

"Mon Dieu! mademoiselle," said the regent, on whom the signs of grief produced their ordinary effect, "what is the matter? What can I do for you? Come to this couch, I beg."

"No, monseigneur, it is at your feet that I should be, for I come to ask a boon."

"And what is it?"

"See first who I am, monseigneur, and then I may dare to speak."

And again Bathilde held out the letter, on which rested her only hope, to the Duc d'Orleans.

The regent took the letter, and, by the light of a candle which burned on the chimney-piece, recognized his own writing, and read as follows:

"'Madame—Your husband is dead for France and for me. Neither France nor I can give you back your husband; but, remember, that if ever you are in want of anything we are both your debtors.

"'Your affectionate,

"'Philippe d'Orleans.'

"I recognize this letter perfectly as being my own," said the regent, "but to the shame of my memory I must confess that I do not know to whom it was written."

"Look at the address, monseigneur," said Bathilde, a little reassured by the expression of benevolence on the duke's face.

[Pg 426]"Clarice du Rocher," cried the regent, "yes, indeed, I remember now; I wrote this letter from Spain after the death of Albert, who was killed at the battle of Almanza. I wrote this letter to his widow. How did it fall into your hands, mademoiselle?"

"Alas, monseigneur, I am the daughter of Albert and Clarice."

"You, mademoiselle! And what has become of your mother?"

"She is dead."

"Long since?"

"Nearly fourteen years."

"But happy, doubtless, and wanting nothing."

"In despair, monseigneur, and wanting everything."

"But why did she not apply to me?"

"Your highness was still in Spain."

"Oh! mon Dieu! what do you say? Continue, mademoiselle, for you cannot tell how much you interest me. Poor Clarice, poor Albert, they loved each other so much, I remember. She could not survive him. Do you know that your father saved my life at Nerwinden, mademoiselle?"

"Yes, monseigneur, I know it, and that gave me courage to present myself before you."

"But you, poor child, poor orphan, what became of you?"

"I, monseigneur, was taken by a friend of our family, a poor writer called Jean Buvat."

"Jean Buvat!" cried the regent, "I know that name; he is the poor copyist who discovered the whole conspiracy, and who some days ago made his demands in person. A place in the library, was it not, some arrears due?"

"The same, monseigneur."

"Mademoiselle," replied the regent, "it appears that those

who surround you are destined to save me. I am thus twice your debtor. You said you had a boon to ask of me—speak boldly, I listen to you."

"Oh, my God!" murmured Bathilde, "give me strength."

"Is it, then, a very important and difficult thing that you desire?"

"Monseigneur," said Bathilde, "it is the life of a man who has deserved death."

"Is it the Chevalier d'Harmental?"

"Alas, monseigneur, it is."

The regent's brow became pensive, while Bathilde, seeing the impression produced by her demand, felt her heart beat and her knees tremble.

"Is he your relation, your ally, your friend?"

"He is my life, he is my soul, monseigneur; I love him."

"But do you know that if I pardon him I must pardon all the rest, and that there are some still more guilty than he is?"

"His life only, monseigneur, all I ask is that he may live."

"But if I change his sentence to a perpetual imprisonment you will never see him again. What would become of you, then?" asked the regent.

Bathilde was obliged to support herself by the back of a chair.

"I would enter into a convent, where I could pray the rest of my life for you, monseigneur, and for him."

"That cannot be," said the regent.

"Why not, monseigneur?"

"Because this very day, this very hour, I have been asked

for your hand, and have promised it."

"You have promised my hand, monseigneur; and to whom?"

"Read," said the regent, taking an open letter from his desk, and presenting it to the young girl.

"Raoul's writing!" cried Bathilde; "what does this mean?"

"Read," repeated the regent.

And in a choking voice, Bathilde read the following letter:—

"'Monseigneur—I have deserved death—I know it, and I do not ask you for life. I am ready to die at the day and hour appointed; but it depends on your highness to make this death sweeter to me. I love a young girl whom I should have married if I had lived; grant that she may be my wife before I die. In leaving her forever alone and friendless in the world, let me at least have the conso[Pg 427]lation of giving her the safeguard of my name and fortune. On leaving the church, monseigneur, I will walk to the scaffold. This is my last wish, my sole desire. Do not refuse the prayer of a dying man.

"'Raoul d'Harmental.'

"Oh, monseigneur," said Bathilde, sobbing, "you see that while I thought of him, he thought of me. Am I not right to love him, when he loves me so much?"

"Yes," said the regent, "and I grant his request, it is just; may it, as he says, sweeten his last moments."

"Monseigneur," cried the young girl, "is that all you grant him?"

"You see," said the regent, "he is just; he asks nothing

else."

"Oh, it is cruel! it is frightful! to see him again, and lose him directly; his life, monseigneur, his life, I beg; and let me never see him again—better so."

"Mademoiselle," said the regent, in a tone which admitted of no reply, and writing some lines on a paper which he sealed, "here is a letter to Monsieur de Launay, the governor of the Bastille; it contains my instructions with regard to the prisoner. My captain of the guards will go with you, and see that my instructions are followed."

"Oh! his life, monseigneur, his life; on my knees, and in the name of Heaven, I implore you."

The regent rang the bell; a valet entered.

"Call Monsieur the Marquis de Lafare," he said.

"Oh, monseigneur, you are cruel," said Bathilde, rising; "at least permit me then to die with him. We will not be separated, even on the scaffold; we will be together, even in the tomb."

"Monsieur de Lafare, accompany mademoiselle to the Bastille," said the regent. "Here is a letter for Monsieur de Launay, read it with him, and see that the orders it contains are punctually executed."

Then, without listening to Bathilde's last cry of despair, the Duc d'Orleans opened the door of a closet and disappeared.

CHAPTER XLIII.
THE MARRIAGE IN EXTREMIS.

Lafare dragged the young girl away, almost fainting, and placed her in one of the carriages always standing in the courtyard of the Palais Royal. During the route Bathilde did not speak; she was cold, dumb, and inanimate as a statue. Her eyes were fixed and tearless, but on arriving at the fortress she started. She fancied she had seen in the shade, in the very place where the Chevalier de Rohan was executed, something like a scaffold. A little further a sentinel cried "Qui vive!" the carriage rolled over a drawbridge, and drew up at the door of the governor's house. A footman out of livery opened the door, and Lafare gave Bathilde his arm— she could scarcely stand—all her strength had left her when hope left her. Lafare and the valet were obliged almost to carry her to the first floor. M. de Launay was at supper. They took Bathilde into a room to wait, while Lafare went directly to the governor. Ten minutes passed, during which Bathilde had only one idea—that of the eternal separation which awaited her. The poor girl saw but one thing—her lover on the scaffold. Lafare re-entered with the governor. Bathilde looked at them with a bewildered air. Lafare approached her, and offering her his arm—

"Mademoiselle," said he, "the church is prepared, the priest is ready."

Bathilde, without replying, rose and leaned on the arm which was offered her. M. de Launay went first, lighted by two men bearing torches.

As Bathilde entered by one of the side doors, she saw entering by the other the Chevalier d'Harmental, accompanied by Valef and Pompadour. These were his witnesses, as De Launay and Lafare were hers. Each door was kept by two of the French guard, silent and motionless as statues.

The two lovers advanced, Bathilde pale and fainting, Raoul calm and smiling. On arriving before the altar, the chevalier took Bathilde's hand, and both fell on their knees, without having spoken a word.

[Pg 428]The altar was lighted only by four wax tapers, which threw a funereal light over the chapel, already dark, and filled with gloomy recollections.

The priest commenced the ceremony; he was a fine old man with white hair, and whose melancholy countenance showed the traces of his daily functions. He had been chaplain of the Bastille for five-and-twenty years, and had heard many sad confessions, and seen many lamentable events. He spoke to them, not, as usual, of their duties as husband and wife, but of divine mercy and eternal resurrection. At the benediction Bathilde laid her head on Raoul's shoulder; the priest thought she was fainting, and stopped.

"Finish, my father," murmured Bathilde.

The priest pronounced the sacramental words, to which both replied by a "yes," which seemed to unite the whole strength of their souls. The ceremony finished, D'Harmental asked M. de Launay if he might spend his few remaining hours with his wife. Monsieur de Launay replied that there was no objection. Raoul embraced Pompadour and Valef, thanked them for having served as witnesses at his marriage, pressed Lafare's hand, thanked Monsieur de Launay for his kindness to him during his imprisonment, and throwing his arm round Bathilde, led her away by the door through which he had entered. When they reached D'Harmental's room, Bathilde could no longer contain her tears, a despairing cry escaped her lips, and she fell weeping on a chair, where doubtless D'Harmental had often sat, during the three weeks of his captivity, and thought of her. Raoul threw himself at her feet, and tried to console her, but was himself so much moved by her grief, that his own tears mingled with hers. This heart of iron melted in its turn, and Bathilde felt at once on her lips the tears and kisses of her lover. They had been about half-an-hour together when they heard steps approaching the door, and a key turning in the lock. Bathilde started, and pressed D'Harmental convulsively against her heart. Raoul understood the dreadful fear which crossed her mind, and reassured her. It could not be what she dreaded, since the execution was fixed for eight o'clock in the morning, and eleven had only just struck.

It was Monsieur de Launay who appeared.

"Monsieur le Chevalier," said he, "have the kindness to follow me."

"Alone?" asked D'Harmental, clasping Bathilde in his arms.

"No, with madame," replied the governor.

531

"Oh! together, Raoul, together!" cried Bathilde, "where they like, so that we are together. We are ready, monsieur, we are ready."

Raoul kissed Bathilde again; then recalling all his pride, he followed M. de Launay, with a face which showed no trace of the terrible emotion he had experienced. They passed through some ill-lighted corridors, descended a spiral staircase, and found themselves at the door of a tower. This door opened out to a yard, surrounded by high walls, which served as a promenade to those prisoners who were not kept secret. In this courtyard was standing a carriage with two horses, on one of which was a postilion, and they saw, shining in the darkness, the cuirasses of a dozen musketeers. A ray of hope crossed the minds of the two lovers. Bathilde had asked the regent to change Raoul's death into a perpetual imprisonment. Perhaps the regent had granted him this favor. The carriage, ready, doubtless, to conduct him to some State prison, the musketeers destined to escort them, all gave to the supposition an air of reality. They raised their eyes to heaven to thank God for this unexpected happiness. Meanwhile M. de Launay had signed to the carriage to approach; the postilion had obeyed, the door was opened, and the governor—with his head uncovered—held his hand to Bathilde, to assist her into the carriage.

She hesitated an instant, turning uneasily to see that they did not take Raoul away by the other side; but seeing that he was ready to follow her, she got in[Pg 429] without resistance. An instant afterward Raoul was sitting by her; the door was closed, and both carriage and escort passed through the gate, over the drawbridge, and they found themselves outside of the Bastille.

They threw themselves into each other's arms; there was no longer any doubt; the regent granted D'Harmental his life, and what was more, consented not to separate him from Bathilde.

This was what Bathilde and D'Harmental had never dared to hope; this life of seclusion—a punishment to many—would be to them a paradise of love—they would be together; and what else had they desired for their future, even when they were masters of their own fate? A single sad idea crossed their minds, and both, with the sympathy of hearts who love, pronounced the name of Buvat.

At this moment the carriage stopped; at such a time everything was, for the lovers, a subject of fear. They again trembled, lest they should have given way too much to hope. The door opened—it was the postilion.

"What do you want?" asked D'Harmental.

"I want to know where I am to take you."

"Where you are to take me! Have you no orders?"

"My orders were to take you to the Bois de Vincennes, between the Chateau and Nogent-sur-Marne, and here we are."

"And where is the escort?" asked D'Harmental.

"Oh, the escort left us at the barrier!"

"Oh, mon Dieu!" cried D'Harmental, while Bathilde—panting with hope—joined her hands in silence, "is it possible?"

And the chevalier jumped out of the carriage, looked round him anxiously, then clasping Bathilde in his arms, they uttered together a cry of joy and thankfulness.

They were free as the air they breathed, but the regent had ordered that they should be taken to the very place where D'Harmental had carried off Bourguignon, mistaking him for himself.

This was the only revenge of Philippe le Debonnaire.

Four years after this event, Buvat, reinstated in his place—and with his arrears paid—had the satisfaction of placing a pen in the hand of a fine boy of three years old—he was the son of Raoul and Bathilde.

The two first names which the child wrote were Albert du Rocher and Clarice Gray. The third was that of Philippe d'Orleans, regent of France.

POSTSCRIPTUM.

Perhaps some persons may have taken sufficient interest in those who have played a secondary part in our history to wish to know what became of them after the events which lost the conspiracy and saved the regent. We will satisfy them in a few words.

The Duc and Duchesse de Maine, whose plotting they wished to stop for the future, were arrested—the duke at Sceaux, and the duchess in her house in the Rue Saint Honoré. The duke was taken to the chateau of Doullens, and the duchess to that of Dijon, and afterward to the citadel of Châlons. Both left at the end of a few months, disarming the regent, one by an absolute denial, the other by a complete avowal.

Richelieu was arrested, as Mademoiselle de Valois had warned him, the day after that on which he had procured Bathilde's interview with the regent; but his captivity was a new triumph for him. It was reported that the handsome prisoner had obtained permission to walk on the terrace of the Bastille. The Rue Saint Antoine was filled with most elegant carriages, and became, in twenty-four hours, the fashionable promenade. The regent—who declared that he had proofs of the treason of M. de Richelieu, sufficient to lose him four heads if he had them—would not, however, risk his popularity with the fair sex by keeping him long in prison. Richelieu, again at liberty, after a cap[Pg 430]tivity of three months, was more brilliant and more sought after than ever; but the closet had been walled up, and Mademoiselle de Valois became Duchesse de Modena.

The Abbe Brigaud—arrested, as we have said, at Orleans—was kept for some time in the prison of that town, to the great despair of Madame Denis and her children; but, one fine morning, as they were sitting down to breakfast, the abbe entered, as calm as ever. They asked him a number of questions, but—with his habitual prudence—he referred them to his judicial declarations, saying that the affair had already given him so much trouble that they would greatly oblige him by never speaking of it any more. Now, as the Abbe Brigaud was quite an autocrat in Madame Denis's establishment, his desire was religiously respected, and from that day the affair was as completely forgotten in the Rue du Temps-Perdu as if it had never existed. Some days afterward Pompadour, Valef, Laval, and Malezieux went out of prison in their turn, and began again to pay their court to Madame de Maine, as if nothing had happened. As to the Cardinal de Polignac, he was not even arrested; he was simply exiled to his Abbey d'Anchin.

These proofs of clemency appeared to Dubois so out of all reason that he came to the regent, intending to make a scene about it, but the regent only replied by repeating the burden of the song which Saint-Simon had made on him:

"For I am Philippe le Debonnaire, Philippe le Debonnaire."

This enraged Dubois so much that the regent, in order to pacify him, was obliged to transform him into his Eminence the Cardinal.

www.ingramcontent.com/pod-product-compliance
Lightning Source LLC
Chambersburg PA
CBHW020605040726
47498CB00003B/644